EXPANSION ON
TRITON

G.D. Wonder

authorHOUSE®

AuthorHouse™ UK
1663 Liberty Drive
Bloomington, IN 47403 USA
www.authorhouse.co.uk
Phone: 0800.197.4150

Published by AuthorHouse 02/18/2015

ISBN: 978-1-5246-2842-0 (sc)
ISBN: 978-1-5246-2843-7 (hc)
ISBN: 978-1-5246-2844-4 (e)

Contents

Prologue ix

1. Journey Into The Unknown 1
2. Beginning Of Dreams 10
3. Mystery Revealed 17
4. The World Is Being Born 20
5. Time Is Running 25
6. Them 36
7. Beginning Of Salvation 48
8. Danger At The Gates 58
9. Awakening 73
10. Step Towards Truth 90
11. Unexpected Guest 107
12. Clash 134
13. Nightmares 150
14. Mysterious Refuge 163
15. Chaos Finishing With Victory 179
16. Secrets Of Hurt 192
17. Gloom Future 205
18. Clash Of The Races 218
19. Changing The Game 230
20. Back To The World Of The Dead 240
21. Closer To The Truth 258
22. A New Day 269

Epilogue 287

EXPANSION ON TRITON

„There is only one tactical rule, which isn't subject to any change: use what is at hand to inflict as many wounds, death and destruction to the enemy in the shortest time possible" - gen. Patton

Prologue

Even though mankind and every living being appreciates life most, the fact, that it managed to survive, scares one the most. Because like any predictions proclaim „the living will envy the dead." Everyone is aware of the fact that one will have to face the destructive power again and is confident that he will fail, because the enemy is so powerful that one can not escape from the battlefield and can only give up and cease to exist.

Nothing like it has ever been before, nor will ever be, because after Zotorigh remains nothing. Those who have made it, are not happy but rather worried, because they know very well that that something they will have to stand in front of, can not be escaped from, nor can not be defeated. Exactly like a dream that comes when a person is tired, just as everyone is aware that he will have to come face to face with annihilation.

It's the year 2345. The Earth was conquered and destroyed by Zotorigh, a remnant of people who managed to escape, roam the galaxies to survive. Major Thomas, at age 46, although it is not clear whether it is his true age, is one of the few people who confronted this cruel race and managed to survive. His stony expression on his face do not reveal any details about himself, and his blue eyes hide many secrets. The only characteristic thing which distinguishes him from other men is a long scar on his face, which is a reminder of his encounter with Zotorigh. Unfortunately, he can not remember any details from the moment when he brushed with death. He does not want to remember those days at the end, when he lost not only his beloved planet, but also his beloved wife and daughter. The few memories of life on Earth appear in his dreams.

Along with a handful of men under his command, and who managed to escape alive, he seeks refuge on remote planets, hoping that the Zotorigh will not reach them. The Galactic fleet consists of twenty-four scarlet destroyers equipped with a plot of neutron-molecular and eight transports carrying people. Those are the remains of the fleet, they managed to save. Most of the ships were damaged after the Zotorigh attacks. The cruisers needed a quick repair, and the whole crew needed time, which they unfortunately did not have.

- Major Thomas, we are approaching the solar system TY-235.

- Give me an analysis.

- The system consists of two planets inhabited by pacifistic creatures. Unfortunately, or perhaps fortunately for us, we have not detected technological development but only technology from the XV century by Earth civilization standards. This race is called Urtringo. Scan performed by NIL ray, got blocked most likely by the structure of the planet.

- What do we do, Major? - asked captain Madox.

Captain Madox was a woman at the age of thirty with blond hair to her shoulders, impeccable manners, velvet skin and soft, very warm facial features as well as a sensual look in her eyes. Just as Major Thomson, she was a very good tactician and had an indisputable reputation as a galactic fleet soldier.

- Major? What do we do? – repeated the captain wanting to know whether they will do a short stop here and complement the stocks, or if they have to fly farther ahead, into the unknown. As a precaution she recalled the scale of destruction of the ship, knowing perfectly well that the onward journey can have more devastating consequences than them being noticed by Zotorigh.

- We will do a short break – said the Major as if he was torn from his lethargy. - Please take care of everything.

He did not have to add anything more, because Madox knew she had to fill gaps in their supply and carry out all minor repairs.

- We do not have much time and we have to be very careful, because on this planet, after all, may be Zotorigh spies.

- You know what to do! - said Major Thomas.

- Yes, we know Major! - replied Captain Madox. Major Thomson stood up from his seat of command and went with a decisive step towards the exit and threw a glance toward the captain.

- Keep me updated! I'll be in my quarters. You take the command, Captain - then he disappeared behind the door.

In the Major's cabin were only a bed and a chair. Major himself, gave up on any unnecessary details, that may distract him. He did not want anything that reminded him of something he did not understand. He did not want any objects from the past, that could remind him of those he had lost. Memorabilia evoke memories and unnecessary pain, that he had experienced in his life.

Opposite the entrance to the cabin was a huge window that took up an entire wall. He walked over to it and began to look at the beautiful, but wild and unknown planet. Although he knew it was impossible he was searching in his imagination, some things, images that could in any way bring back memories of the distant past. He looked at the planet and compared it to the Earth, or rather to his dreams, in which the Earth is the most beautiful place. He dreamed about finding his coveted haven at last, where he would stop and spend the rest of his life.

The planet did by no means resemble Earth, besides the fact that it was shaped like a sphere and even though he already knew the data of this planet and knew that this was a place with a hostile climate for men, he looked at it and imagined it as the Earth. He had secretly hoped that that was the case, however. He was simply just tired of the eternal wandering and escape.

Staring at the planet, trying to forget about what happened during the invasion and attack of the Zotorigh. He tried to forget, tried not to think at all about how he lost what was most dearest to him: his beautiful wife and daughter. Often during the time of the service he had to make decisions about the fighting many enemies. When he won, and he always did, after a long fight he tried to relax in solitude. He closed himself up and imagined himself fighting with Zotorigh. He could see in his mind as it destroys them and saves the lives of the people who believed in him. When his eyelids shut, he was completely cut off from reality, he could not break free from those tragic memories. And those memories gave him the strength as he saw their dread and fear and vowed himself never to allow anyone that trusts him to perish ever again. Although he did not remember any other details, he did however recall one moment, just one moment, which he was not able to explain logically. He wanted to know what or who restrained him, that stood in front of him, when about absolutely everyone succumbed to total destruction. He, who was looking directly into the eyes of the enemy, survived, and the only damage suffered was a wound, which marks his cheek now. They all died from attacks inflicted by Zotorigh, and somehow he defied the power of destruction, which is why he promised himself that because of his uniqueness he will not allow for the destruction of the human race. He knew he had some sort of power that could stop Zotorigh. He just wanted to know what it is. He set itself the objective of never letting the same happen again, what happened on Earth.

-Major! - He interrupted his thoughts with a voice from the speaker in his cabin. - Quickly, please report to the deck!

He became terrified by the fact that it sounded like an order, as no one ever called him in this way and with such tone since the time when he took command, many years ago. Major did not even try to think about putting Madox back in her place, who gave the order, because he sensed that something was wrong. Something so inexplicable that Madox completely forgot about the respect she usually pays her superior.

When the major reached the deck he encountered dead silence, as everyone stared with horror at their monitors.

- What's happening? What happened? Please report! - he asked with a worried voice.

Everybody was quiet, as if they were in hypnosis and were still staring at their monitors, unable to believe their eyes.

- Main screen! - demanded Major, when he saw on the radar a few dozen ships around the fleet, suddenly.- Turn on the shield!

- Turned on.

- Arm everything!

- Unfortunately, there is no such possibility.

- What?

- We can't. Something is blocking the detectors, sensors, lasers, absolutely everything!

- Everyone take your positions! Where did these ships come from? How could their presence not been detected by the radar? Report! And... - he wanted to say „Prepare to fight", but then he realized they did not have such a possibility.

- Yes Major, clenching fists - Captain whispered under her breath, but not quietly enough as the Major heard her. - If we stand to fight. Even if we regained control, with the strength and the number of the enemy's combat ships, we would not stand a chance. Something is blocking the system. Our weapons are inactive, we have no control over the ship, except for the shields that we were able to switch on manually.

- What's happening? - he asked himself demanding answers from others. He felt helpless, for someone who has daily access to the most powerful weapon that have been created by mankind. He hates the feeling of helplessness.

He was not able to do anything.

- Major, what do we do? - Captain asked the question. She also realized that the situation in which they found themselves in, doesn't look good, to say the least.

The whole crew on the deck felt as if they were surrounded by a herd of hungry lions, and they only had slingshots to defend themselves with. They knew that didn't stand a chance, and the fact that the ship wasn't destroyed yet came down to someone's whim.

- What do we do, Major?

The silence continued.

Major suspended his eyes on the monitor and held the air in his lungs. After a moment of stillness he looked at Madox and resumed breathing.

- Nothing yet. We are waiting in combat readiness.

They were absolutely not able to do anything in terms of defense, and the only thing they could do is wait for the course of events. However, everyone asks themself the same question in their heads: why aren't they attacking? They are waiting for something? But for what? If they don't attack, then maybe they are waiting for our movement, our attack – a thought that went through the Majors head.

- Major, we just got a report, saying that these are not Zotorigh ships. These are the ships of the Urtringo.

Major looked at Madox frowning in surprise.

- What?

- These are the ships of the Urtringo. - she repeated, looking at the screen on which it was scanning the entire system of the enemys ships.

Major stood up, walked over to the monitor of Madox and stared at it. In his mind, or rather whispering, he asked:

- How is it possible that this race created such a powerful fleet consisting of so many ships so quickly? - as Major fell into a stupor. - But they could not develop so quickly. Why have they turned off our system, and only left the ability to scan their armed fleet.

- Major, I'm afraid that this is not their whole fleet, but only a retinue welcome.

- Have I been wrong? Check on the radar, what class these ships are. Immediately! - ordered the Major.

- They all are S class!

Major asked himself in a whisper, why have they control over everything, and have let us use the scan to check their weapons.

Madox, although she hasn't been asked directly, replied:

- To show us that they have an advantage over us.

There was silence, all eyes turned to Major. They waited for orders.

- Try to call them out.

- We are trying the whole time, but we have unclear readings with the informtion, that they are sending us a message, but those impulses with a message are addressed only to one computer, Major. To yours.

- What? How?

Major returned to his seat and began reading the information in his mind, that was sent directly to his computer.

Silence continued and everyone was waiting for what the Major would do. No one dared to approach the commander station, because everyone knew that this message is only intended for him. If he thinks he should share the message, he would do so.

- Prepare the spaceglider - said the Major after a moment. - What would happen, will happen anyway. I am flying to the planet to meet with their leader.

„Maybe their help will be useful to us" – A tought that went through the Majors mind.

- I will visit them, personally - Major Thomas knew very well that he did not stand a chance to win a fight against such powerful enemy, like the Zotorigh, but now a spark of hope lit up. He needed allies, he did not have.

- Major, the spaceglider is ready to start and is waiting in the hangar.

- Captain Madox!

- Yes! - She started following the Major. When the major headed with Captain Madox into the hangar, where the ship was ready for departure, suddenly he slowed down and after a while he stopped.

- Major, is everything alright? May I know what the message contained?

- Soon you will find out - said the major.

- Is everything alright? - She repeated the question with a slight hesitation. – Major, what is going on?

- Everything is alright - he repeated as if in a trance and continued. - Madox, I expect an honest answer. - Captain Madox knew that this time, th eMajor does not return to her as etiquette requires, but rather directly as if it has no relation to her professional function. - Do you trust me?

- Yes - Replied captain Madox without hesitation.

- Very well, then. Leave us alone!

When the guard walked away to a safe distance, the Major asked again:

- So, do you trust me?

- Yes, of course and unconditionally - The captain replied.

- You misunderstanding me, Captain. I will say this: I'd like you to take over the command of the fleet, if something was to happen to me on this planet and if I won't return from it. I want you to promise me that you will do everything in your power to fly away when you take such a decision, and when you get a signal from me.

The captain did not know what to say. She was completely surprised by the question. In particular because the Major asked the question not to a soldier, but to a woman. The captain stood in silence, not knowing how to answer this question. Ever since she can remember, the Major spoke to her officially, but not in this way. He always addressed her as a soldier without emotion and without hesitation, but this time she receives a question so simple and at the same time so difficult, that the result was, her ending up being confused. It seemed as if she misheard him, that what she heard was a product of her imagination, because she wanted the Major not only see her as a soldier, but also as a woman.

- You are able to execute this command? - Major asked another question. - Are you? - after a moment of silence that surrounded the major and the captain came the reply:

- Yes I am.

- That's good - said the Major. - Remember that the most important thing is not the life of one man, not even mine, but that of all mankind. This small handful of people on this and several other ships, and if you regain control over your ship and you will see that this whole thing is a trick, I hope you will not hesitate and fly away from here as far as possible. I hope you will follow this advice in the future and will not hesitate striving to realize the dreams of people:

freedom and peace, which we all have forgotten. I live long enough and I'd like to go, if this is the moment, I'd like to be remembered as a man who used to love and has left behind a hope for a better tomorrow, that will follow. Do not take away hope and faith from people. Follow the things that are important - like love.

The captain did not know what to say. She did not expect such words from the Major.

- You will stay, and I believe that you will handle it - said the Major.

- Yes, Major. May God be with you, Major - said the Captain.

Thomas straightened himself up, adjusted his uniform, raised his head and walked away without a word. Very quietly, almost in a whisper, the Captain said: - Goodbye Major – hoping they would see each other again.

When the Major turned and walked toward the hangar, where the spaceglider was ready, the captain stood motionless and saluted the Major with great devotion and respect. During this time the Major sat down behind the wheel. He stared for a moment at the desktop, then pulled the reins towards him and launched off.

1.

JOURNEY INTO THE UNKNOWN

When the spaceglider distanced itself away from the mother ship, the Major issued an order to the computer that was on-board:

- Turn the protective shield on, check equipment.

- Unfortunately, we have no control over our armament - was the reply.

- That's right, I forgot. Everything is secured, let's set off to the planet - has commanded.

With the growing distance to the mother ship the Major stared into the abyss of the kosmos. He glanced at the radar also closely watching whether it has been tracked down by an enemy ship patrolling the planet. In fact, he does not know why he performed these actions, after all there is virtually no control over the ship. He knew, that against his will he is a prisoner on his own ship and when he got into the force field of the planet the Major gave the order:

- As a precaution prepare an escape pod.

- Yes, Major - said the on-board computer. - Everything is ready. Major, may I ask a question?

- Of course, ask - said the major.

- Major, do you know the reason for this mission? My guess is that there is one? - Asked the computer.

- Yes, I know the reason, and I also know that you do too, you know exactly why we're flying now and where.

- Major, I have read the message that you received, but I can not guess the intentions and I can not predict what will happen if you fail to get help.

- I do not know, I really do not know, but I have no time to think about it. Whatever will be, will be - Major replied believing that everything he read was ... Well that's the thing, he's not entirely realize of whether the message was a joke or a trick.

- Major, the composition of the atmosphere is: 78% O^2, 21% N^2 oraz 1% of other elements, which is the same as in our ship.

- How is this possible? - Major fell into a stupor. - But on this planet can not have oxygen. Check thoroughly again - he ordered.

- Major, I confirm: everything indicates that this planet has oxygen that is needed for life. Major, that's not all. On this planet, I noticed a large concentration of places covered with vegetation called savannas.

- Computer! Find out where the closest cluster of dwellings is and immediately headed towards that direction.

- All the sensors indicate that the nearest settlement from us is at a distant of about 150 km north and we have a flight route in this direction.

When they approached the planet with the direction pointed out by the computer, the Major could not stop wondering and could not believe what he was seeing. Suddenly the alarm went off indicating only one thing – battle alarm.

- What's happening?!

- Major, someone took complete control - said the computer. - Three S-class ships, that surpass our weaponry, follow in our direction. What are the orders, Major Thomas?

The Major was silent.

- Major, what are your orders?

- Turn off the engines! We are landing.

- Major, we regained full control of the ship. Turn off the weaponry? We don't stand a chance against them. We must show that we are here in peace and do not want to fight.

The Major began to wonder who and why he decided to restore full control of the ship. Did they wanted to find out about the real intentions of Major, with this approach? Perhaps they want to see whether and how the Major will fight in times of danger?

- The ships will be here in about thirty seconds. Everything is turned off, except of the shield.

- Good. We will wait for their movement.

- Major! Contact in five, four, three, two, one... Stormtroopers in sight.

The Major looked around but did not see anything. Suddenly, before his eyes a stormtrooper begins to appear, he just stared at the ships and sees as the protection that made them invisible to the eye, deactivates, and a stormtrooper becomes visible. Detailed analysis showed a complete, integrated shield. When ships appeared completely, he looked around and fell in amazement, as it turned out that in addition to the ships next to them he also saw – some sort of form of life.

- Since when they are here? – He was surprised, because the radar didn't indicate anyone except himself. They could not come out of nowhere. Stormtrooper took the shape of triangles with black metallic color. In the middle, it seemed, there was a brighter spot in the shape of a circle. Each ship was about 30 meters wide and 10 meters high. The computer issued a statement.

- Major, received a message sent by one of the ships. It's in urtinghani.

- Display it on the main screen – the Major ordered.

- Very well, no sooner said than done!- answered the computer. The message, that was displayed, astonished the Major.

- Is this the correct translation? - he nervously asked the computer.
- Correct?

- Yes! Everything is translated correctly. I receive a signal, which is amplified every few milliseconds and each message is of the same content.

There was an awkward silence that lasted a long time. The Major was leaning against the corner of the desktop staring at the message.

On his forehead appear beads of sweat, that started to run down his temples. The Major was very nervous. At one point he straightened himself up and adjusted his uniform.

- Computer, connect to the database - he ordered.

- Yes, already connecting! - replied the computer. - Major Thomas, we are on.

- Good, good good - he muttered under his breath.

- I have a message for the entire fleet, and above all for captain Madox.

In the command center was only silence. Nobody knew what had happened, everyone looked at each other and the monitor, everyone wanted to know what was going on.

- I do not have much time - said the Major. - I have to tell you only so much, that I think I know how to get out of this whole situation.

- But Major, please tell us what's going on and what happened down there! - Captain Madox demanded an answers.

- I have no time, I have to go – he said firmly.

He wanted to say something else, but it was clear that is nervous and carefully chooses every word he says, because he didn't know, but he hoped that everything will end well. When he was silent for a moment, looking directly at the monitor he shook his head to the left, then to the right, then he concluded:

- From the very beginning, since this unequal fight started, we are fleeing, because we do not see any other way and each of us senses, how it would end, but I believe and do not ask me, please, how I know, because I don't know how to explain it. I know that there will be a different ending.

There was a moment of silence because everyone was waiting for the Major to tell, but the Majors last word, short sentenced ended the conversation.

- Captain Madox take over the command. Let her lead the fleet and let God guide you. We'll see each other for sure and do not worry about me, and ... - than connecting broke off.

- But Major, what's going on there? What's happening? - everyone asked, no being able to hear the Major.

- Nothing. Everything is as it should be - replied the Captain, in her mind, adding, „I hope," then she stared at the screen, where she could only see a black screen. The connection was ultimately closed. The Major disconnected the call. Captain Madox said nothing, but her feelings indicated that everything would be fine.

- Computer, when I get out, and if you still have control of the ship, lock and arm it. In the case of the enemy getting in, destroy the entire contents of my personal computer, so data does not fall into the wrong hands - said Major Thomas.

- Yes, Major! Everything, according to the order - said the computer.

- Now it's time to meet with their leader.

- Goodbye, Major - added computer.

- Time to move - he replied and headed for the exit.

When the Major move away from the ship, heading toward one of the three gliders that were ready to take him with them, he stopped after some hundred meters, he turned toward the ship, and looked at it as if he would never see it again. He took a deep breath and began to walk towards the waiting spacegliders. When he came closer, one of the middle ships slid out a platform to help the Major come on board. When the Major entered the platform, it lifted itself up. The Major wondered what awaits him on the site, and whether what he read on the monitor was true, or was simply just a trap from which there was absolutely no possibility and no chance of escape. Not to mention the ability od show any kind of resistance. When the platform docked inside the ship, he could not believe what he was seeing. Inside the ship, as it turns out, were no indigenous inhabitants of the planet, but there were humans.

When he came on board, ne of the soldiers approached him and introduced himself:

- I'm the commander of this ship. Captain Org. It's nice to finally meet the daredevil and the brave commander.

- What's going on here? - The Major asked.

- Oh, you mean, because people are on this ship?

- Yes, that's what I mean.

- These are not people – said Captain Org. - We only changed our appearance, so we would not cause any fear and repulsion in you. So this will be best. Really Major Thomas. We don't have time. We need to know whether you understood the message that we sent you, and whether you are able to do what we asked for? - the Captain asked the question.

- Of course, I understood and just like you want this too, but I have one question. Why can't you do it on your own? After all, you do have the know-how.

- Yes, we know how to very well, but we are created differently and our bodies simply cease to exist after such a mission. That is why we need your help, because only humans have such a simple muscle tissue system. In other words, we are easily and simply created – Captain Org replied.

- Now, get ready, because in fifteen seconds we fly off to town to meet our lord and king Naroht.

When the Major looked out the window, he saw nothing, just desert and sand dunes.

- I don't see any city, there is nothing here – said the major.

- Yes, there is no city, but have I meantioned it being on the surface? We descend beneath the surface. Prepare for landing - replied Captain Org.

The ships had stopped and lifted themselves up into the air, then the earth began to part. The Major watched breathlessly what happened directly under his feet. He has never seen anything like it. Indeed, he encountered civilizations living underground, but they were poorly developed life forms, but he never encountered whole town that were build under the ground. It was fabulously hidden. As he watched the earth moved apart, thousands of thoughts ran through his mind. He did not know what to think about it. He wanted to ask so many questions. However, Captain Org overtook him by saying:

-All questions will receive an answer, at the right time. There is no point in asking and getting answers you won't understand. Everything needs its time.

At that moment, the Major watched how they penetrated underground. He did not see nothing but darkness. He was not able to see anything.

- But here... - he carefully looked out for anything.

Org caught a glimpse of Major, trying to spot some form of life, whatever it may be - equipment, people, robots, machine.

- Take a look carefully and you'll notice everything - said Org.

The Major did not even asked, even though he had such intent, but received already an answer. Of course he considered that his curiosity and face expression caused the answer to his question and considered that a matter of course, not suspecting anything.

When Major began to stare, he began to nitice more prominent and clearer contours, and he couldn't quite believe what he's seeing. The mighty city began to appear in front of his eyes. Towers, so high that you could not see the beginning or end. Full of ships moving in one direction only. The city seemed to be the most beautiful thing he has seen, or maybe it was beautiful because he didn't expect anything here. Full of greenery, buildings many shapes. Defense towers were built every few hundred meters - each of which was finished with a strange ball, which produced some kind of energy. Everything seemed to be finished in gold and when it protective dome was closed, under which this wonderful city was located, the ship could safely move to the far north-east toward the largest of the buildings. When they flew toward the fortress Morgat, which was the name of the headquarters of the king and ruler of this planet, the ship was surrounded by several smaller gliders.

- These are the escorts of our ruler. They will keep us company. Just for safety - Captain Org explained.

When they flew, the Major stared at these wonderful buildings and works of art. Everything seemed to be so powerful yet small and peaceful. He watched the birds, that were flying next to them - creatures so beautiful and colorful like a rainbow in the sky, that took on every now and then different colors, as they are moving away from gliders and approached back again. Everywhere he looked, everything seemed so quiet and safe.

- We're almost here, prepare for landing - said captain Org.

As the ship approached the landing, Major began to feel calm. Everything was so unreal and he did not know what to think about everything he saw. „The city hidden under the ground – I have not seen anything like this yet, and yet this is just the beginning" - he thought, smiling to himself. Then he realized that everything will be fine.

The glider settled on a circular platform. When Major got out of the ship, he felt a fresh breeze and sunlight on his cheeks.

- Major, please follow me - said Captain Org.

- Of course - said Major Thomas.

As they walked toward the palace, Major could not resist and asked captain Org a question:

- How is it possible that you are such an advanced race, and how did you manage to hide this whole city under the earth? After all ...

- Under the ground? - Asked Captain Org. - We're not underground. We're on the surface. What you saw has been improved by our fathers and ancestors, the dome that protects us from the eyes of foreign races such as yours. We live here in peace on our own, we don't have war or famine. We are self-sufficient and do not want anyone to interfere in our lives and therefore we protect ourselves. I hope that you understood at least a little of what I said. This is a fraction of what really is on this planet, and your technology that you possess is not able to understand or comprehend it all. That is why I will spare you a detailed response - said Captain Org. - You must be very tired? - He asked.

- Yes - said the Major.

- Let the guard take you to your room. You will be able to rest and recharge before you meet our ruler. You could use a rest.

- Actually, these impressions made me tired, and I need to think what's next - Major Thomas said.

- The guards will lead you to your room. Everything you'll need is in place, and if you need anything else, it will be delivered to you. You are our guest. We hope that you wil feel at home - Org expressed his hope.

When Major entered the room, he began to look around. Indeed, like an aparment that I remembered from Earth. Everything was in order. Opposite the entrance was a large wardrobe with a mirror in the middle. On the left side of the door, probably a personal dressing room, and on the right was a large window, stretching almost the entire wall. The furniture was made out of wood. It was a huge room. The bed was just under the window, and by the end stood, or rather hung, a big screen. Bedding seemed to be made out of silk. At the entrance on the right side was a table that was sliding from the wall and chairs standing next to it.

On the wall they were frames with paintings with several types of galaxies. These were vivid images, in which a glowing galaxy gave the impression of reality. Major noticed, when he went towards the window that behind it were simply breathtaking views. A beautiful garden planted with rose bushes and ferns and grewing apple trees, here and there. Major went out and when he reached the end of the terrace, he leaned against the railing. He felt as if he could find happiness and peace here. It reminded him of the wonderful moments with a woman who was his only true love, of who he could not stop thinking about, even though he tried with all his strength. Often, especially when he was alone in other similar places, thoughts would create themselves in his head. Dreamy for a moment, he then said that a bath should do for now when it comes to happiness, so he went to the room, where the door was closed until now.

2.

BEGINNING OF DREAMS

- Major, Major Thomas! Everyone is already waiting in the Chamber for fifteen minutes. Is the Major ready?

Major opened his eyes. He looked around and saw a woman at the door. Horrified by the fact that he didn't wake up on time and that somebody found him asleep. Pondering over the the cause, he came to the conclusion that obviously the atmospheric composition was one of the ingredients that caused him to sleep so long, because something like that never happenes to him.

- Who are you and what are you doing in my bedroom? How long have I slept? - Major Thomas said, slightly confused.

- My name is Sia - said the girl standing in the doorway. - Please forgive me that I am inside, but you do not respond to calls.

Sia was a young, about twenty-two year old girl. She could roughly be one hundred and sixty centimeters tall, beautiful brown hair to her shoulders, drooping more on one side of her face, green eyes and at first glance a silky smooth skin. Although she was wearing a uniform, you could see that she was very slim. Perhaps it was this uniform that caused that you could see her beautiful figure.

- Everyone is waiting – she repeated.

- Of course. I'm coming. Just tell me where my clothes are? - the major asked, looking around the room for something that he could get dressed in.

- There you go - Sia gave the Major a robe similar to that, that he wore every day, except it was in the color blue and was embroidered in brown. - Here are your clothes.

Major took the a robe staring in amazement at the girl.

- And where is mine? - Major asked.

- Do not worry, it is in its place. You can only enter the meeting room in the holy robe. Otherwise we could take it as a contempt for the majesty of our king - Sia said. - Everyone is waiting.

- Ok, I understand - Major put on the robe and they both quickly headed toward the room where the crowd of inhabitants of the planet were waiting.

When the Major came in, everyone looked in his direction. They watched with a penetrating gaze. So much that shivers ran down the Majors body and he felt a strange energy - as if someone or something - some kind of energy flowed through his body.

The Major slowly, but confidently, walked through the middle of the room in complete silence. None of the assembled guests did say a word. When the the major reached the end of the hall following the girl who was, so he thought, his guide, she showed him a place where he could sit back and wait for the arrival of the king. The room where they stood, was huge and had a circular shape. The dome was supported by four columns. At the end of these columns were powerful monuments of kings or rulers or founders of this planet. They could also be images of some gods, but than each one would represent something else. The characters were very intriguing, but Major did not want to ask questions, as he didn't travel to this planet as a tourist.

The Hall had one entry, which was located in the middle, the same entry as the one that the Major walked through. It was finished with smaller monuments of the heir to the throne, Arion, prince of the planet. The entrance was about twenty meters high and was six meters wide. At the end of the room sat the least important members of the royal family who studied herbal medicine for the king. The closer to the throne, that was raised, the increasingly more important members of the family sat next to it. Near the king there were also seats provided for his generals. On the right side sat the representatives of the ordinary citizens of the planet. Each row had a different color corresponding to a residential zone. Most populous were townsmen, farmers, miners and sailors.

„Hmm, could they have all have been waiting for me? And where is the ruler of this kingdom?". When the Major asked himself questions in his mind, suddenly a woman sitting beside him spoke up, saying:

- Yes, we are waiting for two very important persons: for our ruler who will soon arrive, and you.

The Major surprised by what he heard, he looked for the companion sitting next to him, as she looked at the Major, smiled and continued:

- Major Be careful, because what you think can easily be read, or at the people who sit next to you can do so.

The Major startled speechless and after a while he said:

- Excuse me, but when I found out that everyone was here, I thought that the king would be too. Unfortunately, I do not know if I have enough time to wait for your king. My people, or actually the ones that have survived, are waiting for me in our ship that is orbiting your planet, and frankly I do not know what this all means.

- I perfectly understand your concerns, but ...

- How could you understand my concerns, after all ...?

When the Major spoke to the woman, he heard someone with a very high voice saying:

- Our lord and gracious king.

Everyone stood up. At this point the king entered the hall from the left side, surrounded by guards, as well as his wife, Te-ri. The king seemed to radiate and send a positive aura from his body that could be felt from a distance. It was indeed a phenomenal event. No being located in this room didn't expose any energy. When the king took his seat on the throne there was total silence, which he interrupted himself:

-Major Thomas, I know very well why you came to this planet and you don't have to say anything, because I can read everything from your mind.

The Major stood and said nothing.

- Is there anything else you would like to say in front of witnesses and in front of my people? I do not hide anything. My peoples have the right to know what is happening in the universe and what they need to prepare for.

- I'm only losing my time here, and from what I could figure out, I won't find it here either - answered Major.

- Why did you decide to land on our planet? For what purpose? Tell me why you came here? Don't you realize that in this way you can bring us all destruction? Everyone knows exactly what the real danger is now, unfortunately, we are all too well aware that we do not know how to fight it. Our enemy is too powerful and we do not know what it disposes of and what he really knows. We do not know whether they sent spies behind you or not, and so I must ask you to leave immediately the interstellar, because being here, you bring us its attention. Unfortunately I can not help you. You need to leave this planet as soon as possible and never return. Because of what your ancestors did, the Zotorigh killed thousands civilization. As the king I can not allow this to happened to my planet and my people! - the King replied nervously.

Major stood in disbelief. He totally did not expect to hear such words. He was convinced that he would hear something completely different and with frustration sweat started to appear on his forehead. The King suddenly looked at the Major and said:

- I'd like to help you, but I can not risk the existence of my people. The guards will escort you out and to your ship - the king got up and left.

Major stood in a daze and did not believe what he was hearing. It was suppose to go all different. What was this whole charade for? Why would someone reveal their technology, risking the destruction of an entire civilization? Why would anyone invite someone, first demonstrating their strength and capabilities, and than moments later deliver a speech about not being able or wanting to help? He absolutely didn't understand anything. Disappointed and confused, his head was empty, he expected something else.

„I only lost time. What does this all this mean? What the hell is going on? Who and why is making a joke out of him? „.

When the Major stood there motionless, she hall emptied. At some point, an envoy of the king entered the room and addressed the Major:

- The King asks for you. Please follow me.

The Major just wanted to get himself onto his ship and fly away as soon as possible. He was disappointed by all of it. For a while he had great hope that he could find an ally, but now he was alone. He felt a great burden of responsibility for the lives of many people. He did not know what was going on and didn't know why the king asked for him, but he had no other choice.

- Yes, but I would like to quickly finish the visit and return to my ship.

The Major entered the hall, where the king was waiting for him. There were no guards with him.

- Major, forgive me this whole charade. For some reasons I had to do so. The only thing that differentiates us are our bodies – said the king. - When I left the room I experienced a vision in which you were part of. A lot of things will depend on you! You have no idea how important you are in this whole existence of the universe. All the prophecies tell us that someone who will can help us will arrive. The ancients told us that a stranger arrives on our planet and we will be able to help. I experienced visions, and my divination told me that you're the one for whom we are waiting. I'm just surprised that it's you who will need help from us. Now, I'm sure, after what I saw in my vision, that it's you! Yes, it's you! Do you understand what I'm saying? - Asked the king pointing his finger at the Major.

- Yes, I understand, but ...

- What „but"? - The king asked.

- I'm confused. I do not know what to think. I came to this planet straight from my ship, which requires urgent repairs. I did not expect that any creature living here will be able to help us. I didn't even expect a shelter. I just needed time to complete my ship with the necessary elements because our scanners have shown that here you have the elements we need. We stopped by this region just by accident. And then I read a message on my computer. I'm sorry, I thought about refueling and supply us where snacks and refreshments, and here I learn that I am a chosen one here. This is absurd! Are you confident, that it's me? - the Major asked looking at the king in waiting for a response. He believed that the king made a mistake, that this is about someone else.

-Yes, I'm sure it's you! I am sure that you are able to help us. If you don't do this, the whole universe, as well as my people are doomed. Help us, help yourself and those miserable creatures that crawl on this planet.

The Major stood there motionless. He's never before been in a situation like this now. No one ever asked him for anything like this, like the powerful king Naroth is asking for now.

At one point, the king fell on both knees in front of Major Thomas and stared at his face.

- Gracious King, please stand up – he lifted the king from the ground.- I need a moment to reflect and think things through. Because this is, to be honest, something very surprising for me - said the major.

- Of course Major, of course - replied the king.

When they both stood in silence, time seemed to stand still. Finally, the major looked at the king and said:

-Of course, I will undertake this task. How could I hesitate and think about it? I am Major Thomas and my job, and duty, is to defend humanity andanything that wants to live in the galaxy.

There was silence. After a moment, the major spoke to the king, with a question:

- King Naroth, just tell me how do I do it?

- Come and do not ask about anything more - said the king.

They walked down the hallway toward the north wing, the Major thought about what he the king had said. They stopped in front of a

3.

MYSTERY REVEALED

- What is this place? Where are we? - asked the major again.

- This is a teleport - said the king pointing to a mirror located in the hall.

- What do you mean, teleport? After all, they don't exist! You can'tt travel in time! - Major protested.

- But you're wrong, you can and the Zotorigh know it too. That's what they are looking for all over the universe, at the same time completely destroying every planet so no one can get reborn, so no one could go back in time and fix what your race did.

- What do you mean, mine? - He stared in amazement.

- People allowed for this to happen, what the Zatorigh are doing now! Your race is responsible for what is happening now in the galaxy! - Said the king Naroth.

- But that's impossible. You're wrong mighty king! - Major Thomas responded with disbelief.

- If you still think it's a lie, then look at the portal – answered the king Naroth.

Major looked at the mirror, but did not see anything unusual in it.

- But nothing happens and I can't see anything here. What do you want to show me? - Said the major.

- Take a closer look and you will see.

When Major looked into the teleport, the mirror began to distort and after a while it seemed as if water appeared instead of it.

- Now walk up and touch and you will understand - said the king.

When Major came up and touched the mirrors, his mind could play glimpses of what happened in the past. Everything he saw in the blink of an eye. He stood there staring in the mirror when tears started to roll down his cheek, tears that he could not control. He stood there motionless, her lips began to tremble. When the visions have finished, Major could not believe what he saw in them. Slowly he began to recover, wiping his tears of his face. He looked at the king. The king came to the major and touched his shoulder, turning to him with the following words:

- Everyone makes mistakes, and if it's possible to repair the harm that's already done, than we don't have any time to waste. Only you are able to fix what your ancestors did. Remember, the power is in the heart - You have been chosen from among the remnants of humanity, that still exists. You were chosen before you were born. It's your destiny that directs you, not you. Each of us, every human being is created for a purpose. Everyone has their task, even me and it's destiny that ultimately counts! - Said the king.

Major stood there and did not know what to say. After a moment, he looked at the king and said:

- What can I do to save us all? How shall I do it? - he asked the king.

The king pointed to the portal, and replied:

- You will travel in time to the moment before it all started. Are you ready? - the king asked.

- Yes, I am - said the Major.

- Good. Remember one important thing: when something goes wrong, the machine will bring you back here and you'll only have one more chance to go back again in time and fix everything. Remember, also, that no one can know where you are, because otherwise our present world as we know it will cease to exist and everything that's familiar to you and everything that you love won't ever be the same again. It will be a completely different world, one that we both fear.

- It will be dominated by Zotorigh. Remember, you do't have much time and do not waste it! - said the king staring into the eyes of Major.

- I will not disappoint anyone! - Said Major.

- Prepare yourself - said the king. – The teleport will take you to the year 2060. You need to get to a certain person - a young boy who started a course of events. The boy is called Marcus Vortinghton. You need to hurry.

At this point the combat alarm went off and three guards ran into the hall. They fell in front of the king:

- Mighty King, Zotorigh attacked us. They got into our orbit and are now destroying our defenses!

- But how is that possible? How could they have found us? - Wondered the king. - Maintain your positions! We can not allow them to break through our defenses. If this happens, it will be only a matter of time when our end comes - said the king to himself. He turned one last time toward the Major and said:

- Remember, you are our last chance! Do not fail us! Now go and let your god take care of you!

As he spoke, Major went into the surface of the mirror and disappeared.

4.

THE WORLD IS BEING BORN

- Honey, give me the towel? - he heard a woman's voice coming from the room next door.

- Honey are you asleep? - Marcus laid in his bed staring at the door. - Honey, what's wrong with you?

The question was posed by a pretty brunette with hair to her shoulders. The woman entered the room.

- Honey, what happened to you? You are looking at me like you have seen a ghost! Hurry up, you'll be late for work. It is already seven, and you have to be at the base at 7.20. Hurry up, because you will be late and than you can forget about your promotion!

- Ah, I had a very strange dream, felt so real - Marcus said.

- Honey, you can tell me everything later, I'm in a hurry now and I have to rush - she said.

The woman got dressed and left. She slammed the door shut. Marcus was lying in the bed. At this moment, the woman ran back and kissed Marcus on the lips.

- I forgot to say goodbye - she said. - Have a nice day honey. See you at dinner with my parents. Do not forget, just like last time.

- Of course, darling, I won't forget - he promised.

The woman smiled and left.

Marcus stood up and walked to the bathroom. When he was in the shower, he heard noises coming from the bedroom:

- Captain Marcus - he heard. - Are you there Captain?

- Yes, I am - said Marcus. - I'll be ready in three minutes.

When he came out of the bathroom entering the bedroom he saw a young, grizzled blonde man standing at attention.

- The car is already ready. We're late - said Matt, turning to Captain Marcus.

- Ok, ok, let's go - said the Captain.

When they got into the car the Captain was silent.

- You are so silent. Something happened with Tiffany? Or maybe something didn't quite happen in bed? - Matt asked with a smile on his face. - You know, if there is anything I can help with - Matt jokingly responded and wanted to continue. - You see, I, as experienced as I am ...

- No, no - Marcus interrupted. - Everything is fine with Tiffany. I just had a terribly strange dream, last night. Really strange - said the captain.

- Calm down, tell me everything at Brands', while we toast your well-deserved promotion - said Matt.

When Captain Marcus and Lieutenant Mat got out of the car together, Mat looked at the sky turned to the captain and said:

- You have a beautiful weather to celebrate. The weather has been favourable to you.

- Yes sure. It will probably rain when it starts to get late. But, not that's no news. In the morning we have a heatwave, and in the evening downpour - said Captain Marcus in disgust.

When they entered the hangar, they both headed toward the door. The captain began to enter a secret code to access the restricted sector. Only persons involved in secret research on a variety of projects led by the military had access. When the door opened, they both entered the elevator, which took them six stories below ground. The doors closed and the elevator began to descend down very slowly.

- You know, I have a strange feeling about the TX-23 testing – said Marcus. - I do not know why, but I just have a strange feeling this morning, as if something were to happen, or something would go wrong.

- Well, you're right, if it doesn't work, you can forget about your promotion - Matt laughed. - But you still buying drinks - he said.

- Yes, yes, you won't forget about it, will you - said Marcus.

When the elevator stopped, the door opened and they both went into a room filled with various devices for testing, analysis and calculation. In this room there was another smaller, separate room, that were glazed octagonal based prism, about 4 meters high. In the middle of the room was an accelerator to test the TX-23.

- Welcome gentlemen! - Said a man in a white coat.

- Good morning, Dr. Richardson - Marcus and Matt greeted him.

Dr. Richardson was a world-renowned expert on molecular research on the TX-23.

- It's good that you came, because I'm about to started - said Richardson.

- Is everyone here? - Asked Marcus.

- Yes, all of the commanders are here, and I have another surprise: Secretary of Defense Philips has graced us with his presence - said Dr. Richardson.

- Who else? - Marcus asked nervously.

General Stevens, General Portland – they are all upstairs, waiting for the show to start.

- When do we begin, Doctor? I'm starting to get nervous because of the delays - asked Marcus.

- Everything will be ready in 5 minutes. Then the concentration of neutrons will reach its highest level to start a chain reaction - said the doctor. - And before we start everything, I advise you to hide somewhere and leave this room.

- Good idea. Let's go to our retinue. Let's see what they have to say after the presentation - said Marcus.

They both went to the room located on the top. When they entered, General Stevens gave them a cold gaze and said:

- I hope that, that thing that you have created, will work. Otherwise you will have to explain yourself at the Pentagon. The

Authorities have spent a couple of millions on this. It better be working.

- Don't worry General, it will work - said Marcus. - I hope… - he said under his breath, fearing that all his work could be wasted.

When everyone stood by the glass that separated the laboratory from the observation room, waiting for the TX-23 testing to start. Dr. Richardson went to the desktop. He pressed the speaker button and said:

- Ready in 30 seconds. Turning the anti-radiation shields on. The sensors are as standard, the concentration of molecules are as standard.

Observing the indicators, he raised his left hand and placed it on the red button. Far away you could see how his hands begin to tremble and that he was nervous.

- What's this button for? - asked Philips.

- This is the so-called ultimate rescue button - said Dr. Richardson.

- And that means? Please be more specific.

- If all the protections will fail, it is the only rescue. We had to be prepared for any possibility, even the fact that this something may get out, of course we don't want it to see our world, let alone escaped from the laboratory. Was this explanation specific enough?

- Yes, it was.

5,4,3,2,1… In a testing room a light started to appear, that at first appeared to be red but then it got lighter.

- Doctor, detailed report please.

- Everything is according to plan, for now, and I hope it will stay this way - the doctor smiled to himself. - TX-23 reached 100% power in less than a minute. The indicators are beginning to reach their maximum, neutrator thermoplastic shows at 25% of the norm, the concentration of molecules reached almost 80% and are still rising.

They stood in silence watching what will happen. The light that appeared, began to transform into meto-plasma and gained in size, now it was the size of an apple and was still expanding.

- This is going too smoothly – Captain Marcus started to talk to himself. - Something is wrong - he said to Mat. - Doctor, is everything alright? - He asked Richardson.

- Yes, absolutly. Why do you ask? The reaction reaches its highest concentration in 3,2,1, it's ready ...

At that moment a flare bursted in the room where the TX-23 tests were held, it was so bright it blinded people. Like on call, everyone lost consciousness and fell limply to the ground.

5.

TIME IS RUNNING

Marcus opened his eyes, then he looked at the people, who were getting up from the ground.

- What happened? Is everybody alright? - He asked. - Did something go wrong? Dr. Richardson?

- I do not understand, all indicators were at a normal level - said the doctor.

- You have to fix it all. If not, your career is over. You have twenty-four hours. Otherwise, the report reaches the Pentagon! - said General Stevens with a gruff voice turning to Captain Marcus.

- Yes, Sir! - Said Marcus.

The leadership was leaving, while Marcus and Matt saluted standing at attention, looking straight ahead. They both looked acalm, but in reality Captain Marcus, was nervous as drops of sweat were running down his forehead. The moment after the generals and the secretary of defense left the observation room, he pulled out a handkerchief.

- What happened, really? - Marcus turned to Dr. Richardson.

- To be honest, I have no idea. I'll need a few hours to determine what went wrong - said the doctor.

- Well, please keep me updated - said Captain Marcus, leaving with Mat toward the exit.

- You should relax, and I know the right place for it - said Matt, looking at Captain Marcus getting into the car.

- Come on, I'm not in the best mood.

- Well, don't be like that. One beer and you'll feel newborn - Matt tried to convince him.

- You don't understand? I have to go for dinner at Tiffanys' today. As if there could be any other day for it - captain Marcus said with distaste.

- I understand, but you really could use a beer and we could talk about what happened at base and what might have caused it. - said Matt.

- Okay, okay you convinced me, but only one, and really quick - said the Captain.

When the two entered the their familiar pub, they immediately felt like at home. Music that was playing in the speaker was: „Sex on fire" Kings of Lion, and the TV positioned above the bar was running the NFL. As always, the bar was filled with soldiers having finished service, drinking and enjoying themselves while watching the games.

While Captain Marcus took a seat at a table in the corner of the pub, Matt walked over to the bar:

- Mike, two beers please, for me and for Captain Marcus - he said to the bartender.

- You got it - said Mike.

Marcus sat and stared at the window, on which raindrops began to settle on.

„What do you think went wrong? All calculations were correct. Or perhaps, it's actually not possible? „- Wondered Marcus.

- Hold it, a cold Mollet will cheer you up – said Mat, giving the beer to Marcus, and interrupted his thoughts.

- Thanks.

- And what will happen when it turns out, that it was all for nothing? - Asked Matt.

- I don't know. I guess I'll have to devote myself to something else, as I won't have a future at the military - said Marcus.

- I know, well maybe you'll be interested in working in a flower shop?

- Very funny. I need to find out what really caused all of this. It won't give me peace, otherwise - said Marcus.

- Don't worry. The doctor will find out, and everything will be clear by then - said Matt.

Marcus stared at the window and the image began to blur before his eyes, while Matt tried to calm him down. Marcus blinked several times and then stared at window again, but this time his attention focused on a roadster standing in the parking lot in front of the bar between motorbikes. As he was stuck in his deep thoughts, he felt his hands itching, then the car began to distort and float. It hovered ten centimeters above the ground, and in his hands he began to feel a burning sensation, that transformed into small glowing dots on his both hands.

- Marcus, Marcus! Are you listening to me? - Asked Matt.

- What did you say?

- Ok, never mind. I am talking on, and you're just starring at the window, as if you could spot anything - said Matt.

Did you see what I saw? - Marcus asked with a slight hesitation.

- But what was I supposed to see? - Mat replied. - The only thing that draws my attention, is that someone sitting on the other side of the room. Look! Not bad, huh?

- No, nothing, not important. I just ... Never mind, anyway ... - replied Marcus.

When he looked at his watch, he remembered that he was supposed to be having dinner with Tiffanys' parents today. It was a very important for her, because her parents celebrated their twentieth wedding anniversary today.

- It's six pm, and dinner is at six-thirty. I need to go - he said to Mat.

- I'm sorry, I'm really unfocused by what happened in the lab today.

- I understand, don't worry. We'll talk tomorrow on duty. See you tomorrow - said Matt.

While Marcus got in his car, he began to wonder what exactly happened in the pub.

- How is this possible? No, I must have imagined it. I think, I'm just tired - Marcus replied under his breath, and started the car.

At one point, when he stopped at the traffic lights, his head began to hurt. It hurt so much, that it felt like the internal pressure would blow his head up. He pulled off the road, turned off the engine, closed his eyes and visions started to appear in his head. He saw different races, different galaxies, that began to disappear, planets that were on fire, civilizations that exceeded Earth's technology. His vision led him to the planet thousands of light years away from Earth. He felt as if he was there. He felt the breeze on his face as he stood on that planet. He did not believe what he was seeing. He was in the middle of the street between giant buildings. He saw skyscrapers so high that disappeared in the skies, flying spaceships and the entire civilization, that lived on this planet. Suddenly, four fiery meteors appeared in the sky that seemed to hit the planet somewhere. After a while he realized that all these buildings and skyscrapers that surrounded him began to crumble into pieces, in the northern part of the city. He could see an explosion in the south. Creatures inhabiting this planet fled ahead themselves in panic. Captain Marcus wanted to help but couldn't move, he could only watch. One of the fleeing creatures stumbled and fell in front of Marcus. When it tried to get up it noticed the captain, and said:

- Get ready! They're coming for you!

The Captain woke up all sweaty, he looked around to see where he was. He saw that he was sitting in his car, where he stopped.

- That's impossible. I'm just very tired and it's probably the stress. This couldn't really be happening. I'm just too tired, that's all.

He started the car and headed to the dinner with Tiffanys' parents.

When he entered the house, everyone was already there. Calm classical orchestra music was playing in the background. The men were dressed in tuxedos and the women were in their evening dresses. Tiffany's parents were respectable people. Her father, Stuart, was a senator, who in two years was going to be running for the office of President of the State, and her mother, Georgia, he was a respectable doctor.

- Oh, you're here – said Tiffany loudly - I thought you wouldn't show up.

- I promised I'd be here this time, and here I am - said Marcus. - Where are your parents? I would like to congratulate them. Oh ok, I see them - he said, and headed toward them.

- Congratulations on such a long and happy married life together - said Captain Marcus greeting Tiffanys' parents. - You look stunning as always, Mrs. Smith.

- Oh, please. Stop it. - she said, smiling.

- How's your career? Going in the right direction? - asked Stuart Captain Marcus.

- Yes, of course, everything is is just fine - he said.

While they were talking, the Captain phone rang, that he had with him. He was suppose to turn it off before the dinner, but has completely forgotten about it.

- Excuse me, very much - he said and walked out onto the terrace.

When he reassured himself that no one was nearby, he then picked up the phone.

- Yes, hello. Who's calling?

- In twenty minutes on the corner of Forty-second Hamond Street. Be there - he heard someone say on the phone.

- But who's calling?

- I do not have time to explain. We don't have time, everything started. You are in danger.

- But how is it in danger? I do not understand! - He asked with a slight nervousness.

- Be there in twenty minutes, otherwise everyone will die. Time starts now.

- Who ... - the caller on the other end of the phone hung up.

The Captain looked around very carefully. He stood there holding the phone to his ear, then he put it in his pocket. Then he turned and went back to the reception looking for his fiancée. He found her next to the buffet. He grabbed her arm, leaned over and said:

- I'm so sorry darling, I have to go.

- What do you mean, you have to go? You just came! What are you doing? - She asked.

- Nothing. I had a strange phone call. I really have to leave. I promise I will make it up to you and explain everything when I get back - he added, and kissed her on the cheek. - I promise, really, but now I have to go - he said, and headed toward the exit.

Before he got into the car he looked around to see if he was followed by anyone, he got in and started the engine. When we drove to the specified location, the phone rang again.

- Yes? - Answered Marcus.

- In five hundred meters turn left. You are being followed. Try to get rid of them and meet me where we agreed - said the voice on the phone and then hung up again.

The captain looked in the mirror and noticed, that he was being followed by car with unmarked plates. A balck BMW SUV. Inside the car appeared to be four figures. The captain gripped the steering wheel, changed the course and hit the gas pedal. The car, that followed the Captain also speeded up. When the captain tried to lose them, passing other cars left and right, one of the attackers pulled his window down, then pulled out a machine gun and opened fire at Marcus. The captain had no other option but to retaliate. He grabbed the gun he had in his coat, turned his head toward the attackers and fired four shots. The attackers driver maneuvered the car turning the steering wheel sharply to the left and then disappeared out of sight. The captain turned to the right, driving through a road with less traffic. After driving another two blocks he stopped. He tried to calm his nerves and get himself together.

- What the hell's going on at all? - He asked himself, loudly pronouncing every word.

Once he has calmed down he noticed that his left arm was dripping with blood.

- Great, I got shot.

When he tried to somehow bear the wound, he heard the squeal of tires. He looked in the rear mirror and noticed the same car that followed him before.

- Why won't they leave me alone? - He asked himself, then he pressed his foot on the pedal and started to drove off with squealing tires.

The car of the attackers followed after him. Marcus glanced at his watch. „Ihave only ten minutes left, I need to hurry, otherwise they'll get me"- He realized, then he turned onto the road leading out of town. The car of the attackers are approaching at a very fast pace and there are already behind him. When this mysterious BMW attempted to overtake the captain on the left, the captain drove up to the road on the right by performing the same maneuver.

- I don't give up so easily! - He said loudly shouting toward the mysterious car.

When both cars were at the same level, Captain Marcus had only one last chance to avoid them. At that moment, the enemy's car pulled out their guns.

The captain looked at the opponents and loudly shouted: - Choke on it! - Then the attackers rammed their car and hit a standing tree on the roadside.

The captain stopped about two hundred meters behind the destroyed car. He looked over his right shoulder, then sped up and drove off to the arranged meeting.

After a while, four men got out of the car that hit the tree. Everyone was dressed in a long black baggy coat and everyone had a black hat on his head, large enough to completely cover their face. All the characters stood in the middle of the road looking at each other. One of the men walked up to the rest of the them, then turned his head left, then right, up and down.

- This is not the end, Captain Marcus. This is just the beginning. It will be a matter of time before we'll get you.

At the end, all of the men headed toward the city by foot.

When the captain arrived at the appointed place and wanted to attent the wound, he noticed that there wasn't even a trace from the gunshot.

- How is this possible? - thoughts rushed through his head. - I did get shot. I didn't make this up. I need to gather myself and comprehend everything that happend.

He wondered what to do next. After a short wait in silence the phone rang. The captain looked at his phone and hesitated, but after some thought he answers the call.

- Yes, hello? - He answered with a little hesitation.

- Did you have any problems with getting to the place? - the voice asked him on the phone.

- Yes, I did. I was chased by a SUV car. A little bit and they could have got me! And I got shot, I wanted to attent to the wound but it turned out that it disappeared! - Marcus shouted over the phone. - What is happening here? What do they want? - The Captain asked.

- You - he heard on the phone.

- What do you mean, Me? I do not understand - Captain Marcus wondered further.

- There's no time for explanations! You are in great danger - said the voice on the phone.

- Get out of the car in one minute, then go to the bus stop that's in front of you and get into the oncoming bus 4F. You will take place in the last row by the window – he heard over the phone, and the voice hung up.

Captain Marcus looked in the rear mirror and got out of the car, closely observing if he was not being followed by anyone. He walked over to the indicated stop.

- What am I doing? - He asked himself.

After a while he noticed the oncoming bus 4F. When boarding he asked for a ticket to Roseland. He looked around the bus. A few people people sat only there. They seemed to be nothing out of the ordinary. Just ordinary passengers, so he hoped. According to the instructions he sat in the last row by the window and wondered what to do next. After all, he was not informed, what next to do. After a while, when the bus started to move, a man walked over and sat next to him.

- I hope you are alright and that nobody saw you get on this bus - the man said.

- No, ort least I hope not - said Catpain Marcus.

- That's good. I'm Jason.

He was an older man, about fifty years old.

- What's going on here at all? - Asked Marcus - And who were those men in the car?

- These were not people - replied Jason.

- What do you mean they aren't people? Who then?

- You wouldn't want to know, believe me. The only thing I can say is that their objective is to exterminate us all.

Captain Marcus gazed in amazement.

- You still don't understand? - Asked Jason. - Maybe I'll put it differently. Do you know how the secret service works? That's sort of how they operate. First they send people for recognition, then they activate their „plugs" and at the end they send their troops. In this case, for the extermination of the human race a small section of soldiers is sufficient.

- But how is that possible? - Captain Marcus asked.

- Don't ask me about it. I know that you have something that can help us ...

- What? - Marcus asked.

- Certain powers that could stop them, or at least I hope so – He replied - But besides you there are two other people like you, that we have to find as soon as possible. We must find them before they do - said Jason.

- But what powers? I don't understand!

- Tell me, is the last couple of days, did something out of the ordinary happen to you? Or something superhuman? - Asked Jason.

- After testings at base, I sat in a pub, I noticed a car floating in the air at the parking lot, and at the same time some white spots appeared on my hands - said the Captain.

- It's Your power. Your fate. Can you move things from one place to another. That's your weapon. It's very powerful. You don't even realize how powerful it is. We need to hurry and find them before they do - Jason repeated again.

- But how do we find them? - Captain Marcus asked.

- Do not worry. Each of you has something, that can be traced back to you.

- But what is it? - Captain Marcus asked.

- Tell me, as a child have you been gifted with anything? Do you have any scars? he asked.

- I ... - Captain Marcus thought for a moment. - I have the scar. I don't really remember how I got it. I just have it.

- Can you show me?

- There you go - replied Marcus raising his T-shirt.

Jason saw three strokes on his ribs about two centimeters away from each other as well as two dots between the first and second line.

- Yes, this is it - replied Jason. - Do you remember your parents?

- No, I don't remember them. I was raised by my aunt and uncle. They both died, unfortunately. - said Marcus.

- Do you know how they died?

- It was a car accident. They fell into an abyss during a trip to San Francisco.

- They weren't your aunt and uncle. They were your guardians - said Jason. - They guard you from Zotorigh. They died during a fight in the forests of Brazil. They protected to the best of their abilities, but they didn't die in vain - said Jason. - Now you have enough strength. You have enough strength to unite with others and stop them from destroying the planet and their continued expansion onto universe, but we have to hurry because Zotorigh are very close.

While they both sat there in the bus, Captain Marcus phone started to ring. He looked at the phone.

- I have to pick up - replied the Captain. - It's the base, they're calling from the laboratory. - Yes, hello? answered the Captain.

- I was ordered to inform you Captain, as to what was the reason for today's experiment fail was, and why everyone lost consciousness briefly - replied Dr. Richardson.

- Oh, yes. Please continue Doctor.

- What happened today was not accidental. I noticed that one of the cables supplying plasma energy was cut - replied the doctor.

- But who could have done this? - Captain Marcus asked him.

- I don't know, but that's not all - said Dr. Richardson.

- Speak - said Marcus.

- The surveillance has shown that something escaped from TX-23.

There was silence. Marcus didn't know what to ask or even how, because he had heard different things but never anything like this. After a moment, the voice said:

- Hello, are you there?

- Yes I'm here. Could you repeat, because I don't really understand... Hwhat do you mean something escaped ... What? - Marcus asked nervously.

- I don't know how this is possible, but something got out, or someone research it let in, and evidently some portal to another world opened up, or something has been created. I can't gather logical explanations now, but listen, rightnow, what's worse, someone was prepared for it, or knew what was going to happen - said Dr. Richardson.

- I need to know more Doctor - said Captain Marcus. - I need to know who is behind it - said Captain Marcus in a firm voice.

- It will not be easy, but I'll try to find something more - replied the doctor.

- Doctor? - asked Marcus.

- Yes, anything else?

- Please watch out.

- Of course. I'll call you as soon as I will find out something more - said the doctor.

6.

THEM

- We have a little problem - said Marcus to Jason, when he hung up.
- What problem?
- There was an accident in the laboratory, where I worked in and where tests were being held for the TX-23. Someone caused the accident on purpose and ...
- ... And something from another dimension escaped? - Jason interrupted.
- Yes, but how do you know about that? - Captain Marcus asked with surprise.
- I had a dream.
- Who are you at all? - Asked Marcus.
- I, uuuh ... - Jason mubled. - I can't tell you that, Marcus. You will learn everything when the time is right. I'd like to tell you, but I can't. If you want to survive, you must trust me - Jason said with a firm voice.
- Okay, but if you do something that would endangered me, I will kill you - said Captain Marcus. - Then tell me. What are we doing now?
Suddenly, they both felt a huge crash into the back of the bus.
- What was that?

- It's them! Get ready! I do not know how they found us - threw Jason. - And one more thing: watch out for their tongue...

At this point, the bus stopped and in front of it stood one of them - at a distance of about thirty meters. He began to walk slowly approaching the bus and and held in his left hand a sword. Then they felt how a second attacker got onto the roof.

- What should I do? - Asked Marcus.

- Don't get yourself killed - said Jason with a slight smile. - Now I have to deal with this bus. - Jason stood up, stepped forward and vanished into thin air.

Marcus froze. At the same time, he saw how the attacker on the roof pierced his sword into the roof and began to open it as if it were a can of sardines. Captain Marcus rose from his seat with little thought, grabbed a seat in front of him and jumped over getting onto the passage between the seats. He saw Jason appear right next to the bus where the attacker stood. Suddenly, on Jasons' hands appeared something glowing. He aimed a blow to his left fist, then vanished and appeared back behind Zotorigh. Jason induced another blow, but this time to the knee. After receiving punch the attacker fell limply to the ground, but quickly got up and headed toward Jason. He aimed a blow with his sword into his chest, but Jason jumped back being able to avoid it at the last moment, he disappeared and appeared again with his left hand inducing a blow to the right foot. This time the attacker fell unconscious to the ground. Jason stood over the Zotorigh, and in his left hand appeared a sword. The attacker turned his face toward Jason, who thereafter imposed an onslaught to the Zotorigh body. The attacker crumbled into ashes.

Captain Marcus, without thinking, headed for the exit avoiding a strike with the sword. When he was at the door and almost got outside, he felt a powerful hit on his back and fell to the bus floor. While the Captain was lying on the floor, he felt something slick around his neck, then that something began to tighten his throat. Captain Marcus slowly lost consciousness. At this point in Captain Marcus' mind started to appear different images. When he awoke, he didn't feel anything on his neck. He noticed Jason standing over him, shaking his head.

- What happened? - Asked Marcus.

- You don't remember?

- No. I blacked out when something sling around my neck and I just woke up now - said Captain Marcus. - What happened to the Zotorigh?

- You really don't remember? They have been eliminated - said Jason.

The captain gazed helplessly at Jason as he couldn't remember what happened.

- Give me your hand - Jason said. - And close your eyes.

He touched the Captain on his forehead. Captain flashed a „film" of his fight with Zotorigh. He saw himself fall to the ground, the bus lightened with a huge flash of light throwing the attacker with powerful force away from the bus, and he rises back up. With his clenched fists emerges a bright glow. Thereafter, the Captain jumps out of the bus and falls to the ground.

Captain Marcus pulled his forehead away from his hand in disbelief and asked with horror in his voice:

- And who the fuck are you and what the hell is going on?

- Now you know how they were eliminated - replied Jason. - You have a powerful force, which you couldn't possibly dream of...

- I'm asking you, who the fuck are you? - Said Marcus with a gruff voice.

- I'm your friend, you have to trust me - said Jason.

- But I still don't understand anything - said the Captain.

- I can't explain it all, now - said Jason. - We need to get to New Jersey as soon as possible. There is another person like you. With the plane it'll take us four hours from the O'Hare International Airport. We must hurry, we have very little time - said Jason with a firm voice.

- New Jersey? I only briefly walked out of dinner with my fiancee's parents, and now I have to fly to New Jersey. I have to call Tiffany.

- You will call her in a while, because if we won't make it on time, there will be no fiancee and or anyone to call to.

They headed for the nearest car parked nearby and drove away.

While getting out of the car at the airport, they both looked around and walked towards the departure hall.

- I'll go get tickets and you buy us something to eat. Get me water and orange juice. I'll meet you at the entrance to the check in. Be there in fifteen minutes - said Jason.

- Ok - replied Marcus and they split up.

As the Captain was standing in the queue to the cashier, he noticed how two men in suits looked in his direction. One of them was holding a newspaper, where the front page was a photo of him and Jason. He tried to read the text below the photo, but the cashier pulled him out of his thoughts, while counting his purchases and said:

- 4.20, please.

The Captain paid and left. When he approached the check in, Jason was already waiting for him.

- The plane takes off in ten minutes - said Jason.

When both of them were already on the plane and took their places, they heard a voice from the speakers saying:

- Good evening. Here speaks the Captain of the aircraft. The flight will take two hours and fifteen minutes. Please fasten your seat belts during take-off. We wish you a pleasant flight.

They both sat for a moment in silence, then Marcus turned to Jason:

- Can you tell me now everything? What exactly is going on here?

Jason looked at him. He looked for a moment, then he said:

- Ok, what do you want to know?

- Tell me everything you know about me and what role I have to play here.

- Are you sure you want to know? - asked Jason.

-Yes, avery sure. Because within a few hours my whole life turned up side down! Someone attacks me or you are showing me a film in my mind as you touch my head, something squeezed my neck, I see flashes, everything disappears, I don't remember, but I apparently have some magical power like Copperfield!

- Okay. In fact, you and the other people, thet we have to find, will together create a weapon to fight those you have seen and fought against today. - Jason replied.

- I already know, but maybe you can tell me more. What else don't I know? Because the whole time you're just talking very vaguely. I want to hear specifics! - replied Marcus.

- Ok, ok, calm down. Your powers are able to move things, and besides, as you know, you have a powerful weapon in your hands, but that's not all. Five days will be the apogee, and if we can't stop them, hell will break out, like you've never seen before. Everyone you know, will serve as a side dish lunch or as a living incubators for the new offspring of these creatures - Jason explained. - You wanted to know everything, so now you know. Just think: this world has twelve billion people. Half of them will be a snack for the new offspring, while the other half will serve as incubators. Does this outlook makes you to think?

Yes, but if there are other races in the universe that could stop Zotorigh, why don't they do so? - Asked Marcus.

- Exactly, but there is no such breed that could stop them. You and the other two kids are our last resort. You are the last of a race that still has such an opportunity. They're all gone, except you. It was only you and your guardians. They protect you, to the best of their ability - Jason replied.

- And who are you? I don't know anything about you. How did you get here and what is your assignment? I do not understand. You know a lot more than I do. I want to know everything about you.

- Listen to me. If I were to tell you everything, you wouldn't believe me anyway. You know everything you need to know for now - replied Jason. - Now go to sleep, because you might not get the chance later.

Captain Marcus looked at Jason, who closed his eyes and turned onto his left side, covering himself with a blanket, which he got from the flight attendant.

When Marcus fell asleep, he dreamed another vision in which Jason fought alongside him, falls to the ground and doesn't get up again. He also saw how the other two were falling, but he himself can not move. He stands alone with his hands paralyzed and can not do anything.

Marcus suddenly woke up drenched in sweat. When he looked out the window, he saw how their plane approached for landing. He looked around and noticed Jason sitting with his head supported by his hand thinking of something.

- What happened? - Asked Jason.

- I had another vision, and I saw you in it ...

- Keep it to yourself this time what you have seen - Jason interrupted Captain Marcus.

- But ... - he wanted to say something more, but Jason looked at him and said again:

- Keep it to yourself and remember that it will depend on you whether it will be as you saw in his visions - replied Jason.

- Dear passengers, we will approach for landing. Please fasten your seat belts and prepare for landing. It's seventeen degrees Celsius outside. Enjoy your day - they heard the speaker say.

- To work. We need to find the next person - said Jason to Marcus.

Both came out of the plane and passed the check in, when suddenly three men in suits aproached them. One of them turned to them pulling a FBI badge out, saying:

- Come with us immediately!

Marcus did not know what to do. He looked at Jason, who turned to Marcus:

- Well, I think we don't have a choice. Let's go.

And they both were escorted to the interrogation room.

When they both sat in the room the Captain nervously asked Jason:

-And what now? What's your plan?

At this point, an agents came into the room holding two coffees, which he served Marcus and Jason, and then addressed them:

- I am an agent Johns. - He rested both hands on the table and said: - Captain Marcus, you are under arrest for the murder of Dr. Richardson.

The Captain gazed in disbelief. After a moment of silence, he gathered himself and turned to the agent: - But I didn't kill Dr. Richardson! We were friends. When was I supposed to kill Dr. Richardson? - Asked Marcus.

- The doctor has been found in the laboratory, and the last person that has been seen with the doctor was you, Captain Marcus. Anyway, we found bullets from your gun in his body - agent Johns replied.

- But I did not kill the doctor, I swear! - Marcus yelled.

Jason was sitting on a chair, calmly glancing at his watch every now and then.

- Agent Johns, how many people are in this building? - Asked Jason.

- What's it to you? - Johns snapped.

- I advise to take your weapon out and defend yourself against the attackers.

- What atta....

At this point the alarm went off.

- Stay here and don't move anywhere - said Johns.

Jason looked at the captain, then to the agent, and then they heard how someone looked the door from the outside, then he said:

- We have to prepare to escape. Zotorigh are here.

- How here? Now? How is this possible in such a short time? - Marcus asked, surprised.

- Does it matter now?

- How many?

- Enough to kill us if we just continue to sit back and do nothing. Evacuate immediately - Jason yelled to Marcus.

- But how? The doors are locked - asked Marcus.

- Use your power in your hands to open the door - Jason said. - It's very simple, just focus.

When the captain focused his gaze on his hands, white spots began to appear on them, they grew larger and united into one large glowing spot. Suddenly he heard a bang not far away from them, as well as shots and people screaming.

- Captain, please focus, otherwise we'll die - said Jason with a firm voice.

- I'm trying, I'm trying!

He looked at his hands, again overgrown with glowing white spots, which began to grow and combine with each other.

- And now, point your hands towards the door and turn the handle - said Jason. - Hurry up. They're right next door. Thirty seconds they will find us! - Jason screamed.

The captain couldn't stand the force and turned his hand toward the door, and they opened. With surprise he looked at his hands and to Jason sitting next to him.

- We have to go and as quick as possible - said Jason.

He ran out of the room to the left and Marcus ran after him. They both stopped at the end of the wall. Jason looked left and right, first and then turned to Marcus:

- You go first. There's the door, you see? - He pointed with his right hand.

- Yes I see.

- Quick, go!

When Marcus ran around the corner toward the door, he saw Zotorigh coming from the opposite direction. He tried to stop and go back, but he slipped and fell. Zotorigh was coming toward his direction very quickly. Marcus tried to get up and get back to Jason, as he had his back turned to the attacker. Suddenly, he felt Zotorigh's tongue getting caught around his neck with that clutched him. He looked at Jason fighting with two strangers.

- I can't give up. Not today - Marcus said with his last ounce of strength, after which he moved his own body up toward the ceiling with all his strength. As he was at head height with Zotorigh, he looked at him and yelled:

- Choke on it! - Turned his hands towards the attacker, and his hand blew out a powerful beam of white light and hit him straight at the body.

Zotorigh fell down to the ground, freeing the captain's neck. Marcus ran up to him and grabbed his sword, which his opponent had with him, he striked a death blow straight onto the spot where his heart suppose to be. The body turned into ashes and crumbled to dust.

When Captain Marcus has finished with his opponent, he remembered that Jason is still fighting two others. He turned to Jason to help him. He saw that Jason was held by one of them, and the other wanted to strike his sword into his heart. The captain tried to reach the place with all his strength, but it was too late. The sword penetrated Jasons chest, after that he fell to the ground.

The captain stopped and fell to his knees. He didn't believe what he saw. One of the Zotorigh, the one that held the Jasons body, looked toward Captain Marcus smiled and said:

- Now it's your turn - and began to steer toward him, and behind him followed a second one.

- I won't forgive you that! - Marcus yelled clenching his fists and jumped. He stood on his feet and began to run toward the attackers.

When he was in reaching distance to the first Zotorigh, his opponent swung his hand open, which its end was razor-sharp, trying to split the Captains skull. He sensed his intentions, dodged, bounced off the wall with his right foot while turning and hiting him so hard in the face that this face flew off the wall and bounced back from her falling to the ground.

After he was already side by side with the second one, that tried to strike him with his sword, the Captain slumped to the ground, without thinking and was slipping on it. He slipped between the Zotorigh legs and quickly rose to his feet. The attacker was unable to turn, to strike with his sword. The captain was already on his steady feet with hands pointing towards the enemy, who looking at him with hatred and said:

- And what are you going to do now? We are alone you do not have a chance.

- Let's see! - Said Marcus.

Then he began to run toward him and in both hands appeared white glowing balls. At the same time the attacker began to head towards Marcus preparing to his final move with the sword. The captain directed his both hands toward the attacker, and his hands pierced rays through him. The opponent fell to the ground, turning into ashes. The captain ran to the second striker, who he fought first, standing over him, and watched as he slowly passes and asked:

- Was it worth it?

The attacker wasn't quick anought to answer as Marcus hit him with a deadly ray, asking again. Zotorigh vanished into thin air.

As the Captain regained control over himself he remembered that Jason lied limply on the ground. He fell to his knees and suddenly heard Jason wanting to tell him something. He had to bring his ear closer to Jasons face to hear what he wanted to say. But it was too late.

The Captain put his body very carefully on the floor and asked:

- Why did you have to die? Why? - He asked himself. - Not now. I had it in my visions. It wasn't suppose to be like this...

The Captain leaned over to Jason and closed his eyes, trying to hold his tears back. When one of tears dripped onto the body, the Captain noticed as Jason strated to move and breathe. After a moment he saw him open his eyes and comes back to life.

Jason looked at Captain Marcus with a smile on his face:

-Thank you.

Then he turned to get the dust off his clothes, he looked at the Captain, who rose from the floor and asked:

- Can you tell me what other powers I have, or if some kind of unexpected „miracle" will happen again and reveal some of my powers?

- Okay, but first we need to quickly get out of here, because there will be twice of them here soon, and then they'll both die - said Jason to the Captain.

As they passed the corridor, they found bodies of three agents lying on the floor. Jason went to the first one, folded his hands in prayer. Then he raised his hands up, and then lowered them at a very fast pace, and the body of Agent dismentled into several parts.

Another agent turned out to be agent Johns, who was still alive, but had a slit abdomen on his right side. Jason stood over him, he wanted to heal him, but when he leaned toward his the agent pulled himself up so that he could sit straight up and said:

- Don't heal me. I will die soon, anyway. One of them have put something in my stomach and that something is growing. End my agony, because if won't, then I will - He said, grabbing his gun, putting it in his mouth and pulled the trigger. However, the gun turned out to have run out of bullets. He looked again at Jason and said in a pleading voice:

- Please, let me go.

Agent Johns dropped to the floor, closed his eyes and waited for his move. Jason, without thinking, rose to his feet raised his hands and struck a blow that ended the agenta life.

Then he went to the last agent and repeated his actions.

Marcus stood beside all this time, until he suddenly asked:

- Why did you do that?

- If I didn't do it, the Zotorigh would have been here in several minutes, ready for further expansion of doing the same thing to more people - said Jason.

When the two went out from the airport, Captain Marcus asked:

- Where now?

- The person we are looking for, lives seven kilometers to the west, on Dove Road 34, if I'm not mistaken. I hope we get there before them, but I have a feeling that it may be too late.

They got into a taxi. Jason chose a seat in the front, and Captain Marcus sat at the back.

- Where to? - The taxi driver asked.

- To this address, as quick as possible - Jason said, showing the note with the address.

- By highway will be the qucikest. It's only a ten minute drive from the airport - said the taxi driver.

- Great - said Jason. The taxi drove off.

When they they were on their way to the next person, who was also the chosen one, they both sat in silence and looked at the passing cars through the window.

- What brought you gentlemen got to this city? - Asked the taxi driver.

- We came sightseeing - said Jason.

- Here is a delicious pub nearby, where they make amazing pancakes – the taxi driver said with a smile.- So if you're hungry, I would recommend this place - he added the driver.

- Well, thank you for the information. We will try them for sure - said Marcus. Then he turned to Jason with a hushed voice:

- And how do you imagine this encounter? We just go over to that person and say you're the chosen one and you have to come with us, otherwise the destruction of mankind will await us? - Marcus asked sarcastically.

- I have not thought about it, if I'll be honest - said Jason. - But I hope we can find this person like I have found you.

- Actually, how did you find me, because I don't really understand? Is it written on my forehead: I am the chosen one?

- Yes, I know - he replied Jason.- Maybe it sounds silly, but when I got closer to like you, I could feel something like an aura. And the visions, of course.

- What visions? - Marcus asked surprised.

- Well, like you have them. You saw in the about six days ago.

- Are we there yet? - Marcus asked, turning to the driver.

- We're almost there.

- Please stop now. we'll get there by foot - Jason asked the driver.

7.

BEGINNING OF SALVATION

When they got out, they both began to look around the surrounding buildings. Jason looked like as if he was afraid of something, as if he sensed some threat or danger. Jason's eyes suddenly stopped at a four-story building, that stood in front of him.

- This way, come this way - he said.

Like a peevish tourist, Captain Marcus got out of the car and stretched lazily. Jason looked up to the sky and decreed, that it will be raining, for sure. The sky actually looked like it was going to rain. Marcus said nothing. He followed Jasons commands.

Walking in front of themselves, they arrived at an apartment block. Jason gave the order.

- Let's find stairway number 7.

- Hmm ... - said Marcus. - How do you know that's the right number?

- Trust me, I just know - Jason replied, and turned to go around the block. Marcus found the stairway and asked:

- I guess, I stay on the lookout, and you go alone?

- I don't think so - said Jason. - We'll go together. I don't know how this person will react.

Marcus agreed with a nod.

- The apartment should be on the second floor - Jason said.

- How do you know that it's on the second?

- Look, we went inside, we are on the ground floor and there are three doors here. On the first and second floor it must be the same ...

- Well, Sherlock, alright. Lead on, and Watson will follow you, so you no longer have to be afraid - interrupted Marcus.

They walked up the stairs. Jason at front and Marcus behind him. When they reached the first floor, Jason stopped and Marcus accidentally ran into him.

- Sorry, I didn't warn that you would stop.

Jason said nothing, he just turned his eyes upward.

- Did something happen? - Marcus asked, alarmed at the sight of his companion.

- Take care of yourself - said Jason.

- And just what might happen to me?

- Seriously, be careful, I have a strange feeling that something is wrong - Jason said firmly.

- Okay, I'll be careful.

- Thank you - Captain Marcus replied smiling. Then they both moved in search of the apartment number 7.

When they reached the door, Marcus approached and stood at the left side. On the opposite side stood Jason and knocked. No one answered, so after a while he knocked again, louder this time.

- Maybe he's not at home? - Marcus said. - Or maybe he takes a shower. Is there anyone? Hello!- yelled Jason repeatedly knocking again. Still, no one opened.

- Something is wrong - decreed Jason.

- What?

- Move away - said Jason, putting his left hand on the door handle and reaching for his sword with his right hand, which until now was hidden under his jacket. When he opened the door, he could not believe what he saw. The apartment was in complete ruins, as if someone had fought a battle of life and death.

- We're too late? - Marcus asked, looking at Jason.

- Apparently so - said the companion. - We need to quickly look around, because the Zotorigh may still be here. You go this way, I'll go there - the captain pointed out the direction of search.

- What are we looking for?

- I do not know myself. Maybe we can find some traces on where to find this person. One more thing. Do not touch anything with your bare hands - Jason added, giving Marcus latex gloves.- Be careful, because Zotorigh may still be lurking somewhere here, as I feel someone's presence. It is very weak, but be careful.

Captain Marcus stood for a moment, he looked around, then went into a smaller room where he also noticed signs of a fight. While he looked around, he walked up to the closet with shelves, took a random book, blew off the dust and read the headline: „extraterrestrials".

„Sounds familiar!" - Marcus thought, then opened it and began to browse. After a moment he heard as if something was moving in the room. He put the book back on the shelf. He noticed that the door to the closet with clothes were slightly opened and creaked. Captain Marcus began to cautiously approach the closet. When he was quite close, he prepared for the fight, even though he didn't know who he would fight. He began to focus energy in his hands, that began to lighten up the room. Drops of sweat appeared on his forehead. It was evident that he is nervous. He held both hands out to the closet. When he was about to strike, the door of the closet opened and a tiny puppy leaned out. At this point, Captain Marcus breathed a sigh of relief. He lowered his hands and crouched down.

- Come here, little friend – he said, with hands holding out in his direction.

The dog began to cautiously approach Marcus, then he sniffed him.

Marcus grabbed the puppy and said:

- You're probably hungry, huh?

The puppy looked at Marcus and licked his hand.

- You're so sweet. I'll give you a name ...

Suddenly, before he could finish the sentence, Captain Marcus heard a bang in the room where Jason was.

- Oh, shit - he said under his breath, then put the dog down to the floor.- Do not go anywhere - he said to the puppy and ran into the living room.

Running into the living room, he noticed Jason lying on the floor by the wall all curled up in pain. Suddenly, he felt a blow to his face, so strong that Marcus flew against the wall, next to Jason. When Marcus fell to the ground, he mumbled under his breath, „now that's a surprise."

He got up quickly, then felt a hit again, but this time on the left side of his ribs. This hit was also so strong that Marcus got thrown by the window, where he again felt a hit on the other side of his face. Marcus then fell to the floor. He tried to get up, he looked carefully around the room and heard Jason say:

-He's at the corner of the room and comes in your direction.

With little thought, Marcus, drew his left hand in that direction and used his power. When it seemed like that something had been hit, they saw the ball of white light, which he fired, bounces off the attacker, and hitting the wall, creating a hole in it. When Marcus wanted to renew the attack, he felt something grabbing and lifting him by the neck. Jason wanted to take the opportunity and try hit the attacker, but unfortunately nothing worked, as he received a punch so strong that that threw him into the corner of the room. Marcus hovered over the floor trying to grab his throat to prevent him from suffocating. To his surprise, he grabbed an opponent by hand, who didn't seem to have a human form. His touch caused a breach of his protective field and the wave which arose over the body revealed the outline of figures similar to human beings. When it seemed as if everything was lost, Marcus placed his right hand on the place where a human's chest is suppose to be and with his last ounce of strength, striked creating a shockwave. The blow was so powerful that it threw the attacker to the other end of the room. The attacker hit the wall and then fell to the floor. Captain Marcus also fell exhausted on the floor. After a few seconds he tried to get up, as he noticed that the enemy also tried to pull himself up.

Marcus jumped to his feet and then aimed his right hand toward the attacker. When he was about to strike again, he noticed that the attackers cover began to disappear and revealed a human figure. And what was even more amazing, as it turned out, that figure depicted a woman. The protective field that surrounded the fighter disappeared completely. Marcus safely could see the whole shape and was able to accurately aim and strike. As he was about to take a final hit, he suddenly heard attacker say:

- Please don't kill me ...

The attacker fell to the ground and lost consciousness. Captain Marcus stopped the attack. He was very surprised by what he saw and heard. He wondered how is it possible that this girl almost managed to kill them both. At that moment he remembered about Jason, who was lying against the wall. Marcus jumped up and ran to him. He leaned forward to see if his companion was conscious. Jason rolled onto his back and gasped:

- I'm all right, I need a minute to recover. As he spoke, he managed to get up on his feet and sat on a chair that was next to him.

- That girl gave us a hard time. How is she? - Jason asked, staring at the unconscious girl.

Marcus approached her cautiously, put his hand on her and checked if she was alive.

- She's alive, but I almost killed her. Who is she?

- The person we are looking for, I think - said Jason.

- Are you saying, that this girl who wanted to kill us, this is our ...

- Yes, it's her.

- But I thought it would be a man, not a woman - said Marcus surprised. - And what do we do now?

- We need to quickly get out of here. The Zotorigh can sense the opportunity to kill us.

- Well, then, where do we go now?

-Now we have to look for somewhere to stay the night, relax quietly and recharge - said Jason. - We have to find a motel or something, but we can't raise any suspicion.

Marcus looked at the girl, then asked:

- What do we do with her?

- Wake her up - said Jason.

Captain Marcus walked up to the girl, looked at her, then gently grabbed her by the arm and shook her saying:

- Princess, it's time to get up.

The girl opened her eyes. Captain Marcus said:

- Get up, no time for sleep.

The girl stood up, looked at Captain Marcus and Jason and then said:

- I'm sorry, but I thought that you were that something that nearly killed me, a few moments ago.

- Well, it does not matter - said Jason.

- What's your name? - Marcus asked, walking over to the window.

- Emma - she said.

- Beautiful name, but unfortunately I have to interrupt you, because we have to go. We can't stay here any longer - said Marcus.

- Where should I go? - Asked Emma. - I'll stay here. This is my home, I will go nowhere – she said with a firm voice.

- What happened here anyway? - Asked Jason.

Captain Marcus only looked around.

- I was attacked by some creature. I do not know what they wanted. Just before I said anything, they began to attack me, and I just fought back. I didn't know what else I could do. When I defeated them, or killed that is, as they crumbled into fine dust, you came shortly after the incident - Emma said.

- How many were there? - Asked Marcus.

- Two.

- First time you had to deal with such thing? - Asked Jason.

- Yes, for the first time - she said. - When you entered I thought it was them again, so I hid here in the room, and then I saw you - Emma said, looking at Jason. - And I attacked you because I thought you also want to kill me. I had no other choice - she said with a slight fluctuations in her voice.

- I understand, I'd probably do the same - said Captain Marcus interfering the conversation.

- Oh no! Marble, where are you? - The girl ran from the room.

Marcus, along with Jason ran after the girl. Emma ran into the room holding a puppy, that Captain Marcus found. Emma hugged the puppy and held it close to her chest. It looked as if she was suffocating him. The puppy wasn't aware of what was going on, he leaned his snout on her wrist and had a expression of satisfaction on his face.

- That's your dog? - Marcus said with a slight smile on his face.

- Yes - said Emma.

- I found him in the closet.

- I know, because I hid him there - said Emma looking at Marcus. - I was afraid they would kill him.

- We need to get going, because it's not safe here. Now! - Marcus said nervously, staring out the window at the city.

Jason and Emma looked at the Captain Marcus.

- Why are you suddenly so impulsive? - Emma asked, stroking the puppy's head.

- I think we have guests - Marcus said pointing out the window.

- What guests? - Jason asked with surprise, and went to the window to the window with Emma.

- Take a look.

When Emma and Jason looked out the window, they saw armed men were getting out of the truck with the number plate TTG.

- TTG - strike force Commando - said Marcus.

- Where is an emergency exit here? Or maybe the roof? - Jason asked, looking over at Emma.

- There is no entry to the roof, and no emergency exit, because it's a pretty damn old apartment block. - Emma said, spreading her hands helplessly.

- Than we're trapped - said Marcus.

- It's just some soldiers - Emma said in a calm voice.

- Only soldiers? Are you kidding - said Marcus nervous walking around like he was in scalding water, seeking a way out of this situation. - Those are fucking commandos from the elite unit, that were created to fight people like you - Marcus looked at Emma.

- I just remembered something very important, which may be very useful to us - Said Emma after a few seconds of silence, right after what Marcus said.

- What is that? And may it be very important - said Marcus nervously.

- There is a passage to the next building through the attic - said Emma.

- Let's move, we don't have time.

Emma began to head towards the exit, holding her puppy in her hands.

- Leave him, we do not have time for this - Marcus shouted towards Emma.

- I'm not going without him!

Jason looked at Marcus, and he looked at Emma, then said:

- Okay, but you are responsible for him.

Emma only nodded.

When everyone went out of the apartment they noticed how some strikers were already in the building and were approaching in their direction very quickly.

- Lead on, but really quick! - Jason said.

The trio was already on the fourth floor of before entering the attic when Jason stopped and pulled something from his pocket.

- What are you doing? - Marcus asked Jason and looked at his hand, in which he was holding a hand grenade.

- I'm preparing a surprise for them.

- What are you, crazy? It's a grenade! And where did you get it? - Marcus asked, surprised.

- I always carry such gifts with me, just in case, and because we have such a case and we have uninvited guests, we need to give them a gift - said Jason jokingly.

Marcus stared at Jason only.

- Isn't it so? - Asked Jason additionally.

Marcus shook his head to indicate that he agreed and moved on ahead. Jason placed the grenade right outside the door by attaching it to a string and the doorframe. As soon as he closed the door, he shouted:

- Hurry!

- Where now? - Marcus asked hiding behind a pillar in a quite extensive dryng room, to which Emma led them to.

- At the other end, there's the door to another house - Emma said, pointing to the door on the other side of the drying room, a few dozen meters away from them.

- We have one chance and we can't waste it, so do your best - said Marcus.

Emma and Jason nodded, and then began to run toward the door like crazy, that was about a hundred meters away from them. Jason ran last and turned every now and then to make sure that none of the TTG commandos show up behind them. They all reached the second door at the same time, then each one crouched down against the wall.

- A piece of cake, for now - Jason said.

- And that's what worries me - said Marcus.

When they all were already at the entrance to the building, suddently the explosion went off.

- Quickly, inside the other building - Jason shouted.

They began to run in all, one after the other, and Jason ran in as last. Suddenly, he felt a blast next to his face caused by rifle bullets, That were fired in their direction. They closed the door and stood there motionless and petrified. It turned out that a TTG division stood behind the door, armed to the neck and aiming their rifles in their direction.

- What now? - Asked Marcus. - Do you want to surrender?

- No! - Jason replied with a firm voice.

- And you? - Asked Marcus, and looked at Emma.

- I didn't fight with you so that I can surrender now - said Emma.

- In that case we have no choice than to fight - Jason said.

- Stop! Do not move! Hands up! - Shouted one of the commandos.

- There are probably twenty of them - Said Marcus, looking at the commandos, and then looking at Jason.

-To the ground! - Ordered the commando approaching with a cautious step toward them, all the while keeping Jason at gunpoint.

- What do we do? - Asked Marcus.

At this point, a remnant of the commandos moved in equal formation toward the warriors.

- Lie down and wait until they are close enough to attack - said Jason.

Marcus and Emma followed the commandos' commands obediently, only Jason stood there with his hands spread apart.

- Hands on your head, now! - The commando issued another order.

8.

DANGER AT THE GATES

When the commandos were already a few meters from the three, they stopped and pointed their weapons in their direction.

One of the commandos came up to Jason very slowly and held out his hand toward him to catch his wrist, all the while keeping his eyes at Jason. Jason took a step back. The commando tightened his finger on the trigger, but didn't press it fully so that it didn't release any bullet. Jason smirked and looked at the other warriors, and then suddenly disappeared.

Marcus took this as a sign to attack then jumped off his legs, with his hands up. When he was at the height of the commandos' face he bounced off the walls of his feet hitting the commando with his fist in the face, and he fell to the ground like a piece of wood losing consciousness. Emma laid on the floor, and then disappeared.

Suddenly all the commandos started shooting towards the wall, where Jason was a second ago. Bullets of the commandos standing at the back started to hit commandos that were at the front, those who tried to stop Emma, Marcus and Jason just a moment ago.

Captain Marcus dodged so fast that none of bullets that were aimed at him, hit him. He felt their warmth on his skin, as those bullets passed him only by a fractions of millimeters.

Suddenly, Jason appeared with his sword drawn on the left side behind the backs of the commandos. The first commando Jason received a strike on the back, and he fell to the ground limply. At the same time he hit the next one with his a knee to the back of the head, the impact was impressively strong as it threw the commando several meters away. His fall brought two commandos that stood behind him, down with him. The remaining commandos that still stood on their feet, gathered around in a circle with their backs to each other, as each of them pulled the trigger on the machine guns they had with them. They fired at random until everyone of them has drained their bullet dispensers, and threw their empty rifles in front of themselves. Then each of the commandos pulled a samurai sword out, that were hidden on their backs until now.

Captain Marcus stood on the left side, smiling to himself, Jason showed up on the right side of the circle, and the girl on the opposite side. She was not wearing a shield.

The three of them began to create the a triangle, which cut off the TTG commandos escape route.

- Surrender and nothing will happen to you - Marcus turned toward the commandos, the ones that were remaining. None of them moved even a centimeter, neither said a word the whole time, waiting in their positions ready to fight.

- You have a chance to survive! Just surrender! - Marcus said. - Your choice.

The commandos stood in a circle with raised swords without saying a word. They waited with baited breath for the warriors next move.

- It probably means that you are not very clever people - Marcus said under his breath, then held out his hands in front of him, joined his wrists together and smiled. - This is your last chance for survival, after this there will be no turning back - said Marcus the last time. He noted that the commandos tightened their hands on their sword. - As you wish - Marcus said, then after a few seconds you could see how a fireballs began to grow in his hands. With surprised the commandos began to back away, but none of them dropped their sword. They were ready for anything, they were ready to die. Marcus fired, without thinking and without hesitation, five bullets aiming towards the commandos. Each of the bullets reached the commando hitting their chest.

Jason didn't wait long for developments, because at the same time the bullets hit the commandos, he disappeared and a second later appeared behind his back, striking his swords and cutting his spine from the tailbone up to the head. Each of commando was falling like a doll on the ground, and Jason has once again vanished into thin air. As Marcus pointed his fireballs towards the commandos, Emma suddenly disappeared at the same time, and after a few seconds appeared between the two commandos that were still alive. Without thinking and she used the surprise and hit several punches to the face of the first commando, while another was punched in the chest with her knee. The commandos didn't even have the time to swallow, as they fell limply to the floor, Emma smiled to herself and then disappeared again. Jason imposed a series of strikes with his sword to finish off the commandos that were already beaten by Emma.

The warriors attack only lasted less than a minute, and all the commandos were lying limply on the floor. Emma and Jason appeared on Marcus' side.

- I guess it's over and done with - Said Captain Marcus with a slight sneer in his voice.

- I hope there aren't any more surprises waiting on us. - said Jason.

Suddently as Jason finished his sentence, more commandos entered the room from the house from which they were fleeing from. Warriors started to flee toward the other building. Marcus was the last to run out and barely escaped out of the room and ran to the stairwell. He felt a blast of a shock wave on his back, which was emited when bullets hit the wall, just a few meters to their left. The shock wave was so strong that the warriors scattered on the stairwell of the building with their bodies covered in dust and rubble. Jason stood up first. He brushed the dust off and looked around in search of his companions. Emma and Marcus were in one piece, although slightly bruised. Jason looked through the hole in the wall that remained after the rockets. The commandos were heading in their direction.

- They immediately sprinted down the house - Marcus shouted, then threw himself up the stairs towards the exit. Only a few floors separated them from freedom.

Running up the stairs, Marcus grabbed Emma's arm.

- I don't have time to hang around, run all the way down - Marcus said while holding her by the arm, and even pulled her behind him down the stairs. When Marcus and Emma ran down the stairs at a fast pace and were already half way to the exit, Emma suddenly stopped and pulled herself from Marcus' grip.

- What happened? - He asked nervously.

- Where is Jason? - Emma asked, glancing at Marcus, Staring at him without a blink expecting an answer.

- Oh, shit! Jason! - Marcus's eyes widened. He was about to go back to the top when a limp body flew past them. It bounced off the wall and an empty sound dropped to the floor.

- What the hell? - Marcus asked under his breath and looked at Emma, then looked at the body lying on the floor. Emma walked over to the railing and together with Marcus stared at the body the commando. Suddenly, another commando flew near Emma's head, and after him another one past Emma's head by a few centimeters. Emma turned her head up and saw Jason. Not hiding his satisfaction he looked at his work with a smile. Emma shook her head in disbelief.

- I think Jason took up the remaining commandos - she said, looking straight into Marcus' eyes. She didn't finished her scentence and he appeared next to her.

- That's all the commandos, I hope - he said, although it was clear that had strength to fight more.

- Me too - said Marcus and Emma only nodding.

- We don't have time, so all go down as soon as possible, because at any moment even more commandos may appear here, with whom we have a much bigger problem to fight with. If there are Zotorigh it would be even worse, as will would be fresh meat for them - said Jason, and headed down the stairs without waiting for a response.

Emma, along with Marcus didn't thinking much and followed Jason down the stairs, the three of them left the house was in a hurry, but in total silence. The only thing you could hear was the rustle of their pants, with the material rubbing against each other. Jason went down first and looked very carefully each time they approached the next floor. At each floor he clenched his fists harder, making sure that the danger wasn't there, and easing them again. Behind him followed Emma, who just like Jason examined in detail every corner of the corridor, each floor they passed. Marcus followed at the end with a stoney face and looked back every few seconds to make sure that nobody followed them.

When the trio reached the ground floor, Jason, who went first, stopped at the door to the stairwell where they stood, Emma and Marcus joined him and were silent.

Jason looked through the glass in the door of the stairwell, little could see as it only was ten centimeters wide and fifteen centimeters long.

Jason stared at the hole in the door without saying a word, Marcus interrupted the silence that lasted a few seconds.

- Are we waiting for something specific, or shall we wait here all day? - He asked, staring at Jason.

- I'm checking if someone's lurking behind the door, so we won't fall into a trap provided by the TTG commandos or even worse, the Zotorigh.

Emma hasn't said a word, as she stared at the window trying to spot anything.

- But standing here, we won't get smarter - said Marcus.

- That's right - Jason nodded.

- Can we go?

- You're a erratic, or what? - Asked Jason, but Marcus replied with a shrug. - If you are being erratic and in a hurry, please go first and look around - Jason said opening the door.

- I'm not erratic, but I won't sit here for god knows how long - he said.

Jason smiled with the corners of his mouth and then stepped away from the door in order to give way for Marcus.

Captain Marcus leaned out very carefully to look whether some commandos are standing in front of the block. When he stuck his head out, he noticed that in front of them was only empty space, and within about a hundred meters from them stood the TTG commandos van.

- The way is clear - said Marcus, hiding inside his head inside.

- That's great, but what about the commandos van? - Asked Jason.

- It seems to me that it's empty - said Marcus.

- What do you mean, you think? - Asked Jason.

- Well, it seems to me it's empty, because I didn't see anyone inside, and I havn't heard any engine noises, otherwise I'm not a fortune-teller to know whether the car is empty or not. Let's just hope it is.

- We need to be very quickly, I mean REALLY quickly, to get into the van. That should take us about thirty seconds if we're careful. Emma nodded to indicate that she understood. Jason looked at Marcus.

- Are you ready? - He asked.

- Ready - said Marcus.

- That's good, and now quickly to the car - Jason said with a gruff voice and opened the door to the stairwell, in where they stood. Emma came out first out of the stairwell, followed by Marcus, and in the end, Jason, all the while looking around himself. The three of them headed toward the van which was parked next to them, they all wanted to get as soon as possible to the car. Their walk turned into a trot, and then everyone began to run, while looking around very carefully. Captain Marcus ahead of the other two, got first to the back of the van, then came Emma, and Jason got last into the car.

- Almost - he said, then jerked open the door to the cabin of the car on the passenger side, to board as quick as possible. Emma and Jason went to the van, Marcus stood beside it without moving.

- Why do not you get in? - Jason asked, surprised.

- I want to drive - said Marcus.

- Absolutely not - Jason said, slightly surprised.

- Why are you going to drive, and I can't? - Marcus asked, crossing his arms.

- Are you kidding, now you are going to give me an ultimatum. Now, when we are exposed to attacks from all sides - said Jason with disbelief.

- I don't give you any demands or ultimatums, I just want to do something useful - Marcus said firmly.

- Do not know where to drive - said Jason.

- You will guide me.

- Okay, but if you screw up, remember that it wil be your fault - and then got into the vehicle and sat down right next to Emma. Marcus smiled to himself very satisfied, then ran to the door of the van and sat behind the wheel.

- What are you so happy about? - Emma asked impatiently.

- Nothing - she heard in response.

- Move, move - Jason exclaimed. Captain Marcus turned the keys in the ignition. The car didn't start up, the engine only choked. Marcus looked with the corner of his eye at Jason, who crossed his arms.

- What's going on, please start dammit! - Turned the key in the ignition again trying to restart the engine of the car, but it did not react, still you could only hear the choking of the engine. When Marcus tried to start up the engine, Jason noticed the TTG commandos comeing down the stairwell, where the warriors stood just less than two minutes ago.

- I think we got company - said Jason.

Marcus raised his head and looked straight ahead, then turned to Jason

- Great, just the last thing we need, damn it!

- Can you hurry?

- Can't you see I'm trying? - Marcus said drawling through his teeth.

- Than I advise you to hurry more, because they will not wait until we leave - Jason said. Emma saw what was happening, then she leaned more into her seat, where she sat without saying a word. The commandos who came out of the stairwell stopped at a distance of forty meters, stood next to each other and formed a squadron. There was silence for a few seconds, which was interrupted by the sound of the engine for wouldn't start.

- I counted sixteen - Jason said.

- Why won't this piece of junk start? - Shouted Marcus. - Start, for god sake - said angry.

- It will get really hot, in a minute! - Jason said impatiently.

When Marcus took his eyes off the ignition, he noted, as each of the commandos was holding a machine gun, and one of them aimed a rocket launchers at them, as he was waiting for someone to load it in the back.

- If you won't start up the damn car, nothing of it will remain, not even us!

- Come on! - Marcus shouted angrily hitting his fist on the dashboard.

- I think it's too late - said Jason then closed his eyes in prayer. Marcus looked up and looked at the commandos. The Commandos stood with a gun ready to fire, there was silence, which was promptly interrupted by a shot from a rifle of one of the commandos.

A whole series of bullets have been fired, that hit on the windshield, leaving gentle scratches behind and sign of cracks every few centimeters, which had the size of only a few millimeters. Jason opened his eyes and looked at Marcus

- This is an armored van and they can't hurt us - Jason said with relief in his voice.

- Are you sure? - Asked Marcus.

- You saw yourself - said Jason.

- We will change your mind when the bullet will hit your ass, huh?

- What do you mean, don't you see that - Marcus interrupted his argument.

- Maybe one or two will not do anything, but a whole series will pit this vehicle like Swiss cheese – Again, they could hear a loud series of guns, missiles have reached the van bouncing off the car like ping-pong balls bouncing from the table. But every now and then they could hear the bullets penetrate into the body of the car, and glass which sheltered them from the bullets, suddenly started to crack every few centimeters under the onslaught of the bullets.

- If you don't start up the damn car, we won't get out of here alive.

- I'm trying, I'm trying to! - Marcus screamed trying to start up the car the whole time.

- Try more, because a commando aimes a RPG rockets at us, and this won't end very well ...

- What a piece of junk! - Marcus shouted, his fist hitting steering wheel once again. Suddenly, to everyone's surprise, the car started and under the hood they could hear the pleasant and very long awaited purring of the engine.

Marcus, without thinking, pressed the gas pedal to the floor and under the wheels smoke began to rise and they could hear the squeal of tires. The car abruptly moved forward, and Marcus didn't move his foot off the gas, holding the steering wheel firmly and only every now and then pushing the clutch pedal to make the car go faster. They wanted get away as quickly as possible from the commandos and the location in which they were, just a few seconds ago. Emma covered her face with her hands, and Jason breathed a sigh of relief.

As Marcus was a few hundred meters from the commandos, he suddenly braked and turned the steering wheel to the left, so that the car abruptly twisted and changed direction, and accelerated again. As Jason and Emma looked at each other puzzled, they heard a powerful explosion, just a few meters from them.

- What was that? Was that an explosion? - Asked Emma.

Captain Marcus even without saying a word, looked forward, only to look from the corner of his eye to the right and the left mirror, at the end he turned his head and looked at his companions. - We are in luck, any minute, and we would have been in a burning wreckage. I have a reflex - Marcus said with relief.

- What was that explosion? - Emma screamed.

- It was a RPG rocket, I noticed it a few seconds ago and so I changed direction.

- Where are we going now, if I may know? - Jason asked Marcus.

- Ahead of us, unless you have a different plan.

- We should go to the northern coast, as soon as possible - said Jason.

- You got it - said Marcus then changed the lane and went in the direction indicated by Jason.

- Why there? - Suddenly, asked Emma. - And I have one very important question, she said to Marcus, then turned her head toward Jason.

- What question? - Jason asked curiously

- Can someone tell me, what the hell is going on here? What does all of this even mean? The fact that these things drop into my apartment abruptly and hell knows why they attack me with questions. I barely manage to escape alive, the you drop in and almost kill me - Jason and Marcus looked at each other. - Well, those commandos from some kind of squad, are you able to explain that to me? What's going on and what the hell is happening at all?

- I explain, if you will let me - Jason said in a calm voice, putting a hand on Emma's shoulder to calm her.

- Do not play me, just answer what is going on, I'm about to go crazy here - Emma said, spatting through her clenched teeth.

- Alright - said Jason. - As you already know, my name is Jason and behind the wheel sits Marcus.

- I pleased to meet you - Marcus said, nodding toward Emma and smiling at the same time.

- Those who tried to attack you, are invaders from outer space, we call them Zotorigh.

- Are you kidding me? From space? - Emma asked, incredulously.

- Do I look like someone who like to crack a joke? - Asked Jason.

- Those TTG commandos, those are commandos from the elite unit who tracked us to down to catch us and, perhaps, transfer us to strangers, or simply eliminate us as we killed their agents - said Jason staring at Emmas face, who was starring in disbelief.

- And Marcus who is he? - She asked.

- It may sound silly, but Marcus comes from a family of warriors, that from another planet, just like you. You came here together, or actually you were sent here as your planet no longer exists. It was destroyed by the alien race, that one I already have mentioned - said Jason and looked at Emma. There was a silence that was interrupted with Emma laughing.

- And I'm just suppose to believe in everything you just told me? - Asked Emma.

- Believe it or not, but explain to me, please, where did you get your, so to speak, „skills"? - Asked Jason.

- I do not know, I had themfor a long time, since I can remember. That's why my parents gave me up to an orphanage, aftre that a family took me in, but they also learned that I have these „powers", so they told me to go, and so on sixteenth birthday I was on my own. I had to cope somehow, so I used my „powers" to survival.

- Do you mean that you stole from people? - Jason interrupted Emma.

- I call it taking from the rich and giving to the poor, in this case, I was the poor one - Emma replied with a smile on her face.

- Do you remember your parents? - Asked Jason.

- Not really, I was maybe eight years then.

- Do you want the truth? - Jason asked, looking at the girl.

- What truth?

- Actually your parents were with you all the time.

- What do you mean they were with me all the time? - Emma asked, surprised.

- Your parents protect you from Zotorigh. They were with you, even though you did not see them, but they did watch over you - said Jason.

- Why didn't they watch over me today? Huh? - Emma asked upset.

- Because both of them are dead - said Jason, with sadness in his eyes.

- What? How did this happen? When did they die? - Emma asked in a hushed voice.

- They died during a battle in the forest in Brazil, a few days ago. That's why the Zotorigh have found you now.

- Where did her parents die? - Asked Marcus, interfering in Jason's conversation with Emma.

- In the forests of Brazil - Jason said and added the question. - Why do you ask?

- Apparently, my parents died the same way, in the forests of Brazil - Marcus said. - Can you explain this to me?

- Yes, it's true - said Jason. - All four died in the forests of Brazil fighting the Zotorigh.

- And only both our parents died there? Because apparently we're going to find one more person, who is like me and Emma - said Marcus, waiting impatiently for a response.

- Only your parents died - said Jason, who after these words saddened.

Emma and Marcus looked at Jason and silence followed.

- They died sacrificing themselves for you, for your future, if they didn't protect you, all three of you would have been found and killed, a long time ago - said Jason.

The girl sat in silence and pondered on what Jason just told her.

- Where do we go now? - Marcus asked, changing the subject, which started to become awkward.

- If you will pass a motel or hotel, stop by it, we'll stay the night there and have a rest - said Jason.

- Uhum - Marcus nodded as a sign that he agrees with Jason.

- Do you want to know anything else? - Jason asked, peering at Emma.

- Yes, I would like to know, what are you doing here?

- Do not understand the question.

- Apart from the fact that your name is Jason, I do not know anything about you and how do you know anything about what you have just told me - said Emma.

- I ... I just knew them all, I was there with them in the forest in Brazil and I saw how each one after the other died, as one after another fell like a ... - Jason suddenly stopped in mid-sentence and went silent.

- Since they are all dead, why are you alive? - She asked.

- Because I was asked by them, to find and gathered you all in one place so that you will be united with joined forces and to defeated the Zotorigh - said Jason, in his eyes tears gathered.

Emma just sat there and was silently staring at Jasons face, who with difficulty swallowing his saliva.

- Now you understand? - Asked Jason.

- Yes, now I understand everything.

- And would you be able to trust me, just as Marcus did? - Asked Jason.

Emma thought for a moment and then said:

- I think I could trust you - she said with a gentle smile on her face

- That's good - Jason replied smiling back.

- I have one small question - said Marcus, Jason threw a sideway glance at Marcus.

- What do we do with number plates on the car, if I may know?

- It is good that you mention it because I practically forgot that we're driving in a stolen car. We might be easy to track down, so they can we find quickly - Jason said.

Marcus stopped the car, looked at Jason and then asked:

- What do you want to do?

- We have to change the color of the car and take the number plates off - he said.

- Alright - said Marcus putting the first gear on and moving out of place.

Emma sat in silence and stared ahead, trying to reach her sight away from the car. At that time, Marcus was going very slowly, looking carefully for some signs that led to them to a workshop, or an abandoned garage.

- I believed in the existence of UFOs, but I didn't expect to be one of them - Emma said, smiling to herself.

- I founda motel - said Marcus slowing down at the sign, indicating that the nearest motel is located right on the first exit from the highway, a few hundred meters ahead of them.

- Is that one ok? - Asked Marcus.

Jason looked at the sign then nodded.

- That one is fine, besides we don't have a choice as it's getting dark outside.

- Marcus pressed the accelerator and headed toward the motel.

- I have one small favor to sk you - said Jason and put his hand on Marcus' shoulder.

- What?

- Do not drive straight onto the property, just stop at the roadside first.

- Why? - Marcus asked, surprised by the request.

- Because it will be suspicious and may draw the attention of uninvited onlookers and bring us danger - said Jason.

- Have you forgotten, what I was just talking about a few minutes ago? - Jason asked, shaking his head.

Marcus looked at Jason, but didn't say a word.

- Listen to me carefully - continued Jason. - We will do this: you two go to rent a room, and at this time I will look for a place, get rid of this number plate. Is that ok with you?

- That's alright with me, I just hope you come back soon - Marcus said, looking at Jason.

- I'll try to come back in an hour, ok? - He asked.

- Ok.

They had traveled a bit, until Jason said:

- Stop at this point - he pointed to the side.

Marcus stopped, turned on the hazard lights and got out of the car with Emma, and they both began to head towards the motel. Jason switched to the driver's seat and started squealing with smoke off in search of a place where he could to get rid of the number plates and change the color of the car. After driving a few kilometers, Jason stopped the vehicle at a padlocked gate and turned off the engine. He looked in the side mirror, then got out of the car, leaving the lights on. They were facing the factory.

- I hope noone's there - Jason said to himself, after which he walked up to the gate to open it.

- Closed with a padlock - Jason grabbed it with his hands and with one pull ripped the chain that was wrapped around the gate, he then looked around again to make sure that no one saw him. He threw the padlock and the chain into the bushes and hastily opened one side of the gate blocking it on the side, then he got into his car and pulled into the factory, stopping several meters behind the gate. He got out of the car and hastily closed the gate so no one would follow. Again, he got in his car and drove very carefully ahead. After driving just two hundred meters, Jason smiled to himself and stopped the car.

- Just what I was looking for - he said to himself, then he went to the room in which a sign was written: Paint shop.

9.

AWAKENING

- Here we are on our own - Marcus smiled to Emmas direction and stopped in front of the entrance to the motel.

- I hope they have some comfortable beds, because I'm ready to fall asleep - Emma muttered under her breath.

- There's no guessing, we need to find out for ourselves - said Marcus, as they both went into the corridor that led to the reception.

When they passed the corridor and entered the a room that looked like a reception, Marcus walked up to the counter in the middle of the room. Emma stood at the window pulling the curtain and looked around the parking lot.

- Deathly silence - Marcus whispered.

- Maybe ring the bell, and someone will show up - Emma said, pointing to the bell that was placed on the counter.

- You're right, I did not notice - Marcus said gently ringing the bell twice.

After a few seconds a young man came through the door in the left corner of the room. He walked to the counter, looked at the guests and spoke.

- Welcome to the ANAKONDA motel, what can I do for you?

- We need a room with three beds, please - Marcus said, not taking his eyes off the man.

- Unfortunately, we do not have such a room - said the receptionist chewing on his gum.

- So what rooms do you have, if I may know? - Marcus asked, frowning with displeasure.

- I'll check - said the receptionist, and typed something into the computer, that was hidden under the counter. - At the moment, we only have three rooms available, two singles and one double - he said. Marcus leaned against the counter and stared at Emma questioningly.

- Do we stay here?

- Do we have another choice? - Asked Emma

- You're right – he answered

The receptionist stood and watched Marcus closely.

- Have you decided for a room?

Marcus thought for a moment, then said:

- One double and a single.

- Two rooms? - The receptionist asked.

- Yes, something wrong? - Marcus asked. He rested both hands on the counter, and his eyes stared straight into the eyes of the receptionist.

- Of course not - said the receptionist looking down at the floor. - As you wish - said the receptionist, then fumbled again on the computer.

- Rooms 4A and B - he said. 4A is a double and 4B is a single - he added. - Will it be one night or more?

- One - Marcus said firmly.

- Alright, I will get the keys. - the receptionist reached behind his back and grabbed two keys that were placed next to each other. - Do you need anything else?

- No, thank you – Said Emma.

- The payment will be by cash or by card? - The receptionist asked.

- Cash - said Marcus.

- Well, in that case that will be thirty-four dollars - said the receptionist extending his hand for the money. Marcus smiled and then reached into his pocket for his wallet, pulled out the cash and handed it to the receptionist, who smiled and said:

- Thank you and I wish you a good night.

Marcus returned the smile, and together with Emma went toward the room.

- I hope this will be a quiet night, so I can finally relax and close my eye - Emma said to Marcus, grumbling under her breath.

- I hope we can get some rest too.

Marcus and Emma stopped in front of the rooms in which they were to spend the night, Marcus looked at Emma, then smiled and asked a question.

- Do you prefer to sleep alone or with someone, if you don't feel safe.

Emma thought for a moment, then she looked at Marcus and said.

- You know, I think I'd rather be with someone in the room.

- When Jason comes back, I will tell him that he's sharing the room with you - Marcus turned toward Emma, giving her the keys to the double room.

- I'd rather be with you in the room - said Emma and gazed shyly at Marcus.

- With me? - He asked surprised.

- Yes, with you, of course only if you do not mind.

- I do not mind, at all.

Emma smiled at Marcus, and he returned her smile, there was silence, which was interrupted by Marcus after a few seconds.

- Can I ask you something?

- Of course - Emma tried to fix her hair, by brushing her fingers through it and trying to pull it behind her ear.

- Why with me?

- So you don't want to? - Asked Emma.

- Really, it doesn't make any difference to me, I'm just curious, why you don't want to be with him in the room, but with me, asked Marcus.

Emma looked at Marcus and said, after a moment's thought.

- I do not know anything about this man, and you, but I have more trust in you than him. Somehow I can trust you more, I do not know whether it's because of a similar age, or something else, but somehow I feel more secure with you - Emma said with a smile. Marcus scratched his head and then said.

- Thank you - and then handed the key to Emma and added. - Go to the room and I'll look around in the other one, just to see if everything is safe.

- Alright - Emma said turning toward the door to the room where she would sleep with Marcus together.

- And one more thing.

- What?

- If you need help, just shout - he added smiling, then put the key into the door of the other room, he turned the lock, and entered closing the door behind him. Emma stood a moment before entering the room. She looked around, after which she put her key into the lock and opened the door. When she walked into the room she stopped abruptly and turned her head to see if anyone was watching, because for a moment she had a feeling that someone watched at them from a distance. Her eyes stopped on the bushes, which seemed to her that something could hide there and began to slowly steer in that direction. When she got to the bushes and tried to reached out her hands to spread them, suddenly, she heard behind her someone asking.

- What are you doing?

When she turned around, she saw Jason standing at the door to the room with crossed arms.

- I just ... Actually, it does not matter - said Emma.

- Are you up to something? - Asked Jason.

- No. I'm not up to anything.

- Something happened? You behave strangely.

- No, I do not know ... It seemed to me that something or someone is watching us - she said.

- Where? - Jason asked concerned.

- There, in the bushes - she said showing with her hand.

- Wait here - Jason said, and began to head in the direction indicated by Emma... Emma reached out both hands to the front and clenched her fists, at the same time, Jason drew his sword, after which he set himself into a position to attack and they both began to approach the bushes. - Get Ready – he whispered to Emma, seeing that she prepared for an attack.

- I'm ready - she said

When both were about two meters away from the bushes, Jason suddenly disappeared after which he suddenly appeared again in the middle of bushes. He aimed a hit with the sword, but it turned out that nobody was in there, only a frightened squirrel that ran toward the cars parked nearby. Emma sighed with relief dropping her hands and loosening her grip.

- You see, fortunately, there is nobody here, only a poor squirrel – Said Jason, laughing under his breath.

- I thought ... - she broke off the sentence.

- I know, I know, do not worry. - Jason raised his hands up as a sign of victory and said jokingly: - Squirrel zero, Jason one. - Anyone could have thought that they are beening watched, and, well, you're vigilant, this squirrel will no longer mess with us.

The girl breathed a sigh of relief and they both turned toward the door.

- You need to get enough sleep, as we don't know what is waiting for us tomorrow - said Jason to Emma, as he came up to the room. - You'll sleep together in a room, and I'll be next to you - he added.

Emma looked straight into the eyes of Jason.

- Today I will take the night shift - he added, looking at Emma.

- I know.

- You know? You already decided who sleeps where?

Emma did not respond to the question asked by Jason, she just opened the door and ended the conversation with: - Thank you for saving my life, this squirrel was frightening. Have a good night.

Jason froze, even without saying a word, when Emma went into the room, and she looked around. There were two beds, a cupboard and a TV in the room, as well as an entrance to a second room, so she turn on the light.

- We have a bathroom - she said to herself after which she began to undress, closing the door behind her.

When Jason walked into the other room, Marcus was sitting on the bed and holding a picture in his hands. Thoughtful he stared at it.

- What is this photo? - Asked Jason.

- This image is the only thing I have now - he said.

- I can see ? - Jason asked, sitting down next to him on the bed. Marcus handed him a photograph, which he held in his hand.

- Is that your girlfriend? - Asked Jason.

- Yes, this is Tiffany.

- So you have a very beautiful girlfriend - Jason said.

- Rather, I use to have, I mean I do not know now, do not even know if she's alive. Everything that I had so far no longer exists, her probably too.

- Nothing's lost yet, we'll find out eventually, in a few days, everything is still possible - Jason said patting Marcus on the back.

- You know, I'll tell you something about your race, actually about our, as we come from the same planet - Marcus looked at Jason. - We are a very powerful race, you probablt can't remember, but everyone in the galaxy know us for fighting to the last drop of blood and to our last breath. Do not lose faith, nothing is lost, remember that if you don't have anything to fight for, then fight for your existence and to be able to survive another day. Remember, faith makes us very powerful, each one of us, like you and me can work wonders if you believe in something - said Jason.

Marcus looked at Jason, then got up and walked to the door. When he opened it, he turned to Jason and asked.

- And what if eveything I know will be destroyed, what then?

Jason looked at Marcus and then said:

- I don't know, but if there's any hope, it's worth fight for, even if it seems too late. You have beautiful girlfriend, fight for her.

Marcus turned and nodded, then said: - Thank you.

- No, thank you - Jason said, smiling to himself.

- And one more thing - said Jason getting off the bed and heading toward the window.

- Yes?

- Get some sleep, we have little time for sleep, and you will need it - said Jason.

- Uhum- Marcus nodded, then closed the door behind him. Entering the room he looked around in search for Emma, but he couldn't see her anywhere. Very quickly he noticed that the bathroom door was slightly opened, and inside lights were on, he walked over to them, saying:

- Emma, are you there?

There was silence, so he repeated the question.

- You are there? Everything alright?

- Yes, I am – He heard the answer after a while.

- Are you okay? - He asked worried. - Can I come in?

- Yes, you can - Emma replied.

When Marcus went into the bathroom, his attention turned to Emma, who was sitting naked, curled up on the floor in the shower. The water was raining on her head ran down her back.

Marcus, though he entered the room, hesitated, because he didn't know if he could go in any further. An unusual situation in which he found himself in, distracted him, not because he saw Emma naked, but because he saw that the girl had a problem. When he approached her, he noticed that her eyes were red from crying. - Can I help you somehow?

The girl was unfortunately silent, she looked as if she was absent and lost in her thoughts.

When Marcus asked again if everything was okay, Emma looked up and said: - I am afraid, very afraid, you don't even know how much.

Marcus saw exactly how shivers ran through her body, he also saw fear and dread in her eyes.

- What are you afraid of? - Asked Marcus.

- I'm afraid of what might happen tomorrow.

Marcus looked into the air and also realized this true. For a moment, there was silence, which got interrupted by Emma.

- It got to me today, after what happened to us.

Marcus reached for a towel hanging on a hook and handed it to Emma, saying:

- Do not sit on the cold floor, you might catch a cold.

Emma took the towel, stood up and began to dry herself. At that time, Marcus gently turned shyly, despite the fact that a woman's body made no impression on him. Emma seemed to him probably more precious by the fact that they went through so much together. When Marcus stood there with his back turned, he felt her hand rest on his back at shoulder height then turned around and Emma hugged him. Without thinking, Marcus embraced the girl and put his hands around her waist and pulled her closer to him covering her with his arms and towel. He looked her straight into her eyes and gently brushed her hair from her face.

- Do not worry everything will be fine.

Emma looked at Marcus and said: - And if not?

- Surely it will be.

- How do you know, after all you can't be sure - said the girl.

- I'll do everything I can and I know that everything will be fine, trust me.

Emma raised her head, looked at Marcus and kissed him, but Marcus hesitated for a moment. Eventually he returned her kiss, they both stood there for a while gently caressing their mouth, Marcus kissed Emma and Emma kissed Marcus. When Emma started to quickly pull his clothes off and just a few seconds later, Marcus stood there with only his pants on. Emma clung to him, kissing him, after a moment she interrupted the kiss and began to touch his muscular arms and chest. Emma wanted to kiss Marcus again and stroked his cheek with her hands, Marcus grabbed her hand and said: - it would be better if we leave it at that.

Emma stood for a moment and then put her head on his chest and said: - Thank you.

- Why do you thank me? - Asked Marcus.

- Just for being here. Now I feel very safe.

- Do not mention it - Marcus replied, looking at Emma. - Really do not mention it - he added, looking somewhere ahead, as if he saw their future. They both stood there for a moment in silence, the only sound they could hear was the beating of their hearts. Marcus put his hands on her cheeks and gently lifting her head up to kiss Emma on the forehead thus expressing his concern for her. - Now we need to go to sleep, because difficult times await us and we need to get all the rest we can.

- Yes, you are right - said Emma. Marcus came out of the bathroom, stopping by the door along the way. He looked again at the girl and smiled at her.

Emma dried herself up and got dressed. When she entered the room, she found Marcus lying on the bed with his hands clasped behind his head. Eyes fixed on the ceiling.

- Are you thinking about something?

- No - Marcus replied without looking at Emma.

A moment of awkward silence, which was abruptly interrupted by Emma saying: - Jason said he could take today's watch.

- Good - said Marcus, still absent.

Emma laid down on the bed, looked at Marcus and said: - I'm sorry about what happened in the bathroom.

- Nothing happened. Let's just forget about it.

- Well, I suppose that would be best - Emma was slightly embarrassed about the occurrence in the bathroom, so she laid down and closed her eyes. Marcus still stared at the empty space somewhere between the ceiling and himself, then he looked at Emma. The girl was asleep, so he also decided to close his eyes.

- Please do not! - Marcus shouted out loud waking up from his sleep. He sat on the bed all drenched in sweat. His scream woke Emma up, who looked confused at Marcus.

- Something happened? Did you have a nightmare? - She asked very worried.

Marcus looked around the room and in his eyes there was fear and worry. At last, his gaze stopped on Emma.

- I'm sorry.

- What was your nightmare about?

Marcus wiped the sweat off his forehead.

- No, nothing, I had a nightmare.

Emma stood up and walked over to Marcus and sat on the edge of his bed.

- It's all right - said Marcus still wiping the sweat from his face.

- You do not have to lie, I can see you're not alright - Emma stared into Marcus' eyes. - What were you dreaming about? Please tell me, because you shouted so loud, that I'm surprised that Jason didn't come to check on us.

- I do not want to talk about it, please.

Emma stared at him for a moment and said: - We have to trust each other, Marcus. She put her hand on his knee. - You don't have to worry, just relax.

Marcus rubbed his sleepy, but terrified face with both hands. He looked at Emma and said: - I saw the whole earth goes up in flames like ...

- Like what?

- I do not want to talk about it - said Marcus and Emma continued to look at him. Marcus knew Emma wouldn't let it go and will continue to torment him for a confessions. But he didn't dared not finish the sentence.

- Did you see how everyone, how me, how you, how Jason, perished?

Marcus looked horrified at Emma and said: - Yes, that is exactly what I saw.

- Did you see everything you know and saw so far, suddenly ceases to exist?

- Exactly - he said. Emma sat and said nothing.

- And how do you know about that? - Asked Marcus.

Emma closed her eyes and replied: - Because I have the same nightmares.

- But how?- He asked surprised.

- I don't know actually whether I am dreaming or if I daydream, anyway I see things, I see these nightmares, some visions.

- What visions?

- I saw you fight in them and how we all perish. In fact, I usually dream the same thing, but each time it feels like I dream more. Something new always appears. It's like a movie that every dream lasts a little longer and I don't know when it will end - Marcus didn't interrupt Emma, as she went on. - I also have one such dream, in which we all stand on a hill, or rather over a precipice. You, me and Jason, and besides us two other people. I don't know who these people are, but I feel like I know them very well. We all gaze straight ahead, looking in one direction, when I look around I see only clouds that are under our feet. Suddenly, those clouds disappear and I can feel a gusty wind that suddenly hits us on the right side. Over our heads fly four fire comets the size of houses and smash into the ground a few kilometers ahead of us. When I look at you two, to your and Jasons face, I see anxiety and horror. But when I look at the faces of the other two, although they are fuzzy, I can see that they are surrounded by a strange aura, and after a while, this aura of those other fighter goes out. Then they both fall dead, and then Jason's aura goes off, and I can't do anything about it. Then you fall to the ground and don't get up, and at the end I fall to the ground. It all happens very quickly, then I see another man who comes up to us and it all ends. After that I don't see anything - She said in horror. - That's mostly what I dream about and I can't sleep because of that, because I'm afraid - Marcus.

Marcus embraced Emma, hugged her, and whispered: - I will not allow anyone to harm you, and for anyone to happen something to. Everything will be fine, I promise.

Suddenly there was a knock on the door, they both jumped to their feet and Marcus asked with an uncertain voice - Who's there?

- It's me, Jason, can I come in? - He heard the answer with a question.

When Marcus went to the door he pulled the curtain, to ensure that it's Jason. He saw Jason half-dressed how he scratches his back in anticipation for the door to open.

Marcus smiled as the sight of Jason amused him. He reached out his hand to the door handle and when he was about to open the door, his eye glanced at the clock on the wall and it showed 00.55. Marcus wiped his forehead with his free hand, as sweat quite abundantly still ran down his face and opened the door wide. He saw Jason, who was completely dressed with his head down, then raised it up and looked deeply into his eyes saying. -

- Run.

After that word, Marcus felt like a sharp dagger, that Jason held, got stabbed into his heart. After these words, Marcus froze and his eyes began to wander down, straight at Jason's hand that held the dagger stuck in his heart. Limply he fell to the floor.

- Please, no!

And then Marcus woke up in a sweat, and Emma, who was sleeping on the bed next to him woke up as well.

- What happened, what did you dream about, Marcus?

- It was just a nightmare, thankfully - he said.

- What did you dream about? - Shee asked again, and this time Marcus grabbed his chest examining whether everything was alright.

- Oh, God, I saw how... - and he hesitated.

- You can tell me - said Emma, and when Marcus wanted to finish telling her about his dream, he heard someone gently knocking on the door.

- Who's there?

In response, he heard: - It's me, Jason, can I come in?

Marcus's face as filled with fear.

- What's happening? - Asked Emma.

- Impossible, I just dreamed about this - and turned his head toward the door and said, - Just a minute.

- Why don't you open the door? - Asked Emma.

- Because if I open the door, I will die - said Marcus.

- Wait, don't move. sit here and I'm going to open the door, so you won't die - and then got up and started to head towards the door.

- Wait a second, I just check who it is - Marcus said quickly and ran to the door and peeked through the curtain.

- But it's only Jason - Emma said.

- Please, hold on.

Emma listened to his request and didn't open the door.

- Good - replied Marcus at that time checking if Jason was by the door and he saw him exactly like in his dream, Jason's half-dressed, scratching his back in anticipation for the door to open.

- Can I finally come in? How long shall I wait and wait? - Marcus wondered in his thought for a moment and asked himself, how is it possible that he dreamed what's happening now.

- What should I do? He asked Emma, all the while holding his hand on the doorknob. Marcus glanced at the clock on the wall at the last moment. It showed 6.45.

Marcus wondered for a moment. He explained himself in my mind, that what is happening is not for real.

- That's impossible - as soon as he said it, Emma opened the door wide. Jason entered the room and his face was strangely calm. He looked around the room, then he turned directly to Marcus.

- Remember, Marcus, it all depends on you.

After these words, Jason turned to Emma and aimed a powerful hit to the center of the chest. The girl bounced off the wall and fell to the floor. Marcus rushed toward her aid. When he was close enough to touch Jason, he aimed a hit, but before he reached him, Jason vanished into thin air. Marcus bent over Emma. He laid her straight on the floor and then clenched his fists in anger. The plaster on the walls and the ceiling began to crack, the bulb started to blink, and the whole floor shook, causing waves, exactly as those that were caused by throwing a stone in a calm lake. An unimaginably powerful force awoke in him, at that moment. Marcus was not moving, only shouted enraged.

- Where are you? Show yourself! You coward! - And the whole room began to shake.

Unfortunately, no one showed up in the room so Marcus looked at Emma, who was lying on the floor and walked over two steps toward her, because somehow his power almost led him to the middle of the room. He knelt down next to Emma and raising his hands, which caused Emma to levitate to Marcus' outstretched arms. When he held her already in his arms, he took a few steps towards the bed to put Emma on it. Suddenly, beside him appeared Jason with a sword aiming directly at Marcus' heart. Unfortunately, he didn't manage to avoid him and he felt how the sword stabs into his body.

Marcus dropped to the floor like a stone thrown into the endless abyss.

Marcus woke up and it looked as if he escaped from some evil grip. He was drenched in sweat. He got up from the bed, looked at the wall, on which hung a clock. It showed 4.10. He also looked at the bed where Emma slept, with her back turned to him. Marcus sat on the corner of the bed, rubbed his face with his hands and then he said to himself:

- Fortunately it was only a dream - he shook his head and went to the bathroom, passing beside Emma's bed, he paused and looked at her face. It was obvious that Emma sleeping peacefully and didn't have any nightmares, quite the contrary, on her face you could see a gentle smile. „At least you sleep peacefully, without any nightmares" he thought, and went to the bathroom. When he was inside he went over to the wall opposite to the sink with a mirror. He rested one hand on the sink, and the other hand turned on the tap on and splashed his face with cold water. He stared at his reflection in the mirror, asking himself:

- What did I dream? Why? When will this end? This has to end well, pull yourself together, you are able to do anything - He washed his face once more with cold water, not wipping it and walked out of the bathroom. He got dressed and sat on the windowsill to watch the cloudless sky outside the window.

Marcus stared at one point in the sky, which was very familiar. It was the Cassiopeia constellation. He whispered to himself: - I hope that somewhere there it's quiet and nobody worries about tomorrow.

He sat there for a long moment, staring at the sky resting his head on the edge of the wall.

- Why aren't you sleeping? - He heard the question that interrupted his thoughts. He looked at the bed where s Emma was laying and saw her staring at him.

- How long are you awake? - He asked. She did not answer, so he went on. - I can not fall asleep for a long time, just as soon as I close my eyes, I get nightmares. As soon as I fall asleep, some strange nightmares torture me, one's I do not understand, and they always end badly.

- You want to talk about them? - Asked Emma.

- No, there is no need, after all, they will not disappear.

Marcus was staring at the sky through the window, and Emma was lying on the bed, but like Marcus she stared into the darkness outside, where from time to time you could see one falling star after another. Emma stood up and silently walked over to Marcus and once another shooting star flashed in the sky, she said:

- Make a wish.

Marcus looked at Emma surprised.

- When you see a shooting star, you have to make a wish, something you want, and it will fulfill it.

- Seriously? - He asked.

- Don't tell me you did not know.

- I had no clue. Who told you that?

- When I was little, my grandmother said so to me: when there is a falling star, make a wish and it fulfill itself, so I always thought. So try it.

- Seriously?

- Go ahead – she answered, and then Marcus looked at a star that he spotted, fell silent and closed his eyes and after a while he said:

- I'm done, now what?

Emma put her finger on Marcus lips and said: - Now do not tell anyone. This is between you and those who fulfill wishes.

- Then why express any wishes if they can not be told anyone? Marcus asked surprised, but did not get an answer. As Emma summed his question up with a smile.

- Can I ask you something?

- Yes, please do - said Marcus.

- What if everything will be over and done with, and when we win, what do you want to do then?

- You know, I heard that Alaska's forests are beautiful.

- Alaska? - Emma asked surprised

- Yes. I've heard that beautiful deer live in the forests of Alaska, that lakes between large rocky mountains are so transparent that you can see the bottom, from the tops of the mountains. People in Alaska are very polite to one another and time passes very slowly. That's where I'd like to move and grow old when this hell is over- Marcus replied, smiling to himself. The girl just nodded her head, then looked in the window and said: - Not bad.

- And you, what will you do? - Asked Marcus.

Emma was silent for a moment as if wondering which of her dreams of a happy life, she should choose and tell.

- I want to live somewhere in Western or Central Europe, I do not know in which city, but certainly somewhere in the mountains. Maybe in the Alps, I really do not know. I'll think about it seriously, when this is all over.

- Going back to what I dreamed, that I had a strange dream - Marcus said suddenly changing the subject.

- What dream? - Emma asked, surprised.

- I dreamed that we both die, I die first, and then you - told Marcus looking at the girl.

- How do we die? - Asked Emma.

- That's what I do not understand, it's a strange dream, that does not make sense.

- How do we die?- Emma repeated her question, Marcus looked at her and said:

- We both die at the hands of Jason. This is my dream, and then I wake up and it happens really, in my dream again.

- What? - Asked Emma surprised, while making big eyes.

- First, I have a dream, then, I wake up in the dream and it happens really as if I had a deja-vu.

- Wow.

- Jason comes here and attack us, and there's nothing I can do.

- Maybe Jason knows what's going on in these dreams, and can explain all of this? - Emma said.

- I'm afraid to tell him that I have such dreams, because if that's true then... And if it's one big fake and it never happens, I do not know what then?

- No, but if we won't ask, we won't know. Let's ask him, it's best if we ask while driving to the next person, what do you say?

- Uhum – Marcus said and looked at the clock hanging on the wall.

- We need to get going, look it's almost eight.

They started to get dressed, when suddenly they heard a knock at the door.

10.

STEP TOWARDS TRUTH

- Who is there? - Asked Marcus.

- It's me, Jason - was the reply. Marcus thought for a moment and then said:

- Come on in - and Jason went inside looking around and carefully looking at his companions.

- Are you ready? We must hurry.

- Yes, yes - said Marcus putting his jacket on and added: - I'm going to have a look around - and left the room. Emma finished buttoning her sweater and said: - I am also ready.

- Great, because we really don't have time - reminded Jason. Emma looked at him with hesitant eyes.

- What happened? - Asked Jason.

- I don'tt know, but I feel strange.

- Be more specific please, did you eat something bad?

- No, no, it's something else, I get the feeling that someone is watching us.

Jason looked out the window carefully and looking around he said: - Let's go.

Jason walked carefully observing everything, but did not notice anything suspicious. As they approached the car, Marcus was working on something under the bonnet, which was raised.

- You ready? We have to move.

Marcus closed the bonnet by pushing it so it clicked and said: - I'm ready, we can move on.

They got into the vehicle, whose engine was already running.

Once everyone was inside, Emma and Jason looked around the area carefully in search of something strange, Marcus noticed this and asked:

- Is everything alright?

- Drive – che heard him reply, so he hit the gas pedal not asking about the details.

They drove quickly through the first part and just after taking off, Jason and Emma looked around very carefully, to spot anything suspicious. Marcus didn'tt like such an unbearable atmosphere, so he turned to Jason.

- I dreamed about you, you know?

- In what sense? I hope…

- No, no - Marcus laughed and Emma drew a smiley face to their direction.

- Then, what did you dream about?

- You wanted to kill us, me and Emma.

- Heh, I got almost scared there for a minute. May I ask, did you have something like a deja-vu in your dream?

- Yeah, something like that, like a dream within a dream. It's probably something like a deja-vu. How do I interpret such a dream?

Jason did not answer and looked to the side. Marcus pulled up to the side, onto an emergency lane and stopped the vehicle and turned off the engine.

- I do not trust you fully. Please tell me, what does that all mean? I'm really confused and I do not like to be in a situation like that, you know?

- Want to know what's going on? - Jason asked, looking out the window, where his gaze was hung in the empty space.

- Yes, I want to know what's going on and who you are.

Jason looked down at his hands, where one was rubbing the other. It was evident that he is nervous.

- Well, tell me finally - Marcus almost shouted, while clenching his fists on the steering wheel.

There was silence, Jason looked at Marcus and Emma looked at Jason, and after a while Jason looked at Marcus, saying: - You are my son, Marcus. Your name is Marcus Vortinghton.

- What did you say?

Jason did not answer. Emma was breathing heavily, she felt shocked, as if this news concerned her.

- But that's impossible – Marcus said in denial.

- Me, you and the others, all escaped from the planet Daxton right after you were born. And this something that is chasing us, unfortunately it's something I have created myself.

- I do not believe this.

- Believe it or not, unfortunately, it is true, we do not come from this world.

- You're lying - said Marcus confused. - You're lying, lying, lying.

- Unfortunately not, everything that is happening around us, it's true. Look around you, doesn't it seem to you that everything that surrounds you is unnatural, or even unrealistic to you?

Marcus was silent.

- Does it seem to you that what you can do, other people can do, as well?

Marcus was silent.

- You have as much as I do, and you Emma also, a gift, abilities, of that any creature on this planet could never dream about.

- I do not believe it - said Marcus. At that momnet, Jason put his hand to his temple. It seemed as if Marcus had lost consciousness, yet he was fully conscious and saw snippets of a film. In it he was a child, he saw how Jason took him as an infant in his arms, how they play together and many other scenes, one after the other, and suddenly everything disappears. Jason took his hand from Marcus' head and he returned to full capacity. He regained control of himself and listened to Jason's following words.

- We all lived on a planet very similar to Earth, but we didn't have things that happen here, like war, famine, disease, murder, rape, theft. I was a scientist, just like you, and I started to create machines that were intended to help us all. I created machines that had artificial intelligence. It was just as I imagined. These robots helped us in everyday duties, like rescue us from accidents. But one day something went wrong - Jason looked at Emma, then he looked at Marcus. - These machines have killed one of our inhabitants of our planet. After the incident, the supreme council told me to end my work on improving these robots, and also ordered me to destroy them. Unfortunately I did not listen to the order and created another robot. It seemed like the right thing at the time, but today I regret it very much. I created a robot with artificial intelligence, with above average brain structure, with the ability to gain different shapes and forms, after that all hell broke loose. My new robot began to take control of our machines, he began to break into top secret material breaking all the safeguards, and worse, he had the ability to direct other robots. When robots started to take control over our planet, hundreds, thousands of our compatriots were killed, the whole town fell into disrepair. Our leadership decided to create the ultimate line of defense, but unfortunately it failed miserably. Our last chance for our rescue was irretrievably lost. These machines were everywhere, both among soldiers and among ordinary people.

- In that case, how come we have all escaped? - Asked Marcus.

- At the same time, I worked on a capsule that could move to different parts of galaxies, as well as in other dimensions, to planets similar to our own, where we could live on, as space became scares on our planet. The computers found a planet almost identical to ours in another dimension, and it was called Earth. When everything was ready and we were preparing for teleportation, we were attacked by machines. They appeared out of nowhere, we had too little time to get everyone into the teleporter. We have tried to defend our planet, so we sent you first here, after that we closed the portal and the only way of escape. When we lost, you safely fled with the teleports. A powerful king said to me and ordered me to take care of you and follow you, because he had a visions and predicted that three children born with powerful, supernatural powers will overcome all our enemies and there will be peace again in the universe. When he finally got to the last teleporter, I saw how our King was fighting with robots and how he fell on the battlefield - Jason said lowering his head.

There was total silence.

- You are the last living children of our race, and the only ones, who can overcome these terrible and merciless Zotorigh - Jason added, glancing at Marcus and Emma.

Marcus asked – Have I freed them?

- Completely unknowingly and simply by accident you created a machine that opened a portal to the world's alter-space. For now, only four escaped, but try to get other ones to get here too. When they kill you, then everything that you know and everything what is beautiful in your dreams, everything will be destroyed. The only dreams that enslaved people will have, is to have the courage to kill themselves, because the horrors they will face in life will be too awful to bear. The planet will sooner or later be destroyed, just like any other.

Marcus clenched his fists on the steering wheel not believing in what he hears.

- Do you still don't believe me?

- I no longer know what to believe - Said Marcus.

- We better move on - Said Emma, after a while.

While driving everyone was silent, after a while Emma asked: - Why did not you tell us this before?

- I did not know how to tell you all of this.

- I think you are playing us. You are... - He paused to carefully select his words. - I Do not believe you're ... - again he failed to find the words.

Although she did not finish her sentence and did not mentioned the significant word, she was shaking her head to the left and to the right giving him to understand what she wants to say.

I know that I'm pathetic, in fact everything tells me that such behavior, which you were able to observe is pathetic, but how would you react if I stood at your door and said, ‚Hey, I'm an emissary and just arrived on Earth." And then if I told Marcus, he's my son, and thus an inhabitant of another planet, then probably your first legitimate reaction would be to anesthetize me or pointing me in the direction to the next psychiatric hospital.

- Would you have prefered to let Marcus believe that his parents were dead?

- Do not blame me for being heartless. Please believe me that it was for the best. You would you do the same, if you were me. You don't even know how much I missed him and how worried I was about him. You have no idea what it's like to watch someone you love, growing up without you. More than once I cried and regretted my decision, but somewhere in my soul I explained to myself that it would be safer this way. Do you know how it is, to love someone so much and not being able to meet this person? You have no idea. In your life, everything is simple, Emma, so it's easy for you. Believe it or not, but this was the only good decision.

Emma looked at Jason, then lowered her head and fell silent. Jason looked at Marcus and said:

Yes, I do regret what I did and that I didn't let you to believe that I was alive, but it was the only way to protect you. Now, when it is no longer possible, I will not let anyone hurt you, you both - Said Jason staring the whole time at Marcus.

- And now, what do you want to do? Collectall of us here, and after a victory you will just disappear, the same way you appeared? - Asked Marcus.

-No - Said Jason.

-So?

Jason did not answer, he just went silent. Marcus turned his head toward the window and said softly under his breath:

- I thought so.

Silence lasted. Marcus finally interrupted the silence and turned to Jason:

-You know what? I think it would be better, if you did disappear, after all. I copeed without you for so many years, so now I will be able to cope just as well as I did. After the fight I do not want to see you again.

- I know, I expected that. It will be the way you want it - Jason replied in a low voice, swallowing heavily.

- Great.

Jason stopped on the roadside, leaned his head against the wall of the car and then closed his eyes. In the car, there was silence.

- Where do we go exactly? - Marcus asked, without looking at anyone.

- We have to get to Pasadena to the third person - was the reply. -We don't have too much time, we need to be there before eight in the morning, so we have quite a way ahead of us.

Emma asked:

- Why do we have to hurry?

- Heh, so you haven't listened to what I said? But thats ok, I will repeat. It's hard to accept such news and process them quickly, so once again: if the portal is still opened, that is if you do not close this damn portal on time, it's like you had left the door open and informed everyone that you're going on a week's holiday. Someone would plunder the whole house, and in this case there will be no thieves, but just very unpleasant machines- Robots and believe me, they will not plunder the house. Do you understand?

-Now yes - said Emma. - But where is it?

- On the isles - said Jason.

- On what isles? - Emma asked again.

- On the British Isles.

- Where? In England? - Emma asked with disbelief and a frown on her face.

Marcus interrupted Emma's conversation with Jason:

- I do not want to interrupt this charming conversation, but I think we have a tail.

- What? Where? - Asked Jason.

- And where is a tail usually? For several miles, someone drives behind us, but is not approaching. I can not lose him, because he always keeps the same distance - glancing in the rearview mirror he pointed to what he meant.

At that time, Emma leaned to the back doors. She didn't sit behind them but was rather secretly staring from the side so that no one could see her through the rear window. Jason took his place alongside Marcus and was staring at the side mirror asking:

- Is this the black Pontiac? - pointing to the fourth vehicle hiding behind other cars driving about 300 meters behind them.

- How do you know, it's a Pontiac?

- I have a great eyesight - Jason replied with irony and continued asking: - Are you sure?

- Yes, I'm sure - Marcus replied, clutching the steering wheel tighter. - What do we do?

- Yeah, what do we do now? - Asked Emma, who looked at to Marcus, then to Jason, and then to the car, which was following them. - What do we do?

- Let me think - said Jason.

Silence fell. Jason went back to his place at the back, where he began to rub his body with the inside of his palm.

- Should I drive on, or turn into a side street somewhere to get rid of that car? Asked Marcus.

Jason shook back and forth and tried to think of something. Emma began to look more and more anxiously toward Jason and then Marcus, and back and forth.

Maybe we should just stop and ask this person what they want from us?

Marcus and Jason simultaneously threw angry looks at Emma.

-No - Said Jason.

- Why? If you do not, then I will give that person a hard time - Said Emma, with conviction and anger.

Jason looked at Emma, then asked:

- How do you know, that this is a person? You can be sure that behind the wheel sits just a human, and not a Zotorigh? - Jason asked, raising his eyesight towards Emma.

- Well, I'm not so sure, but something tells me that if none of us will do this, we'll regret it - said Emma.

- Meaning..? - Jason asked, looking over his shoulder at Emma.

- I'm just having a feeling that we need to stop and show tham what we are capable of, and that we are not afraid - said Emma.

- We don't have time for this, we need to hurry - said Jason, who anxiously watched in the side mirrors, as well as at Emma and Marcus, all the time.

- Emma's right - Marcus added.

- Are you sure about this? - Jason asked, looking at them.

- I am - said Emma.

-And You, Marcus, you want to stop? - Asked Jason.

- Maybe it will be better if we stop and see if the words of persuasion would be enough for them stop following us. Though this might not necessarily be the case - said Marcus.

- And what if you are wrong? - Asked Jason.

Marcus looked up at Jason then he said:

- Then we will have a problem.

Jason stared at Emma, who was staring with imploring eyes straight into his eyes.

- Ok, as you wish, but remember that you'll have the fate of mankind and the universe on your conscience - Jason said.

- I'm glad you made this decision - said Marcus looking at Jason.

- Turn into the first side road and try move away from the highway as soon as possible - Jason said.

- No - Jason protested vigorously.

- I will not even ask why, but your wish is my command - said Marcus searching for the nearest highway exit.

- And in the meantime we have to think of a plan - Said Jason and approached Emma.

- I thought we would act spontaneously. It would be certainly very exciting. I always love to watch guys, who mindlessly fight with each other.

Jason looked at Emma, but did not say a word, just nodded his head and then turned to Marcus:

- Be ready.

Marcus noticed the highway exit and was ready to turn when suddenly Jason grabbed the steering wheel.

- What are you doing? But ... - his speech was interrupted, as Jason said:

- Not yet. Accelerate as much as possible – Said Jason and looked up to Marcus.

Marcus lifted his head and asked:

- Why not now?

- We have to check if the car is really following us or not - said Jason.

- Uhum – Marcus nodded, then he pressed the gas pedal and the car started to move away at a very fast pace from the car, which probably followed them.

Everyone watched with bated breath, whether the car begins to accelerate and continue follow them, but nothing happened. The car, that has followed them began to recede, and then disappeared far behind. Everyone breathed a sigh of relief, but Marcus did not slow down.

- I think that we are safe now - he said.

- Now turn into a side road as soon as possible - Jason said. - Oh, there - he pointed.

Marcus braked sharply and turned into the road. He accelerated again, when the road that led to the highway had disappeared of the side-view mirror. Marcus slowed down, then stopped for a moment. Everyone stared in the mirror. Marcus looked at Jason and sighed quite loudly, expressing his relief. Emma looked into the rear window. Jason moved toward Emma and touched her shoulder, saying:

- I guess, this time you were wrong.

- I was not mistaken - Emma protested, nodding toward a distant point, which began to approach rapidly in their direction. Everyone, as if on cue, looked in the rearview mirror, then Jason said without turning his head:

- Marcus, move as quickly as possible.

Marcus, without thinking, turned on the gear and pushed the gas pedal with all his strength. The car set off with squealing tires and began to accelerate at a very fast pace, but not fast enough to lose the car, which began to catch up with them. - Well, now we have an opportunity to face someone who drives this car very fast.

Jason stared at Marcus.

- Why fast? - He asked.

- Because we have a bigger problem - Said Marcus, speeding with high speed on a road that was overgrown by trees on the left and right side.

- What's happening? - Asked Jason.

-Hmm, obviously this road is a dead end - said Marcus.

Jason jumped up and approached the driver. He looked in front of the windshield and noticed that the road on which they were driving was coming to an end very fast.

- We have some 1,000 meters left - Marcus opined.

- What the hell do we do? - Asked Emma.

- If you will have the opportunity, make a U-turn so that the car will be facing the enemy before we get to the end of the road - Jason said.

After these words, Marcus swerved and pulled the handbrake and the car turned suddenly a hundred and eighty degrees. Silence fell. Marcus unbuckled his belt and waited for the oncoming car.

- There it is! - Marcus exclaimed, pointing at a car that appeared behind the curve.

- Be ready for anything and do not let them capture you, not to meantion, kill you - Jason yelled toward Emma and Marcus.

- We know that - Emma replied, clenching her fists.

Suddenly, the car that was driving in their direction was about a hundred meters from their car when it abruptly stopped.

- What's happening? - Marcus asked, surprised. - Why has the car stopped?

- Maybe it's a trap? - Emma asked Jason.

- I do not know, but we'll find out soon - Jason said, then opened the door of the cab and stepped outside.

- What are you doing? - Marcus asked Jason, who was already outside the car.

Jason stopped, turned toward Marcus, came up to him and said:

- If the person doesn't attack, it means that it's expected something of us. I need to see what this person wants from us.

- But if it turns out that it's actually a trap, then do everything in your power to avoid being killed.

Jason nodded and began to move away from the car.

- What do we do now? - Emma asked, glancing at Marcus even though both looked ahead, as Jason walked away from the vehicle.

- We wait - said Marcus.

- But if we only wait, then ... - her unfinished speech was interrupted by Marcus:

- Yes, I know what can happen, but we have no choice - he said.

Emma paused and together with Marcus stared through the windshield at Jason, who was walking very slowly toward the standing car. When Jason was halfway between the cars, he stopped, then drew his sword and pointed the blade toward the enemy. Then he lowered his sword to the ground. After about ten seconds, the door of the standing car swung wide open. Jason grabbed his sword in both hands and began to direct a fast pace toward the open door. Suddenly, the man got out of the car. He looked at Jason and pulled his hand toward him as a sign to stop. Jason, little thinking, stopped and lowered his sword on his right side. The man who got out of the car was dressed in a military outfit, and he wore a black cowboy hat. Jason stood and waited for the man's move.

- What's that supposed to mean? - Asked Emma, and began to walk towards the car door.

- What are you doing? - Asked Marcus.

- What do you mean? I won't leave Jason alone with that person - She said, and then got out and followed toward Jason very quickly.

- God dammit - Marcus said under his breath, then got out of the car and followed Emma.

The man who got out of a black Camaro, stood there and stared only at Jason. Emma and Marcus came to stand next to their motionless companion.

- What's happening? - Asked Emma and looked at Jason. - Why doesn't this person attack?

- I do not know, but if it was an enemy, he would have started to fight with me long ago – Jason replied, glancing at Marcus and Emma.

When Jason just finished his sentence, he noticed the man started to approach in their direction, but didn't perform any sudden movements. He walked upright with lowered hands.

- What do we do now?- Marcus asked, glancing sideways at Jason.

- We are waiting for his first move.

- But he made the first move. He walks in our direction. So what are we doing? Marcus asked again nervously. - Do we attack?

- No! Stand still and wait! - Jason replied in a commanding tone.

When the three of them stood and waited, the stranger approached with slow pace toward them. At one point, when the man was about ten meters from them, he stopped, raised his head, looked at all three, then he raised his left hand very carefully and adjusted his hat. Then he reached into the pocket of his coat and pulled out a slip of paper. He folded the paper and threw it in their direction, the paper landed by Emma's feet. The three of them looked at the crumpled piece of paper and then looked at the man. As they stood and stared at the stranger each of them wondered what this person will do next. At some point, the silence has interrupted by the voice of the man who looked at Emma, saying:

- Pick it up and read it!

His voice seemed to be very rough. Emma looked at the crumpled piece of paper lying at her feet. Then, she directed her head towards her comrades without saying a word, and stared at them as if asking what to do.

- I repeat, pick up and read it - The man told Emma again.

This time the tone of his voice seemed to be rougher and colder than before. Emma leaned down toward the piece of paper, while keeping her eyes on the man all the time. She reached the bundle, then raised it very carefully and started to unfold it. When she finished reading it, she looked with disbelief at Marcus and Jason. She forwarded the piece of paper to Marcus. When he read its contents, he stared at the stranger with the same disbelieving eyes as Emma.

- What does it say? - Asked Jason nervous.

- Read it for yourself - Marcus replied, handing him the paper.

Jason took the paper and began to read. When he finished, he asked a man standing in front of them:

- Is it true what is written here?

- Yes, the whole truth - said the man.

- Explain this! - Jason exclaimed.

- What is there to explain? That's the truth - Said the man adjusting his hat. Jason took a step forward, then threw the paper at the feet of a man.

The piece of paper fell very slowly, as if it was lifted by the wind, even though there was no wind to hear in the area. It fell much slower and everyone - all four of them – looked at it how very unnatural it fell to the ground. When the piece of paper finally settled on the ground, about halfway between the three companions and the man, he began to walk toward them very slowly. All three did not move from the spot. The man stopped only about a meter from the trio then said: - You all will die. All your miserable work and your belief in victory, will be for nothing- The man replied.

Everyone looked at the man with great dismay, as if they feared him but at the same time they wanted to destroy him, but something prevented them. The man looked at Marcus and Jason and said:

- I have nothing to you, but I was looking for you for a very long time. In the end, I found you.

Marcus and Jason looked at each other and then at the man. The man raised his head, then he said:

- Do you have any questions?

- Who the hell are you? - Asked Marcus.

- My name is Thomas - The man replied. - Major Thomas - he added - and I know exactly how it might sound to you, but I come from the future.

- Yeah ... - Jason responded with mockery. - And who sent you, what for and how is all this possible?

- But it's impossible to time travel. It's impossible - said Marcus.

- I came from the future and more precisely from the year 2345 - said the man.

- But how is that possible? - Jason asked again.

- After all, time travel machines don't exist – said Marcus.

- Maybe in your times they don't exist, but in mine they do. And I am the best proof - Thomas said. All three looked at Thomas with disbelief and listened to what he said. Emma picked up the paper, unfolded it and looked at it again.

- Is that true, what is written here?- She asked, turning directly to Major Thomas.

- The whole truth. Unfortunately, you all will die, and your entire civilization will cease to exist. I am a Major of a galactic fleet and there are only a handful of us. We traverse the universe in search of a shelter to protect us from that something that you have encounted with recently. I'm on your side and trust me, I need you as much as you need me. I'm here to prevent what is going to happen in two days, and what will be the beginning of the destruction of the galaxy, until my time. Go ahead, come to me and see for yourself - He turned to Jason. - After all, you can check if what I said is true.

Jason stared at Thomas, then walked over to him and touched his head and then pictures appeared in his head of what Major Thomas saw. All the pain, the horror of those people, who remained in the universe, and their flight through the galaxy. He saw Major Thomas fight the Zotorigh race and how he lost, how he arrived on a planet, where he discovered that it is possible to defeat them by going back in time. He sees how Major Thomas arrived on this planet a few days ago, and tries to find them. When he had had enough, as it was the worst thing he could see in that moment, he pulled his hand from his forehead. As he did so, he looked up at Emma and Marcus then said:

- He is right. I saw it in his mind. See for yourself - He approached them and grabbed them by the hand and showed them everything he just saw himself in his mind.

Marcus pulled his hands from Jason, then said:

- That's a lie.

- Why do you think so? – Thomas asked, staring at Marcus.

-Because ... - Marcus paused, then he added. - Because of my visions, they show me quite the opposite.

- What? - Asked Thomas.

- In my dreams and visions everything goes down differently. Sometimes I dream about moments of life as if it weren't my life, like I was someone else. Or how I am already experiencing it and I see how I fight and conquer these monsters. And then I experienced a vision in which the entire galaxy dies. Then again I can see how everything went alright, how I live to an old age and see how my grandchildren are playing in the garden. Then I see how all this is all just a lie, and how I live among the dead, as there is nothing left as all the people I knew are dead - Said Marcus. - I do not know myself what to believe.

The three of them looked at Marcus.

- And what do you believe in the most? What seems the closest version to the truth? - Thomas asked, staring all the time at Marcus.

- The fact that everything will end well - said Marcus.

- Then make it happen - Thomas replied. - Make sure that my nightmare and reality will never be your reality.

Marcus looked at Thomas and then with a slight disbelief and mild pain in his voice he replied:

- But I do not know how to do it.

Major Thomas smiled to himself and then said:

- You do not know yet, but when the time comes, I hope you will be able to choose between what is true and what is fiction.

Marcus lowered his head. Major Thomas turned away from him and began to head towards the car. All three became speechless and stared at Thomas. At this moment, Thomas was already near his vehicle. When he was about to get in, he looked toward the three and asked:

- Are you going to stand there the whole time?

Jason looked at Thomas and asked:

- What are you going to do now? What shall we do?

- I found you, and now we have to go to a place where we can calmly think things through and where we can practice quietly for a moment - Thomas said. - I'll wait for you at the entrance to the highway.

He got into the car, started the engine and drove ahead. He drove about twenty meters and paused, then he leaned his head out the window and shouted at them:

- I will not wait long for you. Better hurry. I easily traced you down, so they can do the same - said Thomas and headed for the highway.

11.

UNEXPECTED GUEST

- Do you have a plan? - Asked Emma.

- Let me think - said Jason.

- Think? We have no time at all - said Emma.

Marcus began to walk there and back.

- What are you thinking about? - Asked Jason.

- I don't want to believe in this all - said Marcus.

- But what exactly? - Asked Jason. - Because I admit that I was already confused.

- Well, Thomas' story that he comes from the future and in general everything is so confusing.

The girl looked at Marcus and shook her head.

- Do you even believe in this? - She asked with a slight sarcasm.

- What do you mean? - Marcus asked nervously.

Emma looked up and asked again:

- Do you really want to know? - She screamed at Marcus.

Marcus stared quizzically at Emma.

- I ask, do you believe in any of that? - she yelled again at Marcus.

Marcus looked at Jason, then at Emma again.

- Yes, I do - he replied.

- Then tell me what do you believe in exactly? - Asked Emma.

- I believe in myself! The fact that all this is a fucking dream that will end when I wake up. Somehow I try to open my eyes, but I can't and I do not know why, I just can't open them! First of all you appeared in my life, then I discover that I have some supernatural powers, and on top of this all I find out that my father was alive this whole time, but I my whole fucking life I believed that he had died when I was little. And finally he turned up, what's his name?

- Thomas - said Emma.

- Yes, Thomas. Thomas appears out of nowhere and tells me that he is from the future and came to help us to save the world! Is that enough? - Said Marcus.

Emma and Jason looked at Marcus in silence.

- And one more thing - he added. - The funny thing is that this whole world, in which I believed in, will cease to exist any day! Understand me. I've simply had enough of this! - Marcus exclaimed, then got in his car slamming the door behind him.

Emma and Jason looked at each other.

- I'll go talk to him - said Jason.

- Uhum - Emma nodded.

Jason went to the door on the other side of the car and got in.

- Can I join you? - He asked.

Marcus looked at Jason and said roughly: - Sit, if you want. Soon, nothing will matter anymore, so you don't have to think about whether I want any company or not.

Jason sat down on the seat, he looked straight ahead and then at Marcus.

- You know, maybe it's hard for you to understand, but I know exactly how you feel - said Jason. - When we were attacked by these machines and after a final attempt to retaliate by our military has failed, you have no idea how much I regretted creating these machines. What am I saying? Every day I regret what I did. I do not even know how it's like, when you dream about all those hundreds and or even millions of peoples faces who have died. But the worst thing is to see how your child is growing up without a father. You don't even know how it feels like not to be able to see the only person you truly love and is still alive, and that's all for their safety. If I could, I would go back in time - said Jason.

Marcus looked at Jason.

- I have just one request to you - said Jason.

- What is it?

- Let your dreams come true, and don't let them only be dreams. Marcus turned his gaze towards Jason.

- I do not have such a possibility anymore, but you do - added Jason.

Jason's eyes began to tear up and started to run down his cheeks, directly onto the piece of paper that Major Thomas gave them. Jason took Marcus hand and said:

- Everything will be fine my son. No matter how long it takes, I will not leave you alone again. Even if I have to die, I will not make the same mistake again - Jason wiped his tears. - I'm sorry.

- You have nothing to be sorry about - Marcus said as Jason took a deep breath.

After exhaling, a gentle smile appeared on his face and as he started to feel better, he straightened up and said:

- We should probably go, as Thomas is waiting for us by the highway.

Marcus looked at Jason and just smiled, as if his smile was him agreeing to what Jason just said.

Emma stood about seven meters away from the car, in which Marcus and Jason sat in.

- Are you getting in, or shall I send you an invitation? - Jason asked Emma leaning his head out the window and gently smiling at her.

- Of course, I won't walk all this way by feet - Emma said, heading toward the car, opened the door, looked at Marcus and got into the car taking the seat at the back.

- Can we go now? - Marcus asked, looking at Emma and Jason.

They both nodded in agreement. Marcus started the engine and followed behind Thomas.

As they drove off, Jason turned to both of them, saying:

- Watch out for yourself, because despite everything that happened today, we must carefully observe Thomas's behavior. I not quite trust him - He addressed the request to Marcus and Emma.

With silence they agreed. As they got to the beginning of the road, in which they turned into, they noticed Thomas' car standing on the left side, and him sitting on the bonnet of the car. They stopped beside him. They were ready to get, as Jason suddenly asked Thomas:

- What are you going to do now?
- What do you mean? - Asked Thomas.
- What are your intentions and plans, because I don't have time and I have a very important matter to attend to.
- What's that? - Asked Thomas.
- We must find the other person as soon as possible before the Zotorigh do.

Thomas got up on his feet, rubbed his hands, then shook his head and said:

- Okay. In that case, we shouldn't wait, but on our way we should establish some kind of battle tactic - Thomas said.
- What battle tactic? What do you mean? - Asked Marcus.
- In the event of an attack we should have a plan B, or at least forsee somehow what to do if something goes wrong. Anyway, I always have a plan B - explained Thomas.
- Good idea – Said Jason, listening to the conversation between Marcus and Thomas.
- So what do you say? - Asked Thomas.
- All in all, I don't let somebody interfere in my way of doing things, but I could always learn something more, or at least it won't hurt - said Marcus.
- And what do you think? Thomas asked Emma.
- I don't really have a say in this. The most important thing at the moment is to get out of this whole mess - she said.
- So everything is set - Said Thomas and began to head towards the car.
- Where are you going? - Marcus asked, looking at Thomas.

- What do you mean where? I am going to drive ahead with my car - Thomas answered the question.

- Under no circumstance - Marcus said a firm voice. - You have to leave your car here, it will be safer if we all drive in one car. That is my condition, or actually, our condition.

Thomas looked at his car and then on the van in which they all were in, then he said:

- Fine - he said with a grimace on his face. - I just have to get my stuff out of the car.

When Thomas began to gather his things at the back of his car, Emma nudged Marcus on the shoulder.

- What are you doing? Why does he have to come with us?

- It will be better if he drives with us in one car, just trust me – He replied in a hushed voice.

- Why? - Emma persisted.

- Because I learned one very important thing in life, it's good to have a friend close to you, but your enemy even closer - he said.

- You mean it will be better to keep an eye on him, than not knowing what he's plotting behind our backs? - Emma asked confused.

- That's exactly, what I mean - said Marcus.

- Oh, now I understand - she said. -But if he'll be plotting something, or even lookat me the wrong way, I'll show him what our race is capable of.

- Well, I give you full rein - said Marcus. - And what do you think about this? - He asked Jason.

- I think it's a good idea. We will have him in sight, in case something happens.

Thomas got into the car, taking a seat on the padded floor of the van and asked:

- Where are we going now and who's the boss? - He asked.

- We're all making decisions, and if it comes to driving I would call it differently - said Jason.

- Meaning? - Asked Thomas.

- It would be better to ask where we are flying to - Jason replied mysteriously.

- What do you mean flying? - Thomas asked, surprised.

- Because the next person we are looking for, who's completely unaware, lives in London. We have a flight in two hours. If we hurry, then we can get there in time. The flight will last nearly ten hours. There will be plenty of time to develop a tactic.

- But we were going to drive to Denver - said Emma surprised.

- Yes, but it was only to mislead Zotorigh, so they wouldn't fathom - said Jason.

The three of them looked up at Jason quizzically.

- You could have said that we are looking for someone in London, so I would take an umbrella with me as the English weather is crap apparently – Marcus said with a slight smile on his face.

- Do not worry about the English weather - Jason said and added -You will miss the hailstorms.

- Can we go now? - Emma hurried them.

- Yes, we're going now - said Marcus. They drove off leaving Thomas' car on the roadside.

As they drove on the highway toward the airport, the four of them sat in silence. Marcus was focused on driving, Emma sat staring at the ceiling, Thomas was sitting on the floor and calculated everything in his head and Jason pulled out a piece of paper and started to take notes.

- What are you writting? - Marcus asked, sitting next to Jason.

- Nothing - Jason said embarrassed.

Marcus looked at Jason and asked again:

- Well after all, you can tell me. Unless you have something to hide? - Marcus asked suspiciously.

- I'm just simply scribbling around - said Jason.

- Fine - Marcus sighed and went back to driving a car.

- I have a request to you - Jason turned to all three of them.

- What request? What is going on? - Asked Emma.

- When we get to the airport, we have to pretend as if we didn't know each other - he replied.

- What? Why? - Emma asked, surprised.

- It's better if they don't connnect us to each other. Besides, if something were to happen, it will be better when everyone is separately so we won't get caught all together - Jason explained.

- Can you tell me, what could happen? - Asked Emma.

- Well, for example, we wouldn't appeal to the guards at the airport and will have a problem that we don't want. At airports they are usually strangely suspicious, and it is enough to just look at the guard the wrong way.

- Maybe we should just fly with a private plane? - Said Marcus.

The three of them looked at Marcus.

- What do you say? - He asked again.

- What are you talking about? What private plane? - Asked Jason.

- I just have a friend who has a private jet, which he can borrow and he won't ask any questions. He owes me a favor - Marcus replied, smiling to himself.- So what do you say? Do you prefer to fly private or huddle together with other people and hide?

- I'm all for it - said Emma.

Jason and Thomas nodded in agreement with Emma.

- It's all set - said Marcus then pulled his phone out, stopped at the side of the road and dialed the number.

Suddenly, Thomas grabbed the phone and looked at Marcus.

-What are you doing? - Thomas asked with surprise.

- Stupid question. I want to make a call. I do not know how you do it, but we just take the phone and calle. If you have a better way to contact someone, then tell me - said Marcus.

- You thought about the fact that you could be traced?

- Well, no, but I have no choice - said Marcus.

- It'd better to call from a pay phone. It's safer. Even if someone tracks us down, the signal will stay at that place and won't be with us - said Thomas.

- You're right. I had not thought about it - said Marcus.

- A few miles from here, there should be a telephone booth. Then we stop and call, and you should throw your phone away, for safety - Thomas said.

-Uhum - Marcus nodded, then threw the phone through the side window. - And gone is my super cool phone.

- Good - Thomas said.

- Can I ask you something? - Marcus turned to Thomas.

- You can, of course. Ask for anything you want - Thomas said.

- Can you tell me, what you have on your left hand? - Marcus asked glancing at the strange device on Thomas' hands.

- This is ... How could I explain it to you the easiest way? - Thomas wondered.

- A phone? - Asked Emma.

- This is a intertemporal transporter - Thomas said.

- What is it? - Asked Emma.

- In other words, it's a time teleporter - he replied and smiled in Emmas direction.

Emma was speechless with surprise.

- But teleporters are invention that only exist in movies - she said.

- In what? - Thomas asked, surprised.

- It does not matter, you do not understand - said Emma.

- Where did you get this device from? - Jason asked curiously.

- I got this device from King Naroth and it's not a human invention, because I can't reasonably use certain things, as it turns out. I also thought that teleporters didn't exist, as it turnes out that they do and they're portable as well - Thomas said.

- You can tell me how it operates and why you can't use it to destroy them, if it is what you claim it to be? - Asked Marcus.

- What do you mean use it? - Thomas asked, surprised.

- Just simply go back in time, to the moment when they haven't existed and prevent their creation.

- You know, I wish it were that simple - Thomas said.

- Than what's the problem? - Asked Marcus.

- This device is programmed to return to the planet from which I was sent. And then I'll olny have one more attempt to travel back in time, if I wouldn't be able to stop them here at this time. I would only be able to go back a few minutes before the last register, so I could fix something that went wrong. After that I will no longer have the possibility to time travel - Thomas said.

- Can you repeat it, but a little bit more specific? - Asked Emma.

- In other words, I have only one jump in time there and forth - Thomas said.

- And tell me, how did you find us? - Asked Marcus. - And how did you know that we were driving this way?

- I got some very unclear indications and I observed you earlier.

- When earlier? - Marcus asked, surprised.

- I'm on this planet for a few weeks, maybe a month - said Thomas.

- Ok, but how did you track us down? - Marcus asked again.

- This device has a target sensor, so to speak - Thomas said.

- What is this target sensor?

- It searches extraordinary anomalies across the globe, such as the use of a powerful force or movement in space without the use of aircraft. In other words, searches for people gifted with supernatural powers and consignees to each powerful energy beam. The first reading I received was a few days ago in a military base, in which you have been working. The next four days ago and then yesterday during your action in the fight against the commandos, and this morning was the last and after that it was hard to find you - said Thomas.

- How do you know about all this? - Marcus wondered.

- About what? - Asked Thomas.

- That I worked in a military base? This classified data. And that I fought the TTG commandos? - Marcus became irritated.

Emma listened to the conversation between Jason, Marcus and Thomas.

- From the Internet, on the radio. The news reported that the entire building got destroyed in strange circumstances, so I immediately associate it with you, and then it wasn't hard to trace you - Thomas said.

- Aha - said Marcus surprised then focused solely on driving.

- Turn here - said Thomas, pointing to the sign of a petrol station. - Here you will find a phone that you can call from.

- No problem - Marcus said, then changed the lane and headed toward the petrol station.

As they turned and were already close to the station, Thomas said:

- Park behind the building, so we don't arouse any suspicions.

Marcus nodded and stopped at the spot specified by Thomas. Marcus left the car and said:

- I'll be right back.

With hope of success he went to the phone booth. He grabbed the phone, pulled out a few coins and threw them into the mechine. Then he dialed the number. As he waited for the call to connect, he looked around to see if anyone was watching. In the handset he only heard the connection signal.

- Answer the heck - Marcus said under his breath.

- Yes, hello? - He heard a man's voice on the phone. - Who is this? - He heard again.

- It's me, Marcus - he said.

- Hi Marcus.

- Do you remember how you still owe me a favor? - He asked.

- Yes, I remember.

- Now I'm going to need your help - said Marcus.

- Hmm, that means? Something happened?

- I need a transport to Europe - said Marcus.

- For when?

- For yesterday, actually for as soon as you can. For tomorrow, or even today? - Asked Marcus.

- How many people will be traveling?

- Four, including me.

- Well, you started to work as a smuggler? That's quite a load you'll be carrying – said the voice on the phone.

- Yes, but never mind the details. Can you help me or not? - Asked Marcus. Markus noticed an awkward silence through the handset. - So, can you? - He asked again.

- You got it - said the man.

- Great! I'll make it up to you someday.

- When do you need the aircraft to be ready? - The voice on the phone asked.

- In 30 minutes, can you do that?

- In an hour, because I have to refuel and enter you onto the list. The plane will be waiting at the place, where always. - said the man.

- Ok thanks. In an hour then - said Marcus. - Many thanks again - he replied, and hung up. When he got into the car, Jason asked:

- And have you taken care of it?

- In an hour the plane will be fully tanked and ready for us. - said Marcus.

- That's good - said Thomas.

- Now we have to get to the airport as soon as possible, in order to make it on time to London. We still have a few hours flight ahead of us and of course in several hours we will have judgment day, and we'll have to deal with Zotorigh as well. What a crap day – Marcus summed up. - We can not be late and we have to be there on time - he added.

- So what are we waiting for? Why don't we move ahead? - Asked Thomas.

- We'll be moving, shortly.

- How far away is the airport? - Emma asked curiously.

- About twenty minutes to half an hour - said Marcus.

When he started the engine, he looked at the three of them and said:

- Keep your fingers crossed, that it all works out.

During the whole trip to the airport, there was complete silence. Everyone looked ahead, and spun in their minds their own versions of the end of this nightmarish adventure.

- You can trust this person? - Thomas asked, glancing at Marcus.

- Who are you talking about? - Asked Marcus.

- Well, about that person that you spoke to on the phone.

- Oh, you're talking about him - said Marcus. - Of course, he can be trusted, he once owed me a favor, and now he's returning the favor.

- That's good - said Thomas.

- What exactly happened in your day? - suddenly fell a question out of Emmas mouth.

- What do you mean? What are you asking about? - Thomas asked with a little hesitation.

- Do you know how to stop it? This race? What's it like in space? Are there any other races other than Earthlings?

Thomas looked up and smiled toward Emma, then he looked up at the sun and said:

- Well, the cosmos. I once dreamed to fly there, and later about returning to Earth. Cosmos is a hell of a large space, which never ends, whether someone likes it or not. You hit on some limits and you think that this is the end of your search. There is a limit, and surprise surprise. Beyond this limit there are exactly the same worlds like this and they are just as endless. It's like an organism in which there are trillions of cells, and it's similar with those worlds. Worlds are born and they die and are struggling to survive. The cell that is already at the end of its life is beeing absorbed by another cell. It will be reborn or will die and that is why we must fight - He looked at Emma. - Billions of cells, which thanks to them you are alive, and it's just like such worlds, but it's damn complicated. There are other civilizations in our space, but you would be lucky to reach any of them. And if you do reach them, you have to hope that they will be more primitive, but no matter how technologically advanced they are you still hope they are friendly creature - Thomas explained.

- But are there other species similar to the human species or similar to our race?

- So far, I met different races of appearances, some of which you could not imagine, but no species resembled us humans - said Thomas.

- I see.

- No, you don't understand - said Thomas.

- Meaning? - The girl asked the question slightly confused.

- I have traveled hundreds of worlds and no species, had ever inflicted so much suffering to its only race like humans do. Calling senseless wars and the desire to destroy each other - Thomas said those words and looked up at the sky.

The car was silent, no one dared to speak the slightest word.

- But there is one trait that makes me respect humans, spite of all the cruelty I've experienced. We are able to unite in strength and able to fight to the last drop of blood. We forget about all the problems and hatred that we have for each other and are able to face the danger shoulder to shoulder. This distinguishes us from mindless animals. The planet, that I remember, was ravaged by ourselves. That's why we travel through space and look for another planet to live on. It's obvious that each planet will get ruined. Zotorigh only accelerated the matter.

- And what, you just want to give up because of that? - Asked Emma.

- Give up? No, I'm not going to give up. I'm going to fight to the last drop of blood. They killed my wife and I lost my daughter, but they won't get me so easily - said Thomas.

Everyone fell silent for a moment, then Jason said:

- We're sorry because of that. It must be very hard.

- You know, it hurts, but not as much as it used to. Everyone I know, lost a loved one. Sometimes whole families, just like me, but what hurts me the most is that our civilization is on the brink of extinction, and I will not allow that to happen. I know they are out there in the heavens looking at me. Sometimes I feel their presence - Thomas said, staring straight ahead.

- How far is it to the airport? - Asked Emma.

- I think it's not far away - Marcus said, pointing to the signs on the road, which indicated the airport being two kilometers away. - We're almost there.

- Great. let's hurry, we don't have time, we must move as fast as possible - said Thomas.

The airport, on which the plane was located, was about twenty kilometers away from the town. There were two hangars, which connected with only one runway. Nearby was a control tower, on which normally only one person would sit, who directed the air traffic.

- I thought it would be a bigger airport - Thomas said a little surprised.

- You thought wrong - said Marcus.

- In which of them is the plane? - Emma asked, pointing to the hangars.

- In the left one - said Marcus.

As they pulled up to the hangar, Thomas turned to the three:

- Something is wrong. Where is the plane? And where's your friend? - Thomas asked, glancing at Marcus.

- He promised it would be here, but it seems to me that not everything is as it should be.

As they reached the end of the hangar, Marcus stopped with a squealing tires, and all four of them froze motionless.

- What's that supposed to mean? - Muttered Thomas.

A figure was standing at the end. It pressed a sword on Marcus' friend. The mysterious character was a young black man aged about twenty-five years. He was dressed all in black, and his face obscured with a hat. As he stood there holding the man, he shouted toward Marcus and the rest:

- Get out of the car or he will die.

- What do we do? - Emma asked quietly.

- Do you have a plan? - Asked Thomas nervously.

- I do - said Marcus. - I'll kick his ass in a heartbeat, so he won't even know his name.

- I will not repeat - said the man. - Get out, now.

- What do we do? - Jason asked.

- Let's do what he asks for, and then we'll see what next - said Thomas.

- Ok, but remember - we fight till the end - Jason recalled.

The four of them left the car and stood in front of the hood. The man raised his head and looked at all four very slowly.

- We have a proposition for you – Thomas said suddenly.

- Really? What proposal? - Asked the man.

- You wouldn't refuse. Release this man, and I promise that I'll be done with you very quickly. So quick, that you won't even feel it - Thomas said, smiling slightly to himself, and feeling very sure of himself.

- Really?

- Yes, indeed - said Thomas.

- Well, in that case I have a better offer for you - said the man.

All four of them looked at each other, then back at the man.

- Surrender, and I promise that I won't kill you.

All four clenched their fists.

- That pisser annoys me - said Jason and ran toward the man. As he was at a distance of about ten meters from him, he disappeared.

The man remained motionless as suddenly beside his face appeared Jason's leg. Without thinking, the man grabbed the leg and pulled him to the ground. Jason fell to the ground so fast that not even he was able to react. The throw was so powerful that a soft hole was created under the feet of a man.

Jason laid motionless, as the other three stood petrified and could not utter a single word.

- What are you waiting for? - Yelled the man, holding his sword next to Marcus' friends throat. -Who Is ready to test me now ? Maybe you Major Thomas? Or you Marcus?

When they heard their names, they were even more astonished, that he knew them.

- What do we do now? - Asked Emma.

Thomas and Marcus looked at each other.

- What the hell do we do now? - Repeated Emma.

- Who is he - asked Major Thomas to himself.

The man stood and looked at the three of them. When Jason awoke and tried to get up and try to attack, the man knelt beside him on one knee and turned to him saying:

- Do not get up you fool, this is not the time to fight but to test your skills only...

Jason was surprised by what he had heard from the man, but did not listen and tried to inflict another blow, this time with his fist. At the same time, when Jason's fist was a few centimeters from the opponents face, Jason suddenly froze and couldn't strike again. It looked like something had paralyzed him. Jason looked sideways at the other three, then at the man.

- And you really wanted to hit me? - Jason heard the question with a little surprised.

All three became cemented and did not know how to react.

- I will not wait for you to think of what to do – Emma said, then headed toward Jason and the stranger.

The man raised his head, looked at Emma, his left arm in front of him and pointed with his hand as if he wanted to point out five points. He frowned and gazed at Emma, who was running toward him and yelled:

- I said STOP!

Emma instantly stopped as if paralyzed.

- I can not move! - She exclaimed. - What have you done to me? - She yelled at the man. - Answer!

The man did not say anything, just smiled, then he added:

- Now it's your turn - looking at Thomas and Marcus.- Attack me! - Yelled the man.

After these words, Marcus and Thomas moved toward him. As they approached the enemy very quickly, the man looked at them, and said:

- ESTRU DE LAXERUDE!

Marcus and Thomas unexpectedly slowed to such an extent that they both looked immobilized, even though they still were running forward very slowly. The man lowered his sword, and began to head towards the four, slightly smiling to himself.

- I did not think I'd be so easy to beat you. All too easily.

- Who are you and what do you want from us? - Emma asked through her clenched teeth.

- You will get the answer to that question, but first I will have to teach you good manners, as you don't have them – as he spoke those words, he turned his left hand toward Marcus and Thomas and said to them: - You two stand there – with the motion of his hand he moved them both.

Thomas and Marcus could not do anything - they were both paralyzed. As he placed them to where he pointed out, using some sort of power, he looked at Emma and did the same - He placed her next to Thomas and Marcus.

- And you, Jason, out of the four you need to learn manners the most. I will teach you them, but first I'll put you where the others are already lined up - then he motioned his second hand and lifted Jason up and moved him to the same place.

- Who are you? - Emma asked again. - And what do you want to do with all of us and this poor man, who's here with us.

- Not so fast - said the man. - I will reckon with you, but him I will let go. He's not needed for anything.

- Who the hell are you ?! - Emma cried out, demanding an answer.

- Here's a little surprise - he smiled at them. - This may sound strange, but I'm one of you. My name is Botteli.

All four of them looked at each other, then Jason turned to Botteli:

- If you were one of us, you wouldn't fight with us.

Botteli aggressively turned his head toward Jason, then composed his hand in the same position as before and almost threw Jason to the end of the hangar and stopped him motionless in the air, shouting in his direction:

- Strange, because it wasn't me who started, but you Jason – said Botteli and Jason instantly returned to the same spot as before, but he still couldn't move.

Botteli walked around him all the time, watching him exactly as if he was looking for some flaws on his clothes. Standing about half a meter from him, his torso drew in his direction, although his feet were all at the same place. He said almost in a whisper to Jason:

- I don't like people who haven't been taught good manners. You are ill-mannered. If you would have asked me who I am and what I want, instead of attacking than things would be very different, but in this case you are at my mercy. Well, at least I have tested you. Now I know what you are capable of – he turned around and walked away a few meters from them. He opened his arms to the sides, palms faced up and picked up all three of them a few meters above the ground. He turned to them on ahead smiled and said: -To be honest, this is not very astounding - these skills of yours.

- But how? - Asked Thomas. - I do not understand, you're one of us, I mean what the hell? - Asked Thomas enraged.

- Go figure - said Botteli. - You are looking for me, right? That means now you don't have to, because I have found and followed you.

They all looked at Botteliego in disbelief.

- And you probably still don't understand - said Botteli, then walked over to Marcus and said: - I am one of three children that have been abandoned on this planet and hide from these creatures, Zotorigh as you call them, right? But unlike you, I have control over my powers and I'm more powerful than you - Botteli said.

- You're talking nonsense! - Marcus exclaimed.

- Really? I talk nonsense? - Botteli said, and in a moment the four of them flew Botteli overhead and fell to the ground. It looked as if they all terribly broke into pieces. Botteli said: - Look at yourselves and look in what miserable situation you are.

All four of them looked at each other, and then their eyes went back on Botteli's face.

- Maybe you're right, but how do we know you're telling the truth? She asked Emma.

- The truth? - He asked, surprised.

- Well, how do we know you're telling the truth about us, and that you are one of us? - Emma asked again.

Botteli stood astride, closed his eyes and lifted himself from the ground to a height of several meters, and after a while he opened his eyes, looked at the floor and said:

- Because I'm one of you.

Emma looked at the other three as if she wanted to give them a message through her thoughts, but they just stared at what Botteli was doing. Because it wasn't hard to guess that he had absolute power over them and that he could turn them into dust with one hand, but they did not let him know that. They wanted to break free at all costs. At that time, Botteli looked up from the floor, then looked at Emma and replied:

- Forgive me dear friends, let's start from the beginning.

Suddenly, from the height at which he hovered, he landed on the ground in front of the four of them. Botteli put them up vertically so that even though they were still in Bottelis power, they stood on their own feet. He walked over to them and said:

- I'm sorry, but when someone's attacking me... - He glanced at Jason,- I don't think

to introduce myself, I only defend myself and forget all my manners, or even don't care about them! I think that's quiet logical isn't it?

He uttered under his breath, and when he was finished, all four of them were freed from his power and everyone sat on the floor freely. Bottelli also sat down and turned to Marcus and the other three:

- I hope that you won't start to attack me again, because, as you already know, you have no chance against me. I am able to predict your movement before you even execute them.

When Bottelli finished his words, the four of them got up from the ground and adjusted their clothes.

- Sit down - Balotelli said, then pointed to the four chairs that were placed on the right side, about thirty meters away from them.

When the four of them looked at Botteli and then at the chairs to which he pointed at, the chairs began to float in the air and were moving in their direction, then gently fell on the floor next to each of them.

- And he? - Emma asked, pointing at Marcus' friend.

- Oh I forgot about him. You my friend aren't going anywhere right? - He said, blocking the man with one motion, who wasn't able to move a centimeter even. - Sit down, please - he said to the warriors again, this time his voice was quite different from that at the beginning. The voice seemed to be more lenient in some way, even delicate. He turned to Marcus' friend and push him onto the chair, which stood at the end of the hangar. - There it should be comfort to you.

The four of them sat obediently on the chairs.

- I started badly and I'm sorry about that, but I had no choice as Jason attacked me. For that, I'm sorry - repeated Botteli. - Just like you, I don't know who I can trust and who I can't.

- Who are you really? - Suddenly Thomas asked.

- My name is Bottelli Martenton - he said.

- How did you know about us, that we are here? - Thomas asked again. - And how do you know our names? - He added.

Bottelli stared at Thomas then he said:

- I am the strongest of the five of us gathered here. But you already know that, as you have seen and experienced it on yourself. I still remember your names from childhood. All your names all got stuck in my head somewhere. When I saw you, I just knew who is who. I just knew it from the beginning.

- And your skills? - Thomas asked. - Since when do you have them, and when did you start using them?

- I have them, since I can remember - said Bott. - Even as a small child at the age of ten I could move things from place to place. One day, I woke up and I really didn't want to get up so I said „dear shoes, please come to me". To my total shock, the shoes began to move toward me across the floor and when I noticed the noise, I looked down and got scared. I started to realize that I can do the same with everything and that's how it begun. I practiced and practiced until I finally began to fly. Just I do not know how I got the scar - he explained.

- What scar? - Asked Jason.

- I have a scar near the heart. It seems to me that the scar means soemthing, I just don't know what - said Botteli.

- Can you show it to me? - Asked Jason concerned.

- Of course - said Bottelli, then he unbuttoned his coat, under which his muscled torso was hidding.

Jason got up and went to Botelli to look at it closely.

- That's impossible - he said under his breath.

- What is impossible? - Asked Bottelli.

- I really don't know where you got that scar from?- Jason asked, touching him to check whether it's real.

- Jason, can you tell us what's with the scar? - Asked Marcus.

Emma sat with a worried expression and observed this whole situation with disbelief.

- My God, it's you - Jason said under his breath, and then fell to his knees.

Bottelli stood there surprised with Jason's behavior. The other three sat on their chairs and didn't know what to do at this situation. Jason bowed, saying:

I'm sorry, I didn't know who you are.

- Who am I? - Bottelli asked, surprised. - Can you tell me? I don't understand this situation.

- You really don't know who you are? - Asked Jason again.

- If I knew, I would have told you already – said Bottelli, turning to Jason.

- Ok - said Jason. - I'll tell you who you are. We have waited for you, for so long. Everyone thought you were dead, that you were gone, that ...- at this point, Jason went silent.

Bottelli only looked astonished, not knowing what to say. Jason laid at his feet like a dog that clung to the feet of his master.

- Stand up! Stand up! - Bottelli repeated. – Tell me, who I am, or who you think I am? You just attacked me, and now you are talking about, that I'm someone, who you have been waiting for so long. What is going on?

When Jason lifted his head, tears started to roll from his eyes. At this moment, Bottelli became motionless and speechless. All three of them were also surprised by this whole situation didn't know how to behave. Jason got up from the ground, wiped his face that was covered with tears. He sat down in his chair and looked at Botteli again.

- You can finally tell me, who I am? As I'am extremely curious - said Bottelli.

- You already know that you are coming from our planet, but do you really know who you are? Bottelli looked up at Jason in surprise. He became very impatient.

- Well, that's probably obvious. I'm Botteli and taking into consideration my skills, I would even say I'm Bottelli the Great. I was sent here to this planet, so these creatures called Zotorigh wouldn't get me.

- Yes, all three of you were sent here, that's right - said Jason. -But do you really know why you're here? What is your purpose and destiny? - Jason asked again.

- Purpose? Can you be a little clearer?

- You are Bottelli Martenton - the son of Xena Martenton and Yma Martenton ... - Jason said.

- And I still I don't understand the whole damn thing - said Bottelli.

- You are our ruler, the son of the emperor and empress Martenton.

Bottelli looked at Jason as though he had seen a ghost. At the same time, his eyes and mouth opened in surprise.

- You hare joking, right? - He almost began to stutter.

- You are the sole and rightful ruler of our planet and our race - said Jason.

Bottelli still stared with disbelief.

- What I think that fall made you confuse things, man.

- I'm not confused - Jason said convincingly. - How do you know these spells? How do you know so much about us, about me and what our names are? How can you predict our next move? And in addition, your powers of course. A normal warrior from our planet isn't capable of what you do. It is true that every few years a child is born with supernatural powers and endowed with extraordinary abilities, but they still couldn't do what you do.

- And how do you know this? - Asked Bottelli.

- Because I personally trained these warriors. I was the commander of the military court of the Emperor! - Jason said. - But when the emperor and empress child was born, they kept it hidden, and no one had the right to get near it, including me. Although, the child was suppose to be trained by me, at the age of ten years. During this training you were suppose to learn everything, and how to be a true warrior. And finally the day has come. You were brought to me. When I saw you, I felt it right away. I could feel such a strong aura coming from you, which I haven't felt from anyone before. Like I could touch it, and feel it. It's very powerful, yet very delicate.

Bottelli was sitting on the floor and listened to what Jason was telling him. Just like the three of them, he looked at Jason and listened to what he was saying.

- When you first stepped onto the mat and a different fighter stood in front of you, I immediately knew what to do. I remember it like today: suddenly a glow appeared around you, that was sprawling in all directions. You began to move so fast that no one could keep up with theirs eyes, quick as an arrow. At the age of ten, you already dealt with a kid that was four years older than you and was already aware of the basic techniques of the Xaonxen military school. Our school was the best in the whole solar system, and you quite easily defeated him in a few fractions of a second and you didn't even get tired. I remember how you looked at me after that. I knew that you would become a really powerful warrior. That was the time when war broke out between us and those robots. I didn't see you anymore. The Empress guards took you. I saw your ship fly off and then it crashed, as it was attacked by the race Zotorigh. And then I stopped sensing your presence. I did not know what happened to you, no one knew. The Empress has lost her only child and heir to the throne. Because of his despair, the emperor stood in the final battle, that could have saved our wonderful planet.

Bottelli looked at Jason.

- I know, because we fought shoulder to shoulder. Until the end, the emperor didn't want to give up. He rather died. His last words, I remember them as if it were yesterday, were: „For my son, may he rest in peace." After that I had to flee to save the handful who did not die in the massacre.

Bottelli looked at the persons sitting on the chairs and asked:

- Is it just you, that managed to survive?

Emma nodded affirmatively.

- I do not understand one thing. Since your ship crashed, and I saw that got on it, how come you are here? On this planet? Because you weren't on the ship that we were travelling with. Only ten passengers boarded the ship. There was no other ship, only our one. So tell me, how could you survive? - Jason asked the question.

He looked at Jason and said:

- I really don't know, as I already woke up on this planet, somewhere in the forest. I do not remember anything that was before that. Sometimes I get these strange visions, glimpses of some pictures, but unfortunately I don't know what they're about... When I woke up, I was walking through the forest for a few days until I got exhausted. Then a man found me, took me in and raised me. When I asked him if he adopted me, he said he found me dying in the forests of the Congo in Africa and took me with him here to the United States. He raised me as his own son because he could not have children himself. When I had my twelfth birthday, I discovered by accident that I have strange supernatural powers.

- How did you discover them? Under what circumstances and in what way? - Marcus asked curiously.

- My father died, so that's what I called the man who found and raised me. Back then it seemed to me as if it was a dream, but then I was involved in a fight on the street. I stood in defense of a weaker child, who got teased by a bunch of guys who didn't want to give him his belongings back. I knew him, he came from a poor family. I decided to help him. Something pushed me to do so. When I stood in his defense and the first of the attackers wanted to hit me, I just stretched out my hand, and it threw him a large distance away. I didn't know what to do and then I realized that I was different. Other people threw themselves on me and at this point I could not take it anymore. Something has awaken in me. something I never felt before. I was as fast as lightning and so strong that ... - Botteli fell silent and lowered his head.

- What happened? - Asked Jason.

- I killed a man. I couldn't control myself, something came over me, it was not me, I did not do it! - Said Bott.

- How did it happen? - Asked Jason.

- I stood in front of him. I looked deep into his eyes, then he floated in the air. He begged me not to do him harm, he said that they were only joking, that it was for fun. I pulled both hands out and I just killed him by breaking his neck. When it all went silent, the body fell to the floor, I looked at my hands, then at the boy, who I was defending. I saw fear in his eyes. He wasn't afraid of the, but me. I felt like a monster. I ran away from there and didn't return to those neighborhoods. The news reported that someone had killed two children. I did not kill two, only one. It turned out that this kid whom I have defended, threw himself off a bridge, the same evening. I know it was my fault. If I had not done anything, they both would have been still alive. I wanted to do something good, and I've done something a lot worse. I really did not mean to. Then, when I was hidding in the woods, I decided I'd start to learn about my powers, how to master and influence them. Within a year my skills have changed a lot. He was able to move objects from place to place. Then I learned to influence people in such a way that they stopped in time. At twenty-two, I was able to do everything, I am able to do now. I searched for various activities that could increase my powers and make them more powerful. Volcanic eruptions, earthquakes, it's all my doing, just like tornadoes, tsunamis, that's all my work. I can control nature and its force, but since a few months ago I began to have strange dreams with you in them. I had very real visions. I've seen hundreds of faces and saw those the end.

- Who are you talking about now? - Asked Emma.

- I'm talking about Zotorigh. A few days ago, when I was jumping from rock to rock at the very top, I saw a strange figure that looked at me. I decided to look at it a little bit closer. As I approached it close enough, I saw this face, that I dreamed about many times. I immediately was ready to fight. I thought it would be easy, but it was not. I started to feel the powerful energy from the depths of its soul. When I attacked, the character just avoided my punches and nothing seemed to work. Until, when I gathered all my power inside of me and attacked a last time. And it worked. After this fight I did not know what was going on, I started to be stronger and faster. My powers have doubled and I began to sense your energy. So I started to follow you. You have no idea how many times you would have died, if it wasn't for me. I already killed about six individuals, but even though I always know who exactly I'm fighting, with them that wasn't the case. When I'm getting closer to you, they are becoming stronger. From what I noticed, I think they are starting to gain momentum, even though I do not know why. - Botteli looked at Jason as if he was waiting for an answer.

- Strange. Are you sure you kill that many of them?

- Yes, I remember exactly how I fought each one. I can replay you every move - said Botteli.

- Strange .. - Jason wondered loudly. - It is impossible that so many of these creatures infiltrated! - He said.

- What? - Bottelli asked surprised.

- Because only four individuals passed through the portal - said Jason.

- Four? So why is there more and more of them? Every time I get the impression that, when I kill one of them, another one comes to help out of nowhere. Are you sure only four of them got through?- Bottelli asked the question, while staring straight into Jasons face.

Jason squinted his eyes, then he said:

- My worst fears come true. They are able to regenerate. When you kill one of them, two come back - he said.

- Fantastic! - Emma exclaimed resignedly. - This means that our battle will be for nothing and everything is already determined – she said.

- Isn't it time for us? - Thomas asked, changing the subject.

- And why do you ask? - Asked Jason.

- Something tells me that we have guests – explained Thomas pointed to the southwestern corner of the hangar, with his head.

When the five of them began to look at the place indicated, they noticed how four figures emerged out of the darkness.

- It's them - Bottelli said through his teeth.

They all got up from their chairs. Bottelli grabbed his sword. Without thinking, Marcus' friend stood up as well, and began to run toward the figure that emerged from the shadows. He ran towards them screaming with fear.

- What are you doing? Stay with us - shouted Emma, who jumped up to run after the man, but at the last moment Botteli grabbed her by the wrist.

- Stay - he said.

- But they will kill him! - said Emma, looking up at the man, who was a few dozen meters away from Zotorigh and was still running and approaching them.

- Are you sure that that's your friend? - Bottelli asked and looked at Marcus, while letting Emma go.

The girl failed to chase after the man, so she stood next to the other four. They all looked at the man, who suddenly slowed down and stopped in front of the figure that became more and more apparent. Suddenly, he began to change his form to those to which he ran toward.

12.

CLASH

- Are you sure it was your friend? - Thomas asked again, looking at Marcus.

- Well, now no.

- And what do we do now? There are five of them - said Emma.

- I knew it was a trap. I felt it in my bones - Thomas threw a glancing at the others.

- We must prepare for battle. We have no other choice - Botteli said.

As he spoke, the five foreign invaders approached inexorably in their direction. Marcus and Thomas clinched their fists and stood in a position ready to attack. Emma started looking around nervously as if she tried to escape, but her body looked relaxed. Bottelli stood legs apart waiting for the invaders to attack, grabbed the sword with both hands gripping it tightly as the end of the sword touched the ground. Jason just as Bottelli, drew his sword, and got ready to fight.

-Don't underestimate them, they are very deadly, especially when there are more and more of them, then their powers grow several times -Bottelli said, speaking to the rest. There was silence. - Prepare, they'll attack soon.

Bottelli has tightened his grip on the sword with both hands, lifting it in their direction. And when the invaders were about fifteen meters from them preparing to resist an attack, they all looked at

Zotorigh with nervous eyes. Everyone wanted to do something, but they couldn't attack first, because it would put them in a losing position. The invaders only waited for them to attack. This would mean that there is no turning back and they needed to start an invasion.

- What do we do? - Emma asked, breaking the silence.

- We are waiting - said Bottelli.

While they all waited and stared from the corner of their eye, Zotorigh suddenly stopped. Five of the invaders were facing five defenders of the planet. They stood in front of, Earths last hope of surviving.

- Why don't they attack? - Markus wondered.

That's the question everyone asked themselves. Surprisingly, one of Zotorigh answered.

- We do not attack, because we want to give you a final chance to surrender and join us.

Marcus stepped out of line and asked:

- And how do we know that what you say is true and is not only a ploy? - Said Marcus.

There was a silence in which you could hear the heartbeats of the defenders of the planet. Zotorigh just smiled from ear to ear, and answered:

-No, You can not trust us, you won't have any assurance. For us, you are really just some more bugs that need to be crushed. If you don't surrender, we will turn this place into hell, the kind of hell you haven't herad about and couldn't imagine. We will kill every inhabitant of this planet, one by one, and you're going to look how we do it and you won't be able to do anything to help them. We promise you that. From each of the conquered planet he have destroyed, from every civilization that we have defeated, and there were as many as grains of sand, only from your planet we took on a variety of fighting techniques and different types of weapons. You are not an obstacle for us. If we felt like it, we'll play around with you or just destroy you in the twinkling of an eye, and maybe even quicker. If you give up now, we will make slaves out of you to make you serve us to the end of your being - he explained with a smile on his face.

All five stood and stared in horror into Zotorigh eyes. Marcus blinked, then he said:

- Don't give us advice, ssuch frightening isn't working for us - he said with a smile on his face.

- Do not believe us? - invader asked again.- That look – he said, then pulled something from his pocket in the shape of a sphere. He put it on the floor of the hangar and straightened himself. - And now look with horror - added with an ironic tone.

When all five looked with one eye at Zotorigh, and the second eye on the ball, which was lying at the feet of the invaders, everyone was waited with baited breath for what was going to happen. Unexpectedly, the device started to move in the direction of Marcus and the rest and stopped exactly halfway and started to whirl around. Then the sphere slowly lifted and from all its sides a light began to emerge that surrounded all five of them. Then there was a flash of white light that blinded all of them for a moment. When they recovered, they saw that they were not on earth but in space, and together with them were Zotorigh.

As they approached the planet that was several times larger than Earth, it was clear that the race living there were well-armed and technologically advanced, everyone saw how above the giant cities were floating powerful stormtrooper and a whole bunch of ships. The planet was run by machines.

-This Is planet Jukiton, we gave the king of this planet, just like you, an ultimatum: either you join us or we will destroy it for good - said the invader. - It is not hard to guess, the king refused - he added.

After a while they could see how on different parts of the planet explosions begin, then the planet collapses inwards, and its center begins to emerge a powerful light. After less than a few minutes, the planet explodes, leaving only scraps of matter floating in space. After a moment, the flash that accompanied the outbreak of the planet, began to fade.

After a while, all warriors were back in the hangar.

- What was all that suppose to mean? - Asked Marcus.

- It was a planet that was destroyed shortly before we arrived on this planet. Only machines lived on this planet, a thousand times more technologically advanced than you, and we destroyed them in just a few moments. Are you sure you still do not want to give up?- The invader asked again.

- We probably won't take your offer! - Bottelli said suddenly with a firm voice, in response.

Zotorigh just looked at their opponents, and they all started to laugh at the same time with a shrill screech, which every moment became more piercing. All five defenders of the planet felt shivers down their necks.

- And now get out of here, or we will be forced to destroy you –Jason threatened and suddenly there was silence.

- Tell me, what are you doing? - Emma asked, surprised by what she heard.

- That's what we should have done right away and not try to get along with them - Jason said.

Zotorigh looked at each other, turned and began to steer towards the exit of the hangar.

- Stop! Where are you going? - Marcus exclaimed, surprised at the reaction of the invaders.

Zotorigh stopped after a few steps, but only one of them turned, the one standing in the middle.

- Why don't you attack? - Asked Marcus. - I thought that that's what you've been waiting for, that's what you wanted.

- Now we'll let you live - Zotorigh answered with a wry smile, then turned and everyone started to recede towards the exit of the hangar.

- I'm not finished with you yet – Marcus gasped in anger and walked briskly after the invaders. He was only a few steps away from them when suddenly Jason stood in his way.

- What are you doing? - Marcus asked with anger in his voice.

- I'm saving your life! - Jason replied firmly. - I'm saving us all.

The invaders did not stop even for a moment, disappearing one by one through the door of the hangar.

- Why did you do that? - Marcus asked again. - I was so close, and you stood in my way!

- Fool! Don't you understand that they have planned it this way? They were only waiting for you to attack them, and then they would have turned you and us into fine dust, don't you understand that? - Jason asked, incredulously.

At that time, the other three joined Marcus and Jason, who were arguing with each other.

- What the hell was that? - Bottelli asked Marcus.

- I wanted to stop them and finish their play, once and for all - said Marcus irritably.

- You wanted to attack them, and then what? - Asked Thomas.

- Look at us, we have no chance at the moment and they would have defeated us with great ease - Jason said. The rest of them just watched and nodded their heads in agreement with Jason. Marcus looked at them all and then he calmed down and became humbled.

- So what you want to do now? - He asked.

- We need to get to Europe as soon as, just as we had it planned. We need to be there before them, and something tells me that might not work out. Time is running out - said Thomas.

- And as to your friend, he almost got us killed - said Thomas and looked at Marcus.

- I have no idea how they knew about him - he defended himself.

- Okay, there's no time for apologies, what happened is done, but I hope that your friend had an easy death - said Thomas ending the topic.

- I also hope so. When we return to the aircraft, I have good news for you - Marcus said with a smile on his face.

- We could use good news, especially since there is no aircraft here - said Thomas.

- Well, you're quite observant, but I didn't tell you that it's on the surface - Said Marcus mysteriously.

- Where's the damn button? - Markus wondered.

- How do you want to find this plane? Just because it's hidden somewhere under us, it does not mean that we will be able to find him - Bottelli said without hesitation and addressed these words to Marcus.

- Do not worry - Marcus said decisively. -Wait, wait, I remember that the entrance should be behind... - Marcus looked around the hangar, stopped his eyes on a few barrels that stood by the wall. - Wait here – he turned to the other four.

- We're not going anywhere - Emma said. She added very quietly, under her breath - all in all it seems to me that we should.

Marcus strolled headed toward the barrels, although he looked around the hangar carefully. When my memory is was right, then here should be a button.

- Hmm, so you do not know where it is? - Emma asked, frowning.

- Easy for you to say, Greg changes the position of a button all the time, thanks to that he avoided theft many times - When Marcus was near the barrels, carefully he began to look at them in search of a device that would open a trap door. Companions watched carefully and joined him. When Tomas asked how this button looked like, Marcus shouted:

- There's nothing for you! When you approach the button, the sensor can sense your presence and the unit is being covered with some kind of crap. And where are Bottelli and Jason?

Emma said: - If I remember correctly, Bottelli went outside hangar to see if there's someone else. I didn't want to stand there like an idiot, I can see how are searching the barrel, I thought nothing would happen if I help you, it'd be faster.

- Well, unfortunately not this time, too much security - said Marcus.

- Well, if you say so - said Emma looking toward Marcus. - You know, I hope that at least you know what it looks like - she said.

Marcus looking in a radius of several meters he said: - I don't know exactly, because I wasn't able to find out, even though I know that it's clearly distinguished from all the other things. It should probably look like a stick or button, I think exactly like this one - he said, looking at the strange object.

Emma turned her head in his direction and said loudly excited: - Is that it?

- Wait a second! - Said Marcus. - I need to check. - He walked over to the device and said equally excited though not entirely with an confident voice, glancing at his companions. - Yes I got it!

- Well, do I understand this right, that you press this button, or whatever you have got there, and the plane will fly up to us? - Asked Emma.

- Wait - he said, and tried to push the button, but was unable to. Emma watched how Marcus' efforts didn't bring any effects, and asked: - Is something wrong?

- Well, not quite, because I push and push and nothing happens - Marcus said.

- It might not be this one? - Asked Thomas. - Or instead of pushing it to its logical direction, since there is so much security here, try to pull the button up.

- Hmm, right observation - Marcus gently grabbed the three centimeters protruding button and pulled it. At this point, four lamps lit up and the alarm went off, quietly informing everyone of some danger. In floor could be heard quiet crackling, and could be felt gentle shaking.

- Well, let's fly to Europe then - Emma said excitedly.

- We'll see what we are flying with - said Thomas, expecting something to happen, but nothing happened. Everyone stood in the middle of the hangar tensely awaiting for something to happen, but nothing did, no door opening, no gate, absolutely nothing moved. Everything fell silent and glowing red lights have stopped flashing.

- And what now? - Emma asked, disappointed.

- Now we take our asses and run to the airport - said Jason, who walked first and unlatched the door of the hangar. At this point, everyone heard a loud thud hinges and could hear the sound of the engine. Everybody turned their heads back and looked at the center of the hangar, where a powerful fifteen meter long flap began to rise, after which a second one began to rise, with the same length and with about five meters width. Everyone froze looking at the opening flap, then Marcus said: - I just remembered that if the flaps are opening, we are not suppose to stand in the middle of the hangar.

- Just in case, remember everything, that is important for us, so we won't miss anything - Jason added.

A private jet started to appear in front of their eyes, with a beautiful FX Pulsar twin-engine, which was the considered the most modern technology. It reached an unimaginable speed, as for those times.

- I recently wanted to buy a ticket and fly to Rome - Jason smiled.

- There you go! Now you don't need to spend a penny, and in a few hours you'll be in Europe and with what a mechine! Get in - Marcus said, turning to his companions.

- Well, well, some got lucky in life - added Emma.

One by one they entered the plane. Bottelli stood and asked: - Who will open the hangar? - At that time, Marcus leaned his head out from inside and said:

- Get in and stop whining, everything is automated - and hid inside. When he entered the cockpit he called Thomas and Botteli to the cockpit and said. - Are you sure you will cope even if...

- Hey, hey, stop. What means „if we will cope" - asked Jason. They all looked at each other in disbelief. Suddenly, Emma came into the cabin and with a disarming smile she asked:

- Can I also fly a little bit? Will you let me? - Silence fell in the cockpit, everyone was watching - He was looking around trying to take in with his eyes hundreds of small lights and indicators that were suppose to inform about the status of the aircraft and the flight development. - So, can I? I flew a little once, so I can manage - she added.

- I think you'll have to, my dear, as Marcus forgot to inform us that he does not know how to handle this thing.

- What? - She asked in surprise. - But Thomas is a pilot - she said.

- I am a pilot, but of a spaceship which can be controled by thoughts. I join my mind with the computer and it just works on its own. I never flew with such thing and I have no idea what all these things are meant for.

- Fantastic - Bottelli sighed, then walked up to the captain's chair, looked at the buttons and said. - Isn't it enough if we just press „start"? - pushing it he heard the engines start up and hear the voice of the computer speak.

- Destination please.

- London - Marcus said firmly and sat behind the wheel and added: - Okay, I was playing, I wanted to see your reaction - he laughed out loud.

Everyone breathed a sigh of relief.

-The fact that you can fly, does not mean that you can just start to walk on the plane. I can't do anything about any turbulence, but from what I understand, this aircraft is equipped with the reduction of any inconvenience, including turbulence - said Marcus.

- Enough of these talks, it seems to me that we should go, because time is running out - said Thomas.

- It seems to me that if we don't move, a few Zotorigh will appear here and some are certainly already moving in the same direction as we - said Thomas.

- Thomas, are you sure you know how to do this, even if I can handle it now, I would need the support of someone on the second seat - Marcus warned.

Emma, Jason and Bottelli took place and everyone buckled their seat belt.

Marcus took the radio and gave the command, despite the fact that everyone was already sitting.

- Ladies and gentlemen, we start. Please take your seats and fasten your seatbelts. Enjoy your flight. – He added: - here is your Captain. Just to be clear. We start.

As soon as the plane left the hangar and wheeled a large circle in front of the runway Marcus grabbed the radio and said.

- Here pulsar XJ, please give permission to start. – The speakers didn't answer, so Marcus said. - Here Pulsar XJ Pr.

Thomas suddenly interrupted him and said move the lever all the way forward: - Do you think that the take-off and safety rules have been changed, because whoever is approaching us in our direction, doesn't have the intention of giving us his permission in writing.

At that moment, Marcus looked through the window in the direction of the control tower. Indeed, a man was running toward them.

Marcus saw him said: - Today I don't care about the permission to start. - As soon as the plane began to pick up speed, a SUV vehicle drove from the control tower heading quickly towards the accelerating aircraft.

- Good decision captain - he heard from the passenger seat.

The voice on the radio said: - It is prohibited to take off from the airport without prior notification of this fact. We do not give permission to fly - Marcus did not respond to calls. He guessed it was a trap.

- Please provide a destination. - Marcus did not react again. It was obviouse whos trap it was. The plane increased its speed when the thrust was almost 90% ready. Marcus wanted to raise the plane, but Thomas grabbed him by the wrist, saying:

- No, we need to accelerate more. Relax, nothing is threatening us.

Marcus waited for the engine power to reach 98%. Then the plane began to take off from the runway, the front of the plane was raised by 40%, then everyone felt how they become heavier, due to the sudden flight upwards. Nobody said a word. Although there was absolute silence, everyone was screaming in thought „faster, higher, higher!" and looked out the window, where each of them was glad that the runway was getting smaller and smaller and the houses and all buildings were moving further away, as they flew higher and higher. At some point, the aircraft made a 180 degree turn and when it reached a maximum altitude Marcus asked Thomas:

- Please press the button that you have in front of you, the red one.

- The one with says power X?

- Yes, exactly that one - he answered and as soon as the button was pressed, each of the passengers felt what it that really meant to fly at 6G speed. Even Thomas was impressed by the sensation, because due to the lack of gravitation such sensations could not experienced in space.

Marcus, along with Thomas looked at each other and knew they had to have a serious talk with everyone, so have turned the DRIVER PILOT button on and went to the passenger compartment. When both of them went inside, Emma looked at the captain and copilot and said:

- Who is piloting a plane?

- Autopilot, my dear. Now we have a break and we can relax and establish everything in detail.

Passengers unbuckled their belts and went toward the table, which was located at the back of the aircraft.

- We have many hours of flight ahead, I have to take a nap - Emma said.

- Yes, that's a good idea - said Bottelli and also threw himself back in his chair. - If the captain does not protest, I also want to join the and report dutifully that I go to sleep. In theory, I'm not tired, but I can always take a nap - he said. - That's how you best regenerated power. Sleep is the best cure for everything, so I also lay down - and unfolded his chair by pressing a button. On the unfolded chair you could feel like inside a real bed, which stood at a height of 20 centimeters above the floor.

Marcus looked at Emma, who was lying with curled up legs, grabbed a blanket and covered her. Emma jumped up scared, apparently already asleep, and unfortunately she was having a light sleep and got frightened.

- Easy Emma, I just wanted to cover you, don't be scared.

- Thank you - she said, then closed her eyes and Marcus turned and began to move towards the cabin. Then Emma opened her eyes and asked:

- And You, Marcus, don't you want to lay down?

- No, not yet. I have a lot to do and think about, but you guys sleep on and take your rest, a lot will depend on you. You must be rested.

Thomas just smiled, even though he guessed what awaits them and then he walked toward the back of the aircraft. After a moment, Thomas entered into the room, after him followed Marcus and Jason right behind him. Thomas asked surprised: - You don't sleep? - Both entering the room replied that they didn't and sat on white, very exclusive seats. The three of them sat on a triangular plan so that everyone had each other in sight.

- No Thomas, don't sleep. It seems to us that we have a lot to talk about. Or are we wrong?

Thomas stood up, walked over to the bar, which turned out to be very well equipped with different kinds of alcohol, he pulled out a decanter and poured in without asking anyone if they wanted some. The situation was difficult and it seemed that everyone want to take at least one drink. Thomas took his glass and made a toast to their health. Each tilted their glass.

- Do you have a plan? - Suddenly the question was asked.

- A plan? - Marcus asked, surprised.

-Yes, yes, a plan. That something that can be done in case, if we believe that something could go wrong - said Thomas. - Does it seem to you that we get away without one? I want to assure you that each of us is experiencing this on their own skin and it's very hard. What happened at the airport, that's not all. You don't know everything.

- And what was suppose to happen? - Asked Marcus.

- How can I tell while not frighten you? - Thomas stretched. – During the meeting at the airport, one of the Zotorigh connected to my mind and pulled out information out of me on where and what we intend to follow - admitted Thomas.

- But how did this happen? - Asked Marcus.

- It took a fraction of a second, but I know that there was a connection. I experienced a brief vision.

- You can be more clearer? - Asked Jason.

- As we all stood in a row, one of them began to fight with me to get access to my mind. It was a test of strength at a distance and I lost. I had a vision and I felt like he invades me in my mind. I couldn't really do anything, when I came to my senses and was able to collect my thoughts and direct them elsewhere, it was already too late. I apologize sincerely - Said Thomas then lowered his head and stared at the floor of the aircraft.

- Do not worry - Marcus reassured him, then he got up and grabbed Thomas by the arm gently patting - this could have happened to anyone.

- Unfortunately, it fell on me - Thomas said lifting his head up.

- There is no point in crying, what happened can't be undone - said Marcus.

Jason was just sitting and staring, and also listened closely to this conversation.

- If they know where we are going and what we're going to do, then maybe we should cross their plans and change the course of events, to surprise them? – finally Jason threw the idea.

- How do you want to surprise them? - Marcus asked, surprised.

- I do not know, we have to think of something. We simply outsmart them and we will be two steps ahead of them. Let them be surprised by the change of the situation and let them know that we should be respected and they should fear us! - Jason said in one breath.

- But how you want to do it, or what exactly do you want to do? - Thomas pressured.

Jason stared at Thomas and Marcus then he said.

- I want to attack them! - Jason replied and turned his gaze at the window of the aircraft.

- I think I misheard! What do you want to do? - Thomas asked in disbelief.

- You heard me, I want to attack them, surprise them, delay their reaction and mess with their heads - said Jason.

- What do you think? - Thomas asked, glancing at Marcus.

Marcus paused for a few seconds, then cleared his throat.

- It could work.

- I thought you would disagree - Thomas said surprised.

- Yes, I had a different opinion, not to attack and run, but in common sense, would it make a difference? This whole escape? We have a few hours to take some steps, because very soon our world will cease to exist! - Marcus said and added: - Now every hour is at great importance, we need to use those well, because we might end up with none soon - Marcus said, looking at Thomas and Jason.

Thomas shook his head to indicate that he agrees. Then he asked:

- How do you want to do it and when?

- The best moment would be when we find a place to jump, I mean teleportation. I can bet that they will also be there and will want to secure it - said Jason.

- Yes, all very well, but in my opinion we are not ready to cooperate, to be able to somehow strike them meaningfully. I know what I'm saying, because I'd prefer myself to smash their heads in. However, we need to practice somehow, gain skill, know when everybody has to attack - Marcus noted.

- Don't worry about that, everything is already prepared - said Thomas.

- How prepared? - Asked Jason.

- We just stop shortly after landing in a place that is prepared for different situations. Don't ask me where it is, as I can't tell you all this now, for security reasons - said Thomas, convincingly.

- What are your plans for Emma and Botelli? - Asked Marcus.

- That's also taken care of, they still do not know, but our whole hope lays in them. They need to find a common key, a common body language and most importantly, they need to fit a hundred percent into the fight, they must be one, one body.

- Don't know how about you, but I think that these few hours will not be enough for for them to become one and to get the proper training and give them advice - said Marcus.

- Yes, I know, but what if I tell you that wherever we are about to stop, time flies by so slowly, that an hour is more than enough for us to carry out comprehensive and complete training - Thomas said.

- You can you be a little clearer? - Asked Jason.

- I can't be any more clearer than that – said Thomas. - After all, you will see for yourself, because you won't believe me otherwise.

Jason and Marcus looked at each other in amazement.

- We want to know now - said Jason and Marcus, who agreed with a wink. - To be more precise, I want to know everything about it. Before I agree to anything, I want to know where you want to take us.

Thomas looked surprised at Jason, then he asked with a slight hesitation in his voice:

- Are you saying that you don't trust me?

Jason smiled to himself, then looked at Marcus and said.

- Of course I don't trust you - he said.

Surprised Thomas looked at Jason, then at Marcus.

- You also don't trust me? - He directed the question to Marcus.

Marcus didn't know what to say, so he just shrugged.

- I do not know what I should think - he said. - You come from the future, you have your device to travel through time, and you know about us much more than you should, in my opinion. Then you want to take us to some strange place, but without explaining any details. I'm just getting lost and every step I take is a great unknown. If you want our trust, then why don't you tell us the whole truth?

- I told you, that I can't tell you everything right away. Zotorigh can not find out everything at once, just let them try to guess our next move.

- And what if you're one of them?

- Who, me? - Thomas asked, surprised. - You're joking, right.

- Why should I be joking? - Asked Jason. Maybe you just want to draw us all into a trap, where we don't stand a chance of escape? You know our next moves, and we are walking in the dark.

- Just try to trust and believe me - Thomas said gently.

- It's not easy to believe everything you say. Maybe you are a robot yourself, huh?

- What, me? - Thomas responded loudly.

- Calm down! - Said Marcus with a firm voice.

- I'm sorry my friend, but this situation is too nerv-racking. A lot is going on, let's try to calm down. Maybe it would be better if I go to bed - said Jason and going out of the room he added: - It seems to me that despite the fact that we are in one group, we do not play together against someone, but everyone wants to beat everyone. How do you want to create a good team in such an atmosphere? With such attitude we don't stand a chance of success.

There was silence. Marcus stopped Jason getting out of the room.

- We'll be ready to create a good team when we trust each other. Otherwise nothing will work out, not even mentioning saving the world.

Thomas secretly agreed with his companion. He became lost in his own thoughts.

- What are you thinking about? - Asked Marcus.

- About how it all will be when it all works out.

- Think about what would happen if our mission fails - Marcus brought him down to ground.

- And if it fails, there will come a day when people won't exist, and the only form of life on earth will be robots. Who knows, maybe then everything will be fine, as it should be, without lies, murders, wars, clear rules for all. - Thomas went to the cockpit, he wanted to be alone. He closed the door separating the cockpit from the passenger area.

13.

NIGHTMARES

- What did you do? - Jason exclaimed, holding the limp body lying in his arms, which belonged to Emma.

- I had no choice, I had to do it.

Botteli, Thomas and Jason looked with horror at Marcus, not understand what had happened.

- She was a mole, I know that one hundred percent, she wanted to kill us - said Marcus.

- That was the plan! She had to join their side, so we could learn about them as much as possible.

- But I think she joined them too much. Why hasn't anyone told me, after all if I'd knew, she would be still alive! - Said Marcus angry.

- That was a mistake for letting you live, but fortunately, it's a mistake that can be undone - Said Bottelli and with eyes fixed on Marcus and began to walk toward him. First slowly, then faster and faster, until he began to run while speaking some words that sounded almost like an incantation. At the same time, Marcus clenched his fists, and suddenly little small rocks began to rise around him in a radius of several meters, the air began to vibrate, and around Marcus static electricity in the form of lightning began to appear. In a moment they were joined by the blue flames that began to wrap around Marcus' body from head to toe. Marcus touched his chest with his wrists and then at high speed he straightened his arms at the elbows as then a sphere with pure energy started to appear in front of him. Marcus looked at Botelliego and said in a whisper:

- You won't ever defeat me.

He threw the sphere of pure energy towards Boteli while he was coming toward him, he unfolded both of his arms to the sides and the ball hit straight at Botteli. To the dismay of Marcus and the rest, Botteli's body accepted the entire sphere which was send in his direction.

Marcus noticed how Bottelli only smiled after his attack and wasn't bothered too much about his powers. As he expected such a development of events, he threw up a white power beam at an angle of 75 degrees, which consisted of hundreds of small energy bullets discharged in Botteli's direction.

Bottelli again spread his arms to the sides in order to accept another huge dose of pure energy, everything happened so quickly that it was impossible to follow with the naked eye. The massive amount of energy struck again and again onto Botelli's body, as Botteli didn't expect the huge amount of power, suddenly he began to scream. At one point, he crouched down on one knee, his face broke into a grimace of pain. He disappeared in a hail of hundreds of fireballs of clean energy.

Marcus suddenly stopped the attack, loudly gasping and trying to catch his breath. Hands limply hung along the body. The space around him began to lighten, and Marcus stood gently swaying on his feet, trying to keep his balance.

Marcus looked at Botelli or actually the place where his body should be and was terrified because what he saw could not be put into words.

Bottelli stood on both legs staring at Marcus. On his body were no signs of attacks that just moments ago caused him so much pain.

- You wanted to kill me, but it didn't work out! Your efforts and your miserable power is all for nothing. Now, you will die - Baloteli said.

Marcus saw that his attacks had almost no impact, so he decided to repeat them, but they weren't impressing the opponent at all.

With each attack, Marcus, not Botteli increasingly lost his strength. He wanted to attack Botelliego with his last strength, and when he started to prepare, he heard s whisper in his ear: - You can't harm me.

Marcus froze, he felt tremendous heat in the chest and began to slide down to the ground. Suddenly all the energy they emitted around themselves while fighting disappeared. Botteli stood right by Marcus with his head bowed down. Slowly, his head began to turn to the left side and looked at Jason and Thomas smiling.

- No! - They shouted almost as if on cue, both even though nobody gave such a command. Botteli won the uneven fight. Marcus's body slumped to the ground. Bottelli straightened up next to the frail not moving Marcus, his eyes closed and his head reeled as if he wanted to stretch his stiff bones. When he was standing upright, he looked like he was relaxed. He opened his eyes and slowly, very slowly turned his face toward Thomas, on which he drew a smile of a winner. He pierced him with his eyes, and Thomas began to feel terrified.

- Now you, Thomas – he took a step toward him.

- Wake up! Are you alright? – Emma asked, sitting next to Marcus. - It was just a bad dream - she added.

Marcus rose up on his chair and leaned on his elbows, he stared at Emma as if he didn't know what was going on around him. Still he was wondering in his head, whether it is just a dream, or he was already consciouse.

- You're all drenched in sweat, what did you dream about? - Emma asked.

Marcus looked around the room, he looked at Jason how he was sleeping tight, then looked through the window, and after a while his eyes turned back to Emma.

- Can you tell me, what did you dream about? Are you going to stay silent? - She asked again.

Marcus stared still at the girl without saying anything. In the end, he said.

- What time is it?

- Almost six o'clock - Emma replied.

- You look like you have seen a ghost or something worse. Tell me finally, what did you dream about? You were jumping terribly in your chair and said something delirious in your sleep. Tell me what it was, or I will be guessing, until I'm right.

Marcus rose up on his chair, folded his hands on the back of his head and ran them through his hair.

- I had those nightmares again - he said.

- And what exactly?

- As always, only now as if there were more of them. I dream about them almost every time I go to sleep, I don't know what to do, whether I should sleep, or wait until I drop from exhaustion. Every time I lay down I'm affraid that these dreams will haunt me again. Everything gets mixed up and confusing in them.

- Meaning?

- One time I dream how Jason wants to kill us, another time tabout Botteli. I don't know what's going on, what to believe, whether all these dreams are conscious or whether they are a dream. I'm afraid to even think they might be conscious visions.

Emma just looked at Marcus, saying nothing. Marcus sat down in his chair, dropped his feet on the floor and then got up and started walking toward the cockpit.

- What are you doing? - Emma asked, getting up from her chair. - Where are you going?

- The cockpit, find out where we are and when we land, because I can't wait. I wish we were already in Europe.

When he was almost in the cabin, he turned to Emma and said:

- Do you want to learn how to fly a jet?

- You know, I don't walk very well, I mean I am able to stumble on my own shadow, and you ask me to fly a plane – she smiled slightly and added: - Besides, there are so many tiny buttons. I might do something wrong. That's not the time to learn.

- As you wish, but an opportunity like this won't present itself again, so think about it.

- After all, no thank you.

- If you change your mind, I'll be in the cabin - Marcus replied smiling to Emma, then closed the door behind him. When he walked in, he noticed Jason sitting on the right side, so Marcus sat in the left seat and put his belt on and heard the question.

- Everything alright?

- Yes, just fine, except for one hell of a big detail. Where are we?

- According to the map and devices we should be hitting the UK soon - said Jason.

- Well, in that case, I change the direction now and enter the new coordinates for Weymuth - ordered Marcus. - And in the meantime I'm going to wake Thomas, he'll know what to do.

- But we were flying to London? - Asked Jason.

- Yes, we were but plans have changed - Marcus said then stood up and left the cockpit heading toward Thomas, who was still sleeping. He wanted to wake him up gently by shaking his arm, but he barely touched him, Thomas grabbed his wrist, ready to fight. He looked for a moment at Marcus and loosened his grip. He sat down on the chair he asked:

- Where are we?

- We're almost there.

- That's good - summed up Thomas.Then he rose to his feet, rubbing his face and went into the cockpit. A step behind him walked Marcus.

- Could you leave us alone? - He heard the question coming from Jason.

- No problem. As he passed Thomas, he stopped him.

- Jason?

- Yes?

- Can you ensure that nobody will disturb us? - It sounded mysterious, but he agreed.

- It's nothing important, just for safety reasons.The less people know about your task the bigger the chance of winning. When it comes to each one of you, no one knows more than he should, and not enough to spoil anything. It's important that despite the lack of information everyone can trust one another.

- All good - said Jason and then left.

- So far everything is going according to plan –Marcus said when they were alone.

- That's good, I just hope that Zotorigh won't be able to follow - Thomas said.

- So what do you want to do there? - Asked Marcus.

- Where do I want to do what? - Asked Thomas.

- Well, where we are flying to.

- Soon we will see, the most important thing is that land safely, because the start is one thing - said Thomas.

- Yes, I know, but do not worry, I got familiar with the plane - Thomas said.

- I know what you dream about - he added without notice.

Marcus felt strange, but said nothing.

- I dreamed exactly the same thing as you did - Thomas said bluntly.

Marcus, not knowing what to say, he just leaned against the chair back, took a deep breath and said: - What are you going to do? What is your plan, are you going to let yourself get killed? According to what we know if this situation actually would to occur, then Botteli will kill us.

- I'm afraid of him, he's powerful, Zotorigh are a powerful opponent and I know that they can kill us. If we don't do anything, they will destroy our civilization. I'm not afraid of them because I know that they are the enemy. And they will remain the enemy. On the other hand Bottelli is more dangerous because he's one of us, and has such tremendous power - Thomas said.

- Uhum - Marcus agreed.

- Look - Thomas said, pointing to the sky. – You could say that today is a beautiful day to die.

- Yeah, it's just that I'm not used to the thought of dieing in such beautiful weather - Marcus said.

At that time, Thomas watched closely guidelines and course, what he followed.

- Can I ask you something? - The question came from Marcus.

- Yes, ask about what you want - Thomas said.

- How did it happen that it was you, who was chosen for this trip? - Silence. – If you do not want to, then don't respond.

- All in all, I'm not really sure myself. Several ships full of people, who remained alive were crossing the galaxy, well actually we have escaped from what destroyed the Earth in the forst place. We arrived at the planet which looked like Earth, which was inconceivable to us, with greenery, lakes, groundwater, the only thing missing were people, so we came to the conclusion that we would stop on this planet, and supply in necessary things and continue our journey. This planet seemed to be very underdeveloped technologically, or so we thought. Those were the data that we have received, because as it turned out this planet was several times more technologically advanced than our Earth shortly before its destruction. I was invited to meet their ruler, then I found out that I'm some kind of... How did they call me - the chosen one, able to save the entire galaxy, but unfortunately, to do that I had to move to you, to your time to stop them from destroying the galaxy - Thomas said.

- And can I ask you one more question? - Asked Marcus.

- Yes, sure.

- How many people survived, if you know the answer?

- On all ships there were about ninety thousand people who survived, maybe less - said Thomas. – You know, a few moments before my teleportation, they attacked the planet - Zotorigh and I don't really know whether all people have died if we have defeated those nasty creatures, though I hardly believe it. I know what they can do, and what they are capable of - continued Thomas.

Marcus stood and stared at Thomas.

- What else do you know about Zotorigh?

- They can take any form and look like anyone, of course, they have to kill that person first, as they have to take the data from the spinal vertebrae -Thomas finished, then looked at Marcus.

- How do you know about them so much? - Asked Marcus.

- We were able to detect these creatures on our ships a couple of times, as they wanted to penetrate deeper into our population and destroy our ship from the inside, but fortunately we have a machine, that is able to detect these cruel Zotorigh and eliminate them - Thomas said.

- I'm really sorry for what happened - assured Marcus.

- Clearly it was suppose to happen - said Thomas.

- I believe in destiny, that if something happened, it would happen anyway and you wouldn't be able to change the course of events - said Thomas.

- If so, then why have you agreed to do this trip? - Marcus asked? Thomas looked at Marcus and then fell silent.

- I can't answer you to this question, I never really gave it much thought. It was a moment, just an impulse, I did what I think anyone would have done to save people - said Thomas.

- I don't know, what I would have done, considering how some people are. Sometimes I feel so angry with people that I would like them all to go to hell, and that the human species would just stop exist, and then it all started.

- Are we there yet? - Suddenly they heard behind the door Emma's question.

- What's the hurry? We land in about ten minutes, actually you can already prepare for landing - said Thomas.

- Okay, but please don't make it shake, I always get sick when it shakes too much - asked Emma, then walked away, her steps could still be heared for a while.

- How much time do we have to prepare? - Asked Marcus. Thomas hesitated to answer.

- Two hours - he said after a moment.

- Two hours? So in two hours you want to train us and turn a handful of warriors, who dont believe in themselves and feel like strangers become a great team, who each would be prepared to die for each other? Where have you been raised? Or who do you think we are?

- It's simple my friend, for a moment we will be in a place where time almost stops for us.

- What will happen?

- Basically, one minute here, will become one hour at the place to which we are heading. This means that two hours would give us a few days to prepare and improve our fighting techniques. Well actually, your fighting techniques, because I don't have any powers except that I'm good in fighting humans – Thomas added, while smiling toward Marcus.

- Wait a minute, I was in a secret military unit that knew about everything that was happening on this planet, and also had knowledge about all the strange places that have been found or constructed by man, but so far I haven't heard of a place that you described. You can tell me how you know this place, or where you have learned about it? Or even better, if you could tell me who built this place? - Marcus said, looking at Thomas.

Thomas smiled.

- Actually, you couldn't have known about this place because I was the one who built it - said Thomas.

- What do you mean you built it? - Marcus asked, surprised.

- Well, in my time such training rooms weren't nothing new, they were on every ship, that was flying in our fleet, they were created to train soldiers in a very short time. Thanks to them, a full training wouldn't take months or years, but only days.

- That's very interesting, what you are telling me - said Marcus. - I think it's time to land, right? - He asked, looking at the navigation system in the jet.

- Yes, it's time to get ready and land - said Thomas.

-Buckle up - said Marcus to Thomas, who obeyed. He grabbed the railing with both hands and clenched it firmly with his hands.

Marcus noticed and asked: - What happened?

- No, nothing happened - said Thomas. - And why do you ask?

- Because look – he smiled to himself. - You are squeezing the railing, as if you were about to rip it off.

- Oh, you mean that. That's nothing, I just really hate the whole landing part - Thomas replied. - This may sound strange, but I hated it even in my time.

- That's normal, you have nothing to be afraid of. I have the same. You see, we do have something in common.

Thomas just smiled to himself, after these words Thomas slowly loosened his nervous grip on the railing. He calmed down slowly.

- Attention all passengers - Marcus said grabbing the radio. - I hope that everyone buckled their belts, as we are approaching to land. We are flying through thick fog, so please expect turbulence, but don't be afraid, everything is under control - he added smiling.

After these words, he put the radio into place and grabbed the steering with both hands. Then he turned to Thomas.

- When I tell, then grab the red lever and pull it with all your strength toward you.

- Okay - said Thomas. - And can I know what it's for?

- Well, it's nothing important, but if you don't pull it as I ask, then instead of landing we will all crash.

Thomas looked at Marcus with a serious expression. - You are kidding me?

- This lever is being used, to create thrust to slow down the fall. This will allow me to land the jet safely - explained Marcus.

- Oh, now I understand everything - Thomas said with relief in his voice.

- Well, now grab the lever and hold it straight with all your strength, don't spin it either to the left or right, keep it in a straight position - Marcus said, pointing to the lever.

Thomas listen carefully to what Marcus said.

- And these indicators are to be set at zero - said the pilot.

- No problem, Thomas replied.

Marcus hit a few buttons, then also grabbed the lever, which he had in front of him and just like Thomas, tried to keep it in a straight position.

-What's the altitude? - Marcus asked Thomas.

- Five thousand meters and it's decreasing.

- We'll feel some turbulence, soon – After these words, Marcus shouted into the radio: - Hold on!

A few seconds after it, first there was a gentle vibration, then it turned into a more violent gust of wind from the left and then the right. After a few seconds the plane was thrashing in the air like a cloth thrown to the wind.

- I did not expect such turbulence - said Marcus.

Thomas just shook his head.

- Altitude?

- Two thousand seven hundred meters and descreasing more and more.

- I can see the airport - Marcus cried with relief in his voice.

At the same time, passengers clung to the seats with death on there faces. No one wanted to admit that they were afraid, everyone expected the worst, but one thing was certain: nobody wanted to just die under such circumstances.

- Now grab the lever and pull it toward you, now! - Marcus said loudly and firmly.

Thomas didn't expect the lever to be so resistant.

In spite of his efforts, the lever didn't even move a millimeter.

- Jammed!

Marcus looked with cool gaze at Thomas.

- Try, otherwise we'll all die in a few seconds! - Marcus said through his teeth.

At the same time Marcus pressed a button on his left side. This way, he released the undercarriage.

- I doesn't want to! Thomas repeated nervously, his voice was filled with terror as well as fear.

- We'll crash in ten seconds, there's no time for hell-sakes! - Marcus exclaimed.

Thomas grabbed the lever harder and with his last strength he began to pull the lever.

- One thousand meters, nine hundred and fifty, nine, eight hundred and fifty - Marcus counted aloud. Sweat began to appear on his forehead.

- Aaa! - Thomas cried out and with his last bit of strength he moved the lever towards him, at the same time they could feel a strong pull as the plane began even out. - We are too low! This is it! - Marcus exclaimed.

The only thing they saw in front of them was the runway, which unfortunately was already too close to make any maneuver.

Marcus closed his eyes and after a second felt an impact so strong that he lost consciousness.

The planes hull dug into the runway, and the impact was so powerful that it tore the plane into two parts. The rear part of the detached plane flew several meters away, while tumbling several times. The front part of the fuselage plowed into the ground like a piece of meteorite. The two aircraft parts were about twenty meters from each other. Around the scene, smoke started to appear from the engines that began to burn for a short time. Marcus and Thomas were still in the cockpit, both their faces overhang limp facing the steep ground.

After a few minutes Marcus regained consciousness, and had a slight wound on his head. When he began to open his eyes all he could see was fog. He raised his head and looked at Thomas. He saw how he began to move and tried to say something as if he was delirious. Marcus' head seemed to be many times heavier than usual. A sleepy feeling started to embrace him, that he tried to fight against, but he didn't have the strength. As he hangs limply, he heard a bang, as if lightning struck next to him. On the spot where Thomas was, it was empty.

Marcus didn't know what was going on, but he was sure that he had to get out of this place as fast as possible. There was a danger that Zotorigh may already know about their location.

When he started to reach for the belt in order to free himself, staring at the ground, he knew that the fall would be painful as he was hanging about two meters above the ground. The problem increased when Marcus realized that between him and the ground were sharp plane parts that fell off the plane after the collision.

Marcus made a decision and chose to escape injured, than to get killed in that moment.

When he started to unbuckle his belt, he closed his eyes, as he didn't want to look how he falls and how sharp rubble pierces his body. He just wanted to get it over with.

He grabbed the handle and with one firm stroke he unbuckled his belt. When he started to detach from his chair, he felt how someone touch his arm, and after a split second grabs his hand.

- You're not going anywhere! - He heard a familiar voice, but couldn't recognize whose voice it was. He felt a tug, after which he noticed that he was lying on the ground. Thomas, Jason and Emma were also laying next to him. He tried to get up but fainted from the exertion. From moment to moment he regained consciousness. Through the fog he saw someone lifting him from the ground, and carrying to a strange place. The next time he woke up, he saw Thomas by his side. Before he could gather his thoughts and could say anything, he fainted again.

14.

MYSTERIOUS REFUGE

When Marcus awoke once again, he noticed that he no longer was lying on the ground, but in the bed, dressed in pajamas and covered with a blanket. When he looked around he noticed that to his right were two spare beds. He noticed Emma's and Thomas's clothes on them.

Marcus propped himself up on his elbows. The room looked like a hospital room, but he could not see any medical apparatus. There was a window with blinds in the room and beside his bed was a chair with his clothes on it.

Marcus stood up, he noticed that nothing was hurting him, and all the wounds had healed.

- Where the hell am I? - He muttered under his breath.

He sat on the edge of the bed, he gently put his feet on the floor trying to get up. He did it very carefully and slowly as he didn't know if his legs had suffered any injuries or fractures. But when he stood on his feet, he noticed that nothing was wrong with him. He didn't feel any pain and could stand on his own. He changed from pajamas into his everyday clothes. Just when he was finished, Thomas came into the room.

- Oh, you got up already.

- Where am I and how long have I slept? - Marcus asked bluntly.

Thomas looked at Marcus and then replied in a calm voice:

- You slept for four days and we are at the place where we had planned to go - said Thomas.

- Four days?

- Calm down, you actually slept only a few minutes' - Thomas said.

Marcus looked at Thomas a little surprised.

- I do not understand.

- Don't worry, you'll understand - said Thomas.

- Where is everyone? - Marcus asked.

- In the main training room.

Marcus stood up and started to head towards the window.

- You're going to train today or just hang around?

Marcus stopped and turned toward Thomas.

- Who has saved me?

- Botteli - said Thomas.

- Botteli?

- Bottelli has saved us all - said Thomas.

Marcus sat back down on the bed. Thomas sat down next to him.

- We were very lucky that Botteli was with us, otherwise we would have all died. On the runway when we landed, you were saved last and it was literally on the last minute. He barely pulled you from the wreckage, the plane burst into flames.

Marcus did not answer, just nodded.

- So what are you going to do now? - Thomas asked again.

- I do not know - said Marcus confused.

- Listen to me carefully - said Thomas. - If you will sit here, we'll learn nothing from each other, we are here to get in sync and to increase our strength. This place is great, you do not even know how great, so I'll ask again. Are you going to sit here waiting, waiting for the end of the world or do something to avoid this end?

Thomas gave Marcus a bundle.

- What is it? - Asked Marcus.

- Those are your clothes for training.

Marcus unfolded the material on the bed. The garment looked like a wetsuit, but without a zip. It seemed to be very small, like for five-year child. The material was very stretchy and two-colored - black and blue.

- And I'm suppose to fit into this? - Marcus asked, surprised.

- This is a suit with onyx-kepler - Thomas said.

- With what? - Marcus asked, surprised.

- Onyx Kepler is a very durable material, which hasn't been invented on Earth. It is a thousand times stronger than steel. You can say that you can't destroy it.

- But how am I suppose to fit into this? - Asked Marcus.

- You might be surprised, it could even be too big for you – Thomas said with a smile.

- Too big? - On Marcus' face appeared surprise, that was difficult to conceal.

- Try and see - Thomas said.

Marcus took the clothes.

- I'll wait behind the door - said Thomas, then got up from the bed and left the room.

To Marcus' surprise, the suit was very stretchy. He fit into it with ease. Indeed, it suited him very well.

Marcus looked around the room and began to head for the exit.

- Oh, you're ready. We must quickly start your training, because you have a lot to catch up with – Thomas said to Marcus, who had just left the room.

- Everyone is waiting for you at the training room - Thomas said.

ith – Thomas said to Marcus, who had just left the room.

- Everyone is waiting for you at the training room - Thomas said.

Marcus wanted to say something, but before he did, Thomas gave him something in his clenched fist.

- What is that?

- Take it now - said Thomas, giving Marcus a pill.

- What is this pill?

- Too much to explain - said Thomas.

- Why are you giving this to me? If you won't tell me, then I won't take it! – Marcus said with a firm voice.

- Just take this pill and don't ask any questions - Thomas said.

- Over my dead body - said Marcus.

Thomas looked at Marcus and then nodded.

- Ok, I'll tell you – said Thomas. - This pill is your breakfast, actually all our breakfast.

- Breakfast? what breakfast?

- This pill replaces real food, but it's just as nutritious as a full blown meal - Thomas said.

- And I'm suppose to believe that? - Asked Marcus.

- Believe it or not, but if you don't take it, I guarantee you, you will run out of energy during training very quickly.

- Everyone takes this for breakfast? - Asked Marcus.

- No - Thomas said.

- So why am I only taking this?

- Excuse me, I need to be clearer. I didn't tell you something very important and essential about this pill - Thomas said.

- I'm listening - said Marcus.

- You only take this pill once before a workout.

- Why do you insist that I take it?

- I'll tell otherwise – Thomas went on to explain. – If you take this pill once before a workout, you don't need to eat anything else until the end of the workout.

Marcus laughed.

- Do you want me to tell me, that this pill will replace all of my meals for the next few days? - Asked Marcus.

- Yes, that's exactly what I want to tell you.

For a moment, Marcus stared in Thomas' eyes, then took the pill in his hand and put it into his mouth.

- And what, was it so bad? - Asked Thomas.

- Well no - replied Marcus, slightly embarrassed. - But I still don't believe you.

They walked down the hall toward a door, which was about a hundred meters away from them. When they got there, Thomas grabbed the door handle and before he opened the door, he said:

- Are you ready?

- Ready, yes, but at the same time a bit stressed.

- Stressed? About what? – Thomas asked.

- You know, actually about nothing important.

- Are you sure? - Thomas asked again.

- Yes, I'm sure, it doesn't really matter anyway.

- Well, as you wish – Thomas said while pressing the handle.

- Wait - he heard the words spoken by Marcus.

- What happened? - Asked Thomas.

- I ... I'm just afraid - Marcus said, looking at the floor.

- Afraid? Afraid of what?

- What's behind the door - said Marcus.

- Behind the door?

- I expressed myself the wrong way. I'm not afraid of the workout. I'm afraid that we won't be able to save the world. I'm afraid that it will all be for nothing.

Thomas walked over to Marcus, grabbed his arm, then said:

- Can I tell you something in confidence?

- Yes - said Marcus.

- I'm also afraid but that won't change anything and even though we have a good chance, I also know that this is our only chance. But I don't want to try anything. I prefer to fail than not having tried to save the world at all.

Marcus said nothing but stared at the floor.

- Don't worry, just fight - said Thomas.

Marcus raised his head, looked at Thomas and smiled.

- Feeling already a little better?

- Yes, a little.

- That's good - said Thomas.

He turned the handle and opened the door.

- You're ready to put your power to the test?

- Yes, I'm ready. What doesn't kill us, makes us stronger - said Marcus.

- That's good, so go ahead - said Thomas and pushed him to the front door.

They went to the training room. Marcus came first in, closely followed by Thomas. Marcus could not believe what he was seeing.

The room in which they stood, turned out to be bigger than he could imagine. Around them was empty space. The room was so big that they couldn't see any walls. The room was all in white except for the blue floor. A few meters away there was a small pond.

- That's a joke, right - Marcus said out loud.

- What is a joke? - asked Thomas.

- You did not tell me that this room is so big that you can't see the walls. - How could you have built something like this on your own? Isn't it impossible to build something like this?

- This won't be the only time I'm going to surprise you - said Thomas smiling at Marcus.

- Tell me, how did you do this?

- It's simple, in my time such things are not uncommon.

Marcus looked around the room, every now and then rubbing their eyes in amazement.

- Where is everyone?

- They train somewhere here. Believe me, when they saw it for the first time, they were just as surprised as you are. Emma almost fainted with shock.

- I'm not surprised, I almost did get a heart attack - said Marcus. - And this pill has nothing to do with it? - Marcus asked suspiciously.

- To do with what?

- Well, to do with what we see here. Maybe it's a hallucination?

- No, don't be stupid. Everyone took the same pill – you, me, Emma. It's nothing more than a typical training room from my time.

- Okay, whatever you say, but I still didn't want to believe it. Something seems to me that this is nothing but an illusion.

- Time to start train - Thomas cut off the conversation.

- Well, taht's what we are here for.

- Stretch youself, and I'll call the rest.

Marcus laid down on the floor, then began to stretch.

Thomas pulled out a tiny device from his left pants pocket and pressed a button on top of it.

- What is that? - Marcus asked curiously.

- It is a communication device. You'll also get one –he said to Marcus, giving him a bracelet from the other pocket.

The bracelet was black, and in the middle of it was a yellow dot.

- What is it and what should I do with it?

- Put it around your hand - said Thomas.

- But tell me, what for?

- I see you're an unbeliever.

- I just like to be in the know. Tell me what and how and I will be happy.

Thomas extended his left hand toward Marcus. He had the same bracelet on his hand.

- How does it work?

- When you press this button, a LED light located in each bracelet tells us that we should meet at an agreed location. See for yourself - said Thomas by pressing a button.

Bracelet suddenly began to glow red, and when it began to gently beep, which was interrupted every two seconds with silence.

- Now you know how it works.

- Yeah, I know, but fast do the rest get here?– Marcus asked, putting his bracelet on his left wrist.

- Speaking of the devil - Thomas replied, pointing his hand to Emma who was approaching them.

Marcus looked at Emma, then rubbed his eyes as if he wanted to see her better.

- Something happened? - Thomas asked, looking at Marcusa who seemed surprised.

- You're joking - said Marcus softly under his breath.

It seemed that Emma was floating in the air. It was very hard for Marcus to believe.

- I'm so glad you are feeling much better, we all thought we have lost you. Fortunately Bottelli saved you, like all of us – said Emma approaching Thomas and Marcus.

- You can fly? - Marcus stared in disbelief at Emma's feet.

- Well, of course, she can – He said, smiling toward Marcus.

- But how is it possible, you didn't fly before, and now you can?

- You know, it is thanks to these workouts. It turned out that I was able to do so much more than I thought.

At the same time, when Emma was responding to Marcus questions, Jason and Botteli approached in their direction.

They also floated in the air.

- I wonder what else you will surprise me with - Marcus turned to Thomas.

- Like I said, will be surprised more than once.

- Good, that you already feeling better - Balotelli said, then patted Marcus on the back.

Marcus smiled towards Balotelli.

- Someone explain to me, how it will look like now?- Marcus asked the others.

- Simple - said Jason.

- We have to learn to fight together and help each other during battle against these Zotorigh.

- There are enough of us and we have enough time to learn about the connection of bodies, souls, and the synchronization of movements. We have a few days for it to make it work perfect. To stop them invading, and most important thing is to close the portal and destroy it once and for all – Thomas said. - And we have to remember that we only have one chance to attack and to win.

- So what are we waiting for, let's get to work – Marcus said excitedly.

- Now I'll take care of Marcus - Jason suddenly said to the others. - And you go and relax, as you practiced a few hours - said Jason staring straight into Marcus' eyes.

- And what is Thomas going to do?

- Thomas does not have superpowers, so he has another job.

- And what? Can you tell me? - Asked Marcus.

- Thomas has to destroy the teleporter, and we have to clear his way and keep him safe, because the success of this mission depends on him - Jason said, looking at Thomas.

Thomas agreed, nodded and then said:

- If all goes well, then we will enjoy a great victory, one which you couldn't have dreamed of. What every day was a nightmare for me, will become just a nightmare from which I could wake up from and perhaps return to my world, not the spaceship. I hope I will return to Earth such beautiful as yours, I just hope it will succeed, because otherwise everything's lost.

- And what would happen if we fail to close the portal, how much time would we have for defense? - Asked Marcus.

- For defense? - Asked Thomas.

- Well, yes.

- Maybe an hour, maybe even less, then your whole world will turn into a state of war that will last a day at most. Everyone you once knew, will serve as a restorative material for Zotorigh, in other words, will be absorbed by them, some will be used as guinea pigs and experience unimaginable pain. Some will serve as an incubators for their offspring - continued Thomas.

- What do you mean for the offspring? - Marcus asked as if he wanted to make sure he'd heard correctly.

- Well, at your times, these beings were unable to reproduce by themselves, so they need help. They needed incubators, laying tiny Andromeda in their bodies, and fed on those bodies from the inside. The worst part is that they did it when the individual was still alive and wasn't able to do anything about it. Imagine that you are being eaten from the inside piece by piece and you can not pass out or die, because you're sustained alive by them and can feel everything inside. For the storage of spores special conditions are required, which men don't fulfill, but women do.

Marcus looks with horror at Thomas.

-Unfortunately, it sounds scary, but it's true. Initially, every woman who was still alive, was replaced into an incubator. Then Zotorigh learned to cope without the support of humans.

Emma turned pale after hearing what Thomas said.

Marcus clenched his fists the whole time and everyone could see that he was very angry.

- You wanted to know, so now I have told you - Thomas sighed.
- So, as you can see, we have no other choice but to win, or else all hell will break loose on earth and will continue throughout the galaxies - he added.

- I lost my appetite after what I heard - Emma said, then turned around and walked toward the door that led into the room in which Marcus woke up.

- Where are you going? - Asked Thomas.

- As far from here as I can. I've heard too much - Emma said, then disappeared behind the door.

- I'll do the same as Emma - said Bottelli and headed in the same direction.

- I'm sorry for what I said, but that is the whole truth, I wanted you to realize what would happen if we lose - explained Thomas.

- I understand - said Marcus.

- Well, what are we waiting for, let's get to work - said Jason.

- Go and have some rest, and I'll take care of Marcus - said Jason to Thomas.

Thomas also disappeared behind the door.

Jason stood in front of Marcus, and said:

- Now it's time to see what you're capable of.

- Yes, but what exactly do I do?

- Do you see this fountain? - He pointed at it with his hand. - You need to concentrate enough to be able to lift the water from the fountain.

- Are you kidding? - Marcus said with a slight smile.

- Do I look like, I'm kidding? - Jason asked with a serious expression.

- Well, no - said Marcus.

- Then just focus and do it! - Jason ordered firmly.

Marcus looked at Jason, then he directed his gaze toward the fountain. He was staring at the fountain the whole time, as beads of sweat appeared on his forehead while trying to complete the task with all his strength, but ... in vain.

- I can't do it - He said, gasping.

- What do you mean you can't do it? Look how it's done – Jason said, then pointed to the fountain with his right hand, and stared at it for about five seconds when, suddently, the water began to vibrate gently. After about a minute, all the water, which was in the fountain, started to float above it.

Marcus gazed with astonishment at what Jason had just done. It was evident that Marcus wasn't convinced on whether what he just saw was an illusion or a dream.

Jason nodded his palm down, and all the water sung with great force, back into the fountain.

- Sthis is how it's done - he said pleased and looked at Marcus.

Marcus only scratched his head.

- Now you try again - said Jason pointing to the fountain.

- Okay, one more time - said Marcus.

Marcus turned his gaze back to the fountain. It was obvious that he focused entirely on what he was trying to do. A distended veins appeared on his forehead.

Marcus took a deep breath, then braced himself, all the while staring at the fountain.

- Wait – he heard Jason speak.

Marcus looked surprised at Jason.

- You're doing it wrong.

- What do you mean?

- You're focusing too much on what you have to do, at the moment.

- Well yes, I focus because I have to raise the water from the fountain, and I need a little concentration in order to do that.

- Well, not really - said Jason.

- Not? - Marcus asked, confused. - But I have to concentrate in order to do it - said Marcus again.

- The problem is that you have to raise it with your will. It will only float if you want it, not because you have to lift it. You're so focused on what you have to do, that you wouldn't even notice if someone would attack you, and consequently, you wouldn't be able to defend yourself.

Marcus listened with interest.

- Not exactly, I don't only just focus on what I should do.

- Are you sure about that? Jason asked.

- Yes I'm sure - said Marcus.

- Then try to raise the water again and defend yourself of my punch - Jason said.

- No problem - Marcus said with a smile. - This will be a piece of cake.

- Let's get started.

- Let's get started - said Marcus.

When Marcus was busy focusing on the task, suddenly, Jason hit him in the face. Marcus didn't manage to do avoid it. The blow was hard enough for Marcus to take two steps back and to grab his cheek, instinctively.

- See, you're too focused on what you have to do. You don't see what's going on around you.

Marcus lowered his head. He agreed with his teacher.

- Look at me - said Jason firmly to Marcus. - You have no right to give up, we are here to practice. Its' hard for everyone at the beginning, over time you will become better.

- I didn't even have the time to react - said Marcus disappointed.

- Well you did, but unfortunately too late - said Jason. - You have a lot to learn still.

Marcus wink in agreement with Jason's conclusion.

- Okay, now let's take a break. You look very tired - said Jason.

- I'm not tired.

- We have to regenerate regularly. We are using a lot of energy.

- But I do not ... - Marcus tried to say something.

- Listen – Jason interrupted him. -So far, you're not doing well, you have to relax. Believe me, you're too tense and too tired.

- Ok - said Marcus, though he did it reluctantly. He didn't like to lose. He preferred to go straight for success.

- Let's go back to our room.

They headed slowly for the exit. When they were close to the exit, Marcus stood still, as if in denial and said:

- I want to try again.

- Not now, now get some rest.

- No, now!- Marcus said in a loud voice.

- I told you! - Jason exclaimed.

- You won't tell me what to do! - Marcus answered back.

- What did you say? - Asked Jason.

- What you've just heard! Do you have a hearing problems? I want to try again!

Jason walked over to Marcus and stood dangerously close, their faces almost touching. He kept his eyes on his.

- Listen to me carefully. You're too young to to be this rude to me. Hide your little aspirations. I manage this training and you have to listen to me - he said through clenched teeth.

Marcus looked down. His blood began to boil.

- Do you understand? - Jason asked again in a commanding tone.

- Yes, I do - said Marcus.

- That's good - he said taking two steps back. He kept a close eye on Marcus. - Now come on, it's time to rest - he added gently.

- But you do not understand.

- What don't I understand?

- I can't let Zotorigh destroyed the whole world. Now, if I don't prove to myself that I can move the water, I will never be able to do this! Do you get it? - Marcus asked bitterly.

- And this is the reason why you were ready to fight with me?

- Yes - Marcus replied without hesitation.

Jason smiled.

- I like that you are assertive and determined.

Marcus stared at Jason awaiting a permission for one more attempt.

- Well, try again, but for a last time, and if you fail, we'll go back to the building and make a break, will you? – Asked Jason.

- Okay, it's a deal.

- Then show what you can do - Jason encouraged.

Marcus looked at the fountain, stood with feet apart, lowered his hands along his body, took a deep breath and then closed his eyes. Jason didn't interrupted, he just watched. After about five seconds,

Marcus began to feel a tingling feeling in his arms. He opened his eyes, glanced at the fountain, then at Jason as if to check whether he was really watching. He made sure that he watched and closed his eyelids. After a moment he opened them again and stared at the fountain, at that moment, stones and dust on the ground began to tremble and float. At this point, all of the water which was in a fountain shot into the air to form a water column which was fifty meters high.

Jason clapped with recognition.

- That's already enough! - Jason said, looking at Marcus, who smiled proudly.

- Are you satisfied?

- Yes, I am, very much indeed - said Jason.

- Now that you're happy, allow me to put the water back where it belongs?

- Of course.

Marcus slowly began to drop all the water back into the fountain. His face didn't stop to smile.

- Do you want to relax now? - Asked Jason.

- With the greatest pleasure.

They headed for the exit.

- Can I ask you one more thing? - Jason turned to Marcus.

- Sure.

- I know this may be a trivial question, but I would like to know, how come you were able to do it the first time?

- But it was not the first time - said Marcus surprised.

- For me it was as those attempts don't count, because you didn't even get tried, and there you go, with your first attempt, you did it - said Jason.

- To be honest, I don't really know how I did it. Then, when I wasn't able to raise even a drop of water, I wanted to so much. All the time I told myself that I must do it, but when we almost started to fight, I realized that I simply have to do it and I know I'm able to, after all we are the same race, right? Besides, let's not forget, you're my father, and that means that I have to be able to do such tricks like you.

- Thank you, - said Jason. They both smiled. At that point, they grabbed each others arms and Jason patted Marcus on the back.

- Very well done, I'm very pleased with you, my son.

Contrary to expectations, Marcus looked depressed.

- Is everything alright?

- Yes, everything is alright – said the boy. - And why do you ask?

- You look worried.

- No, I'm not worried about anything, really.

- I can see that something is wrong - Jason insisted.

- Really, everything is just fine - said Marcus stubborn.

- But you can tell me anything.

- Just leave it, really it's alright.

Jason looked to Marcus with an unsatisfied face.

- I don't really believe that everything is alright. Speak, I don't want to torture you all day.

- Fine.

- So what's going on?

- Do you even love me? - Marcus asked, looking straight into Jason's eyes, who totally didn't expect this question. - You are my father, I didn't know about it until a few days ago, when you showed up. As a child I was thrown from one caregiver to another as if I were a toy. None of the caregivers told me, what I really wanted to hear from you. – Jason swallowed. Suddenly, he ran out of words. - Answer to that very simple question, do you love me or not? - Marcus repeated the question.

Jason lowered his head.

- Just as I thought - Said Marcus disappointed and opened the door.

- Of course I love you - suddenly Jason replied.

Marcus stopped at a standstill.

- Then why did you take so long to answer?

- Because it wasn't a simple answer, and certainly not a simple question. You don't even know how afraid I was, of you asking me this question one day. Every day I wondered, when I would see you and when you would ask me this question - said Jason.

Marcus listened attentively to every word his father spoke. After a moment, they hugged. Jason said:

- I really do love you, you don't even know how much.

When they both stood there huddled for a moment, Jason turned to Marcus.

- We can go?

15.

CHAOS FINISHING WITH VICTORY

- We traced the chosen ones - one of the Zotorigh reported, opening his eyes and putting a book back on the shelf.

Five Zotorigh stood staring out the window, suddenly one of them turned around very slowly and walked to the Zotorigh who just put the book down. He put his hand on his shoulder, then closed his eyes. He opened them a few seconds later. He smiled and then walked to the other Zotorigh, and stood in a row with them.

- They only have a few more hours and then we destroy them – said the Zotorigh standing on the right side.

- Let them gather their strength. But they can't avoid what is destined for them - said the Zotorigh standing on the left.

- Everyone already knows where they are, it's time to begin the final phase - added the Zotorigh standing in the middle.

Everyone stared out the window.

Zotorigh, who put the book down, turned and headed toward the door.

All four left the apartment, which was attacked by special commandos a few days earlier. Zotorigh stopped only when the last one of them left the apartment. Everyone stood facing each other, then one after another vanished into thin air.

When Marcus was sitting on the bed Botteli came to him. He glanced at Thomas and spoke.

- Congratulations to you - he said.

- Congratulations, for what? - Marcus asked, looking surprised at Balotelli.

- I heard what you did, I'm glad that you slowly begin to control your powers.

Marcus smiled softly under his breath.

- At the beginning it was very difficult. I couldn't move even a drop of water, but when I realized that I had no choice but to do it, as I had to prove it for myself then there was no turning back - said Marcus.

- I understand you very well - nodded Bottelli.

Marcus smiled again, then directed his eyes at the wall. Bottelli put a hand on his shoulder.

- About that situation with Jason before, I wouldn't worry if I were you. Jason's like that to everyone.

- I know and I don't worry about it - Marcus said, looking at Balotelli. – Besides, it's all clear now - he added.

Bottelli stood up, patted Marcus on the shoulder once again, smiled benignly and left. When the door closed behind him, Marcus started to look around the room and look at the people that gathered there.

Emma was lying on the bed staring at the ceiling. It seemed that that she was thinking about something. Thomas sat on the bed and stared out the window.

- What are you thinking about? - Marcus asked him.

Thomas turned his head toward Marcus.

- What?

- I asked you, what you are thinking about.

- About nothing, I just sit. What would I be thinking about?

- I don't know, I asked before, but you didn't say anything.

- Oh - Thomas said slightly confused.

- So, what were you thinking?

Thomas opened his mouth to answer, when the megaphone had spread the words:

- We ask everyone to appear at the gym.

- I think we have to go – Thomas said, jumping on his feet. Marcus and Emma also rushed toward the door. Marcus suddenly grabbed Thomas' sleeve.

- What happened? - Asked Thomas.

- When you looked out the window, you were crying. I saw tears on your cheek. If something is happening, can you tell me - said Marcus.

- Nothing happened, really - said Thomas.

- Don't lie to me - Marcus said in a firm voice looking straight into Thomas' eyes.

Thomas looked down.

- It's really nothing.

- Girls, are you going to walk or stand around and chit-chat? - the question was asked. Emma returned to the bedroom. – I forgot to tell you that everyone has to go to the gym.

- I repeat, all warriors are asked to go to the training room - fell an order from the speakers.

- I have a bad feeling about this - Emma said, standing in the doorway. - Hurry up - She adds and ran out of the room.

- Really, it's nothing.

- As you wish, if you don't want to say. I just hope you won't regret it - Marcus said then he and Thomas ran very quickly out of the room.

When Tomas and Marcus came to the gym, everyone stood in a circle and was silent.

- Something happened? Someone died? - Asked Thomas.

- Nobody yet, but that could change very quickly - said Botteli. They all stood in silence.

- Can someone tell me what is happening here and why everyone has such serious faces? - Asked Thomas, looking one by one at each of them.

- Do not look at me, I do not know, I was with you - Marcus said, raising his hands.

- The fact is that we have very little time - suddenly said Jason.

- Why? What's happening? - Emma asked, horrified.

- We thought that we would be able to continue to practice here, but unfortunately Zotorigh have tracked us down - explained Jason.

- In that case, how much time do we have? - Asked Marcus.

- I'm afraid, less than five hours - said Bottelli.

- That's a long time. Calculated here, that's some few days - said Emma.

- Calculations are right, the problem is that we have five hours here. Behind the door, we only really have five minutes or less, they are already some hundred kilometers from us heading in our direction the whole time - said Botteli.

- How do you know all this? - Asked Thomas.

- I can feel it, when they began to move in the air - said Botteli.

- What do you mean move? - Asked Emma.

- They are simply fly toward us, very quickly. When I started to gather you here, they took off from somewhere in the United States. Until the moment when you all gathered here, only five minutes have passed, but in real time they are halfway here. The fact that they flew a hundred kilometers in just a several seconds, means they are very quickly approaching. I could barely even feel them.

They stood motionless with fear and terror painted on their faces, which couldn't be compared to anything they ever felt before. Only Thomas seemed to remain calm and for a moment even smiled.

- What's so funny? - Asked Botteli.

- You mean me?

- Yeah, you, you can tell that you're somewhat happy about this meeting - says Botteli, clenching his fists.

- Relax, don't get upset.

- How can I not get upset if we will face these monsters, at any moment...

- And we will fight as best we can! Until the end, until the last of us! Until the last drop of blood! - Yelled Thomas. Everyone in the room looked at him.

- Anybody want to add anything else? - Asked Thomas. Nobody said a word. - Listen to me carefully. I know that we don't have much time, as Botteli said, we have about five hours left here. And in the real world, behind those walls, we only have a few minutes, so please let's not waste this time. So that when we exhale our last breath, we will know that we did our best and nothing was in vain, believing that it will not be the end of us, but it will be the end of these tiny Zotorigh. I'm tired of hiding from them and the constant waiting, it's time to face them and fight for what is most important - to fight for the future, for a better future, bright, with no dark clouds in the sky. Let the sky be as clear as the galaxies, and trust me they are very beautiful because I know what I'm saying, I saw a couple of them. Thomas smiled to himself, then his smile disappeared very quickly from his face. Are you willing to sacrifice yourselves in exchange for a future without us? - Asked Thomas.

There was silence, Emma walked over to Thomas, then hugged him. Everyone, especially Thomas, were surprised by what Emma did, but it was clear that this was her way of showing that she's willing to sacrifice her life for the cause.

- I won't hug you, but I can tell you that you can count on me - said Jason.

Botteli expressed his consent by nodding his head, then Marcus did the same.

- I am glad about your decision, I'm proud of you - said Thomas.

- After all, each of us come from the galactic race of warriors - summed up Jason.

- Yes, that's right, and now show your true powers - continued Thomas. - Now you can stop cuddling, I understood your answer – He said trying to detach from Emma.

- It wasn't my answer, I just needed it, but the answer is yes. It's not like I'm going to stand around and watch as others fight and lose their lives, so can just I hide like a mouse - Emma said smiling.

- Well, then let us set one thing straight: we're all relying only on each other, that's why there is no space for any mistakes. We need to establish a plan of action. Emma and Marcus start practicing together and please, don't waste this time standing around - asked Thomas. Emma and Marcus moved into the northern direction.

- And you ... - Thomas stared at Boteli and Jason. - You're going to train me. Emma and Marcus! - He yelled to the retreating couple. They stopped and turned around. — Remember to come back here in about two hours, so we can all unite and team up - said Thomas smiling in their direction.

- We won't be late - they both nodded, then they turned around again.

- Why are you smiling? - Botteli asked, surprised seeing the smile on Thomas' face staring at the back of Emma and Marcus.

- I'm smiling, although I don't feel like laughing right now. Now I need you to train me - he laughed.

- Yeah, especially since you will get a decent bashing and we won't be easy on you - Botteli promised.

- I can see that you dreamed about kicking my ass - said Thomas.

- I wouldn't say I was dreaming about it, but if there is an opportunity then why not...

- What about you, are you going to just stand around and be silent? - Asked Thomas and looked at Jason.

- Of course not, but how's that supposed to be like?

- You don't have any superpowers. I'm a little scared to hit you, I don't want to hurt you – Jason said, looking straight into Thomas' eyes. - It's a little strange.

- What is strange?

- Well, you know, beat someone older than myself - Jason scratched his head.

- Do not worry. You'll be surprised. Imagine that these creatures that will appear in your time are nothing compared to those that appeared in my time. Those which we are going to fight with, are the first generation of Zotorigh and are underdeveloped. Unfortunately, in my time such machines do not exist. You have no idea what they are capacle of and how much they have developed. I fought with them a few fights and somehow I survived, but it was not easy. So believe me, I am able to fight, and I'll manage somehow.

- Are you afraid that an old man will beat you? - Thomas said, smiling playfully.

Jason, in turn, looked at Thomas contemptuously.

- Ok, but I hope you won't regret it.

- In that case, who wants to start? - asked Thomas looking at Jason and Baloteli. None of them came forward. - Do not tell me that you're afraid of fighting a mere mortal grandfather?

- No no, of course not – Baloteli answered.

- So what are you waiting for? Keep moving, because I can not wait.

Bottelli stood there and looked to Thomas and then to Jason.

- Okay, well, if you don't want to fight me, then maybe you can show each other what you are capable of? - Suggested Thomas.

- That's a better solution - nodded Botteli. - What do you think about it? - He turned to Jason.

- I was about to suggest the same.

- So, ladies, what are you waiting for. Let's start - ordered Thomas.

Thomas stepped two steps back and waited for Botteli's or Jason's first move. Jason stared at Balotelli and stepped back, just like Thomas. Bottelli did the same and closed his eyes.

There was silence.

Bottelli stood there waiting for Jason to do something. Suddenly he vanished into thin air. Jason stood astride looking very carefully around, but he was not able to see Botteli, who just seemed to be right next to him. He couldn't see him, but he could feel his presence.

A few drops of sweat appeared on Jason's forehead.

Jason stood very focused, but his body looked relaxed. But when Thomas looked closer, he noticed how Jason's whole body started to tremble as he was nervous. As Thomas wanted to give Jason advise, suddenly behind Jason's back Botteli appeared and struck a blow with his clinched fist onto his back.

The blow was so powerful that Jason got thrown some ten meters away. Botteli disappeared again.

Jason did not even had time to fall to the ground, when suddenly Botteli appeared in front of him and aiming another blow, this time with his knee to the face. After that, Jason fell to the ground. For a while, Bottelli stayed in the same position in which he executed the attack, then dropped his leg and looked at Thomas.

- Are you sure you want to train with me? - He asked.

- Of course! - said Thomas. - Is that all you can do? – Jason started to rise from the ground and brushed the dust of from his clothes.

- No, of course that's not all - Said Bottelli looking at Jason.

Jason wiped his mouth, then spat blood on the ground.

- I just thought that after these blows you wouldn't be able to pick yourself up, so I stopped attacking. I thought, I hurt you.

- Please, frankly, I felt a mosquito bite from a few days ago more, and not those pseudo blows of yours - Jason laughed.

- I see you are trying to annoy me, but you won't succeed - assured Botteli.

- So what are you waiting for? Attack, but seriously, as I'm getting bored.

- No problem, you'll regret that you picked yourself up of the ground – Botellie's face grew serious. - Watch and weep.

After these words, Botteli folded his hands together to a cross, he whispered a few words in a strange language and stared at Jason. When Jason was waiting for Botteli to attack, suddenly two strange lights which began to become brighter appeared on Botteli's both sides, until they suddenly exploded. The blast was so powerful that Thomas who was standing about thirty meters behind Botteli felt it firsthand.

When the dust settled, they could see two fireballs that exudes a powerful energy floated next to Botelli.

- What's that supposed to be? - Asked Jason.

- You'll see - said Bottelli, then closed his eyes. At the same time, those fireballs that were on Botteli's left and right side began to be doubled, those began to split and doubled over and over, until about fifty fireballs were behind his back, and each of them was the size of a watermelon.

- And what do you think? - Botteli asked, looking at Jason.

- I must admit that I did not expect that.

- That's good, because that's not all - said Bottelli.

After these words, Botteli opened his arms to the sides, and the fireballs began to move toward Jason. One by one, faster and faster, until they turn speeds so great that Jason could not even speak a word when the first ball reached him and exploded, followed closely by continues ones.

Botteli didn't seem to care that Jason could barely stand on his feet. Despite of that, he has didn't end the attack and fired another fifty fireballs. Only after then he paused. The place where Jason stood turned into one big fireball, and with each subsequent attack it expanded in size. The diameter of a large fireball was about forty meters and then started to decrease. When it completely disappeared and before the dust settled, Botteli could see the outlines of a man standing in a defensive position.

- That's probably a joke - Bottelli said under his breath.

When the dust completely settled, Jason brushed it off, and looked at Botteli an said:

- I thought would try more, but you disappointed me.

Bottelli only dropped his hands, then smiled to himself.

- Tell me, is there something more you are able to do? Because I'm running out of patience with those miserable attacks of yours – shouted Jason to Botteli's direction.

Thomas watched closely the whole time and couldn't believe what just took place in front of him. What Jason did, exceeded all expectations.

„After all they both come from the same planet and are part of the same race" - Thomas told himself in his head.

Bottelli looked at Jason with disbelief and horror at the same time. „What's going on with my powers, after all I am the strongest of them all" - wondered Botta.

Jason stood with lowered hands and stared at Balotelli, then started walking toward him in a very slow walk, all the while looking around.

- I'm not done yet! – Botteli exclaimed, clenching his fists with all his strength.

Thomas saw and felt Botteli's anger, energy that elapsed from him, reached even Jason.

Jason stopped and stared at Botelliego with amazement, and the smile on his face began to disappear.

- Now you really made me angry! I am the greatest warrior in the galaxy! - exclamation Botteli loudly.

Jason wanted to step back, but something stopped him and so he stood motionless.

-I can not move! - He shouted in Thomas's direction with horror in his eyes.

Thomas wanted to approach Botteli and calm him down, but before he took any steps he spoke through clenched teeth, saying: - Do not even try!

- You wanted to make fun of me! Show that you're stronger than me, but this time you crossed the line! - Bottelli said in a loud voice toward Jason.

When Bottelli approached him at a distance of about two meters, Jason began to float gently above the ground, then suddenly began to turn a hundred and eighty degrees, until he stopped upside down.

Bottelli smiled again.

- So are you going to fight? - Jason asked enraged.

- A fight is a fight, most important is the end and how it will turn out - said Botteli.

- What are you going to do with me? - Jason asked with fear in his eyes.

- Now I'll show you how weak you really are. Your abilities are for nothing.

After these words Bottelli walked over to Jason and stopped about twenty centimeters in front of him. Jason hanging in the air could not move or even turn his head.

- Do not what we agreed on this bofore the training! - Jason said through gritted teeth.

- I know that, but, as I already said, most important is the end result.

After these words, Botteli clenched his fists, and a light began to appear around them, which was becoming increasingly brighter.

Bottelli closed his eyes, then directed his fist toward Jason.

The blow was so powerful that when Botteli's fist reached Jason's body, enormous energy was released which threw Jason several hundred meters back.

Jason flew with great speed, at the same time Battoli disappeared from the place in which he stood when he returned to Jason slumped flying track, he then gave him a blow, this time directing his body to the ground.

This time the impact was very powerful, it would seem that it was even more powerful than the one before. At the time, Botteli's fist contact Jason's body, the impact produced a ball of energy that swallowed both Botteli and Jason, at the same time.

The bang that was created, could be heard at a distance of several kilometers.

Thomas stood there, horrified by what Bottelli was doing. He knew very well that he couldn't do anything, and even if he wanted to, it wasn't able to, because he didn't have enough strength to take Botteli on. After all, he was only human.

After the dust settled that surrounded Jason and the furious Botteli, he could see how Botteli grabbed the already unconscious Jason by his throat.

- That's enough! - Thomas exclaimed, horrified.

- We'll finish when I say! - Replied Botteli. - I'm just getting warmed up - he said throwing Jason, who was unconscious up in the air. Then he disappeared.

When Jason was lifted to a height of fifty meters, he woke up and saw how Botteli appeared over his head and inflicts hail of blows to his body.

Blows that were inflicted by Botteli were so fast, that Thomas was not able to see them. He saw how Botteli appeared from the left and the right. All the hits that Botteli aimed were very precise and always hit the target. While Jason seemed like a rag doll, which was thrown in all directions. A few moments later, he saw Jason who hit the ground with a bang. Jason's flying body hit the ground right next to Thomas. Botteli's whole attack lasted only several seconds.

Without hesitation, Thomas ran to Jason and knelt next to him trying to raise him by the arm.

To his great surprise, on Jason's body were no signs of any impact, and Jason became conscious and started to grin from ear to ear.

- What's happening? - Thomas asked, surprised.

Jason looked up to Thomas, who was clearly confused, then he said.

- Now it's my turn.

After these words, he rose to his feet and crossed his arms. Bottelli approached towards Jason very slowly, then he disappeared and appeared on the doorstep prepared to attack Jason.

Jason was ready to aim a strike exactly towards Botteli's body, Botteli as if he predicted Jason's movements ducked down and avoided the blow.

Without thinking, Botteli reciprocated, hitting Jason with his fist in the chest. Blows reached its target. Jason tried to dodge, but Botteli was very fast. Jason jumped several meters back, looked at Botteli, who was smiling and stood ready to repel the attack, then he proceeded to the counterattack.

When Jason aimed his blow towards Botteli, who dodged without any problems. Jason did not give up and punched to the left, then to the right.

From time to time, Thomas saw the very fast, almost invisible to the naked eye, blows that were aimed to Botteli's ribs and the face. Unfortunately, none of Jason's blows were fast enough and strong enough to cause Botteli any harm.

Botteli was faster and didn't have any problems with blocking Jason's blows. At some point, Jason began to speed up his movements.

Finally, the blows began to reach the target. Jason's blows completely changed their quality, they become stronger in impact, hitting the face, the body, the legs. Jason didn't only use fists, but also hit with his knees. It was apparent that he was fighting with his whole body, he did not spare his legs and hit the opponent in the head.

Botteli also didn't spare Jason, who was hitting his fist on Botteli's chest, who countered with a blow with his knees that reached Jason's abdomen.

At one moment, Jason and Botteli distanced themselves from each other by about twenty meters, landing on the ground and standing face to face with clenched fists. Then they both stood up straight and relax their clenched fist. They both turned around with a smile to Thomas, who stood motionless with his mouth open.

16.

SECRETS OF HURT

- What was that? - Emma asked, grabbing Marcus's hand.

- But what do you mean? - Marcus looked with amazement at Emma.

- Did you feel, what I just did? - Emma looked around.

- Yes, I felt it, it didn't come from a normal warrior, someone has tremendous power and is becoming increasingly stronger – Marcus said, looking toward the place where Jason Thomas and Botteli were training. - But do not worry, I feel it's a good energy – Marcus assured her with a smile on his face.

- I thought so, but I wanted to make sure – Emma said swallowing.

- Remember that we have less than two hours, and time is running out - Emma remembered, glancing at Marcus.

- What do you want to start from? - He asked.

- Maybe we should just start to fight with each other and beat each other black and blue - said Emma, smiling innocently.

- Not a bad idea, but it may be better if we work on our consistency.

- Meaning? - asked Emma.

- Just improve our current abilities and work towards perfecting them – he said. – I've seen what you are capable of, but to me it seems there's more.

- What do you mean? - Emma asked curiously.

- I have noticed on myself, that when I'm with you I feel stronger and more effective - explained Marcus.

- What? - Emma was surprised.

- Gee, how do I put it more simply? - Marcus went on. - When I'm with you, it seems to me that you can charge me up when I'm losing power. When I'm out of of energy, I have the impression that you are, my so called, battery - Marcus said, looking over to Emma. She started laughing. - I do not understand why you are laughing? I'm serious.

Emma became serious and stopped laughing.

- Well, if you do not believe me, then see for yourself - Marcus said, then pulled away from Emma a few steps back and spread his hands.

- What are you doing? - Emma asked curiously.

- Do not move and do not try to defend yourself.

- Are you attacking me? - Emma asked nervously.

- Yes, but please do not move, I need to focus.

Emma was silent and look carefully at what Marcus was up to.

When they both stood in silence, something strange began to happen next to Marcus, who started to float in the air. It seemed as if he was touching a surface with your fingers.

Emma didn't believe what she saw and rubbed her eyes in surprise.

Marcus was floating in the air the whole time, opened his eyes and steam began to emit out of his hands. His hands seemed like they were glowing.

Marcus slowly began to fall to the ground. When he stood with both feet on the ground, little sparks and microscopic lightning bolts began to appear on his hands. It seemed as if all the energy he possessed was concentrated in his hands. At some point, flames appeared in his hands and Marcus began to change slowly. His muscles were tensed and little veins began to appear on his body.

Emma looked surprised and curious what will happen next.

Marcus ahd his eyes closed the whole time, when he suddenly opened them his blue eyes changed into black. The hair on his head lifted and became spikey.

Marcus stared at Emma, then gave her a blow with both hands together, and a giant energy hit Emma.

When Emma felt the blow, and her body disappeared in the deep smoke.

Marcus only stood and watched at the place where Emma was attacked and tried to spot her.

When the smoke began to disperse he noticed Emma lying on the ground. The blow was so powerful that the Emma's body got thrown about ten meters away.

When Marcus look closely, he noticed there was a wound on Emma's abdomen, and she was lying in a pool of her own blood.

- What did I do? – He cried aloud, then ran to Emma grabbing her head. He hugged her tightly to his body. - What have I done, what have I done? - Repeated Marcus constantly.

While Marcus held Emma's head, Emma suddenly awoke.

- Do not die here now, you have no such right to do that! - Marcus said in a tone of command.

- Who said I'm dieing? - Emma asked, surprised.

- You got a hole in the body - Marcus said, looking at Emma's body.

- Maybe I do, but let me tell you that I do not feel anything and it is very strange – said Emma. Her body suddenly began to regenerate.

Marcus suddenly stood up on both legs and could not believe what he saw. Emma's body began to close up the wound, which was caused by Marcus's attack. The tissue began to reconnect and soon after that, there was no trace.

Marcus just swallowed hard and did not know what to say.

- A normal person wouldn't be able to stood up with a wound like that, let alone recover - Marcus said very surprised.

- Maybe you're right, but remember that we are from another planet and each of us has different gifts. Each of us were born with other abilities.

Marcus looked at Emma with disbelief.

- Obviously, othet than disappearing, I can also regenerate and renew my body - said Emma.

- Apparently so - said Marcus, but he was still in shock.

- Do we continue practising? - Emma asked, smiling toward Marcus as if nothing ever happened. - Now, I can not wait to fight with Zotorigh.

- You can't wait to fight with them? - Marcus asked, surprised.

- Yes.

- Can you explain why? Because a few hours ago you were afraid to fight, and now you're the first to fight with them.

- I mean, now I can regenerate myself, as if I'm immortal - noted the girl.

- Maybe so, but will you be able to stop them from destroying the Earth - Marcus asked.

Emma was silent.

- Okay, end of chitchat, let us fight - Marcus said. - We have less and less time – he added, glancing at Emma. After that, he stood legs apart again and looked at Emma.

- What do you want to do now?

- Attack me.

- Are you sure?

- Yes, attack, we do not have time.

- As you wish.

Emma started to head towards Marcus. Marcus clenched his fists and waited for the attack. When Emma was about ten meters from Marcus, she suddenly vanished into thin air.

- Damn it, I forgot that she's able to disappear – Marcus muttered unhappy. Suddenly he felt a kick in the back. He tried to turn around and hit Emma, but before he could do so a huge blow hit his stomach. When he tried to protect himself, he felt another blow, this time directed yo the face with a knee. After a series of attacks, Marcus fell on his right knee and Emma suddenly stopped attacking. Emma appeared smiling, about two meters next to him.

- I can see that punching me gives you great pleasure – Marcus said spitting blood.

- You do not know how much - Emma replied, grinning from ear to ear.

Marcus stood up on both legs, gazing at Emma the whole time.

- Someone's not good enough, somehow you fought a lot better at my aparment. I'm punching you like a rag doll, and you can not deal with it - Emma said looking up at Marcus, who seemed to be getting more angry.

- You think you are so smart, only because you are able to disappear - said Marcus.

- Well, you know, everybody has a gift, and that's mine.

Marcus stood enraged and looked at Emma.

- Attack me again - he said.

- With pleasure - said Emma, then vanished into thin air.

Marcus stood and watched with focused around the whole space, in order to spot the slightest movement.

- Where are you? - He is talking to himself under his breath.

Suddenly, behind him came the reply.

- Right here - right then, he felt Emma's knee lands on his back. The impact, that Emma inflicted was so powerful that Marcus fell to the ground. When he tried to get up, he quickly felt how his ribs received a further blow from her foot.

He tried to roll out to avoid further kicks, then he felt a gentle breeze on his cheek, and right in its place appeared a powerful blow.

- Now I know everything, I can see thru you - Marcus mumbled under his breath. He jumped to his feet and waited for Emma's next attack.

When Marcus stood focused and ready to receive another blow from Emma he could feel like something was coming from the left side toward his face. When he pulled his left hand in that direction, he felt how a leg hit him. He was able to defend himself. Immediately after the impact, literally a fraction of a second later, he felt how Emma tries to hit him from the opposite direction, straight into the body. In reply, Marcus punched in that direction and could feel his fist reach and hit first. Soon after, Emma's fist reached Marcus' chest, but this time the impact was much weaker than the previous ones. Emma punched on, but Marcus increasingly blocked her punches.

- Enough of this - Emma exclaimed, then she suddenly appeared on the right side of Marcus, about three meters away from him.

- I can see that you start to feel where I am.

- Well, I succeeded in the end - Marcus said with a smile.

- You're right, but not quite. The real fight starts now - said Emma, and then vanished.

Marcus stood and watched around him very carefully, you could see gentle anxiety on his face as sweat began to appear on his forehead. Marcus wiped it off with his left hand, he wondered whether it was caused by nervousness, or just fatigue.

Suddenly he felt a powerful blow to the face, the impact was so strong that Marcus was thrown about ten meters into the air.

„What is happening with me?" - he wondered and asked himself in the depths of his soul. „I have to concentrate."

When he fell down he felt a blow again, but a strong kick comparative to the first strike that made him sunk into the ground like a stone thrown into the water and falling to the bottom.

For a moment, Marcus did not move even a millimeter, he laid limply and seemed to have lost consciousness, but after a few seconds when the dust which was created after Marcus' fall or mucg rather after Emma's attack, settled, Marcus suddenly got up and brushed himself off. He looked around in search of Emma. Again, she appeared not far from him.

- You want to relax? - Her arms were crossed on her chest.

Marcus stared at Emma not saying anything, he just smiled at her.

- So what? Do you want to rest or not? - Emma asked again glancing at Marcus.

- I do not need a rest - said Marcus.

- I think that you could use a little rest, because somehow you don't get any better - said Emma.

- Let's resume our training and not chitchat, as we are only losing time - Marcus said in a calm voice.

- No problem - Emma said and then vanished into thin air.

Marcus jumped to his feet and clenched his fists, waiting for Emma to strike, he knew that it would happen, but he did not know from which side.

While Marcus wondered, he suddenly turned his head to the left side and pulled out in that direction both fists with great speed. When he barely straightened his arms, he felt something bounce off from his fists and fall to the floor. Marcus, without much thought, began to shower this place with punches with increasing speed and force, until light started to emit from his fists.

Suddenly he jumped back two steps, then directed his fists to the spot where seemingly Emma was laying, and fired several fireballs of energy.

When the fireballs hit the targeted spot, a massive explosion broke out.

Marcus stood and tried to see behind the firepillar, but the light which emerged in contact with the ground, was so bright that it blinded him. He barely managed to cover his eyes when he suddenly felt a blow t the left side of his ribs, and soon after that, a hit in the face. After these two blows he fell on his knees and supposrted himself with his hands on the floor.

Marcus looked around he saw Emma standing over him, shortly after that she disappeared again.

At this point Marcus leaped to his feet, then stretched out his hands in front of him hitting Emma in the corpus. Emma has become visible again. Marcus, without thinking, inflicted Emma additional blows, with his fist, with his knee in the chest, and he tried to surprise Emma and hit her with his head. After the last blow given from his head, Emma fell to the ground.

Marcus stood over her, smiled, and held out his hand toward her in order to help her stand back on her feet.

Emma took this move as a gesture of attack and covered herself with both hands and curled up into a ball. Marcus suddenly felt a powerful force hitting his body and got thrown several meters away and fell like a ragdoll to the ground.

Both Marcus and Emma laid unconscious for a while, but after several seconds, Marcus began to rise up. When he managed to get up, he saw how Emma began to move and tried to get up. She couldn't get up on her own and every time he raised herself on her hands, her body collapsed with a hollow bang on the ground.

Marcus walked up to her.

- Do you need help? - He asked with an uncertain voice.

Emma looked at him and held out a hand to him, accepting his help. When Marcus picked Emma up while looking her straight in the eye, he asked.

- Can you tell me, what this was? - he asked curiously and nervous at the same time.

- But what?

- Well, what happened a moment ago - said Marcus.

- I do not know what you mean.

- Are you kidding me? - Asked Marcus.

Emma shook her head to the left and right in a gesture of response, trying to tell him that she has no idea what Marcus exactly means.

- Are you telling me that you had nothing to do with it? - asked Marcus upset.

- I really do not know what you're talking about - explained the girl.

Marcus thought for a moment and then asked.

- Are you telling me that you don't remember anything?

- I'd tell you if I remembered, but I still do not know what you're talking about! – Emma started to get upset.

- You can tell me, what's the last thing you remember? - Asked Marcus.

- Ok, no problem – She thought for a moment looking at the sky. - I know. The last thing I remember was when you hit me in the body and when I fell to the ground. After that I don't remember anything, until when I got up and you also got up from the ground about ten meters away from me.

Marcus's eyes widened.

- Exactly ... Why were you so far from me?

- I can explain, but let's have a seat.

Emma sat on the place, that Marcus pointed out for her and he took a seat next to her.

- Well, how can I explain, when you fell to the ground, and I went over and pulled out a hand to help you get up, you curled up into a ball and covered your face. When you did that, at the same time an enormous power began to radiate from your body which threw me several meters away - said Marcus.

- So what are you saying? - asked Emma, surprised and not quite believing in what Marcus just told her.

- I do not know what to tell you, but it seems to me that when your body is in a hopeless situation it starts to release a huge amount of energy as a final defense, which immediately formes a shock wave and everything around you is wiped out.

Emma laughed.

- Why are you laughing? - Asked Marcus. - You do not believe me?

- Believe or not believe. It doesnt matter, I don't think that I could do something like that.

- Clearly it happens unconscious. You may not have influence on it, maybe it's an ultimate line of defense.

Emma calmed down and for a moment she stared thoughtfully into the distance.

- What are you thinking about?

- I'm trying to remember if it ever happened to me before.

- Try to remember.

Emma and Marcus sat for a moment in silence, Marcus was looking at Emma all the time.

- What do you want? - Emma asked, knowing that Marcus looked at her. - I feel a little embarrassed, when you stare at me like that.

- You really can not remember any situation? - Asked Marcus.

- What situation? - Asked Emma, baffled.

- Situations such as this now, when your film suddenly breaks off and you have a gap in your memory - said Marcus.

Emma was silent.

- Something happened? - Asked Marcus.

- I know!

- Tell me, maybe we'll find out something.

- I remember something from my childhood, but it's probably nothing – She stopped and starred at the floor.

- Please tell me - asked Marcus and smiled towards Emma.

- Never mind, it just seemed to me.

- It seems to me that this is not unimportant, but you're afraid to tell.

- No, really, appeared to me like it was something - defended Emma.

- I do not have to lie to me. I see that you're hiding something - he added.

Emma looked at Marcus and then lowered her eyes again. Marcus didn't wait even a second and walked toward Emma, grabbed her hand and asked:

- Are you okay?

- Yes, yes, I'm alright - said Emma slightly confused.

- You can tell me everything – Marcus assured her holding Emma's hand still. The girl hugged him unexpectedly. For a moment totally surprised, Marcus stood like a statue and didn't know what to do. Finally, he returned her hug.

- What happened?- Asked Marcus again.

- I don't want to talk about it - said Emma looking at Marcus' face.

He could see the sadness in her eyes as tears emerged that gathered at the corners.

Marcus swallowed.

- You know that you can tell me all about it - assured Marcus.

- But I didn't want to talk about it - Emma said with a firm voice. Marcus hugged her tighter and stroked her head. The girl pressed her face into his body. The boy did not give up.

- Did this happen a long time ago?

Emma did not answer. Marcus said.

- A long time ago?

After a few seconds of total silence, Emma looked at Marcus. She released him from her shoulders and wiped her eyes of.

- When I was little, I was only twelve years old. I was in an orphanage because my parents died in a car accident, or so I was told. Now I know that it was not true. At the orphanage, I found myself a friend so I wouldn't feel alone. The rooms at this orphanage were double and triplerooms. Nothing out of the ordinary, gray walls that didn't add any comfort, but on the contrary, made the surroundings even more depressing. Anyway, back in those days it was probably the standard - Emma said after a moment's thought. - One evening, we stayed with my best friend together alone in the room because we didn't feel too well. We sat all day in our room, in fact, each of us was lying in her bed. I remember it like it was yesterday. We talked and imagined what our future will look like. Suddenly our guardian entered the room and took Jessie. He locked himself and her in the room next door. I heard strange noises, she asked him to stop, but nothing seemed to help. After a while there was a frightening silence – Emma said, swallowing hard and tears running down from the corners of her eyes.

Marcus sat and listened numbly clenching his fists with all his strength.

Emma looked at Marcus and then continued.

- After a while he came into my room and sat on my bed and started to stroke me on my head. I remember how his cold hands tightened around my neck and he said, „everything will be fine". After that I don't remember much, except waking up again and seeing his body, or actually the remains of it, thrown like a rag doll and laid in the corner.

Marcus swallowed and breathed a sigh of relief.

- Right after that, I got up, got dressed and ran away from there and never returned again. I was afraid of the consequence of what happened then, so I was hiding all the time. As a little girl there was not much I could do, only give false information, so no one could find me.

Marcus pulled Emma closer and said.

- Do not worry, with me nothing will ever happen to you, no one will ever hurt you again, and if they try, I'll kill him. I promise - he said, and hugged Emma again.

Emma wiped her tears and tried to gather herself.

- Now it's behind me and I know how to deal with it.

Marcus forced a smile on his face.

- I see that now I will not be able to beat you - Emma said, changing the subject.

- What do you mean? - Marcus asked, surprised.

- Now, every time I will attack you, you will be able to calmly hit me. Can you tell me how come that you understood so quickly how I work?

- That's what you want to know.

- Yeah. Explain it to me, then maybe I won't make such mistakes anymore.

- Easy - he said. - At the beginning when I received punches from you, I didn't quite know where you were and what your next move would be, but with each blow I started to feel a vibration in different places on my body. And then your fist or knee appeared. These vibrations grew stronger and more intense. When one of your blows and the vibrations were really strong, I could see your outlines and literally a fractions of a second later, I saw how you appear and you hit me. Then, until it occurred to me that this was not just any vibration or any hallucinations, but it was just you.

- Me?

Marcus smiled at Emma.

- I do not know how it happened, but I knew where you would arrive and where you would hit me, before you even got there.

- I do not know if I believe it - said Emma.

- Than why could you do anything to me at first and then I was able to block you?

-I do not know, but I do not believe you, tell yourself what you want - said Emma.

- As you wish, but you will see, I hope soon that I'm right.

- What do you mean?

- Well, I hope I will be able to show you what I mean when we fight those Zotorigh - said Marcus.

- Oh no, what time is it? - Asked Emma.

- We still have a little time - said Marcus. - Do you want to check something? Or practice more?

- I do not know, it seems to me that we should get going, it is better to be early than too late - said Emma and smiled at Marcus.

- Ok, fine. But remember if we get some pounding from them, it will be your fault - said Marcus.

- Well, I take it upon myself - assured Emma.

- It is time then for us - said Marcus and began to walk towards the place where Thomas, Jason and Botteli were training.

Emma stood for a moment and looked at Marcus who was retreating from her. When Marcus saw that Emma was standing and wasn't moving, he stopped turned around and asked:

- Are you coming or staying?

- I'm coming - she responded, interrupting her thoughts. She rushed to Marcus, who has put his right arm around Emmas neck, he smiled at her and said:

- Do not worry, I won't let anyone hurt you, even if I have to sacrifice my life for it.

Emma said nothing. They walked in silence towards the other defenders of the Earth.

17.

GLOOM FUTURE

- Attack! - Thomas exclaimed, looking at Battoli.

- Are you sure you want to fight me? - Asked Bottelli.

- Yes, actually I do not know, what are you waiting for?

Jason stood on the side and looked at what was happening at the gym.

- I'm telling you, even though I am a few years older, it won't be easy to fight me – Thomas said sneering.

- I'm not saying it will be easy, but I fear for your health - said Botteli.

Thomas stood with crossed arms.

- So what, will you move or shall I send you a special invitation for this event? - Thomas asked impatiently.

- Okay, as you wish, but I hope you won't regret it later – said Botteli, clenching his fists and standing firmly on both feet, lowered his head and remained motionless.

Thomas stood for a moment, waiting for Botteli to attack. He clenched his fists also. He kept his eyes on his opponent.

- I thought you would attack, but I see that I have to take trouble to get to you – Thomas said annoyed after waiting.

Bottelli opened his eyes and lifted himself up above ground. Thomas stopped curiously. His face gave fear away. Bottelli suddenly disappeared.

Thomas wasn't even able to swallow when he suddenly felt a punch on his back, and after that he felt a series of punches on his body. Then he fell hard to the ground. All this lasted only a few seconds.

Thomas was lying limply on the ground and seemed to have lost consciousness for a moment. He tried to get up, but his trembling arms couldn't hold him up.

Jason looked at Thomas. In his eyes you could see terror and helplessness. He swallowed and then spat on the ground next to him. Then his head fell to the side hitting the concrete.

Bottelli stood by with a sneering smile and watched as Thomas curled up in pain.

Jason, without thinking, jumped up and ran towards Thomas to his rescue.

Suddenly Botteli held his hand out toward Jason, who suddenly froze.

- What are you doing? - Jason yelled toward Botteli.

Bottelli replied nothing, he just stood above Thomas and starred how he suffered, then smiled softly, and directed his other arm toward Thomas, who was still half-conscious.

- Can you stop now? Enough is enough - Jason exclaimed in a firm voice.

- Enough? I haven't even started yet – said Botteli in a serious yet firm voice.

- Do not be stupid! – Jason exclaimed surprised at how very seriously Bottelli takes this training.

- What do you want to do, dammit?

- What I should have done at the very beginning.

- Meaning what?

- You'll see for yourself - Bottelli replied, then directed his hand at Thomas who was still lying on the ground, and began to fire tiny fireballs.

- What the hell are you doing? - Jason yelled terrified.

- Watch and learn – Said Bottelli and released his fireballs that struck the spot where Thomas laid.

Jason looked in horror and couldn't bring a word out.

As the place, where Thomas laid, was covered with smoke, Bottelli smiled again to himself and looked up at Jason.

- Now you know what I wanted to do? - Asked Botteli.

- Kill Thomas? - Jason asked through clenched teeth.

- Kill? - Botteli replied surprised. Then he noticed a fist in front of his face, but it was too late. It reached Botteli's face, whose legs buckled under the impact. He dropped to one knee.

- I think you missed! - They heard a voice that seemed to be the voice of Thomas.

Immediately after these words, Thomas's figure emerged from the smoke. Botteli stood up. He was surprised by the whole situation, he did not know how Thomas managed to escape.

When Thomas finished his sentence, Bottelli wanted to say something, as noticed how Thomas's knee was directed toward his face. And he was not able to avoid to blow. He fell to the ground and Thomas launched an attack. When Bottelli looked into his eyes, he only saw revenge in them.

- But that's impossible! - Bottelli cried aloud. - After all, you are an ordinary person, not a fighter, I am a fighter from the galactic family and I'm the prince! - Botteli shouted toward Thomas without taking his eyes from him.

„That's impossible, that I can feel blows of this ordinary mortal" – Botteli told himself in his mind. Suddenly a fist appeared in front of his face. This time, he managed to move his head to avoid the blow. He jumped back and landed on firm legs. He clenched his fists and moved confidently toward Thomas.

Thomas dodged his whole body to the left, he did it at the last moment, as Botteli's both fists passed his face by a few millimeters. Bottelli turned in the air on his back and directed his left knee toward the opponent's face. Thomas did not managed to do any evasive action and Botteli's blow reached the target. He fell to the ground. When Bottelli reached Thomas's face with his knee, he did a backflip in the air and fell to the ground on both legs. The landing ended with a crouch.

Thomas was on the ground, looked at Botelliego and smiled again.

Botteli looked at Jason with surprise, who obviously was totally confused, and did not know what was going on.

Thomas brushed the dust and dirt off and asked bluntly: - Are you surprised?

- I thought Botteli is the most powerful fighter. I didn't expect you to execute such strong strikes - Jason replied.

Thomas just smiled, then asked Botteli: - And are you surprised?

- I thought you are a human - he replied evasively.

- Yes, I am human.

- Something is not right - Botteli said. – Your punches were too strong for an ordinary earthling. If you are human, how come you have such powerful blows?

Thomas looked at Jason, who came up to Botteli and asked: - Exactly, can you explain? Unless you have something to hide.

- I do not see any problem - said Thomas.

- We're listening.

Thomas took a few steps several times, to the right, then left, took a deep breath and finally said.

- In my day we have a technology, about which you can only dream about. I'm wearing a suit that gives me power, speed and strength. It's a typical suit from my time.

- Are you sure? - Asked Botteli.

- Meaning? What am I suppose to be sure about? – Thomas did not understand his doubts.

- You know very well what I mean - Botteli said.

Thomas swallowed and said: - You can clearer? I do not know what you're talking about.

- I feel that you are hiding something from us, if this is so, it's best to tell us the truth now. Besides at the airport, I've seen for a split second, that in your time you are probably someone important - said Botteli.

Thomas lowered his head and fell silent. Jason wanted to say something and opened his mouth, when suddenly Thomas raised his head and said:

- Yes, you're right, I'm hiding something from you. And this is probably not the best time to hide anything.

Bottelli smiled and sat on the ground, Jason just swallowed and breathed a sigh of relief.

- Then again, we're listening again.

- So, as you know, in my day I was, I mean I still am, a Major of a galactic fleet. We had a powerful fleet, which was the most powerful in the northern parts of our galaxy, not much of it remained, unfortunately. By the continuous fight against Zotorigh we lost almost one hundred percent of our frigate. Only a few ships survived during the battle for our second earth in the lightning constellation, this was a few years after the destruction of our home planet, our beloved Mother Earth. Maybe I'll start from what had happened before the end of existence of my race.

Jason and Bottelli listened attentively and none of them said a word.

- Our race expanded throughout the whole galaxy, we settled even on planets that were hostile to life, where the day turned into hot and burning ones, and at night everything was freezing. Thanks to our technology we could colonize even such planets as those. Our fleet had hundreds, if not thousands of ships. Imagine a sky covered with thousands of spacegliders hundreds of meters long, and some are even several kilometers long. Imagine if they were all to fly over your heads. Not only would they cover the whole sky, but they could continuously for several days. We were so powerful that many races wanted to join us and live in peace with us, and we gladly let them. We colonized hundreds of planets, our race had more than four hundred billion lives at its peak, alone on planet mother earth lived more than eighty billion. We colonized all planets in our solar system, including Venus. We only failed to conquer the Sun, because after all it's naturally impossible. Besides, that's not the point. The most important person for our race was obviously the president of all nations and races, and of course his headquarters were on Earth. In the event of the president's death, the Major of the galactic fleet took over the authority. And as I mentioned before, that's my function. After the president's death, which occurred as a result of a battle with Zotorigh, I was appointed as the new chief. I was suppose to carry out a retaliatory attack – Thomas' eyes twinkled and he proudly spoke every word. - We have sent the most powerful freighters to avenge our planet. To our surprise, it was going quite easily and we have suffered relatively small losses. – Thomas said like in a trance. - Unfortunately, at this time we started something we knew nothing about and Zotorigh had everything planned out very well. After each attack by those hideous creatures, we lost more and more ships and people, and we did not know why. Attacks on the part of the aggressor were increasingly brutal. With time we understood why they won with us so easily. Unfortunately for us it was already too late, they didn't just kill our people but they also changed them to their own. Zotorigh destroyed us from the inside – Thomas interrupted thoughtfully.

- You can go on? -Bottelli asked who wanted to know what happened next.

- Yes - Thomas said, and continued his words staring straight ahead as if he wanted to spot something in the distance. - When we were fighting for the planet Galaxon, on my ship have served many soldiers from every civilization we met. Back then I stood on the deck, and next to me was Captain Stevens and was giving orders. He was a very brave soldier, if it wasn't for his missing hand that he lost in battle, we would have still serve and fight. With every attack and moveing ahead of the fleet, we lost more ships one after the other. The most important moment was when Stevens stood on the deck, and then another Stevens came into the room. Yes, exactly – Thomas said, noticing the surprise on Botteli's and Jason's face. – Everyone who was on deck, was speechless. We arrested the two of them and questioned them one by one. Unfortunately, with no results, each of them knew the same, spoke the same, even had the movements. At the end, we had no other choice but to put the two side by side, targeted our weapons at them, but both dis not response. It seemed that we wouldn't be able to recognize the true Stevens, but we did. We noticed that in the moment of stress, Zotorigh don't show one typical human reaction. They don't sweat. When we finally realized that, the doppelganger began to change its form. What we saw, exceeded all our expectations. The very sight of them froze the blood in our veins and caused fear. Not only were they nasty and frightening, but it was almost impossible to destroy them. Before we defeated one individual, I lost over a hundred people. These creatures are so fast that you can barely see them. But returning to the point – Thomas corrected himself. - It turned out that on the ship that I commanded, unfortunately there were a few more like him. When one changes its form, the others do also. It's a signal of willingness to fight. For the first time we understood why we were losing ships so easily. During an attack, when he sent ships full of people like xeol's, morgon's, and many other races to fight, one ship could be filled with thirty to fifty thousand soldiers. During battle we sent at least ten of such ships, and in addition even smaller ones as well. The real battle didn't take place in space between their ships and ours, but inside our ships. First they blocked our SOS message to our other ships, and then they began to hunt for us down and slaughter, killing all one after the other. Before the real fight in space took place, everyone on board was already dead. Then they seperated, and got rid of the bodies of our soldiers. They took on their appearance and were so clever that they even took on their wounds. Rarely our real soldiers returned to our ships. In this way, we learned how very naive we were, because no one even thought about searching our shipwrecks in space, especially since usually there is nothing to search for. We started to learn from our mistakes, and the Supreme Council of the Galactic Fleet decided to never commit such a trivial error. For this purpose, special units were created. Their aim was to find changelings and to eradicate them for good before they spread in on our fleet.

- But how did Stevens survive miraculously? - asked Jason

- A very good question - said Thomas. - Well, at the hearing he said that he actually was on board, in the armory, where he barricaded himself along with several stexon's and a few ours. They were defending themselves, exchanging fire with Zotorigh for over ten hours without a break. They were surprised that they were still alive, as Zotorigh don't usually play around with the enemy. One of the soldiers discovered that they were standing right over the nuclear-fusion capacitor where, an explosion could release such a huge energy that everything within a radius of hundreds of kilometers, if not thousands, gets destroyed. You might as well compare it to an explosion of a mid-size planet. Such a nuclear-fusion capacitor is placed on every major S class ship and destroyer ships of class alpha. Where it is located knows only to the captain of the ship and of course a major of the galactic fleet, in this case me. They attacked this place in first place to disarm the charge. Zotorigh pulled from each captain information with deceit, in order to disable security. Then they killed him, as his existence and was already foregone, because Zotorigh don't take any prisoners - Thomas said. All the warriors listened to him attentively. – So, as I said, Stevens barricaded himself along with several staxon's for several hours and they were defending themselves. Once everyone was slowly beginning to weaken and started to run out of ammunition, they came to the conclusion that they would be dieing anyway, and their only chance is to get away from the ship. Fortunately, they were just a few meters from the escape capsules.

As they attempted to escape, at the beginning everything went smoothly without any obstacles, they overcame meter by meter without a Zotorigh at sight. Once they were at the cabins and were about to board the capsules, all hell broke loose. In just minutes, they almost all died. Stevens was also going to die, but suddenly the last stexon had pushed him into the capsule, and saved his life by covering him with his own body. Unfortunately, a piece of Zotorigh claw hit him in the hand and got wounded, which resulted in a subsequent amputation. The capsule flew automatically from the ship, and it flew to the nearest fleet. He flew a couple of days and when he got to the fleet, it turned out that the fleet was empty, there were only ships filled with ghosts, without crew. Previously, Zotorigh attacked that ship in the same way as they did on his ship. Stevens looked for the nearest fighter plane, this took him several hours because he had to sneak around very carefully so he wouldn't encounter any Zotorigh. Those are their tactics, that after the attack they leave at least two of them behind on each ship, ready to fight in case if help had arrived from other fleets.

When Stevens got into the fighter plane, he tried to start the plane several times, in the end he succeeded. When he flew off to the headquarters, he fell into an asteroid belt and when he tried to avoid it, he used sudden evasive moves. One was so sudden that it had thrown him out of the chair and hit his head on something and lost consciousness. When he regained consciousness, he could not remember anything about himself. A reconnaissance patrol fleet had found him. Unfortunately for us, we went to the back of the fleet, instead of to the main command ship. When they asked him where his ship was and what happened to him, he could not remember anything, not even his name. They took him for tests. They said he would regain his memory in a few, maybe several days and that's what happened. He remembered all the tragic events and asked to be transferred to the command ship. When the real Stevens boarded our ship, our soldiers were a little bit amazed, as he had left the command ship in such a crucial moment and asked him to get immediately to the deck, as we were going to battle for Galaxonos in a few hours, which was the last planet that was still under our control. His place was at the commanding deck. Stevens said he had just arrived on our ship. He so strongly persisted that someone finally believed him. It turned out that it wasn't the real Stevens who sat on the commanding deck. You know the rest.

After the appearance of the real Stevens, Zotorigh started a massacre on board. We have lost more than five thousand of our men before we killed Zotorigh, these enormous losses were caused only by four Zotorigh. Fortunately Zotorigh that were on other ships didn't know anything about it, because they weren't able to send each other messages at such a great distance that separated our ships. We were able to catch some living Zotorigh and conducted tests on them, practiced on them, and learned from them, how they look and how they behave. After a few months we have created a unit as I already have mentioned, that's designed to track and eliminate bugs on ships, and single Zotorigh specimens, so they no longer present a major problem. This way we cleaned our ships one after the other, and during this time our scientists succeeded in creating a material that is as resistant as nothing that has been produced so far. This material proved to be not only very robust but also lightweight. We started to produce our armor made with this material on a massive scale. Unfortunately, someone decided that only senior soldiers get the new armor, cannon fodder remained in the old ones.

Thomas looked at Botteli and Jason, both stood there petrified.

- For a brief moment we won every battle with them. We did not know that they, like us, will also learn from their mistakes. Every day, they are were getting stronger and it got harder to defeat them, and again we lost against them. When we started to defend Galaxon, where we never had any problems with defeating the enemy, we lost it, and then decided to strike with all our strength. We have agreed with others who also wanted to destroy Zotorigh, and by joining forces we wanted to end the war and destroy them. We have put together everything we had and what could be used for the fight. In total there were about eighteen thousand different kinds of fighter jets smaller and larger once, from class Fury to class Alfa, which we had dozens of units. Due to the high cost we were not allowed to build new ones. Zotorigh had only a few hundred units of middle class Jupiter. So we had an advantage? Of course! No one ever had a greater advantage as we did then. Of course we circled them on each side, we were not able to be beaten, but they have put on some extraordinary resistance. They joined their cover of their ships in one and unfortunately we not able to get through it.

I wanted to continue our grip on them so we could finally break their defense, but other generals wanted to quickly destroy them, so they decided to split them into two smaller targets which seemed to be the weaker ones. After the vote we decided to let in several ships to break down their defense, just as it was done during the wars from the times of Napoleon and the famous hussars on Earth. We separated them, by driving a wedge into the tight group, which weaked the fighter. We wanted to capture the survivors and give them to our scientists, because victory seemed close. For a moment I was wondering if it would be a good command, but I had no choice because the generals have insisted on such a scenario. I gave the order in accordance with the decision of us all, to send the most powerful destroyers ahead, that broke through the guard and when we started to boast a victory seeing how their individual vessels fall, our radars detected something behind us that no one expected. A huge number of their ships.

So when we went to defend Galaxonos, we did not think it would be a trap, because nothing indicated it. After arriving in the middle of the Zotorigh fleet and as we stretched our fleet we got attacked by hundreds of fighter jets of a class, which so far I am still not able to determine.

All our squadron were in their hands as we let them use their action within their cover, and at the back we were deprived of any protection. Every time we fired at a Zotorigh ship, they answered more firepower as if they stored the energy from our attack. The high commanders could only watch helplessly and do nothing.

The fleet, which was our last hope was completely destroyed. On the screens we saw how nearly twenty thousand ships droped to fifteen, fourteen, twelve, ten. Those ships that were operating inside the protective field were not able to escape to fight and defend us. Nobody could have imagined that this would be the end. Their ships were faster, more manoeuvrable, even though they were less armed, they still had an advantage over us. Millions of lives have been swallowed, and only a few stormtroopers from our fleet managed to escape along with several fighter jets.

The fleet, which was suppose to bring us victory, became our destruction, but it was rather our vanity, which didn't anticipate. The command ship where I am serving and commanding was the biggest ship and housed more than one hundred thousand lives on board, all of which only eight thousand survived the attack. Seeing what was happening, we decided to assemble the people to flee.

This armor, which I am wearing now is the last piece that was not destroyed by aliens. It can knock down not just one Zotorigh. In my time Zotorigh learned to defend themselves from it, but here they do not even know of its existence.

\

- So we are lucky- Botteli blurted out. It seemed that he was not breathing for a long time but when Thomas had finished the story, he suddenly remembered to do so.

- Luckiness is a relative term - said Thomas. - Maybe we are lucky, that one such armor remained, but on the other hand, if it wasn't for me, then nothing at all would have happened, Zotorigh would not exist, and no armor would be needed. Maybe it would have never been created?

- Generally I agree with you, but not entirely - Jason said.

- What do you mean not entirely? - Thomas walked over to Jason. - Explain it to me, immediately.

- Calm down, calm your nerves - said Jason, looking up at Thomas and taking two steps back.

- This is the answer, what was that supposed to mean? - Said Thomas.

Botteli was sitting with legs curled up and eyes closed.

- And what would be if you never appeared in our time, and they would have? Our world certainly would cease to exist, just like yours.

- Then it wouldn't be of interest to me - Thomas said shortly.

- And it seems to me that just before your death you would ask yourself one question: if there was something I could have done differently – Jason said and added: - You are a Major of a fleet, right?

- Yes, I am, but how does this matter at the moment?

- So if you are, then you probably swore on your life and death, that you will do whatever int takes to defend the inhabitants of other worlds, right?

- Yes, that's right - Thomas said, shaking his head.

- So behave like a real Major would – Jason said dryly. – Remember that this planet is still alive, and so far everything is ahead of us. Everyone here trie with all our power to keep at least one world, so one planet would still be left. What happened in your time, isn't your fault. A human is just a human, not a machine, so it has the right to make a mistake. If you can, then please don't take other's hope away, if you have lost yours - said Jason.

Thomas lowered his head and had become sad after just a second.

- I hope I haven't offended you – Jason asked gently, looking at Thomas.

- It's alright - said Thomas. - Don't worry about me.

- Someone is approaching us - said Bottelli suddenly, while opening his eyes and jumping off his feet. He stared into space in front of them and tried to spot the strangers.

18.

CLASH OF THE RACES

- Who is this? - Asked Jason.

- I'm not really sure, but the energy of this person is very strong and I've never sensed anything this strong - Botteli muttered through clenched teeth. - I was wrong! Now I sense two very powerful sources of energy - he added.

Jason and Thomas stood with clenched fists and looked around.

- I feel that energy! - Thomas said suddenly, and his eyes turned to Emma's and Marcus's direction.

- I also sense it – Jason added after a few seconds. He looked in the same direction as Thomas.

- That's impossible! - Said Botteli and widened his eyes with surprise. - But that's Emma and Marcus - said Bottelli. All three breathed a sigh of relief. The young warriors approached them briskly.

- There's only one very important question that's troubling me: how come they have gained so much power? - Botteli asked.

- Strange - confirmed Thomas.

- We shall see in a moment – Jason said, smiling toward Marcus and Emma who approached them. Suddenly they stopped.

- What are you just standing around? - Emma asked, looking at Botteli.

- Weren't you suppose to practice? - Marcus added.

- We already have finished, and actually we stopped, this may sound silly, but we sensed you from far away - said Botteli.

- Oh you sensed right - Emma repeated under her breath then smiled, which immediately was followed by a smiled from Marcus. When Emma saw that only them both were smiling as the others had serious faces, her smile disappeared.

- Really? - She asked.

- Does it looks like we're joking? - Asked Botteli.

- No no - said Emma looking at Marcus, who just as her got serious. There was silence for a few seconds neither commented.

- I don't want to interrupt such pleasant silence, but I can't believe that you have become so powerful - Jason broke the silence.

- Powerful? - Asked Emma.

- Your strength and your inner chakras are enormous. We sensed you long before we saw you.

Emma looked at Botteli with great surprise and could not quite believe what he said.

- You were absent for a moment, and your power can be felt from afar. I can't wait to see what you have learned - said Botteli. – Actually what are you already doing here? Time for training isn't over yet.

- He had not finished, but we felt it was time to get going - Emma replied. – They are getting closer.

- That's true, my calculations show that we had only two minutes left outside - confirmed Botteli.

- I remember, from what you told me, that the gate to teleport is located somewhere in Europe. In that case what do they want here? - Asked Emma.

- They want to kill us before we get there, they want to get our heads, because when they do then nothing will stand in their way to the complete the destruction of the universe and then my mission fails - said Thomas.

Emma just swallowed and looked everyone present, then said to herself.

- I hope it will be different.

- They're already here! - Botteli exclaimed suddenly. He turned his gaze toward the exit of the gym.

- I also sense them - admitted Emma and clenched her fists, just like Botteli.

- I think each of us can sense them - he added.

All five stood with clenched fists and turned toward the entrance. Five Zotorigh entered the Hall. Each of them looked almost identical, nothing distinguished them from each other. There was was no fear in the eyes of the warriors. Two days have passed since their last encounter with Zotorigh, during which they gained a lot of strength.

- And what are you going to do? - Marcus whispered, looking at Thomas.

- We are waiting for their move, because it's the only chance to survive – He replied.

- What chance, what are you talking about? - Marcus asked, surprised.

- You'll see, and now focus and be prepared to fight, because I don't know what they intend to do - Thomas said without taking his eyes from Zotorigh.

Zotorigh stopped just twenty meters from the warriors, each stood in front of one fighter, and then each Zotorigh began to look very carefully at the warrior what stood in front of them. Each of the Zotorigh had a stoney face, each of them stared at his opponent as if they wanted to drill their gaze through them.

Each of the Zotorigh wore a long black coat that reached to the ankles, and each of them had massive black boots with skewers on them, while the head was covered with a black cowboy hats which covered their whole faces almost.

- Do any of you know what they are doing? - Emma asked, surprised.

- They scan us, I think - Botteli said while pulling his sword from behind his back.

- I wouldn't do this, if I were you - suddenly said the Zotorigh standing in the middle.

Bottelli froze.

- You think that you pull your sword out and you will be able to defend yourself. You think it will be easier and safer with it, but believe me that won't be the case. If you pull it out, the only thing you'd do is encourage us to fight. And trust me, you wouldn't want that - said Zotorigh and took two steps forward.

Botteli lowered his arm back very slowly and stared Thomas.

- Do not be silly, join us and we promise you that nothing will happen to you - After he spoke those words one of the Zotorigh smiled softly under his breath.

- We won't argue with you - said Marcus.

- We know that you will not, so you leave us nothing but to destroy you – Zotorigh standing in the middle spoke again. He stood astride and clenched his fists. - Now it's your turn.

- Don't do anything - Thomas said nervous through his teeth.

- So we don't do anything, they ask to be attacked! - Jason exclaimed.

- Yes, they ask us to attack and know how we are going to attack, theyit will destroy us in a few seconds. They have it all calculated – Thomas said.

- How do you know? - Asked Emma.

- Because they did it this way in my time, and we, like fools, we fell for it. They now control us completely, so don't do anything what they ask you to do, because they are only waiting for it – Thomas explained.

- You don't want to fight or are you just afraid? - Asked Botteli.

None of the five had not said a word.

- We know what you want to do and we are telling you that it will fail – Zotorigh said.

- We don't care anything, what you're thinking and what you are going to do, you want to fight then I invite you to, start to fight, and we will prepare a living hell for you! - Bottelli exclaimed, looking straight into Zotorigh eyes.

- I see that you are outspoken, prince, but don't worry, in a few minutes it will change when you're lying on the ground and whimper like a dog - Zotorigh said.

Botteli smiled, although he was surprised about Zotorigh's knowledge.

- If you know that I'm a prince, then as a prince I command you to introduce yourself, if you have a name, of course - said Botteli.

Zotorigh just smiled, then turned to Botteli.

- Where are, like earthlings say, my manners? My name is Bazz – Zotorigh said, smiling in Emma's direction, after which his smile disappeared on his face and was replaced with a stoney face expression.

- Do you have any questions or can we get to the fighting, so we can destroy this thing, you call Earth? - Asked Bazz.

Botteli didn't speak, but reached for his sword again, that was on his back.

- Don't do that! - Thomas exclaimed, but it was too late, because Bazz already saw what Botteli intended to do, Bazz smiled, then clenched his fists and began to head towards the five.

Botteli didn't remain passive and grabbed his sword in both hands and began to float in the air and head towards the forthcoming Bazz with great speed.

- What shall we do? - Emma exclaimed, looking at Thomas and the remaining three.

- What we have left is to fight and not get killed - said Thomas.

Bazz stopped and from his fists rays began to be emit. He turned his hands toward Botteli who was coming toward him. When he was close, he stopped, dropped his sword and spread his arms to the sides.

- What is happening with me? - He asked himself surprised. Suddenly, with all strength he hit the ground. Botelli, the most powerful of the five, got beaten by Zotorigh. The rest watched horrified.

- What the hell is going on? - Emma asked, horrified by what she saw.

- I have no idea - said Thomas.

When everyone stared at what was happening to Botteli, suddenly Marcus said.

- You are going to just stand and look, or are you going to do something?

- Of course we are – Jason said and ran towards Botteli, after running just a few meters he stopped at a standstill and fell to the ground.

- I can not move! - he exclaimed to the others.

- What do you mean ... - Thomas began, but didn't finish.

Some unusual force pressed him also to the ground.

When Emma barely begun to understand what was going on she also felt alien force that knocked her to the ground.

- You see, now you are my rag dolls - Zotorigh said, smiling.

- What have you done to us? – Emma screamed, who couldn't even move a finger.

- What do you mean? Can't you see? - Asked Bazz. - I deprived you of all movement, you soley rely on my mercy - Bazz said.

Emma didn't know what to say, she lowered her gaze to the ground and fell silent.

- You don't know what to do now? You are probably wondering, what will happen to you? - Bazz asked, walking over to Emma.

Emma didn't dare to even nod.

Bazz stopped by the girl, then crouched down by her head.

- My dear - began Bazz. – Oh, excuse me, if you can call you that of course. I'll tell you what will happen – Said Bazz and touched Emma's hair and adjusted it at the forehead, so that she was able to see all four of them.

Now, I will finish you all one by one, I'll play a game with you all and it's called the endurance game. This game is about which of you guys can withstand being tearing apart as long as possible because I'm going to remove your limbs, piece by piece, arms, legs, head, and in the end your heart. And each of you will be able to watch until the very end because I can also keep you alive even after this game. In the end I will deprive you of your life energy, because the more we have it, the stronger we are - Bazz said.

Emma froze with horror.

- How can you do that? I don't you have any feelings? - Emma asked, her voice was filled with helplessness.

- My dear, for me it's all about the destruction and that each world, that we conquered was helpless and couldn't do anything, even if they tried hard. All the rest does not matter, I draw pleasure from all the suffering – Bazz said with a smile on his face.

Emma looks straight into his eyes. But he stood up, smiled and turned away without emotion. He began to direct his steps to each of them lying on the ground. He first came up to Botteli, when he was with him, he waved his left hand up and Bott got up from the ground and hung in the air. He did the same with Marcus, Thomas, Jason and in the end he came up to Emma, and also raised her in this way.

- I'm missing something here.

- What? - Asked Emma.

Emma stared at Bazz with increasing fury, she wanted to make to hit him in the face with all her strength.

- If you worry so much about others, I have an important task for you in this game - Bazz said, smiling.

Emma stared at him, not understanding what's going on.

- Do not worry, it will be the best entertainment for you. You will decid who will be the first to suffer, and which part of the body we will start from.

Emma stared into Bazz's face, in her eyes there was anger mixed with hatred.

- I see that you are too much in the mood to talk to me or maybe you have already started to choose who is closer to your heart, and who isn't? – He walked around her body, that was hanging limply in the air. His smile was becoming increasingly difficult to bear. It was obvious he was going to begin his game. He approached Emma, their faces were maybe ten centimeters apart. He grabbed her by the hair and pulled back, and on her face was an expression of pain. Despite this, the girl didn't scream.

- From whom shall I start?

Emma is shocked at how angry and what force Bazz said this brief sentence.

- Who did you chose. Asked Bazz

So far, Emma tried to find a little bit of humanity in Bazz's face. Now she gave up and stared at the ground.

- I thought so - said Bazz. – If you can't decide, I will choose for you. I choose, therefore, Marcus, because you have special feeling for him.

Emma said nothing, her eyes were only just slightly furtive at Marcus. Marcus surprised by what he heard, he looked at Emma and asked:

- What is he talking about, Emma?

Bazz turned his head toward Marcus and said - Don't tell me that you didn't know.

Marcus didn't answer.

- Remember what happened in the bathroom in that deserted town - Bazz said.

Marcus did not know what to say, and Bazz said: - If you can't choose, then let me spare you. And just so you are aware that you will left alive to the end.

All four Zotorigh walked to the other warriors from out the back, each one for each one of them.

- Watch how I rip Marcus's body apart piece by piece - Marcus' body suddenly began to rise higher and higher, and when it was more than a meter over their heads, he was struck to the ground with powerful force, and at the spot where he fell, clouds of dust hovered over. Emma watched at what happened to the body of her friend, but did not blink an eye.

- I see that you're trying to be unimpressed. In that case, let's try something a little more sophisticated.

He walked over to Marcus' body and raised it with one hand and squeezed him behind his neck hard enough that after about five seconds Marcus began to have convulsions, and he opened his eyes and grabbed Bazz by the hand that held his neck with both hands. Unfortunately, Marcus was so weakened that he couldn't free himself from Bazz's grip, and his face became more and more red. After a while he began to drift away, all the while trying to escape from

Bazz's grip, with every strike Marcus became weaker and weaker, at one point he grabbed Bazz by the hand with both hands trying to break free one last time. He does not make it, and his body became limp.

Bazz smiled, then let go of Marcus's body. Marcus fell to the ground like a doll, his head hit the floor, causing him to suddenly recover consciousness and tried to catch a deep breath and writhing in pain. He tried to crawl away from the captors but Bazz stopped him by stepping his foot on his back and pushing him to the ground. Emma just stared at Marcus, and tears began to flow from her eyes. Bazz looked at the others and saw that each of the warriors tried to keep cool, but they didn't succeed, because each of them hid their indifference in their eyes but the fear was impossible to hide.

- Do not worry, it's not the end of attractions for him – he said, and when he spoke these words, he picked Marcus up from the ground, but this time he picked him up with his back to him inverted slightly slowly clenching his fingers around Marcus' neck. Bazz smiled at Emma and when he held Markus by the neck he put his second hand to his back and clenched his fist, thenhe aimed a blow to his spine with all his strength. The blow was very strong, so strong that from Marcus' mouth started to flow blood.

- How did you like the show? - Bazz turned to Emma.

Emma stared coldly at Bazz, and said:

- You will die. I'll kill you, and all four of these freaks, you are whores who shouldn't have existed in the first place.

Bazz wasn't impressed by what Emma said, he smiled, while holding Marcus's neck he added: - Say goodbye to him while you have the opportunity. - He hit Marcus in the spine, then again and again, and his hand reached Marcus more often. When he stopped striking, Marcus' body rocked in the air for a moment. Moments later, his body was thrown by Bazz and fell under Emma's feet. Marcus hit his head on the ground, but did not flinch. He was unconscious, but Emma feared most, that he was dead. She fell to her knees and pressed his body to her. Tears fell from her cheeks onto Marcus' face.

Bazz came ambling at Emmy, put his face closer to her ear and whispered: - And how did you like it, little flower? - He laughed unpleasantly.

Suddenly, Emma's memories appeared. She remembered her mother, who always said that to her, everytime she wanted to express her love for her. For some unknown reason she always held back and didn't want to say out two simple words.

Emma clenched her fists, which were stroking Marcus' head until now and hit Bazz in the body. Its impact was so powerful that it created a shock wave through which Bazz fell a few meters away. He rose quickly on his legs.

Bazz looked at Emma, who stood in a gentle straddle. Baz wiped the blood dripping from his nose.

- I see that I underestimated you, do you have something else that you can surprise me with? - Bazz said.

- Come on, and I'll show you - She responded very cool with a confident voice. When Bazz approached her, microscopic lightning bursts began to form around her that grew brighter and there were more and more of them. Emma smiled looking at Bazz with a cold gaze.

Bazz began to run towards Emma, but when he was just within her reach, his body was rejected with great force to the back. He fell and looked at Emma. Flashes around the girl changed into flames, which initially occupied only her hands, and then rapidly spread to the chest first, then the whole body. Initially they wree white after a few seconds they took on a yellow color, and seconds later they started to become more and more red. Eventually the storm of red flames covered Emma's whole body.

- Is this what you are trying to surprise me with? - Bazz said, then walked toward Emma, as she stood in place and just held her arms out in front of him. A stream of light that shot from her hand, hit her opponent in the chest, piercing through him. Bazz looked at himself with disbelief. Then he fell to the ground.

All gathered watched in disbelief, shocked by what Emma had done. She was surprised and stared at her hands.

- Wow, it's something completely new - The girl smiled. Zotorigh stood speechless. Suddenly, behind her a voice said.

- And I thought you are capable of much, much more.

Emma froze and turned uncertainly.

- You are not suppose to be alive - She stammered.

- Relax, no hurry, wait, we'll see - He laughed aloud and added: - I can also be surprising.

Emma shook her head, unable to come to terms with what she had witnessed.

- Well, I see you still don't believe in what you see, so come here you disbeliever and put your hand on my wound - He laughed loudly. Emma clenched her fists.

- I promise you will not suffered for too long.

- I like suffering, it ennobles and strengthens – Bazz said philosophically.

The two opponents started to run to each other with great speed, the distance between them decreased and they both turned into flying missiles. Their hands were stretched out in front of them, and when their bodies collided, the impact created powerful light and great forcefield. Everyone present in the room felt the strength of this forcefield. The light was so blinding that Zotorigh covered his eyes with his hands not to get blinded. Suddenly the light disappeared. It has become apparent that both inflicted their powerful strikes with superhuman speed. The impacts were very fast, so fast that noone could hardly see them. After a moment they stopped the fight.

- I am impressed, you have learned a lot, really, respect - Bazz said, walking toward the girl.

- Haven't seen anything yet, and believe me, I can surprise - Emma replied brushing of the dust that fell on her when she used her power.

- But no matter how much I would be surprised, I do not have time to play with you. You're starting to bore me, I won't play with you anymore.

On Emma's hands appeared small lightning. The girl stood in place and wasn't retreating, even when the opponent walked straight at her. Her strength and confidence surprised Bazz. He didn't expect such resistance. The girl created a new protection field, which was in the shape of a dome. Bazz stopped in front of the field surprised. Emma took an unexpected step and pulled Bazz into the field from which he wasn't able to get away. He looked around and searched for an escape, but the more he tried to escape, the smaller the field became and Bazz came closer and closer to Emma. The girl raised her hands up, as if she was trying to push a ball ahead with all the strength, that was above her. In her hands she held a huge fireball that turned into white flames. Bazz looked horrified at Emma and didn't even notice that it was the end of it, when Emma dropped her hands.

- And girl, you overestimated your strength, as I'm... - He began to weaken, then directed his head down and his eyes rested on his chest and saw that he had the huge hole. He looked at Emma. - What is this? What have you done to me? - the field began to fade, and so did his strength. – What have you done to me? – He whispered slumping to the ground. He tried to get up but Emma put her foot on his shoulder and then pushed him so that he fell to the ground again.

- I haven't done anything yet, I'm just starting.

Again, the girl's whole body was covered in red flames.

Bazz couldn't get up. He just watched as Emma collected energy and was attacking him with hundreds of small fireballs, which began to tear his body apart. Emma walked over to the helpless Bazz and then stood over his head. She saw how each Zotorigh standing by the remaining warriors grabed everyone by the neck and lifted them off the ground. None of the defenders of the Earth could not move, they were all paralyzed.

- And what are you going to do now? Who do you save? - Bazz asked, but it was the last action for which he had the strength. After that his body began to stratify and tear. His skin had melted, revealing the exoskeleton of unusual molecular structure. Emma looked from the corner of her eye at the other warriors, who were held by the neck by Zotorigh. A sword was stuck in each of their belly. Emma managed to scream: - No! - Then she fell to the ground.

19.

CHANGING THE GAME

When Emma began to revive, she only heard „Emma, Emma, wake up, halo, Emma, can you hear us? Emma!". When she opened her eyes she saw how all warriors leaned over her body.

- Emma, ok? - The girl was lying on the ground not moving at all, only her eyes wandered to the left and right, and when looked at everyone, she heard:

- And we thought you were dead - Thomas replied, smiling.

- What happened, where am I, where are Zotorigh? - she stammered out trying to understand what happened and why she couldn't remember.

- How did this all happen? - Marcus asked, surprised.

- Well, where are they? - Emma asked again, and began to look, shaking her head left and right in search for Zotorigh.

- You really do not remember? - Marcus asked again.

Emma looked straight ahead, saying: - If I could remember, I wouldn't ask, and can someone tell me why I'm lying on the ground?

- My dear, thanks to you we are all live here ... - said Botteli.

- What?

- You defeated them all literally in seconds - added Botteli.

- But I do not remember anything, Ouch, my back – Emma hissed, trying to get up.

- It is clear that your best skills show up when you're in a hopeless situation – Marcus replied, giving Emma his hand so she could get up from the ground. She grabbed his and stood up.

- It was amazing, Emma, I didn't think that you would be able to do something like that – Said Botteli and suddenly hugged her.

- Without exaggeration, I wouldn't have been so courageous if it wasn't for you, as you know, you exaggerate it - Emma laughed.

- If you can do so, then surely we can too, but we haven't gotten there yet. If we all were cable of that, Zotorigh would cease to exist.

- I would not be so sure - Thomas said.

They all looked at him in surprise.

- Don't even joke, did you see what she did with them? - Said Marcus.

- What Emma did was great, but I'm afraid that what I saw, were not machine from my time - said Thomas.

- What do you mean not from your time, you said it yourself? - Said Botteli.

- Yes, I know I said so, but unfortunately I made a mistake - said Thomas.

- You are bloody joking, then who were they? - Emma asked furiously.

- I'm not joking, besides why would I lie, I only saw that they have changed slightly - said Thomas

- Then what was it then? That something that I fought with?

- In my time Zotorigh look exactly the same, yet different from those here on Earth.

- What is the difference? - Asked Botteli.

- As you have seen with your own eyes, those individuals break up into small pieces, right?

- Well, we have seen - said Botteli.

- The ones I know, do not decompose in this way.

- And how do they decompose then? - Emma asked?

- In my time, just a heap of scrap metal remained after them.

- What do you mean with all this? - Asked Jason.

- I do not know, but I certainly see such a complex model for the first time. This one was made as if with living tissue inside, all of them have a living organ within that somehow breaks down in a few seconds. They have the same appearance as Zotorigh in my day, no doubt, even fight the same way, but in my time they are less complex. I'm afraid that they have been improved.

When Emma looked down at Thomas' hands she saw how they were shaking with nervousness. Everyone stared at Thomas and didn't know how they were suppose to understand his words.

- In a word, these copies are more modern.

- What? - Botteli asked incredulously. He wanted to say something, but the squeal of Thomas' device, that was in his hands interrupted him.

- What was that? - Asked Emma.

- Nothing - said Thomas.

- Don't lie, I see in your eyes that you're lying, and you are starting to sweat - said Emma.

- It's really nothing.

- If it's nothing, then why are you sweating?

- Do you have something to hide? - Asked Botteli.

- I have nothing to hide - Thomas said slightly annoyed.

- If you have nothing to hide, then tell us what it was! - Jason screamed.

Thomas looked around and then said: - My computer gave me accurate data on the defeated Zotorigh.

- And? - Jason asked.

- Unfortunately, I do not have good news for you.

Everyone stared at Thomas and waited for him to say something. He typped something into the machine. Finally, he spoke.

- The CVT Mercur computer calculated that we don't have a chance against those machines.

- And now what happened, huh? - Emma asked, staring at Thomas and the others. – If we have no chance, then why did we defeat them?

- Explain it to me now - Botteli added, coming up to Thomas and standing in front of him. Marcus stood in silence and brooded over something with his hand on his chin. His fingers tapped out a known rhythm.

- Can you explain this somehow to us? - Jason asked in a calmer tone compared to Botteli.

Thomas said nothing, he did not speak for a moment, everyone stared at him and waited for what he would say.

- You said that this computer is a teleport, right? - Suddenly Marcus asked.

- So as I said, but you don't want me to...– Thomas paused in mid-sentence.

- That's exactly what I think.

- I can't do it, you know that – Thomas said looking up at Marcus.

- If I move to the future, and actually return to my own time, then you know very well that I wouldn't be able to repeat it again. The entire computer system will be exhausted almost to the maximum, and the only thing that I would be able to do on it is to read the data and nothing more. Well, unless you have a propulsion for it, but I dont believe you do.

- What kind of driver are you talking about? - Jason asked out of curiosity

- One moment - Thomas said, smiling toward Marcus. - A neutron-exostratic propulsion, my dear warrior.

- What? - Asked Marcus.

- I know how it sounds but I'll explain - Thomas said, then pressed a button on his computer and began to stare at the screen, it took him a few seconds, Marcus saw how the computer displayed some information. - I already tell you, I'm sorry that it took a long time, but I had to become familiar with some details, because I don't remember exactly each device of our fleet. I mean a neutron-exostratic propulsion or simply said, do you have a nuclear bomb somewhere in the garage?

- So you're talking about a bomb?

- Well, not quite, because it is a thousand times stronger, but it is incredibly powerful. It has such a great potential that it's unimaginable. As soon as we discovered it, it turned out that we didn't need anything at all anymore. This energy is everything, I admit that we only just started working on this, but unfortunately we weren't able to finish our research, and that's in such a tiny device. Now you understand why I am reluctant to go back in time to the moment when I set off - Thomas said.

As everyone looked at Thomas again, the signal of Thomas' computer went off again.

- What does your computer say now? - Asked Emma.

- The computer calculated the probability of our success of my mission.

- What exactly?

- If I were to go back into the future, according these calculations, the success of this mission would fall to virtually zero. There is no guarantee that I would be able to come back to you.

- To explain to us like human to human, how is it possible that these creatures changed within a few days, tand that you haven't even heard of their existence? – Asked Jason.

- I do not know, and I'm afraid to even think about it - said Thomas.

- Can I ask you something else? - The question was asked by Marcus.

- Ask if you want, but don't know if I can answer - replied Thomas

- Why has your computer calculated the chances of returning here to zero?

Everyone listened intently to what Thomas had to say.

- I knew this question would fall and I was afraid it would - said Thomas. - In my time, as you know, isn't very colorful as we were completely destroyed, and the Earth was conquered and destroyed by Zotorigh long ago. When I teleported to you in time, the planet on which I found myself was a fight between Zotorigh and the powerful Urtringo nation that was ruled by King Narost. At the time when I teleported from the kingdom, they broke into the kingdom and then I heard how they got into the castle and that's all.

- In that case what are you afraid of? You didn't explain anything to us - said Marcus.

- I'm afraid that when I get back, the world will not exist anymore, and therefore I will also cease to exist, because I'll get straight into Zotorigh hands, and that's something I really wouldn't want to happen - Said Thomas, as sweat appeared on his forehead.

- Really that an idea like that came to your mind? - Asked Thomas.

In his eyes he could see the glint and glimmer of hope that perhaps Marcus' idea, which he suggested, wouldn't come true.

- What is it, do you have some other plan? - Asked Thomas.

Silence answered him.

- Do you really want me to go back now?

No one spoke.

- We have no plan, just like you are not sure if you will be able to come back to us.

- I see that you have decided - said Thomas.

- No, Thomas, we have decided nothing, but look at it from our perspective, you come here and all this began.

- Do you think it's my fault?

- The fact that you came to our planet and now we are in trouble, as until recently everything was ok - said Marcus.

- You're a fool - said Thomas to Marcus, who was standing almost next to him and looked at him with rage, exactly as if all this was actually his fault.

- It was you who have created these monsters, because when I was born this fight lasted for a long time already. I came here to stop them precisely at the beginning of their development. This moment is the most important, because, I do not know, but for some reason people smarter than me decided about it this way. It is you and your scientists who are responsible for all that, not us, I was only elected to save not only people but entire galaxies and the universe.

Thomas walked away from the whole group, but no one wanted to stop him.

- I despise you all - suddenly fell from Thomas' mouth.

Marcus was literally speechless and was unable to express himself. He did not expect that from Thomas.

The others responded similarly, they didn't expect what Thomas just said.

Silence fell.

- Gentlemen, calm down, without nerves - said Jason. - I know you're upset, tired of it all, but really there is nothing to argue about, what's done is done.

Jason stared at Thomas and said to him: - I can only sympathize and apologize for our race. We want the same thing as you, to destroy them, right?

Thomas nodded.

- We also we want that, so please don't be mad at us, because just like you, we have lost our loved ones too - said Jason.

- Excuse me very much, I didn't mean it exactly that way - Thomas wanted to rectify what he had said. - I got carried away by it all, once again I beg your pardon - said Thomas.

- No need to waste time, you need to act - said Jason.

- I see that I really care about it, okay then. I'll come back and see why these creatures have changed. I hope that I can come back, because I admit that I am also concerned about what happened to them. I don't want things to happen what I am afraid of, because it would mean the end of it all.

Emma suddenly hugged Thomas, which surprised him a little.

- Come back to us quickly - the girl said.

- That's what I intend to do - Thomas smiled.

He looked at the transporter and pressed a few buttons. When he had finished, behind his back suddenly appeared a tiny light that grew brighter and brighter. When it had grown to the size of a watermelon, it suddenly shattered in all directions. In place of the scattered light appeared a plasma in a shape of a door.

Everyone froze in disbelief.

- I imagined a teleporter a little bit differently - Jason said under his breath.

- Do not worry, I also imagined this device differently, but believe me, this model is better and safer than previous ones - assured Thomas.

- And there were other ones? - Jason asked curiously.

- There were a few, but as I said, they didn't cut it. They have abandoned works over them, king Naroth decided to use the last functioning one, only in the face of danger.

- And what was wrong with the othere ones? - Asked Jason.

- Calm down, time is pressing us - interjected Botteli.

- Calm down, nothing will happen if I stay here for a moment – Thomas said with a strangely calm voice.

- So what was wrong with them?

- How can I say this, while teleporting individual were separated into two parts and sometimes a into more - Thomas said.

No one ever mentioned the teleporter issue again.

Thomas looked once again at everyone, then approached the device.

- It's time for me – he said at the end. – Remember, don't start the party without me.

- We promise that we'll wait, but you hurry, or else I'll kick your ass – Marcus exclaimed.

- I promise not to disappoint.

He touched the device on his hands, then the teleport closed instantly and the plasma door fell to the ground disappearing in all directions. Only a stain of the steaming plasma remained, everyone watched it until it disappeared completely.

- And what now? - Bottelli said breaking the silence.

- Now we have to go ... Shit! - Emma screamed.

- What happened? - Asked Jason.

- Thomas didn't tell us where we should go exactly.

- Since we are here, everything indicates that it's somewhere in the UK.

- Bravo genius, and can you be more precise? - Asked Emma.

- How big was your lab? - Jason asked, turning to Marcus.

- Well, it wasn't the smallest - said Marcus.

- But be more specific: size, shape of a square, circle, something special? - Asked Jason.

- It had a diameter of about twenty meters and it was placed in a circle of course, and structural columns were every few meters apart. Why do you ask about my lab? - Marcus asked out of curiosity.

- Listen carefully, it hit me, where it might be - said Jason.

- Wow, not bad how you have enlightened me - Emma said. - Can we get more details?

- Think of where such a place is known for in the UK. I'll give you a hint. It's standing there for several thousand years and is considered to be a teleporter and to another galaxy. Most importantly, it's a circle - told Jason.

There was silence. Emma suddenly jumped up and looked at Jason.

- Do not tell me that it's Stonehenge?

- Yes, exactly. That's the place where we have to go.

- Are you sure?

- Yes - he smiled. - And you know what something else? - Jason asked rhetorically. - We are constantly moving in this direction, look. - Everyone gathered around the map that Jason unfolded. - That's where we landed, right?

- Yes.

- That's where we are now.

- So the direction is simply straight ahead.

- By car, we'll be there in about two hours, and remember how Thomas glanced at the map and didn't want to tell us where we're going, but said he'll be there in two hours?

- And so what?

- It's only about one hundred and fifty kilometers away.

- Now, time plays the most important role, because from what Thomas said, it's today around midnight when it all happens. We have just a few hours. We must hurry.

Bottelli applauded by being impressed. Emma asked: - How do we want to get there? Wagon? We can't pay by credit card, and I did not take cash unfortunately.

- What if we borrow a car? Tmaybe this one that's over there - Jason said, pointing to the head of a pickup truck parked about two hundred meters from them.

- Well great, I have to admit that your brain's quite slow, I just said that we can't pay by card - Emma murmured.

- Who said we have to pay?

- You want to steal a car?

- Borrow it for a moment, that's completely different.

- You can't just steal it, do you think no one will notice?

- I hope, moreover, that the theft will save someone's, and the whole galaxy's, ass – Jason said in his defense. - So what, are you coming or not? You'll stand here and wait for an invitation from me?

Everyone rushed towards the car parked, which was several meters from them.

Jason walked over to the driver's side of the car, looked around, then pulled at the door handle, to his surprise, the car wasn't locked. He smiled to himself and got in quickly.

- Lucky me.

The remaining fighters got inside.

What are you waiting for? Start the engine - ordered Botteli.

- Wait a second, first I need to find the cables.

- What? You do not have the keys? How to start the car then, genius?

- It should be those cables, I should be able to short-circuit them and it'll work – Jason said, burying his hands under the wheel.

- Isn't it better to use keys? - asked Emma.

- I told you I do not have any - Jason snapped.

- Maybe you should check here? - reaching under the armrest She felt the keys and handed them to Jason while smiling at him.

- I think we're really lucky - said Jason and turned the key in the ignition.

20.

BACK TO THE WORLD OF THE DEAD

- Major Thomas! Major Thomas! - Major opened his eyes, he rose
to his feet and looked around, suddently a plasma missile flew over
his head and literally passed him by a few millimeters.

- What the hell? - He felt a sudden pull on his leg, then he
slammed to the ground.

- Don't get up and crawl up to me – He heard. In the corner of the
room he noticed lying guardian of the imperial army, who stretched
out his hand.

- Please hurry - ordered the soldier. Without thinking, the Major
began to crawl to the guard, as plasma missiles were flying over his
head all the time.

- Please follow me - fell a command, Major only looked at the
soldier.

- Please, just don't raise your head, otherwise you will lose it,
that's for sure – the soldier added with a wry smile, and began to
crawl to the door which were a few meters away from them. When
they passed the door, or rather what was left of them, Major Thomas
wanted to get up and go, but the soldier immediately grabbed Major's
shoulder and said, :

- It would be better if we will continue to crawl.

Major nodded. They crawled some eighty meters until they were sure that the stray of bullets or a laser beam won't reach them anymore.

- Can I get up now?

- Trust me, not yet – he heard in response. As they mooveed away from the place, where Major Thomas was at the beginning, the sound of explosions started to fade.

- It is safe to get up now – Said the soldier rising from the ground. - Fortunately, we have found you, because at any moment you could have lost your head.

- Why?

- Because this place will be destroyed in a few minutes.

- What?

- The Emperor ordered to destroy it. It won't stop Zotorigh, but it will certainly slow their operation down.

- Where is the Emperor? - Asked the Major.

- The Emperor has been evacuated to a safe place together with his personal guard and his wife.

- And something more, where, how?

- Unfortunately, I can't say anything more because I don't know. Let's hurry, because the extent of this destruction will turn us into ashes. They were about five hundred meters from the place where they started from, when suddenly they felt and heard a loud explosion.

- Wow, we're lucky - the soldier said.

- Take me to your commander.

- I'm sorry, but I have to refuse to execute this order.

- Refuse how, you are a soldier and I'm a major.

- Yes, and I got orders from my superiors, so I follow them no matter what. I was suppose to find a major and guide him away from the front lines, I have to stay here and maintain my position. We've already lost the front fortresses, and we can't lose this one here as they will otherwise have a quick access into the city center. Besides, individual Zotorigh are here, and someone will shows up for you in a moment, I sent a report to the control that you have been found.

Now we need to move to a safer place. A Zotorigh patrol will come this way in a moment.

- Zotorigh patrol?

- Yes, patrol, as we are in their territory.

- Which day of the fight is this? For how long have I been absent?

- Which day?

- Days or months, well, how long have I been absent for? - Asked the major.

- I would say hours - said the soldier.

- Hours, what do you mean with hours? What hour of fighting is this?

- Some twenty.

- Twenty?

- And how many hours did you think?

- But I wasn't here for a few days, I don't understand how on Earth was I there for a few days and here it's only been twenty hours – Major wondered in the head.

- That's impossible - the soldier said. - I was with you when you set off, and I know that it wasn't a couple of days ago but only a few hours, maybe my time runs differently there but ...

- Where there – The Major interruped him. - Time flows the same way.

- Quickly, let's hide – cried the soldier suddenly out and opened in a narrow passage for the major. At the end of the corridor was a door. – After you - the soldier pointed to the major to go first. Major warily stepped through the room in which there were only two chairs. The room was small, it might be two by three meters.

- What is it, where are we? Can you tell me what happened when I was absent?

- You'll find out everything in a moment, Major - soldier pointed to a chair.

They sat down.

- So when you were sent to the past, at the same time we were attacked by Zotorigh. To be honest, we didn't expect that it will happen so quickly, but what can you do, these are the charms of war. Zotorigh knew exactly where everything is located.

- Meaning? - Major asked curiously.

- They knew where our cannon artillery were, our emplacements, and even knew where the main command center were - the soldier said.

- It's very interesting - said Major Thomas and fell into a moment of reflection. The soldier interrupts him.

- Why did you come back? If the Major does not want tell me, then don't if it's a secret. I'm just asking out of curiosity.

There was a silence that was interrupted by sounds of explosions further and closer ones.

- I came back because something began to worry me. I don't know how much time has passed from the moment when I started, but right after me came Zotorigh to Earth, better than those with whom we are fighting here. New, improved models.

- What? - The soldier was astonished. The thought of more powerful Zotorigh scared him.

- Yes, as if they were more advanced, never mind. I need to get to the headquarters and talk to your emperor - said the Major. - How much longer do I have to wait?

- I'll check – He looked at the computer on his wrist with a map that showed the location and said: - A few more minutes. I got a report that the ship had to change the route, because it ran into the Zotorigh resistance fighters fleet. Fortunately they did not suffer much, according to the computer damage were calculated at nine percent – The soldier informs Major Thomas.

The soldier looked at major strangely. It was obvious that he wanted to ask him something and finally dared to do so.

- Major, how does your earth look like?

- Why do you ask?

- I've heard a lot about your planet, apparently it's one of its kind – The soldier's eyes were glowing in anticipation.

- It's beautiful. I have spent a few days or a few weeks on Earth, I don't really know to be honest, and I can confidently say that I will never forget it. It is really beautiful, I saw a beautiful sky blue, you have no idea what it feels like to feel the breeze on your cheek. It is impossible to describe the feeling of fresh rain in the morning and cut grass, it scent is irreplaceable. I've never felt anything like this before and I hope I will be able to feel it again - Said Major Thomas looking at the soldier and smiling.

- I don't know whether I imagined it well - said the soldier. - It is a strange description.

Major Thomas was about to complain about the absence of the ship when suddenly he heard and saw it above his head.

- Just in time, I do not have time to wait for the end of the world.

- I got the information that they are ready and are waiting for you. Major are you ready? - the soldier asked, glancing at Thomas.

- I'm ready from the moment I landed on this planet - Major Thomas said with irony.

The soldier nodded. It was a signal, after which the ship gently lowered its flight. When it was sufficiently low, a circular platform slipped out of it and fell slowly to the ground. Two soldiers of the imperial guard appeared on this platform.

- Well, finally - Thomas sighed impatiently.

- Sorry, we had small complications.

- No worries – the major said, remembering how many times he risked his life trying to get from place to place. - I hope you get back safe and sound – He glanced at one of the guards.

- We'll do eveything we can.

- Good luck – Major said to the soldier who got him out of the battlefield, then stepped onto the platform. It was launched by the guards word and began to rise up.

- Once again, our apologies, Major, we had small problems – Repeated the soldier.

When they were all on board, the man of the escort said: - I will show you you're place.

Just a few steps were enough and Major stood at the end of the vessel from which he could see everything in a distance of several kilometers, enough to see the approaching enemy fighters and attack.

- When do we get there? - He asked.
- If the gods will lead us safely, it will take us a few moments.
- Great.
- Who is the captain of this ship?
- Me, sir - the man said, saluting.
- It you will be probably able to give me an answer to the question of what we are we waiting for? If I remember correctly, in such situations, you need to make quick decisions about distancing - Major Thomas said.

The captain gave the order – Turn the protective filed on.

- Fields are turned on, sir - said someone. - Radar height?

- We head to the northern side of the citadel – The captain said, issuing an order, and the ship began to rise gently, then pivoted. They could feel how it gently started to accelerate. Looking at the citadel they could seen how ships with soldiers take off and fly away to the front line every now and then to fight with Zotorigh. Suddenly, on the whole ship battle alarm went off and they could hear information from the speakers: - Two stormtrooper pierced through the defense, contacted will be made in two minutes.

- We go into battle mode and prepare for battle escort – ordered the captain, then he turned in the direction of Major Thomas, saying: – It should stop Zotorigh for a while.

- What is the chance of winning?

- Unfortunately, according to calculations we have just three percent chance of winning.

- What are your weapons?

- Thirty-molecular-plasma missiles. self-charge and renewable type kama cannon, it operates destructive as short-range mbeta and, just in case, a nuclear-submaterial gun– calculated the captain.

- How strong is the shield?

- A plasmocytolymphatic-chrome shield is sufficient for only forty seconds, with the full fire force of course - said the captain.

- They won't stop with a single attack, knowing life they will shoot with eveything they've got - Major Thomas said under his breath.

- What are your orders? - Ask the captain.

Major Thomas looked at everyone gathered on the deck and nodded. Everyone stared at Major expecting him to draw an ace from his sleeve. But he said:

- I see no other choice but to use the full force of everything we have.

The captain stared at Majors face, nodded, then replied:

- Do you think Major, that it'll give some result, given the advantages that Zotorigh have?

- I do not think we have the slightest chance - Major said looking around the deck. - We do not have a choice.

- I also do not see any other way - said the captain then gave the order.

- Prepare! Rise to the fighting altitude. Turn on everything and set it for maximum firepower. This could be our last journey, so let it be spectacular.

- I agree - added Major Thomas.

- Contact will accure in fifty seconds – everyone heard from the speakers.

The ship's captain stood in the middle of the deck, looked out the window where at any moment he would see the enemy ship, leaned on the lectern and closed his eyes. It looked as if he waited for the inevitable.

- Why are you standing there and do nothing?

- What am I suppose to do?

- How on earth have you become captain? - Major Thomas growled furious.

- We still have a moment to think about how to get out of this situation, and you immediately give up?

- I'm not giving up, but according to the computers calcula...

- I'm not interested in some computer calculations.

The Captain looked at Major surprised.

- It's just a computer, just as I suspect what we are fighting with. It is programmed and when something is programmed, it can be infected with the virus.

- Computers are never wrong, according to calculations that have been carried out, it sent us information from the main computer and gave us a unique and accurate data. Our computers are never wrong – Said the Captain with conviction and guided his sights on the Major. The Majors face flushed as he clenched his fists and said firmly:

- Listen to me carefully, as I don't have time and I won't repeat myself. It don't care who you are, you can die here yourself, as it suits you, but don't write everyone else's death sentence. Take the lead!

The captain did not seem to believe what he just heard.

- How dare you, you will not be commanded on my ship.

- Tell that to the emperor, when he comes to ask you, why he and his men must die.

There was silence, the Captain along with Major stared at each other straight in the eye.

- What would you tell them?

The captain swallowed hard.

- I thought so.

- Contact in twenty seconds.

- So how's it going to be? - Asked Major Thomas

The captain stood and said nothing.

- Would you rather die standing idly by, or will you allow to save your ass? Decide quickly, because you heard yourself how much time we have.

- The Major takes over the command - said the Captain immediately.

- Thank you, homing missiles, start tracking.

- Done.

- When I give the order, you fire.

- Yes, Sir.

- The first escorting trooper turn left and one to the right.

The Captain looked surprised at the Major.

- And what about us?

- You'll see - Major smiled.

- Contact in ten, nine ... - said the voice of the computer onboard.

The Captain acted with his hands on the desktop.

- Rockets fired.

- Good.

- Five, four ...

- Stormtrooper turn left - immediately! Immediately, turn off all engines - Major Thomas yelled as they all felt a very violent jerk and fell down. The computer has changed the message:

- Collision with the ground in four, three ...

- Align, immediately - Major Thomas gave the order before the computer counted to two. The ship stopped magically in the air, hovering only a few meters above the ground.

- Immediately ... - Major Thomas could not even finish the sentence, because a powerful explosion rocked the boat like jelly. - What was that? Report!

- One of four Zotorigh ships got destroyed, and was shot down by our rocket – The tactical Lieutenant said.

Major smiled, then without hesitation issued another order. - Start the engines and fly low to the ground towards the fortress between the buildings.

The captain looked in amazement at what the new commander in chief was up to.

- I hope that this ship is very agile, as we really need it to be now.

Two more explosions had spread in the vicinity of the ship.

- They just destroyed one of our fighters while escorting and we destroyed another enemy's machine – Lieutenant checked again. - It's still two left - he said softly with a mocking tone. He was very confident and knew how the battle would end.

- Return immediately - Ordered Major Thomas.

- Done - Said the steersman and they felt a sudden turn.

- We're no longer fly to the citadel? - Asked the captain.

- Change of plans - said Major Thomas. - Do it.

- It's a full turn - He heard from the steersman and suddenly began to fly straight at the enemy's ships. The captain looked at the Major and smiled. Major Thomas took it approvingly and then said:

- I'll show you now what it means to win the fight in a big way.

- Now the chance of winning is fifty-fifty, please tell the fighterjet fighters to attack with full firepower, when we are in ... - Suddenly everyone felt another powerful explosion just two hundred meters from them. The explosion was so strong that there was a surge for a split second and the ship had lowered its flight path a few meters, then it returned to the same altitude.

- They destroyed our fighterjet – Repoted the Lieutenant.

On the deck it went deathly quiet.

For a few seconds the Major said nothing. Finally, he ordered: - Let's continue the attack.

- Yes, sir.

From the speakers they could hear interruptive noises.

- Report, what is it?

- They surrounded us.

- What? - Information! - In slit seconds, on his desktop appeared all the information.

- We were surrounded by five enemy ships like „Foxtrot", and three flew ahead of us. They have the firepower ten times greater than ours. There are also two ships at the back with a firepower comparable to our - said the on-board computer.

- But where did they come from? There were only two ships and now suddenly there are five? - Major Thomas shouted looking ahead and fluched with the rage.

- They fired five rockets in our direction, destroying a „xenon". They will reach us in ten seconds! - The computer said.

- What percentage of chance of survival?

- The first three rockets will destroy our shiled, the other two will destroy our ship to forty percent, the next attack will destroy our ship fully with all the people on board - the computer said.

Major Thomas stared in disbelief at the lectern with the monitor counting down the seconds until impact.

- Immediately repel the attack with missiles - Major Thomas screamed.

- Rockets fired.

- Collision with enemy missiles in three, two, one ...

Suddenly they all felt how the whole ship shuddered, then everything returned to normal.

- Missiles destroyed and repelled the attack - the computer said.

Major Thomas grinned and gave another command, not waiting for the enemys move.

- Immediately recharge nuclear-submolecular missiles.

- Yes - said the computer.

- How it works nuclear-molecular? - Asked the Captain with surprise staring in horror at Major Thomas.

- Did you hear something wrong? - The Major asked.

- Do you know what you are doing?

- I want to destroy the damn Zotorigh once and for all - Major Thomas said, looking from the captain to the on-board computer.

- Firing the rockets in our planetary area you will destroy the entire planet!

Major Thomas looked up at the captain and then fell silent.

- Major, missiles ready for launch - reported the computer.

Silence.

- Shoot the missiles?

Major hesitated to answer.

- What are your orders, Major Thomas?

- I want to end this once and for all, but I don't want to destroy our only chance of survival - Major Thomas said quietly, under his breath.

- Major Thomas please give your order, missiles are loaded - pressured the computer.

Everyone is awaiting a decision in horror.

- Warning, Zotorigh ships have launched another attack, this time missiles maxbet were fired in our direction. They destroy the shield and the computer. Contact in for five, four ...

- Release mbeta rockets. Immediately! Dodge to the right and then left.

After these words, everyone on board felt a sharp turn to the right, and when the ship began to bounce to the left they felt a powerful blow knocking everyone of their feet to the floor. After a split second they felt the second blow that was even stronger than the one before. The impact tore a hole in the fuselage.

The strike threw everyone located on the deck a few meters to the left and then to the right. Major Thomas along with the Captain were thrown off the deck of command.

Major stood up, brushed himself off and looked around.

The crew slowly gathered up from the floor.

- Everything alright? - The Major asked strecthing out his hand to the Captain.

- A little bit banged up, but so far, except for a few bruises I'm fine.

- Computer, report the damage.

There was silence.

- Computer! Report the damage! - Said the Major.

- The ship is damaged in in in six six ty percent.

Major Thomas looked at the captain, and the Captain looked at Major.

- You check whether the equipment works.

- Unfortunately ly there are no possibi li li ty of repell ing another atta ck ck ... – the attack in fact damaged the computer.

- Please give details - said Major Thomas.

- No unfortunately I can can not perform any any cooommmaaaands – The computer stretched the last word, and finally fell silent.

- Provide data! - Major Thomas screamed loudly, and with all his strength and fury hit the lectern with both fists.

- Captain! - Major Thomas said through his teeth.

- Yes, Major - the captain stood at attention.

- Is it possible to do something useful on this ship?

- I do not understand.

- Is this rattletrap suited for anything else, or are we simply in a wreckage and are waiting for a pitiful end – Frustration spoke through the Major.

- Sorry, Major, I haven't seen any of our ships in such a state like this. unfortunately you can't do anything now - Said the captain, and immediately an alarm went off indicating that the ship was drifting toward certain destruction. As the fight destroyed most of the sensors, protection and weapons, enemy rockets were fired. Major Thomas looked at the captain, and then his eyes scoured the deck, on which the crew were standing. It was evident that they were determined to fight and resigned to their fate.

- My service with you was a real challenge for me, and to serve with you was a pleasure and honor – The Captain stood up and saluted paying tribute to the Major and the crew.

- It was a privilege for me as well.

The monitor showed that seven enemy's missiles were flying toward the ship. Major Thomas closed his eyes, then scrolled through his entire life so far in his head. It reminded him of all the memories, to his surprise, especially the good ones.

Complete silence reigned on the ship, everyone were waiting silently for their end as they were aware of the approaching missiles and when they were just a hundred meters from the ship, there was a series of explosions that destroyed the rocket. The entire crew of the ship felt a powerful shock wave of detonation. Major Thomas staggered, grabbing the railing and looked out the window and could not believe what he was seeing.

Around the ship were hundreds of ships of the Urtingo fleet that either took on the missiles or simply fired at them.

Along with the Captain, the entire crew and Thomas were shocked and speechless. Hundreds of ships of the Urtingo fleet dealt with enemys ships, in the blink of an eye. Zotorigh resistance was unsuccessful and another enemy units ceased to exist.

Major Thomas gulped with relief, looked at the captain, who also didn't hide his relief. He wiped his forehead and said:

- Did you know anything about this, or are you just as surprised as I am?

The captain smiled.

- I knew that help would come, but I did not know weather they would make it.

- Why did not you tell me? - Major was furious.

- If I would've told you, then Zotorigh would've destroyed us long ago, they wouldn't hesitate to attack.

- Are you saying that you thought that I was a spy? - Major asked, clenching his fists.

- No, nothing like that, Major, the point is that Zotorigh are well aware of what is going on in your head and any message that you bring immediately goes to them - the captain said

- What?

- We know that they read your thoughts, but we don't know when and where and how they do it. They know exactly what you're planning and know your next moves step by step. Somehow, they managed to take control of your brain, but considering what you have done, it appears that you have managed to trick them. There were many things they couldn't have predicted. Do you have any other questions? - Captain asked brushing the dust off his uniform.

- Are you saying that they read my brain, like an open book?

- Exactly.

- But what ... but how ...?

- That, we do not know, because they surpass our technology. It is good that we detected it during your visit to the palace of the king because we wouldn't stand here now.

- Wait - said Major Thomas suddenly remembering something. - On Earth, in the past Zotorigh have exactly the same capabilities as now, and yet that's where it all began - said Major.

- Yeah, exactly that's where it all began - Said the Captain.

- I don't understand one thing – Major didn't give up. - It couldn't happen on Earth in the past.

- We did not say that it happened just on Earth, but we have such suspicions. If we conclude that it didn't begin on earth, then obviously it began here in our time of present - Said the captain.

- Oh God! - Major Thomas exclaimed suddenly.

- What happened?

- If it happened here, that means they knew my plan along and what we intend to do next. I brought them here and it's my fault what's happening rightnow.

- Calm down, Major - The Captain turned to Major.

- But how can I be calm when I realized that it was all my fault? It's my fault, I flew here unnecessarily, I could have die and I would have spared you all this! – Major shouted in despair.

The captain took two steps back and looked at the Major furiously, his eyes suddenly changed color to black and he spoke.

- How dare you say that it's your fault! Do not even try to carry all the blame on yourself! What happened, just happened and there's nothing you can do about it, Major, and the fact that you came here, was obviously because fate wanted it to happen this way, not you, not me, no one wanted it, but destiny - Said the Captain, and when he finished he became calmer. Major Thomas suddenly straightened up, it was obvious that what the captain of the ship just did scared him.

- It's ok, Major – The Captain said gently, as he noticed how his speech made an impact on the Major. His eyes returned to its natural color.

- How on earth did you find out, that they have control over me?

- In the hall, when you talked to our king, some of us began to feel something strange, right after your statements.

- Meaning?

- Other brainwaves in split seconds - Said the Captain, Major Thomas looked at the Captain quizzically, giving him to understand that he didn't really understand anything. - In other words, for a fraction of a second we felt that you are not yourself - Said the Captain.

- But how did this happen?

- We do not know exactly when, but we know that by contact with Zotorigh. They invaded your mind. – The Captain said then looked at the Major.

- You do not want to tell me that I am one of them?

- No, you're not - Said the Captain.

Major went to the window. He leaned against the railing and lowered his head.

- What are you thinking about?

- For the past period I didn't have any contact with Zotorigh, so I have no idea when and how they got into my mind.

- You don't know or you can't remember?

- I really don't know - Said Major Thomas quite convincingly.

- And when was the last you stood eye to eye with Zotorigh?

- Recently other than Earth, in past times, but as you said, this happened before I time travelled, so it had to be... - Major Thomas stopped suddenly, then touched his scar on his cheek.

- Do you want to tell us something? – The Captain asked Major Thomas grabbing his arm.

- That's impossible! - Major started to look around the deck like a madman.

- So when was the last time you dealt with Zotorigh? – Captain demanded an answers.

- It's impossible, and yet... The last time I stood face to face with Zotorigh was when they gave me this scar – He pointed to his cheek and then lowered his gaze to the floor.

- It's ok. Spit it out - Urged the Captain. There was an awkward silence, everyone on the ship fell silent and waited for Majors move, and were curious what he would say. After a long moment he raised his head and said:

- Then when they inflicted me this scar, then something died in me. Our entire fleet got ambushed, we retreated the cargo ships with people on board. These were people who survived the Zotorigh invasion on planet Triton, one of Oxylesa moons. We had just six transports and about thirty ships of the attacking fleet. We were surrounded by hundreds of Zotorigh destroyers, but somehow we were able to deduce all ships with people on board. Me and the entire leadership decided to defend the ship and repel the attack. When the fleet was quite far away and we safely ordered the retreat, suddenly Zotorigh appeared on our board. We didn't know back then that they can take on human form. A few individuals bursted onto our deck and began the slaughter. They slaughtered almost the entire crew and several civilians that were located on the lower decks, they hunted us like ducks. They caught one after the other, then kidnapped me and a few lieutenants and told me to choose who was going to die first, and how we would die. – Major looked around the deck. Noone even flinch. - Shall I continue? - He asked looking at the Captain.

- If you don't want to or are unable to then don't, I understand.

- I want to get it over with - said Major Thomas and continued. - When I was told to choose the first victim, I did something noone had expected, but for me it was the most obvious thing in the world. I think everyone would do the same.

- So what did you do? - The Captain asked curiously.

- Do I have to say it, or are you just too lazy to read my mind?

- We don't have the habit of rummaging through someone's mind while talking - Said the Captain politely.

- Oh, so where was I? And yes, I know! - exclaimed the Major quietly. I told myself I prefer to be the first to die than to choose someone from the crew.

- You signed yourself up for a certain death? Why?

- Because, the most valuable thing for me is the life of other people, I was chosen to guard the freedom and lives of all creatures, and not send them to die unnecessarily.

- A wise answer. But it still doesn't explained to us how they took control of your mind.

- And yes, I'll tell you - Major Thomas said. - So when I picked myself instead of someone else, one of the Zotorigh came up to me, grabbed my head and said, I should look at them very well as it'll be the last time I ever see them, then he grabbed me by the neck and put a firm grip on it, he put a pointy claw to my throat and whispered into my ear: „Now watch how the others die. You will die last with the thought that you didn't save them". Then he ordered his men to start the fun with each in turn. I do not know what happened, I suddenly felt a surge of strength, broke somehow free from this creature, and when it tried to give me a blow, I managed to dodge, then grabbed his knife which was tucked in his belt and stabbed it in the body of this disgusting creatures. Suddenly I felt a blow to the back of the head, I fell to the ground. For a moment I did not know what was going on, but I felt like something grabbed my legs and lifted me up. In the hall I heard the moans of pain of my soldiers. Then I felt like something very, very cold tightened around my neck. I couldn't move because I had no strength, I only felt how the greatest treasure escapes my body – my life.

- Is this the end of your story? - The Captain asked curiously, when Major interrupted his story.

- When I woke up I already had this scar on my face. There was nobody in the room. I didn't know how I managed to survive and where Zotorigh disappeared, or who saved my life. There were only body of soldiers laying around with me in this room, there were no traces of foreigners, literally as if they vanished into thin air.

21.

CLOSER TO THE TRUTH

When the platform moved a meter away from the ship, the Captain pressed a button on the device on his wrist. Then something strange began to happen, the platform got covered with something in the form of an armor or protective field. Major Thomas watched in surprise.

- I didn't notice this thing on your wrist earlier, Captain.

The captain looked at Major and answered with a slight smile, and Major Thomas said.

- What is your plan Captain, if I may know?

- Now we wait for the transportation shuttle that will take us out to our king, and in a moment we'll find out how long we have to wait. The last report, we were given, repoted that the ship will arrive here in about ten minutes - Said the Captain.

- Great, can't we take one of the ships of the fleet. that destroyed the Zotorigh?

- Unfortunately not - the captain replied.

- Strange - Thomas muttered

- What's so strange about that?

- After all, hundreds of ships float over our heads, and none of them can take us to your king? With all due respect, but something here seems wrong.

- Let me explain Major. These vessels are not suitable for transporting anyone, since they are only computerized. There isn't living soul on board. Those are drones.

The captains answer obviously cooled the Major Thomas down as he didn't say anything more and just looked at what was happening around. When the platform reached the ground and touched it gently, the first soldier stepped off the platform, walked a few meters, then looked around himself. Then he turned to face the Captain, who gave the order:

- Operational readiness.

The captain fumbled at the device on his wrist. A moment later, all the crew of the ship started to become invisible. They were all covered with the protective shield.

- Is something going on? - Thomas asked, concerned.

- No, everything's fine, it's just a framework of security and just in case they attacked us.

- Great, everyone is in a protective suits, except me - Major Thomas said under his breath.

- We need to send a special invitation for Major Thomas to donned the armor? – The Captain teased.

- No, you don't need to, but I do not have such a device - said Major Thomas.

- And what do you teleport with then? It has only one function?

- I have no idea what it's useful for. Anyway, I didn't have the possibility to learn more about this device.

- Where do you have it, Major?

- Here, I have it on my wrist the whole time - Major raised his hand.

- Major Thomas, then put your protective shield on - Said the captain pointing to the keyboard attached to the device.

- And how am I supposed to turn a protective suit on?

- In your case, you only need to speak the order to the keyboard for it to work. „Suit" or „armor" - that's enough.

A tiny square cube appeared from the computer attached to his wrist and began to cover first his hand, then it spread over the entire body in all directions, covering the chest, legs, and at the very end his head. When it finally formed itself into shape, it then changed its color from green to black. Only the eyes were exposed .

- I did not expect this - said Major Thomas with a big surprise.

The captain wincked at the major: - Believe me, that's not the last time you will surprise you.

- When will the transport arrive?

- According to computer calculations and the report that I got from the command center, transport it is not possible for the time being because of a very heavy enemy fire by Zotorigh ships and enemy troop movements - said the captain.

- Do you have details?

The captain looked at Major Thomas, but did not give any answer.

- Can I ask in a different way, is there any chance of someone coming for us?

- Unfortunately no, we can only rely on ourselves.

- You have to be joking? - Major Thomas said.

- Do I look like someone who'd joke in a situation like this?

- So what is your plan, Captain?

- Me?

- Who else?

- From what I remember, it is a Major deigned to take charge –
The Captain smiled ironically.

- You're right - Thomas replied confused.

- So what are the orders, Major Thomas.

He had no idea. He looked around and he had no idea. Guard were waiting for orders. In the end, he said curtly. He didn't like to lose.

- Captain, please locate our position immediately, and please give appropriate orders to the guard.

- I like that.

- Don't discuss! Execute immediately.

The captain's eyes widened and began to dispatch people.

- You and you - pointed with a nod to the two soldiers. - Take on positions twenty meters in front of us and observe any suspicious movements. I count on quick reports.

- Yes, Sir.

- You and you - the captain pointed the next two soldiers. - Do the same just behind us and report immediately, when something unsettling happens.

- Yes, Sir - said the other two with one voice.

- And you two protect at all costs, even your lives, Major Thomas. – he said, pointing to the last two soldiers.

- Yes, Sir - The soldiers stood near the Major.

- That's very kind of you, but I'd prefer a ship instead of the escort.

- I also wanted a ship, but we don't have any transportation for now, and if, God forbid, Zotorigh attack and will kill you, then our whole plan will backfire - said the captain.

- Captain!- Exclaimed one of the guards standing at the front.

- What's happening?

- We have company! Three objects approach us, sorry four.

The captain froze for a split second, then looked at the Major and said:

- Do not worry. We'll show you now how we should fight these creatures.

- Captain!

- What's happening?

- I got the latest report.

- Report immediately - Ordered the Captain.

- Recent data indicate that ten hostile objects are approaching, contact occurs in thirty seconds – The soldier starred helplessly at his computer.

- What are the proportions of winning?

- If we take the fight, our chances are zero, and if we start to escape, the computer displays, our chances are equal to sixty-two percent.

- What is the quickest way to the Emperor, which way? - Asked Thomas.

- We're running away? - He asked the surprised captain.

- No, we're not - Major Thomas said.

- What do you want to do in that case?

- What do you think?

- Well, it looks like we're running away to me.

Major Thomas looks with pity at the captain, and said:

- I fought them and I know that even if we were thirty, we wouldn't manage to beat them.

- There's only one problem – The Captain said suddenly.

- What?

- I, as a soldier of the imperial guard, I can not escape, it would be a disgrace to me and I could not forgive myself if I ran away – Captain grabbed his gun clinging belt.

- You have to be joking?

- No, I'm not joking.

- You will die! I knew what only one Zotorigh can do with the whole regiment, let alone ten of them!

- Sorry, Major, our paths diverge here. You have to go alone. It's time for you - The Captain said without hesitation pointing with a nod in which direction the Major should go.

- They are here! - Shouted the soldier standing next to the captain.

The captain looked at the major.

- Get out as quick as you can, and don't worry about us.

Major finally started to escape in the indicated direction. When he was a few meters behind the Captain he heard.

- Soldiers prepare and you shall be filled with glory and bravery!

After what he heard, the Major accelerated and disappeared around the corner.

When he ran only a hundred meters he heard a scream, and recognized the voice. He heard his terrible cry for a few seconds, then it stopped and there was complete silence.

Major Thomas immediately accelerated when he ran just five hundred meters he felt that something was watching and chasing him. When he looked over his shoulder he saw Zotorigh running in his direction in a fast pace. Thomas accelerated even more and turned his head back, every time he looked back Zotorigh was getting closer. Thomas ran with all his strength ahead. At a distance of thirty meters he saw a small passage where only he could squeeze in.

„This is my only chance to escape" - Thought Thomas, and with all his strength began to run toward the gap between the buildings.

When he looked again, he saw how Zotorigh who was a few seconds ago behind him at a distance of fifty meters, now was only eight meters behind him, and was approaching very quickly. When he reached the gap, Major Thomas suddenly stopped and stood still. He swallowed hard and stood prepared to fight.

- Easy, Major Thomas - Zotorigh suddenly said, standing in front of the gap.

Major Thomas did not say a word the whole time just starred at the Zotorigh who spoke to him, all the while watching another Zotorigh from the corner of his eye. Suddenly, the Zotorigh standing at the back to Major Thomas turned around and then ran off into the unknown. Major did not expect such a maneuver. Major clenched his fists after which his spacesuit started to cover his face and his protective shield started to cover his whole body from head to toe.

- Calm down, I intend to do nothing unless you want me to - Zotorigh suddenly added unexpectedly. - I've got a proposition for you

- I'm not interest in any proposition of your, I despise you, I'd rather die than argue with you, you miserable creatures.

- Creatures? - Asked Zotorigh approaching closer and closer to Major Thomas.

- So you think that we are the creatures? - Zotorigh asked. - You are a fool, thinking that we are cruel and sow destruction across the galaxy.

Major Thomas stared at Zotorigh then furiously punched his face, which suddenly, split into two parts under the pressure of impact. Zotorigh backed away very slowly, as the two parts of the face began to reshape and stick back together. Major Thomas tried to move with all his strength, but his body wouldn't twitch a millimeter.

Zotorigh came to Major then he said:

- Where was I? You think we're horrible? That only we spread destruction? If you looked at your race you would recognize that we are just like you, anyway, do you want to know what happened to your planet?

- It was destroyed by you! - Thomas said drawling through his teeth.

- And here you are wrong, the fact is that we destroyed your planet, but it was already dead. You have destroyed it yourselves well before us, destroying more species than we have, you people act like parasites! First, you gradually enter a different world, study it, and then destroy everything you encounter on your way, occupying space, piece by piece, until the you damaged it to such an extent that there is nothing valuable left on it. When you take advantage of all the raw materials, the you move deeper until you have destroyed everything around. On your planet called Earth, there were more than a trillion species, and you all destroyed them, and polluted oceans. You were the reason why the earth was flooded with water, which melted because of climate warming, killing millions of species, and that all just in two centuries - said Zotorigh, who stood with his back to Major Thomas. - And you still want to tell me that we're cruel?

- Tell yourself what you want, I won't believe you anyway - Thomas said through closed teeth.

- And if that wasn't enough, you started to conquer other planets, because on yours there was no room and it was impossible to live on. You conquered one after another, each of which was able to host your kind of life for your apparently better race, or you kill everyone on the planet, or kept them as your slaves, and when you've used all the resources of the planet tehn you started to destroy that one as well – This is the truth about your race, the great and powerful species called human. After all, you are one of them, right? Major?

- I do not believe you!

- No, maybe this will convince you – After these words Zotorigh touched Major Thomas' forehead and in his head appeared thoughts of other creatures, including images of the planet Earth before it was destroyed by humans. He had seen and felt the suffering of animals killed by other people, veered images of destruction, devastation of nature. He saw war, floods, explosions starting with the atomic bomb, ending with a plasma bomb that could kill millions of lives in a few seconds.

Zotorigh pulled his hand away from the Majors forehead then looked at him and asked.

- You still do not believe me?

- You are ridiculous - said Major Thomas

Zotorigh grinned from ear to ear and added:

- I almost forgot that you are arrogant and self-centered as well.

- I do not care what you say and what you showed me, and I don't believe you anyway. If you want to kill me, then do it now! - Major Thomas screamed trying to break free from the invisible shackles.

- As I said earlier, I have a proposition for you.

- What?

- You'll see for yourself - After these words Zotorigh touched his forehead again. A planet similar to Earth appeared in his head and on this planet were all kinds of beings from different planets, that lived together in harmony and peace. The planet was half covered in water, and thousands of tiny islands and on one of them he saw his wife who was playing with their daughter. When they approached to a distance of about three meters, Major Thomas' wife looked up to the sky, hugged her daughter and returned to play.

At this point Zotorigh pulled his fingers from Majors face, and asked bluntly.

- Do you want to join them?

- But that's impossible - Major Thomas said with shock as tears began to flow from his left eye.

- So, my proposition is as follows. Do you want to spend eternity with them, I know you want to see your wife and daughter and touch them one more time. Therefore, I offer you a life after your life, and

I promise that when you die you will join your loved ones. In return I want your teleporter.

Thomas laughed his opponent straight in the face.

- I see that you are not willing to cooperate - noted Zotorigh.

- Even if it were true, I still wouldn't believe you. Even if you offer me eternal life on this kind of planet I do not believe any word you say. You are a lying race. I'd rather die in agony than to get along with you – Major spat violently to the ground.

Zotorigh smiled.

- What are you waiting you freak of nature? Finish me! I'm not afraid of you - shouted the Major.

Zotorigh held out his hand and it began to change shape. After a while the whole hand turned into a couple of limbs.

- What the hell is that?

- That, my dear, is a penetrator.

Thomas's eyes widened.

- I'll explain how it works – he put those limbs to the Major chest. Major tried to flee, but he still could not move.

- You do not have to worry and don't think that you will die soon - Zotorigh said. - This device works in a way that it inflicts maximum pain while keeping the victim alive. At the beginning you will feel a hell of a sharp twinge that will allow tiny needles to stab into your body, after a few seconds the needle will be increase in size to a tennis ball, ripping your bones and muscles apart. When they grow to this size, one after another will follow in the farthest reaches of your body by penetrating them piece by piece. When you think it's the end, you'll be begging for death, as it's not the end.

- You will feel and see how your body begins to decompose, centimeter by centimeter, you can't even imagine how horrific painful it is, but don't worry, I'm sure you won't miss anything. Your brain and heart will still be working. You'll see and feel all your organs one by one. Everything will be migrated to the main penetrator, which will eat your body. All parts will be absorbed by it, but it won't take your consciousness, which is why you will witness this suffering for all eternity and you will be experiencing this over and over again.

Fill your eternity. So what are you still brave, or will you be begging for mercy?

- You already know my opinion – Major Thomas said, looking straight into Zotorigh eyes.

- As I thought.

The opponent lifted a finger pointing to the penetrator, that immediately stabbed one of those limbs into Major Thomas' chest piercing into his exoskeleton.

Major Thomas howled in pain.

Zotorigh looked at Major Thomas, then suddenly he grabbed his chest and fell to his knees and the penetrator fell out of Major's body and landed on the ground. Major also fell to the ground and when he looked at the enemy he saw that his body was pierced through by something like a spear. Zotorigh turned his head back in disbelief and then began to decompose and immediately turned into ashes.

Major Thomas being tired lowered his head for a moment. When he raised it up, Zotorigh was already gone, but a well-known figure appeared to him in the distance.

- Holey cow, how on earth did you manage to survive? - Said Major Thomas through his teeth writhing in pain.

The captain smiled and offered his hand to the Major.

- As you can see, I have my ways to beat these creatures.

- I heard you scream.

- Are you sure it was a scream of pain?

- Well, I'm not, moreover, I have no idea what sort of screams you use at different moments of his life – Major replied evasively.

- Exactly. I see that these creatures and their toys started to have fun with you - Said the captain looking at the wound inflicted by the penetrator.

- Well, as you can see.

- Do not worry, we'll fix this somehow - said the captain, after which he went to Major Thomas and grabbed his hand, which he had placed on the computer. He typed something in it.

- In a few seconds you should be better.

Major Thomas looked at his chest. The more he looked at it, the better appeared the wound to him. In the place where the suit got destroyed new material molecules appeared. The suit was already repaired.

The Captain smiled toward the Major.

- You can feel the gentle itch for a few seconds, but do not worry. In a few minutes you'll be as good as new.

- I feel great - Said Thomas after a moment.

- And that's how you look - The Captain replied.

- And where are the others? - Major Thomas asked a question while looking around.

Captain looked at Major then became sad and then said,

- Unfortunately, not all of us can enjoy the sun.

Major Thomas walked over to the captain and then grabbed him by the shoulder and said.

- I'm sorry, may they rest in peace.

- There is no reason to be sad, they look down upon us and know they did everything they could. They will watch over us.

The captain began to move.

- Where are we going?

- Behind these buildings transport is waiting for us that will take us directly to the citadel, where our ruler is waiting for you – Said the Captain, then lowered his eyes as a sign of respect for their ruler.

Major Thomas, for some unknown reason, he did exactly the same.

- When the ruler is finished with you, you will go directly on a journey into a world where they are waiting for you - said the captain.

- But I need to know ...

- Don't tell me.

- Oh yes, I forgot that you can read my mind.

- That's not it, you can't say anything because you're controlled by Zotorighów. So what, are you going?

22.

A NEW DAY

- Do any of you have a plan for what we do and how we arrive at the place? - Emma asked the question looking at each in turn.

Jason was looking from the corner of his eye at Emma, who was sitting in the back, and said:

- I do not know about you, but I'm not going to allow Zotorigh to expand onto our planet and destroyed it completely.

Emma leaned forward.

- And what if Thomas said proves to be a lie? And it was all the other way around?

Jason suddenly stopped the car and turned towards Emma.

- What do you mean, the other way around?

- Well, what if it turns out that all this was meant to bring us to this place, and we will be presented to the Zotorigh on a silver plate?

Jason stared at Emma and didn't believe what he was hearing.

- I know this may sound stupid but I thought that when Thomas suddenly disappeared, it may not be a coincident.

- You are really stupid if you think so - interjected Botteli.

- What? - Asked Emma not believing in what she was hearing.

- Do I have to repeat myself?

- How can you say that to me? I only share my concerns!

- I know it might have crossed your mind, but say it out loud, that's another matter – Botteli said. - I believe Thomas.

- I Do not know about you, but I believe him as much as Botteli does -Added Marcus and Jason nodded as a sign that he agrees with them.

- Well, I won't say anything more, in fact it was stupid on my part - Emma said and turned her head toward the window.

Jason returned to driving the car. After a while, Botteli spoke up.

- I'm sorry about what I said, but you know if it wasn't for him, we wouldn't even know about these monsters. We wouldn't have the opportunity to be here and to be able to save our future and the planet, and what's more, the entire universe, because all of us would have all been dead by now.

Emma looked and smiled at Botteli, then nodded and went back to staring out the window, watching as they get meter by meter closer to the goal.

- Are we there yet? - Asked Marcus.

- Good that you ask, because we just arrived - Jason said, looking in the rearview mirror.

- Well, this is about to start - said Botteli stretching.

- What do we actually have to look for? - Asked Marcus.

Jason while parking, replied: - You will see a circle. A stone circle.

Jason pulled into the parking lot.

- It starts to get dark, you think it will happen at night? - Asked Botteli.

- It does not matter if it happens now or later, it's important that Thomas comes back with good news – Jason replied, Bottelli said while looking around:

- Well, then let's get to work.

Emma, along with Marcus left the car and began to look around for the stoney circle.

- Look, from what I remember, this Stonehenge is on the hill - Marcus said, pointing to the place that was less than a half kilometer away, then began moving in the direction indicated.

- Let's not split - Emma interjected. - It will be safer this way.

- But why? Is something threatening us?

- I have a strange feeling.

- Well, maybe it would be best.

- Super - Said Emma smiling, then walked over to Jason and kissed him on the cheek.

- And what about me? - Bottelli asked, spreading his arms out to the sides.

Emma loked at Botteliego, not knowing what he meant.

- I also want a kiss, I think I deserve a nice moment before what's going to happen next - Bottelli said, looking at Emma,

- Ok, fine, you're right – Emma said and kissed him on the cheek.

- Thank you, - said Balotelli and walked on in silence.

- I think we should hurry - Jason suddenly said.

- What's happening? - Asked Marcus.

- I think it started – he said, pointing to the stone statues standing on the hill. Small lights began to appear between the stones.

- Hurry to the circle! - Jason screamed and ran powerful forward, without thinking, the rest of the crew also started to run straight ahead. As they approached the circle, the light became more and more clearer and more light appeared which suddenly began to move in different directions. But none of them went beyond the circle.

When Jason ran ahead from the others at a distance of several meters, he reached the stone statues, as suddenly lights disappeared, then complete darkness fell, and he could hear a whispering everywhere in every language on earth. After a few seconds, the remaining ones reached him and also stopped suddenly, and were looking in every direction.

- Where are they?

- Do you also hear this, or am I imagining it? - Jason asked, looking at each in turn.

- These strange voices? - Emma asked, looking around trying to see people denouncing whispered words.

- I can not help but feel that something bad is about to happen - Said Botteli grabbing his sword. The silence was really frightening. - I really do have bad feelings about this – he said a little louder.

- I know what you're talking about my friend, I also feel a strange uneasiness - said Marcus

- This silence does not herald anything good - confirmed Emma.

Something moved, behind one of the stones. The warriors were ready to fight. A second, two and behind the stone came out ... a cat.

- But nothing bad will happen – Emma said grabbing the cat and stroking it.

- Let him go – Marcus ordered.

- Why, what could happen? – Emma asked, not looking away from the cat.

- Damn it, put the cat down!

- Alright, fine - said Emma then put the cat on the grass, the cat looks at Emma then meowed and ran through one of the stones gates. Suddenly, the cat meowed shrilly and ran away.

- What was that? Did you hear that? - Asked Jason.

Botteli said: – I told you that cats bring bad luck? – He tightened his grip on the sword.

- What are you talking about, after all... - Emma did not manage to finish the sentence when a Zotorigh came out the gate, walking with very slow steps towards the warriors.

All the warriors as if on cue, stood in a line preparing to fight in concentration. Zotorigh passed through the gate, stopped a meter from them, adjusted his coat and looked at the warriors.

- I see that you are on time - he said.

Nobody said nothing, everyone was waiting for his move.

- Do you really don't feel like talking before the fight?

- I see anger in your eyes – Said Zotorigh approaching Botteli. – I do not understand its source. Are you angry because you weren't able to save your planet, or because you will fail to save another one? Or maybe because you couldn't do anything when we killed your father?

Bottelli fought with himself. He would not give up to the provocation.

- I am glad that so many gathered here. I won't have to travel and look for you throughout the universe. - Zotorigh put his hand into his pocket and pulled out a tiny ball that he threw behind him, and everyone looked at it curiously. The ball fell to the ground and began to shine in a yellowish color, then he began to move towards one of the monuments. When it reached and hit it, it began to flash with a white light. Then it shattered into small pieces.

- If you think that you can impress us with your tricks and we will get scared, you are wrong - said Jason.

Suddenly, between two rocks appeared a vertical surface of water. Warriors were determined to win.

- Prepare for battle! - Shouted Marcus.

Emma became invisible. Marcus clenched his fists, then on both his hands fireballs appeared. Jason drew his sword in front of him, raising it as if he wanted to cut down the side of the obstacle.

- I see that you really, really want to lose the whole fight even before it even began.

- We won't lose - said Jason.

- Do not say you have a plan to win this? If you say so, I wish you good luck. I wish, however, to make this fight even. You are four, I'm alone. This should be changed.

- I won't let you do this – Marcus shouted, then runs toward him, clenching his fists.

Zotorigh looked slightly to the right over his shoulder and saw Marcus running toward him. He smiled broadly. He waited for this move.

- Stop! - Emma shouted, grabbing Marcus's arm.

-What are you doing! - Botteli stopped Emma.

When Marcus came close to Zotorigha, he aimed a blow with his left hand toward the back of the head, his right fist punched him in the back. When both blows reached him, Marcus jumped back two steps and looked at Zotorigh.

- Is this all you can do? - He asked his opponent.

- This is just the beginning - said Marcus

Zotorigh turned around to the face Marcus and said – And I thought this was it.

Zotorigh was standing in front of Marcus, he raised his hand up and then pointed a finger at Marcus.

- I don't even dare to open the gate – Marcus said through gritted teeth. - I will not let you open the portal, even if I have to die!

Earlier strikes and now threats didn't impress his opponent at all. He looked at Marcus and closed his eyes, turned toward the portal and touched the pane. Marcus started to run towards Zotorigha and stroke him with a few blows with his fists, but Zotorigh didn't make anything out of it and continued to open the portal. Zotorigha finger touched the pane, and it immediately turned into ice.

- Unfortunately, you can't stop me! In a few minutes this planet will cease to exist - Zotorigh said, turning toward the approaching comrades, who came Marcus to help. Marcus continued to attack all the time meted out further blows, ever stronger, Zotorigh stood there and did not move a millimeter.

Marcus jumps back, then bounces off his left foot from the ground and jumped on Zotorighs head height and struck his knee into the head so that not only the head but also part of the torso bended quite significantly, then returned slowly to his position.

Bottelli and Jason stopped still. Marcus, who after hitting dropped to the ground, stood there not continueing any attacks.

Their enemy is gently shaking his head to the right, then left. He stood up and said:

- I've had enough of you!
- But that's impossible - said Jason.
- What is impossible? - Zotorigh asked ironically.
- After these blows, you have no right to stand up, let alone fight - Marcus said, horrified.
- You call those blows? In a moment, I'll show you a blow, after which you will not get up - Zotorigh said and started to look at the gathered warriors.

They all tightened their fists, waiting for what might happen and watched Zotorighs every step.

Zotorighs gaze stopped at Emma. The enemy began to move in her direction.

Emma took two steps back, then stood ready to repel the attack that was going to take place in a fraction of a second.

- Do not worry, I'll play with you a little bit first and then I'll throw your scraps to the remaining warriors so they'll see, how pathetic and weak you all are - Zotorigh added.

- Do you think it will be easy to win with me? - She asked Zotorigh.

- I guess, we'll see.

- So you don't underestimate me - Said Emma, then screamed out loud and suddenly vanished.

Emma disappeared, her opponent stopped.

- I knew you would run, who's next? - Asked Zotorigh.

Jason looked at Marcus and Botteli and gave them a sign that he was going to attack and started toward him, saying:

- We will not run away, if that's what you thought.

Zotorigh suddenly vanished into thin air when Jason tried to impose a stroke.

- Where the hell did he go! - Botteli exclaimed, looking around very nervously clenching his hands on the hilt of his sword. Suddenly everyone heard a loud bang and looked toward one of the stones, which began to disintegrate into small pieces. Zotorigh began to rise from under the rubble and you could see how it ences on his feet. Everyone saw Emma behind him, who began to materialize and after a split second, when Zotorigh looked at her, she disappeared again. When Zothorigh didn't finish to turn his head back, something or someone hit its head, but noone could see who it was. Suddenly, he fell with powerful force on a second stone. Emma materialized again and inflicted her opponent a final kick.

- Well, I have to admit I did not expect that from her - said Jason.

- I loved it too - Added Botteli smiling.

- That means, we are ready - said Marcus.

- Did you like the show? - Emma approached them. They applaused her. Emma bowed.

Botteli looked towards the lying Zotorigh and said: - We shouldn't celebrate yet.

Zotorigh got up from the ground.

- And I thought, we would have peace of mind - Muttered Bottelli.

- Something seems to me that we are not the ones play for time - said Jason.

- That's right - said the enemy. – I'm just beginning to play with you. He held out his left hand to the front, directing it toward Jason then spread his fingers to the sides and a fiery glowing ball appeared in front of his hand that was stretched out towards the warriors.

All the warriors stood like petrified, not knowing what to do. Everyone was scared, but didn't want to show their fears of what the next step of Zotorigh would be.

- And how do you like my show? - Zotorigh asked smiling.

Nobody said a word, everyone stared at the fiery ball, which suddenly began to increase in size, until it reached the size of a grapefruit.

- In addition to this surprise I have for you another one.

Bottelli swallowed, glancing sideways at his companions.

Fireball divided into three smaller ones.

- Were Zotorigh able to produce something like that in your world? - Jason asked, addressing these words to Botteli.

- I do not recall.

- Of course you can't remember, because we were not able to - Zotorigh interjected in Botteli's sentence.

There was silence.

- Before I kill you, I will explain to you why I delayed your death.

Nobody said a word, everyone just starred at Zotorigha.

- The answer is very simple, easier than it might seem to you - Zotorigh said with a smile. - Previously, I wasn't able to do that, because you were too strong for me. Everyone of you had unimaginable powers, which simply scared me, but now I do not have to worry about.

- Why?

- Emma it's rude to interrupt someone's sentence. As I said earlier, I couldn't kill you, but now I can because I have the same powers as you. You still don't understand? During the fight I had a chance to touch you. And you know that by a touch we gain knowledge about you, right?

The Warriors took a step backward.

- No matter what powers you have, we will not let you open the portal.

- But you already have.

Fireballs began to move towards the warriors.

- Prepare for battle! - exclaimed Botteli then vanished into thin air. The bullets suddenly accelerated as if they were fired from a cannon in the warriors direction. Bottelli suddenly stood in front of the bullets and took on all their energy.

- No! - Suddenly shouted Zotorigh seeing what Botteli did, whose body fell limply to the ground.

- I won't forgive you this! - Marcus yelled, clenched his fists and tensed himself with all his strength. flames appeared from his hands suddenly that started to glow brighter. The earth began to shake and tiny pieces of stones lifted off the ground.

- Finally, something's happening - Said Zotorigh then vanished into thin air.

Emma and Jason looked around. Marcus stood there the whole time flexing his muscles as around him tiny electrostatic discharges began to appear.

At that moment, dozens of Zotorigh appeared around Marcus and were punching him in the body, followed by a kick with the knee in the stomach, after which Marcus fell to the ground like a rag doll.

Zotorigh just watched, how Marcus' body fell limply to the ground.

Emma dropped her hands helplessly and started to run toward Marcus. When Jason saw that Emma was running toward Marcus, he started to do the same and jumped up without thinking about what would happen next.

Zotorigh smiled to himself, put his foot on the ground, and then vanished in the air again.

When Emma reached Marcus' body which was lying motionless on the ground, in front of her appeared Zotorigh holding his hand in front of Emma's face.

Emma stopped and directed her gaze at Zotorighs face.

- Burn in hell.

- You first.

Then a light emerged out of his hand and hit Emma, after which she fell to the ground. Zotorigh disappeared again.

Jason suddenly stopped and yelled at the top of his lungs.

- Fight like a true warrior.

And then he began to look around.

- I see that you are very angry - Asked Zotorigh and appeared several meters away from Jason.

- I'll kill you! - Jason said with anger in his voice.

- No, my dear Jason, you can't kill me, as you can see I easily can defeat stronger fighters than you. You're like a little harmless cockroach, which must be crushed!

Jason clenched his fists and said with a smile and calm voice.

- You know what is so fascinating about cockroaches?

- I'm not interested!

- The fact that no matter how you destroyed cockroaches, weather you crush, step or beat it, it always arise. They can't be destroyed. Not even by an atomic bomb.

- Not only is it funny that you are going to die, but also that you still believe that you can beat me. I'm impressed - said Zotorigh.

In the distance, stood Marcus with a serious face and clenched fists. Around him were more and more lightning. Zotorigh was surprised to see him on his feet. The flames on Marcus' hands became stronger and brighter, until they finally blinded Zotorigh, who backed away, not knowing what was going on.

- How did you increase your strength?

- This question will torment you until your death.

Jason was looking at it all and couldn't really understand where Marcus power came from.

Zotorigh suddenly stopped and smiled.

- Whether you're stronger now or not, and will die anyway – and he vanished into thin air.

At the same time, Marcus was doing something that Jason couldn't understand. It looked like as if Marcus wanted to hit someone that was standing behind him, even tho no one was there. Suddenly it turned out that Zotorigh appeared on this spot, who didn't realized and fell to the ground. The blow was so strong that it literally threw Zotorigh several meters back.

When Zotorigh flew limply in disbelief of what is happening, he stared at Marcus, who disappeared shortly after giving him the blow. Before Zotorigh fell to the ground, he felt a strike with a knee on his body.

Marcus did not wait a second longer and lifted himself several meters into the air and stretched his hands towards the whole, which was created after the impact of Zotorigha hitting the ground. He released several fireballs of pure energy from his hand, that flew directly toward the hole. When the fireballs reached its target, it created a huge explosion which shockwaves was so strong that Jason, who was standing a few meters from the battlefield got thrown back.

Marcus hung in the air for quite a few seconds and then disappeared and suddenly appeared next to Jason, who was trying to get up from the ground.

- How did you do that? - Asked Jason who got pulled up by Marcus by his hand.
- You have to see what's happening with Botteli and Emma.
- But they're dead, I saw how Zotorigh defeated them.
- They're alive.
- What, how come? Jason asked
- They're alive, but they are in a serious condition.
- Till dawn it's less than half an hour - said Jason.
- Unfortunately, we have less time - said Marcus. - In a moment, Zotorigh will recover and then it will be strong and don't know if I'll be able to stop him. I won't be able to stop it, and if Thomas does not appear soon with good news, it'll be it for us. Go to Bottelego. I'll go to Emma.

Emma was lying drenched in her own blood. Marcus lifted her gently and leaned her against a massive boulder that was lying beside her. Emma opened her eyes and asked.

- Did you beat it?

- Not yet, I'm waiting for you - Marcus smiled.

- Unfortunately, I think I have to disappoint you.

- Don't talk nonsense.

- I know my time is coming - she squeezed Marcus' hand.

- Don't say anything.

- I won't be able to defeat Zotorigha, but you have a very good chance – Emma was weakening with every word.

- Remember how I told you how I want to spend the last moments of my life?

- Yes, I remember.

- Now I know I would like to spend it with you - said Emma.

- And that's how it's going to be - Marcus assured her.

- Maybe so, but in a next life, my dear.

Marcus looked at Emma, and probably sensed what she wanted to say and wanted to protest, but she wouldn't let him say anything. She grabbed him by the neck and kissed him, and after she tore her mouth from his mouth, she said, looking him straight in the eye: - You will become stronger and more powerful when you combine my life force with yours, you know that right?

- What are you talking about Emma? - Marcus said.

- Don't say a word, you know what to do, when you do you will gain strength, so strong noone has ever dreamed of.

- I don't agree, Marcus protested.

- Marcus it's too late, I am dying, and you do your last job.

Marcus closed his eyes, and tears streamed down his cheeks when he opened them, Emma only smiled. Marcus felt how a new, unfamiliar strength enters his body begins to revive. When he looked back at Emma, she fell asleep.

Marcus felt a terrible tear, he felt like losing a beautiful friendship. His eye color changed to green, and his hair suddenly lengthened by several centimeters, his whole body tensed and he started to grow unimaginably.

Marcus took a deep breath and began to float up, he could see the earth to the horizon. Then he gently dropped next to Botteli and Jason.

- How are you? - Heard Bottelli.

- Not the best, I think I have broken ribs.

- Not good.

- And Emma?

Marcus didn't look at Jason, who asked the question. Out of Marcus' eyes flowed tears, and both Botteli and Jason figured out what that means.

- I'm sorry.

- The beast will pay for it, I swear by god, it'll pay for it. Can you fight with a sword? - Marcus asked Jason.

- Yes, I can.

- That's good because I will need your help.

Bottelli tried to move and got up with big effort, creating a powerful trinity along with Marcus and Jason.

- I will also do everything that's in my power to help you.

- I know my friend, I know, together we will revenge Emma and won't allow the destruction of the Earth.

And when Bottelli finished his sentence, the earth began to shake and Zothoring jumped out at high altitude above the ground with great force. Then it slammed into the ground creating a large crater.

Zotorigh stared at the warriors then looked at Marcus and said:

- I admit that I am impressed with your strength, even though you know you can't win this fight and you're still trying to do something to save this poor planet. I do not know why you care so much for it, but that's not my business.

Marcus was silent.

- You're weak, give up Botteli.

- I won't give up. The son of the Emperor never gives up.

- Well, of course.

Zotorigh again moving farther stopped at Jason's height and said to him:

- Jason, give up.

- Do not count on it!

- For you, Marcus, I have a special task. You can choose who will die first.

- Choose?

- Yes, choose - said Zotorigh disappearing into the air.

- Choose who has to die first.

- Fight me.

- Jason or Botteli?

- What if I decide, you will do as I please?

- Yes I will, I will the killed one whom you point at, Marcus - Jason and Botteli got paled.

- I want to die, so fight me.

- You will all die!

- No, nobody except you will not die today! – Marcus shouted, then in his hands appeared two fireballs of pure energy. Around his body appeared smoke.

- I think something really starts to happen - Said Zotorigh excited.

- I've had enough of this contempt for people, you killed a really fantastic person and I won't allow you to hurt anyone else.

- And that's where you are wrong - Said Zotorigh and literally moved his body from the place where he stood, to behind his back in a split second.

Marcus felt a huge pain on his back, which began to move his body from the feet to the very top of his head. As he fell to the ground he felt his body stopped a few centimeters in the air before the collision. The ground trembled.

Bottelli started to run at Zotorigh. He aimed several blows with his sword at a very fast pace, appearing like lightning in the sky, but that it didn't make the slightest impression on Zotorigh who avoided every blow with great ease.

When Bottelli realized that his attacks weren't effective, he jumped back, then he took two steps to the left side, bounced off the ground and jumped on to Zotorigh's head height, then struck with his knee with full force into his head. Zotorigh body bended back so that his head almost touched the ground, but he didn't fall completely, he stopped and smiled.

When Botteli fell to the ground gasping anxiously, he froze and was unable to move even a millimeter, not knowing what was happening, he looked at Marcus.

Marcus looked at Botteli, and directed his gaze at Jason who just like everyone else, could not move a centimeter.

- What happened? - Asked Marcus nervous.

- You see, my dear Marcus, – Zotorigh said, grinning from ear to ear. - as if I played with you on time, because in a few minutes, the gate will appear, and I'll be needing you.

Marcus still wasn't able to understand what was happening.

- I see you're surprised. When I said that I will need you, I wasn't joking. With the four of you gathered here, I will be able to open the portal. On the other side, thousands of Zotorigh are waiting.

When he finished his sentence, Emma's dead body raised up, then began to move into the center of Stonehenge, where it took one of the four places in the circle. Then Zotorigh did the same with Botteli's body, despite the fact that he struggled and tried to break free, even though he couldn't do anything.

- But Emma is dead, so now you've lost your chance to win - Marcus said through clenched teeth.

- And who said that she needs to be alive?

- All I need is your body and powers.

Marcus stared at Botteli's body, that took another place in the circle.

- Do won't forgive you this!

- Do not worry and do not get angry. You will be one of the first, who will see the death of this planet - Zotorigh said. - Till dawn were only five minutes left.

- You see, you couldn't do anything - Zotorigh added, looking at Marcus, who helplessly tried to free himself.

Zotorigh took a deep breath, staring at the body of Marcus and Jason that took their adequate space to open the portal. Zotorigh walked over to Emma's body and slit her wrist his his knife-sharp fingernails, and blood spurted like a fountain. Zotorigh licked his fingernail.

- Tasty - he said and suddenly appeared next to Jason, then he moved to Botteliego.

Marcus didn't even blink when Zotorigh did exactly the same thing to Botteli, and the blood which began to flow from Botteli's body began to direct itself in the center of Stonehenge.

Marcus had time to blink only once, when Zotorigh suddenly stood in front of him, staring into his eyes continually smiling.

- Noone could beat us, no race, no uxendon, no mologowy, not even your funny race did manage to beat us, even though its thanks to you that we broke free. Weak is your race.

After these words, Zotorigh slit Marcus' wrist as he had done before with the other three warriors. Blood soaked the ground and began to move into the center of Stonehenge. When the blood of the four warriors reached the center, where the gate was already prepared, it suddenly began to break into tiny crumbs that began to fall to the ground, revealing a crystal clear coating. On the other side they could see thousands of Zotorigh.

- When you all bleed out, and all the blood from your body reaches the portal, it will completely open and my brothers will prey on your eight billion meaningless lives.

Marcus closed his eyes, then lowered his head. Suddenly he heard.

- I think you're late, my dear Thomas – Silence was broken by Zotorigh.

Marcus raised his head, in his eyes appeared a glow, which couldn't be seen in any of the other warriors.

Thomas was standing in front of Zotorigh.

- And I have the impression that I have arrived just on time.

After these words, a fireball of pure energy appeared in Major's hands. He didn't wait even a split second and released it towrad Zotorigh.

Zotorigh didn't even manage to react when the energy ball hit him, the force of the impact was so powerful that he fell to the ground like a leaf in the gusty wind.

Under the impact, all warriors regained their movement and fell to the ground.

Major Thomas smiled and said:

- I told you I was coming. Remember how I told you, that everything will depend on you? Not only the human lives but the whole galaxy?

- Yes I remember - said Marcus.

- I learned what to do to stop Zotorighów.

Marcus clutched his chest. In the middle of it a blade was stuck.

- Why? - Marcus asked slumping to the ground.

The warriors stood there like enchanted. Again, they couldn't move, but this time with disbelief.

When Marcus slided to the ground he saw how Zotorigh sprang up from the ground and ran with a very fast pace toward the warriors. He drifting away while watching how Zotorigh tore Thomas's body apart.

Marcus stared at Major Thomas, who tried to crawl to Marcus with his last strength.

- Why?

Major Thomas stopped and smiled for the last time.

Marcus turned his head toward Botteli, he saw how Botteli tried to defend against Zotorighs infuriated attack with his last ounce of strength, but his defense did not last long. Zotorighs fist penetrated Botteli's body like through a piece of paper and Botteli's body fell limply to the ground.

Marcus noticed how Zotorigh headed in his direction. Unable to do anything about it, he said:

- I didn't expect such an end.

Zotorigh nodded. Marcus fell unconscious.

Epilogue

- Honey, can you give me the towel? - A question was asked.

Marcus opened his eyes and noticed, he was in a bright room while lying on the bed.

- Honey, can you give me that towel? - A question was asked again, this time louder.

Marcus looked around the room, his eyes rested on a chair, on which a towel was hanging.

- Yes, of course - Marcus whispered getting out of bed. He reached for the towel. He didn't understand where he was yet, but walked toward the sound of water. When he went into the bathroom, she stood in the doorway and became speechless.

Emma looked at Marcus, she smiled and then asked:

- Something's wrong, honey?

Marcus stood silent and motionless for several seconds.

- Honey, what happened? - Emma asked again.

- No, just ... no, nothing happened - Marcus said, walking over to Emma. He grabbed her and hugged her tightly to his body.

- Are you alright? You look like you have seen a ghost - Emma asked, glancing at Marcus.

Marcus looked at Emma again. He smiled and replied:

- Now, everything is alright.

Printed in the United States
By Bookmasters